A CRISIS AT TRANQUILITY!

SCHUYLER M. WOOD

CONTENTS

ACKNOWLEDGMENTS

When I needed a cosmic event to cause the crisis for the crew of *Tranquility*, the requirement for bigger brains than mine became apparent. Little did I know that I would end up interacting with people who would be so generous with their time and knowledge.

But the most important thank you's must go to the people in my life.

My wife, Marilen, has been so supportive and encouraging of my writing *A Crisis at Tranquility!*

My mother, who taught me the ways of life so I could meet its challenges head-on.

David F., Sara F., Maria W., Dave H., Adam H., John M., Bill S., and Calvin W. who allowed me use them as templates for some of the characters in my story.

Stuart S. and Martin B. have passed on from this life, but will live on by being in my book as one of the pilots of the *Hestia* and as The Keeper known as Machete.

Now, to thank the big brains who helped make the science accurate.

The people who answered my first set of questions pertaining to possible space objects to cause headaches for the crew of *Tranquility* were at the Hayden Planetarium. It was because of their enthusiastic response to my idea for the story that my wife bought me a laptop so I could write anywhere.

The people at The Planetary Society gave me a tour of their headquarters in Pasadena, California, and shared information about Solar Sails.

Dr. Kenneth E. Phillips and Devin A. Waller, of the California Science Center, were so gracious with their time in answering the many questions I had.

The people at the Chabot Space and Science Center also fielded several of my questions.

And a multitude of friends and random people I talked to about my story were so positive and excited about it.

My editor, Paul Weisser, was so patient with me.

To all these people, and many more who gave their input to make *A Crisis at Tranquility!* a reality, I thank you and wish you much happiness.

Schuyler M. Wood

AUTHOR'S NOTE

This story has quite a few real scientific terms, as well as some from my imagination. To give you a better understanding of them, I have added a glossary at the back.

I hope you enjoy the story, which has given me so much pleasure to write.

For Marilen.
The love of my life.

CHAPTER 1

To Insanity! And Beyond!

A large silver-and-black cylinder orbited the Moon. As it spun slowly, the metal hull sparkled like a polished gem.

The Moon passed below, uncaring that Marc was about to be annoyed.

"Marc! Marc! Wake up!" said a female voice.

"Humph?"

"Marc! Wake up. Tony's burning the butter. *Again*."

As Marc's bloodshot hazel eyes pried themselves open, his nose confirmed what Irma said. Tony had indeed burned the butter.

Again.

He looked at the computer monitor on his nightstand with the head on it of a pretty blonde-haired lady with green eyes.

"Alright, Irma. I'll deal with it. Now, shoo!"

Irma giggled as she was sucked away by a computer-generated tornado and gave a giddy "Weeeee!" as she disappeared.

Marc let a low grumble loose as he rubbed the sleepy-seeds out of his eyes and toyed with the idea of calling Irma back to tell her to turn the fire extinguishers on. Letting Tony get turned into something resembling a glow-in-the-dark mutant by the non-toxic foam would be amusingly satisfying, but the kitchen had just been serviced, and Marc wasn't going to be denied cooking a proper opening meal. Besides, having a fluorescent blue mutant greeting the guests would be a bit much.

Marc threw the bed covers off and stretched his five-foot-nine body. He then reached over to a control pad on the nightstand to press a button. The curtains covering the window split apart and retracted into the wall. The outside revealed a second-story view of a lush green garden with enough foliage to give the room privacy. The light coming through the window showed a room that was filled with books plus the odds and ends of a person well-traveled. One shelf was dedicated to figurines of Disney characters and old TV shows.

After rolling out of bed, he stuck his feet into some well-worn slippers, stumbled out of his quarters in his dark blue PJ's, rubbed at the stubble on his face, and ran a hand through his thick dark brown hair as he walked down the hallway. He waved at the haze of smoke coming from the doorway down the hall. When he reached the kitchen, he slapped the switch to start the overhead hoods that sucked out the smoke and restored the air quality to normal. Glancing at the magnetic strip holding a collection of assorted knives, he thought about using one to carve a reminder into Tony's arm about turning on the hood. But that would only result in himself needing medical attention. One did not pull a knife on a Marine. So, he did the next best thing. He threw insults at him.

"How is it that someone who can field-strip and reassemble a pump-action shotgun in less than a minute can't cook an egg without fucking it up? You're the only person I know who can screw up melting *ice!*"

Standing at the six-burner stove in khaki shorts and a black t-shirt was Tony Rhodes. At five-foot-ten, he was a well-built man who could easily have been mistaken for an ancient Greek statue that had walked off its pedestal—an image that was reinforced by his Greek ancestry, whose lineage, rumor had it, could be traced back to legendary Spartan warrior, King Leonidas. At first glance, he appeared to be in his early thirties, but his black hair, peppered with grey and cut in a military style, revealed that he was in his early fifties.

Tony shrugged his shoulders and, with a lopsided smirk, said. "It's a talent. Want some?"

Grabbing a towel, Marc walked over to the stove, used the towel to remove the scorching hot pan from the burner, and contemplated the charcoal that had once been eggs.

"No, thanks. Apparently, you think that being a carbon-based life form requires us to eat carbonized nutrition. And what were you doing cooking food when you know I'm making an Opening Breakfast?"

The Marine looked sheepish as he shrugged his shoulders.

"I thought I could help this time, if I could only manage to figure out the temp to cook the eggs at."

Marc gave his friend a are-you-kidding? look.

"For starters, don't use a flame that rivals the exhaust from a ship leaving Earth's orbit."

Tony frowned. "You cook with insane flames all the time."

With practiced ease, Marc placed the pan in the sink and poured water on it that released a cloud of steam.

"I happen to know what I'm doing in a kitchen. You, on the other hand, shouldn't be allowed to touch a cookbook. It would most likely burst into flames in order to save others from you using it." Marc then washed his hands and turned on the burners for the flat-top grill. "Go see if there are any more eggs. I'll start making the coffee."

Tony grunted an acknowledgment and wandered off.

The Crew Kitchen was something Marc had worked hard to upgrade with the top-of-the-line equipment and keep it clean. This was the spot where most of the Core Crew had their meals and where Marc spent most of his off time—not just to cook, but to keep Tony from triggering the fire extinguishers again. This was where he could think and develop new ideas for the *Tranquility Casino*.

⠲ ⠠⠦⠃⠰⠂⠔⠄ ⠿ ⠠⠱⠃⠄ ⠙⠻⠦⠲⠔ ⠐⠫⠿

The *Tranquility Casino* was a centrifugal gravity tube, also known as an O'Neill Cylinder, that was in synchronous orbit above the northeast part of the Moon. It had once been a resupply station that made the ships exploring the Solar System possible in the early 2100s by converting the ice on the Moon into hydrogen for the ships. It was now a marvel of engineering that had the reputation of nearly zero waste and minimal need for air or fuel.

When Star Base One, the largest station ever built, went online in 2169, it replaced the supply station, which then became an obsolete floating eyesore. Marc knew that since the ultra-rich love space travel, they would want to have someplace that would cater to their needs and desires, but was far away from prying eyes.

After years of planning, making a deal with one of the richest people on Earth, Marc was delighted when the *Tranquility Casino* was finally open for business. He had decided on the name *Tranquility* to tie into the Apollo 11 Moon landing paraphernalia housed in the casino's Main Bar. It was the biggest collection of that famous event anywhere, with its crown jewel being Neil Armstrong's spacesuit. The collection was very popular with the customers, particularly the hologram Video Booth in the casino where they could pretend to be Armstrong stepping onto the Moon for the first time.

When *Tranquility* opened for business, it was an instant hit. Open for three weeks at a time, with two weeks off for restocking, *Tranquility* had a waiting list of six months to board the transport ships for a week's stay.

For the Core Crew, *Tranquility* was home.

⠲　⠐⠍⠃⠂⠵⠒⠂⠄⠆⠐⠣⠄⠘⠏⠳⠂⠇⠄⠐⠻⠆⠒

A tall, slender, wiry-tough man with steel grey eyes and long wild silvery grey hair that hung down past his shoulders slinked into the kitchen. McFarland wrinkled his nose as he sniffed the air while tucking in his t-shirt, which had "I'm a Kept secret" printed on the front. His lips slightly curled at what he smelled, and in a voice that sounded just shy of a tiger's growl, inquired, "Tony been cookin' again?"

Marc pointed a thumb over his shoulder. "There's a couple o' hockey pucks in the sink that might be useful for the next BBQ."

McFarland grunted. "I'll pass." Then he walked to the reach-in freezer and removed some frozen fruit. "You want a fruit smoothie?

It'll help balance the carb and fat-laden breakfast you're about to make."

Marc grinned. "And yet, you still have seconds when we do the Opening Breakfast."

McFarland went to a large blender and started adding the fruit. "I can't help it if you make the food too good for me to say no to. You want one or not?"

Marc nodded. "Sure."

"Make one for me, too," said Tony, returning with a basket of eggs and down feathers fluttering about him.

As McFarland watched the feathers get sucked up by the overhead hood, he asked, "Did you have fun with Ginger and her sisters? Do they have any feathers left? Or are they like most girls you leave? Naked and not sure what the fuck happened."

Tony brushed at his shirt, releasing another cloud of feathers. "They're pissed and said, 'Screw you and the elephant you rode in on.'"

McFarland frowned at that. "Shouldn't it be a horse?"

Tony shrugged. "They're stupid chickens. Who knows what they think we ride?"

With a harrumph, McFarland turned his attention back to the smoothies. "That's true," he said, placing some more fruit in the blender. Then he got some plain yogurt from the reach-in refrigerator and started making the smoothies for them.

Marc took the eggs and washed them before expertly cracking them into a bowl one-handed while whisking with the other. He paused for a moment when he heard something. From the hallway leading to the kitchen came the voice of *Tranquility*'s Chief Engineer.

Richard Vanderbilt could be counted on for two things: to fix anything that had a mechanical function, and to be silly. His five-foot-ten body came in singing as he mimed a stage performer who was carrying a top hat in one hand and a cane in the other while doing high kicks:

Hello, my baby

Hello, my honey

Hello, my ragtime gal

Send me a kiss by wire

Baby, my heart's on fire.

It was antics such as this that had earned Richard the nickname "Wingnut." His performance came to an end when he saw the glare from McFarland and bowed to him.

"Good morning, McFarland. *Eat* any good books lately?"

McFarland turned back to the blender. "It's a good thing we need you. Singing before I've had my coffee is a killing offense."

Wingnut bounced up and down on his toes excitedly as he clapped his hands together. "What constitutes a paddling? I haven't had a good paddling in a while."

McFarland rolled his eyes. "I'll see if I can pencil you in after breakfast."

Marc and Tony looked at each other, shaking their heads.

Marc continued his work with the eggs as he asked Wingnut, "Anything to report on the Laser Sails?"

The engineer poured himself a cup of coffee and, as always, took too big a gulp of the hot liquid and quickly swallowed it, which caused his eyes to water. He sucked in air to cool his mouth as he responded to Marc. "Nope..., no problems..., went... without a... hitch.... *Tranquility*... is in... proper... orbit... until the... next adjustment."

Tony shook his head at the brilliant but silly man. "Careful. That may be hot."

Wingnut gave the coffee cup a spiteful glare and shook a finger at it. "I told this cup yesterday I wanted a proper temperature coffee. You would think, after five years, it would listen to me."

⠴⠂ ⠠⠶⠞⠃⠄⠎⠆⠎⠐ ⠆ ⠠⠙⠃⠐ ⠹⠏⠇⠄⠰⠆ ⠠⠆⠒⠖

Tranquility's Laser Sails were a part of the orbital alignment system that brought the station from Earth's orbit, where it was constructed, to save on building costs. The huge sails were deployed every few months to adjust *Tranquility's* position without using fuel other than the lasers that were directed at the sails from the four Ion-Whiskers. The Whiskers were state-of-the-art Ion-propelled satellites that added a thousand-fold stronger stream of photons from the lasers' emitters to the Sails than the Sun could provide. They also had a full array of scanners, telescopes, and sensing equipment that provided constant surveys of the Solar System. Being deployed full-time around *Tranquility* made them the early warning system for NEOs—Near-Earth Objects—that might endanger Earth, Star Base One, or *Tranquility* itself.

⠴⠂ ⠠⠶⠞⠃⠄⠎⠆⠎⠐ ⠆ ⠠⠙⠃⠐ ⠹⠏⠇⠄⠰⠆ ⠠⠆⠒⠖

An electronic pop of the Com-System sounded from the wall speaker.

"Bridge to Crew Kitchen. Marc, are you lurking down there?"

Marc pressed the Com-button. "What's up, Grey Wolf?"

"I wanted to let you know that the Chaos Twins are thirty minutes away. Thought you'd want a head's-up to cook your fabulous french toast for us before we unload the supplies."

Marc smirked. "I thought I'd let Tony do breakfast this time."

Grey Wolf's panicked voice wailed out of the speaker: "Oh, god, *no!!!*"

Tony leaned toward the Com-System with a sneer. "I'll remember you said that during our next training session."

A groan was heard from Grey Wolf. "Great. I'm a dead man. Thanks, Marc."

They could hear Steven's voice bellowing with laughter on the Bridge: "I'll bring the popcorn! You make the movie, McFarland."

McFarland grumbled into his smoothie. "Oh, goodie. Another snuff film to add to my collection."

Marc rolled his eyes. "Alright, everyone, we have a lot of work ahead of us today. Grey Wolf, get updates on the auction crew arrival. Steven, give Susan, Eileen, and Kimberly a call and tell them that the twins will be home soon. And I'll get started on breakfast."

Grey Wolf and Steven acknowledged and cut the connection.

Marc continued to work on the egg mixture by adding fresh ground nutmeg and real vanilla extract. Then, looking over his shoulder, he said, "McFarland...."

Grey eyes narrowed at Marc as McFarland wiped his mouth with the back of his hand.

"What?"

Marc pointed at a shelf near McFarland. "Hand me some amaretto for the french toast."

McFarland eyed the bottle and grunted less than enthusiastically. "Oh, okay."

Marc watched the silver-haired curmudgeon slowly get up, grab the bottle, and bring it over to him. Opening the bottle, Marc added a few splashes of the liquor to the eggs.

"Woe is you, the so put-upon man," Marc said. "Unfed and uncared for. How do you manage to put up with such demands on you?"

McFarland got some coffee and sat back down. "Killing sarcastic morning people seems to help."

Marc, Tony, and Wingnut chuckled at that.

A few minutes later, a lady in her late twenties, with wavy dark brown hair, entered the kitchen, wearing flannel Snoopy PJ's and a thick white robe.

"Gurd murnnning," she mumbled, as she headed straight to the coffee.

Marc watched as his sister, Kimberly, picked up a coffee cup, placed it under the spigot for the coffee, leaned forward to look closely at the mug, turned it right side up, and filled it.

"Another late-night studying for your pilot's license, Sis?"

"Mmm hmm," she grunted after carefully gulping a few mouthfuls of coffee. Then she refilled the mug and sat down at the table, putting her head on her arms, and only lifting it enough to sip some more coffee.

Next came a short, dark-red-haired woman with a smile that lit up any room she walked into. Susan greeted everyone in her ever cheerful voice: "Good morning! How is everyone? Oh! I see we lost Kim already."

Kimberly grunted an acknowledgment as she held out the now empty coffee cup, waving it back and forth.

Susan pulled the cup from Kimberly's hand, which flopped like a dead fish back to the table.

"Allow me to refill that for you," Susan said with a sympathetic smile.

Sitting across from Kimberly, Wingnut regarded the dead hand. "Maybe, if we made a pot of coffee with energy drink instead of water, we wouldn't have a zombie at the table."

Susan placed the coffee cup in the Auto-Wash and got a bigger mug for Kimberly. "A friend of mine did that once," she said. "They claimed to be able to see sound waves."

"Hmmm...," pondered McFarland. "I wonder what Grunge music looks like."

"I'm guessing about nine-point-six on the Richter scale," said the next woman to enter the kitchen. Eileen was of average height, with shoulder-length brunette hair and sparkling brown eyes. Her work as a CMT—Certified Massage Therapist—had given her arms and shoulders a strong look, and yet she was every inch a lady. After greeting everyone with a smile, she saw Kimberly's comatose body, moved behind her, and started to massage the sleepy girl's neck and shoulders.

Kimberly's eyes shot open and then relaxed in absolute bliss. "I just may survive today, thanks to you," she said.

"Here," said Susan, placing the filled coffee mug in Kimberly's hand. "Drink some more coffee, and between the two of you, you can seize the day. Or throttle it. Whichever comes first."

Two men walked into the kitchen, talking about computers in a way that sounded like a foreign language to the others. Steven's short, stocky stature was highlighted by Grey Wolf's tall and lanky body. To completely separate how they looked, Steven wore casual dark slacks and a dark green polo shirt, while Grey Wolf wore an untucked black t-shirt, denim jeans, and a denim vest. Although they were vastly different in appearance and personality, together they formed an unrivaled computer team.

Steven went straight to Susan and gave her a hug and a kiss. "Sorry I wasn't in our quarters when you got up."

Susan nuzzled his cheek with her nose. "You're forgiven. This time. But next time I may have to divorce you."

As Grey Wolf filled two coffee mugs and handed one to Steven, he said, "You can blame me, Susan. I had a problem with the Bridge systems that needed his touch."

Susan looked at Grey Wolf with a smile. "I'd find some way to drag you away from your one true love, but I like Irma."

Irma appeared on the wall monitor, looking shy while batting her eyes. "Aw, shucks. How's a girl to get any work done around here with so much affection being thrown at her?"

Tony muttered to Marc, "Who brought all these weird people here?"

Marc grinned. "Me. One of the better ideas I've had."

Twenty minutes later, a pile of french toast was being attacked by everyone as coffee was being guzzled. Marc stopped eating, listened for a moment, looked longingly at his plate, sighed, and pushed back from the table. Then he stood up and walked toward the hallway, from which he could hear the unmistakable sound of marching feet, followed by two chanting voices.

"O-Ee-Yah! Eoh-Ah! O-Ee-Yah! Eoh-Ah! O-Ee-Yah! Eoh-Ah!"

The Chaos Twins, Vincent and Kevin Pierce—a.k.a. Thing I and Thing 2—were identical twins who stood a little over six feet tall, with neatly cut dark brown hair and lean bodies. When they wore the same clothing, as they did now in their dark grey flight suits, the only way to tell them apart was that Vincent was a tiny bit taller and had a slightly slenderer nose.

Kevin, Vincent, and Marc were founding members of a group of friends called Team Chaos, who believed that friendship starts with trust, and anything else not nailed down can be thrown out the window. And considering the parties they had thrown over the years, many things had gone out the window.

Tables.

Chairs.

People.

If you were invited to a Team Chaos party, you were guaranteed to witness an interesting time. Last month's video of the twins' "Floor Buffer Chariot Race" went viral with over two million views in the first hour.

The Chaos Twins were crazy, but Marc trusted them with his life.

When they entered the kitchen in lockstep now with each other, they stopped and bowed to Marc with flare. "Hail, Mutant! We have come from afar at your request!"

Marc returned the bow and chanted with them in sync: "Life is like a beer mug. Full, with lots of head!"

This ended with the three of them saluting each other by punching themselves in the side of the head and yelling, "*Ack!*"

The rest of the crew ignored the display of insanity. Every supply run by the twins was completed with this ritual of reporting to Marc.

Kevin looked at McFarland, who still hadn't brushed or tied his hair back, pointed an accusing finger at him, and complained, "You started the electroshock treatments without us. You promised!!!"

McFarland moved his coffee mug farther away from the twins and grumbled. "It's too early for this shit!"

Marc pointed at the food he had made. "At ease, you two. Coffee is brewed and french toast is done. When you're ready, I've got a ton of prep to discuss with you, Kevin, and all departments have a lot to do after we unload the supplies."

The twins saluted with a fist to the side of their heads and proceeded to fight over the french toast.

"That one's mine!"

"Fine. I get the one in the middle."

"You got that last time!"

McFarland removed a plastic spider that magically appeared in his coffee and growled, "Someone's gonna die."

Irma's head appeared on the monitor. "Shall I start recording for you, McFarland? I could edit it with sound effects."

The sound of something wet getting punched, followed by a blood-curdling scream, came out of the speakers.

"Maybe later," grumbled McFarland as he threw the spider at Vincent's head.

"Hey!" yelled Vincent as he looked down at the floor and picked up the spider. "I've been looking for that." He stuffed it in his pocket.

Susan patted her mouth with her napkin. "Eat up, everyone. The fifty casino guests arrive in four days, six hours. The AuctionHouse team in two days, three hours. And the Auxiliary Crew with the Marines in twenty-eight hours."

Grey Wolf and Steven looked up from their plates.

"How the hell does she know the updates when we just got them?" Grey Wolf asked.

Susan looked at them over her coffee mug and batted her eyes. "It's how I earn the big bucks, guys."

"She's a witch," Kevin managed to say around a mouthful of french toast.

Susan lifted her hand and moved her fingers as if casting a spell. "Careful, you. Or I'll turn you into a newt!"

"Too late!!!" the rest of the crew all said in unison.

Irma appeared again on the monitor. "Hey, guys! We're on the news!"

She vanished, and a lady with extremely white teeth and long black hair, which was tied back so it wouldn't get in the way when she was in Zero-G, looked back at them from the monitor.

"This is Rachel Connolly, reporting from the *AuctionHouse 5* transport ship on our way to the Moon-orbiting casino, *Tranquility*. As you most likely know, in five days *Tranquility* will be hosting the first off-Earth auction, where legendary items of Hollywood and Rock 'n' Roll will be up for grabs to the highest bidder. This transport ship is jam-packed with those items, and when we arrive in two days, I'll give you a firsthand look at them before the auction, as well as interviews with the crew of *Tranquility*. When *Tranquility* opened for business five years ago, it was the one and only time that reporters were allowed onboard, and what they found was a place of wonder and style. Throughout those years, interviews with the guests have painted a picture of incredible service, entertainment, and food, unlike anything found on Earth. I'm looking forward to experiencing what only an elite few have had the pleasure of. I'm Rachel Connolly, and I'll be your guide to the Auction at *Tranquility*."

As the monitor went dark, Irma reappeared. "Is it just me, or does she need a brightness control for her teeth?"

Steven barely contained his spit take into his mug of coffee, while the others chuckled and nodded in agreement.

McFarland pushed his half-eaten plate of food away. "Being reminded that I'm going to be interviewed by a news hound has killed my appetite."

Susan pushed his plate back in front of him. "Don't act like you didn't know this was happening. We all signed off on this."

McFarland growled. "Just because I know something's gonna happen doesn't mean that I'm gonna like it."

Susan couldn't argue with that, and didn't. "Rachel Connolly is to be given every courtesy we give the guests. She already knows about the areas that are off-limits, unless she's accompanied by one of us. That's it. Back to our regularly scheduled insanity."

The twins bumped their coffee mugs together. "To insanity! And beyond!"

Then they guzzled the last of their coffee before going to refill their mugs.

Marc cleared his dishes and placed them in the Auto-Wash. "Just do us a favor, McFarland, and don't make things difficult for her. None of us like having a reporter nosing around, but it's a necessary evil to have the auction here. Now finish your food like a good boy, and you'll see the pretty girl on the plate."

McFarland narrowed his eyes at Marc, looked down at his plate, grabbed his fork, and pushed the remainder of the french toast away from the center of his plate. Nothing appeared. "Where's the girl?"

Marc smiled. "You must have been a bad boy."

McFarland stabbed a bit of french toast. "You say that like it's something new."

Marc turned for the door. "I'm heading down to the main kitchen to get it ready for the supplies. I'll meet you all in the Loading Bay."

A chorus of affirmatives followed him.

Marc took the elevator to the first floor. In contrast to the homey feeling of Core Crew's living quarters on the second floor, the first floor was spotless and well lit. The walls were an off-white with lightly textured Fibonacci and fractal patterns, so the lighting wouldn't glare off the surface. The dark burgundy carpet had gold trim, and the polished redwood ceilings gave the hallway a feeling of elegance and style. Between the elevator and the main entrance to the dining hall, there was one of two small alcoves. Marc stopped, tapped on the access pad for one of them, scrolled through a list of musicians, and made a selection. "Good morning, boys! Ready to get to work?"

Inside the alcove, there appeared two holograms of seated cello players who were dressed in classic Renaissance outfits befitting musicians. The two dark-haired men saluted Marc with their bows, and then the one on the left replied. "Of course, our good man. What may we play for you?"

Marc smiled at the 2Cellos. "I need something to start the day off with some energy. How about 'Wake Me Up'? I leave it to your discretion what to play from there. Please pipe it into the main kitchen."

The cello players nodded to Marc. "As you wish."

The music they started playing was fast-paced, with a bouncy beat. Perfect for doing any number of chores. When the guests arrived, the cellists would change to chamber music, but while the crew was busy getting *Tranquility* ready, the music leaned toward a more Rock style.

Marc looked at the alcove across from the cello players and considered activating the grand piano player, but decided not to.

Continuing down the hall, he stopped at a doorway that had a brass sign above it with the words *Dining Room* on it. After tapping on a panel next to the door to adjust the sensors from standby mode to active, he entered when the doors quietly slid open. It was nearly pitch black in the room, except for the softly glowing lights at each of the doors. After five years, Marc could walk the entire station blindfolded. With ease he made his way toward the kitchen as he called out. "Irma? Would you please start the 'Opening Day' program?"

Irma's voice softly echoed in the empty room: "Sure thing, Captain, My Captain."

The lights slowly came up to full illumination as Marc entered the kitchen. He knew that the lighting throughout *Tranquility* was being turned on. Out on the hull, a series of lights glinted through the gaps of the solar panels that made the casino sparkle as it rotated. Marc felt that they had the best "Open" sign anywhere.

The main kitchen, which was well designed and orderly, gleamed with cleanliness befitting that of a world-class restaurant. Marc checked all the walk-in refrigerators and freezers to make sure they were running at the proper temperatures, then tested every burner on the stoves and all the other equipment. He took note of a burnt-out light in the pantry and then headed out to meet the others to unload the *Camel.*

⠲ ⠐⠍⠃⠂⠊⠰⠂ ⠐⠆ ⠠⠩⠃⠄ ⠌⠳⠦⠨⠇ ⠐⠦⠒⠖

The Class 6-C cargo transporter was known as the *Camel.* Its cargo holds were temperature-controlled so that it could hold perishable food, and it had a separate area for frozen food. Its massive water tanks were refilled once a month at the Earth-orbiting factory that processed the asteroids brought in from the Asteroid Belt by robotic ships. Its large tanks, called the Hump, could hold 1.6 million gallons of water, which fit into *Tranquility*'s hull. This meant that docking was something that only specialized pilots were allowed to do, and guaranteed that the cargo didn't float freely about once the *Camel* docked.

⠲ ⠐⠍⠃⠂⠊⠰⠂ ⠐⠆ ⠠⠩⠃⠄ ⠌⠳⠦⠨⠇ ⠐⠦⠒⠖

The *Camel*'s Loading Bay was a hive of activity as the exoskeleton loaders, which could move 800 pounds of supplies, were being operated by the twins in ways that defied reason.

Tony often felt that he was watching an insane form of square dancing with heavy equipment. There was even a bit of arm-hooking with the loaders so they could make tighter turns.

The two brothers had a connection that only twins seem to have, and no one else understood. When any of the others tried to unload the supplies, it always took two or three times as long to finish, compared to what the twins did. There wasn't any communication between them, other than a random "hup!" or "hi-ya!" to indicate which way they were going or who should go first. They just moved around each other, missing hitting by mere inches.

The crew had learned long ago to stay out of the way as the twins set down the pallets on the docking bay.

Susan was taking inventory as the items were separated by the others and loaded on the Auto-Carts, which delivered their loads to the departments without the need for anyone to operate them.

To refill *Tranquility*'s water supply, Wingnut connected hoses to the *Camel*'s storage tanks, which made up seventy-five percent of the volume of the ship. After several years of unloading the Camel, the crew had the supplies heading off to their departments in record time.

As Kevin maneuvered a black container out of the cargo hold, he asked, "Who placed an order for a coffin? Are we planning on sending a guest home in a box this time?"

Wingnut waved his hand at him. "That's for Ross. It's a new Čapek unit for him."

Kevin grinned at his brother. "Hey, Vince! Go long!" Then he pretended that he was going to toss the box to him."

Wingnut crossed his arms and wasn't fooled for a second. "That's two-point-three million dollars out of your pocket if you break it. And you get to explain to Marc why it will be necessary to order another one."

Kevin pouted as he lowered the box to the floor. "Oh, sure. Pull the Angry Mutant Card and ruin all my fun."

Marc entered the Loading Bay with a concerned look. "And what, exactly, would I have to be angry about, Thing Two?"

Kevin smirked. "Vincent and I jumping rope in the exoskeleton with the water hoses."

Marc stopped, considered the idea, and shook his head. "That would surely be another first for you guys. But let's not destroy the exoskeletons. Unless you wanna unload the *Camel* by hand."

Kevin's eyes got big at the thought of that. "No thanks. I really don't want firsthand experience at moving sixteen tons."

The twins went back to unloading the supplies while singing The Cas Carnaby Five "Sixteen Tons." Everyone else joined in, enjoying the silliness of the friendship they shared.

As soon as the last pallet was placed on the dock, the twins started their tradition of sumo wrestling with the exoskeletons. That was the others' cue to quickly finish unloading the pallet and find something else to do. It only caused them to have acid reflux to see equipment being used in such a manner. But if the twins didn't blow off steam after being cooped up in the *Camel* for nearly a week, they would find some other way that would cause heartburn for the rest of the crew.

⠲ ⠐⠡⠗⠊⠎⠞⠀⠕⠋ �⠑⠆ �⠏⠥⠄⠊ ⠐⠩⠶⠏

The main kitchen always required the most attention, because of the need to keep food at correct temperatures, so everyone chipped in to put things away. When Kevin arrived, he claimed victory over his brother and started directing the placement of items with the finesse of a crazed drill sergeant.

As soon as the kitchen was stocked, the Core Crew would help the others until everything from the *Camel* was stored away. Each department head took great joy in giving Kevin a taste of his own medicine. Once the departments were as ready as they could be without the Auxiliary Crew, the Core Crew gathered together in the Main Bar to have drinks.

Wingnut walked up to Marc and placed a bottle of Chivas Regal Scotch in front of him.

"My cousin Lawrence sent this bottle as an apology for stealing your recipes, and asks you not to send any more Marines to his restaurant."

Marc eyed the bottle. "I guess he's learned his lesson about swiping a cook's recipes. Tell him that it'll take at least one more bottle for me to forgive him."

Wingnut grinned and set two more bottles in front of him. "He thought that would be the case."

⠨⠂ ⠠⠐⠷⠂⠒⠂⠂ ⠰⠿ ⠠⠯⠷⠄ ⠒⠿⠂⠲⠄⠂ ⠐⠿⠒⠆⠆

When Lawrence had been part of the serving crew during the previous year, he had managed to download *Tranquility*'s top-secret recipes. Shortly after that, his restaurant in Portland, Oregon, was visited by a group of Marines, who bought several rounds of drinks for the house, broke all the legs off all the stools and chairs, and then left a nice tip after creating a smoldering hole in the solid oak bar. Sometime during the mayhem, a computer virus was released that scrambled all the restaurant's recipes and deleted all of *Tranquility*'s.

⠨⠂ ⠠⠐⠷⠂⠒⠂⠂ ⠰⠿ ⠠⠯⠷⠄ ⠒⠿⠂⠲⠄⠂ ⠐⠿⠒⠆⠆

Marc pushed the bottles toward McFarland, who could always be found behind the bar. "Would you add these to my collection, please?"

McFarland opened the lock to Marc's private stock. "Sure thing." He pointed at some green bottles in the case. "I see you restocked on Midori. You planning to make your Vulcan Mind-Melds again?"

Marc grinned. "Yep!"

The twins' heads turned in unison as they enthusiastically shouted, "YES!!!"

Tony groaned. "People say Marines are nuts when they cut loose. Is Team Chaos gonna set the bar higher for insane behavior again? You know there's still a tomato stain on the ceiling in the kitchen from the food fight the last time you made the drinks. And I'm locking up the floor buffers. It took Wingnut *forever* to get them to work right after the twins had their 'Chariot Race.'"

"But, mom!" whined the twins. "We were just having fun!"

Tony pointed at Marc and the twins. "You guys are a handful just by yourselves. Turning two or more of you loose when buzzed always makes me think the Devil should be taking notes."

Marc smirked. "We do enjoy spreading the chaos."

Kevin, Vincent, and Marc put their mugs of beer together and chanted. "Chaos powers activate! Shape of a disaster area! Form of a lawsuit!!!"

Tony shook his head, wondering if he should triple-lock the floor buffers and anything else not screwed down. He was dreading the madness that was coming.

CHAPTER 2

Saved by the Marines

The next morning, both Marc and Tony were up early, jogging in *Tranquility*'s Botanical Garden—a forty-yard-wide section around the entire inside circumference of the station. The pathway they were running on wove back and forth to carefully showcase the assorted trees, flowers, and plants. The diversity of the plant life was a thing of great pride for the Core Crew because they were the first to have a self-sustaining garden in space. It even had a small pond with a creek that was home to butterflies, ladybugs, and dragonflies. In a protected area that was off-limits to guests, there was a beehive. Without the tireless worker bees, the plants and flowers would never be as lush and plentiful.

The "sky" reached all the way to the central hub that slowly spun in the opposite direction of the station. Without this counter-spinning hub, *Tranquility*'s stable orbit would not be possible. With an assortment of different wavelengths given off by the light sources attached to the hub, the effect was as close to Earth as one could achieve on a station. People could even get a sunburn if they fell asleep for more than five hours on the open grass area. Also, attached to the hub were large fan blades that gave a gentle breeze and cast shadows as if clouds were passing overhead. Along the South Wall, there were windows to the guest rooms; and along the North Wall, there were the windows of the employees' rooms. Above those were the windows for the Core Crew.

All the living quarters were identical in size, but the wall between the bedroom and the living room in each could be adjusted to the occupant's wishes. The living room had a computer terminal with a large monitor on the wall that could play any number of programs or movies. The windows in both rooms looked out onto the garden and had several types of curtains that could block out the sunlight or shade it. All the living spaces also had a small private bathroom with a shower.

Given its distance from resources, *Tranquility* relied on using recycled water, which was filtered and then sanitized. The system cycled the potable water through a pond, which in turn fed the small creek that weaved throughout the garden. A section of creek turned into mild rapids, aerating the water, which then dropped into the pond, where the Japanese koi could be found.

Marc pointed at some purple flowers. "Looks like the bees are enjoying the new lavender plants. That should add some flavor to the honey for Kevin to use."

Tony frowned. "I know we need them to keep the plants healthy, but I'm never gonna like seeing them buzzing about."

Marc wiped some sweat from his forehead with the back of his hand. "Oh, c'mon, Tony. In our five years here, there's been only one case of someone getting stung, and that was *me* when I rolled over on one while I was sunbathing. I have to say, it's kind of funny that a big badass Marine is afraid of such a small critter."

Tony quickened his pace, pulling ahead of Marc. "You've never witnessed a full-scale swarm of angry bees, have you? It's something I can do without ever again."

Marc caught up to Tony and matched his speed. "If I recall that story correctly, it was Yellow Jackets, not bees, and you were nowhere near them."

Tony upped his speed again. "Never let the truth stand in the way of a good story."

Marc called out after him. "Strange…, you don't look Irish," and ran to catch up.

The bracelet on Marc's wrist started to vibrate and beep, indicating that someone was paging him. He whistled at Tony and pointed at the bracelet, so they stopped under a willow tree for him to answer it.

"Marc here."

Susan's cheerful voice responded. "The Auxiliary Crew and Marines will be arriving in one hour, Marc. I thought you would want a heads-up, so you can get presentable before they get here. Unless you plan on smelling to high heaven for them."

Marc smirked. "In some cultures, the scent of a male's sweat is arousing to the opposite sex."

Susan's amused reply was, "Name one group who spends time in space in confined areas with dozens of other people."

Marc tried to quickly think of one. "Umm…, hmm…, well…, can I get back to you on that?"

Susan sounded victorious. "Sure. You now have fifty-eight minutes. See you both at Docking Elevator One."

As Marc cut the connection, Tony said, "How did she know I was with you?"

Marc pointed a finger to his head. "She's got ESP?"

Tony raised an eyebrow. "Then, why does she always lose at our poker games?"

Marc shrugged. "She's addicted to losing?"

Tony headed down the pathway. "Works for me. C'mon, time to put our game faces on."

They jogged to the exit, which gently blew air against them and into the garden to help prevent any of the flying critters from escaping into the rest of the station.

⠴⠀⠠⠐⠷⠄⠡⠒⠐⠀⠿⠀⠠⠋⠷⠐⠀⠿⠷⠠⠂⠄⠐⠊⠀⠐⠿⠴⠢

Susan watched from the bedroom window as the two men exited the garden. "Those two guys are sure dedicated to keeping themselves fit."

In the other room, Steven called out, "What was that, honey?"

Susan turned from the window and walked to the living room. "Have you considered joining Marc and Tony for their morning runs?"

Their home had a warm, almost cabin-like feel to it. The walls and floors were both covered with real wood paneling, and wooden tables and chairs completed the look. The only items that didn't say "Rustic Home" were the computer on the desk and the large monitor on the wall.

Steven was sitting at the desk, downloading some new designs for computer components. "Considered running? Yes. Doing it? No. The pace they keep would kill me. Besides, I thought you liked my love handles."

Susan wrapped her arms around Steven's shoulders and kissed him on the neck. "I love everything about you. It was just a thought. I have to get ready for the ACs' arrival." She took off her shirt and dropped it playfully on his head. "You could join me in the shower."

Steven lifted the shirt from his eyes to see her in the bathroom doorway, beckoning him with a finger and a seductive grin.

⠰⠂ ⠄⠐⠏⠂�⠂⠒ ⠐⠢ ⠠⠫⠓⠐ ⠹⠏⠡⠄⠄⠇ ⠐⠢⠶⠏

When Tony finished showering, he started to get dressed. It was evident that his time as a Marine hadn't been easy on his body. His back and legs had multiple scars from bullets, knives, and surgical operations. They were all well healed and faded, but still quite visible. He put on some tan slacks, a black belt, a grey t-shirt, and a black dress shirt.

His quarters were neat and organized, a habit that had followed him from his years as a Marine to his civilian life, with mementos from his service around the world.

He gave a quick look in the full-length mirror, nodded in approval, and headed for the door.

⠰⠂ ⠄⠐⠏⠂⠒⠂⠒ ⠐⠢ ⠠⠫⠓⠐ ⠹⠏⠡⠄⠄⠇ ⠐⠢⠶⠏

The transport ship *Hestia*, named after the Greek goddess of family and home, arrived with the Auxiliary Crew and the Marines. As always, Marc, Tony, and Susan were at Docking Elevator 1 to greet them. The Auxiliary Crew disembarked first, since most of them were females, and the Marines were gentlemen. The ACs were warmly greeted by name and treated as old friends.

The last crew member to exit was a five-foot-tall older lady with short black hair, who was wearing a loose dark blue blouse and black slacks.

Marc stepped forward to give her a hug. "Thanks for coming, Dawn. I always breathe easier when you're in Sickbay."

Dawn smiled up at Marc. "Glad to lend a hand, Kiddo. This time, I'm aiming for no visits."

"I'll let Kevin know that he's on his own if something happens in the kitchen," said Marc as Dawn headed down the hallway, waving her hand in acknowledgment.

Tony leaned toward Marc. "I like that old lady."

Dawn looked over her shoulder. "Who are you calling old?" But she didn't stop walking down the hallway.

Tony gulped as he pretended to be fascinated by his fingernails.

Marc and Susan started giggling when the sound of the returning elevator brought the three of them back to the moment at hand.

⠲⠀⠄⠦⠓⠄⠔⠒⠂⠆⠀⠆⠀⠠⠊⠣⠄⠀⠿⠃⠥⠄⠄⠆⠀⠴⠙⠶

When the Core Crew first opened *Tranquility*, they decided that they needed some sort of security to dissuade anyone from taking advantage of their being so far from help. Tony hand-picked retired and honorably discharged Marines to provide security. In five years, they had only needed to break up a few drunken fights among the customers. The job was easy and paid the Marines three times what they could make at any other security job. That made working at *Tranquility* a coveted position for the Marines.

⠲⠀⠄⠦⠓⠄⠔⠒⠂⠆⠀⠆⠀⠠⠊⠣⠄⠀⠿⠃⠥⠄⠄⠆⠀⠴⠙⠶

When the five Marines entered the hallway, they formed a line, came to attention, and saluted. Tony stepped forward to return the salute.

"At ease, gentlemen. Welcome back to *Tranquility*. You have your room assignments and already know the drill. Relax and report to the Main Dining Hall at nineteen-thirty hours. Dismissed!"

"Ooo-Rah!" replied the Marines, who saluted and quickly marched down the hall.

Susan sighed. "I live for this part of opening the casino."

Marc asked, "Does Steven know you fantasize about five walking masses of muscle?"

Susan continued to watch the Marines until they disappeared around the corner. "It's only fair. His eyes bug out whenever the Dallas Cheerleaders jump around."

Tony narrowed his eyes as he looked at Marc. "Watch who you're calling 'a walking mass of muscles,' butterball. They only salute civilians they respect. Each one of them would walk into a hail of bullets for both of you."

Marc looked at Susan. "He's got a point. I've never been disappointed with their service or manner of conduct."

Susan threw a last glance toward where the Marines had gone, and sighed. "Nor I, but I'm still gonna drool a little each time they march by me."

Tony complained, "How come you don't drool at me?"

Susan looked aghast. "Oh, now that would just be wrong, on so many levels."

"Akin to eyeing a brother, I would imagine," Marc said.

They all turned to the elevator as it returned to greet the two pilots of the *Hestia*. The older of the pair had greying, dark brown hair, a five o'clock shadow goatee, and a smile that equaled Susan's for warming up a room. The shorter pilot, who had shaggy blonde hair, was younger, but not by much, and grinned like a maniac at seeing them.

Marc stepped forward to extend his hand to the older man. "Stuart, good to see you. Fred, are you keeping this old man in line?"

Fred shook Marc's hand. "Only when I can keep him away from the strip clubs."

Stuart pointed a thumb at Fred. "Which he takes me to."

Tony shook their hands, and Susan gave them hugs.

"We have your room ready for you two," said Tony as he waved them down the hallway. "Dinner is at nineteen-thirty hours."

Stuart's shoulders slouched a bit. "We got a message just before we docked that the transport ship *Annabel* has engine trouble. We need to get back to Starbase One and pick up some delegates. So much for spending our anniversary here on *Tranquility*."

Marc looked at Susan and Tony, who were all frowns, and then at the two pilots. "Well, that sucks square rocks through a long garden hose. We'll have to set you guys up with some food to go, as well as the cake that Kevin made for you. No way are we letting two of the best independent pilots get away without letting us do some sort of celebration for your seventeen years of marriage. How long can you delay your departure?"

Stuart looked at Fred. "What do you think? An hour? Maybe two?"

Fred scratched the side of his head as he thought. "Hmmm…. If we do a longer burn toward SB-1 and do a heavier deceleration, we should gain about…, two and a half, three hours. That means using up a lot more fuel, but it'll be worth it to spend time here."

Marc turned to Tony. "Would you mind contacting Kevin to let him know that there's a change in the dinner plans for Stuart and Fred?"

Tony nodded and started the process of getting them some food to go.

Marc then addressed Susan. "Would you let Kimberly know that their rooms are not gonna be needed.... Oh, I see you're already on that."

Susan looked up from what she was doing and smirked. "You say that like you're surprised."

Marc brought his hand up in surrender. "Surprised? By you? Only when you drop the ball on something."

Susan squinted. "When have I *ever* 'dropped the ball'?"

Fred spoke up. "I'm guessing, never?"

Marc chuckled. "And you would be right, my friend."

Susan beamed with pride. "Darn tootin'!"

Tony motioned them down the hallway. "Alright, you two, let's get going. While Kevin is whipping up a to-go order that you are most likely going to be eating the whole way back to SB-1, let's head to the bar to get you a few drinks.... I know, nothing alcoholic," he added when Stuart was about to say something.

Stuart nodded. "It's a curse to stand by the rules sometimes, but the no booze forty-eight hours before a flight is one we never break."

Marc placed his hand on Stuart's shoulder. "And that's one of the many reasons we entrust you two to transport our crew."

"Kimberly is up to speed," said Susan, "and will meet us at the bar with the gifts."

Stuart and Fred looked at each other. "Gifts?"

Marc started to lead them down the hallway. "Don't get too excited. It's just a little something we got everyone."

Fred shook his head in wonder. "You still stock that fabulous ginger ale?"

Tony smiled. "Ordered a case of Bruce Cost just for you. I'll have McFarland pull it to take with you."

Stuart exhaled heavily. "Trying to explain to people the generosity you guys have here is impossible. No one believes us."

Marc shrugged. "We're only like that with people we like."

Tony added, "We've ruffled a few feathers here and there."

Susan leaned closer to Fred. "He means Marc."

Marc glanced at her. "I heard that."

Susan looked away, finding that some of her hair needed straightening with her hands.

Laughter followed them down the hallway as they headed to the bar.

⠂⠄ ⠐⠌⠏⠄⠌⠄⠌ ⠐⠋ ⠄⠯⠡⠄ ⠌⠯⠏⠦⠄⠌ ⠄⠏⠭⠖

Two hours and thirty-five minutes later, the whole Core Crew escorted Stuart and Fred back to the elevator. Waiting there was one of Kevin's cooks with a service cart loaded with food.

As Stuart looked at the cart, his jaw dropped. "There's no way we're gonna eat all that in a day and a half back to SB-1."

Fred rubbed his hands together and licked his lips. "I'm game to try!"

Kevin moved over to the cart to thank and dismiss the cook. Then he said to the pilots, "Some of this is for the trip back. The rest is for you to throw a proper party when you get home."

Marc grinned. "I added a bottle of Chivas Regal to make a proper toast."

The pilots looked at each other with tears of joy and then back at the Core Crew. Stuart stepped up to Marc and gave him a huge hug. "There are no words to express our appreciation for all this. Thanks."

Fred wiped the tears from his face. "You have a brother who needs a boyfriend? I know a nice guy."

Marc laughed and pointed at Kimberly. "Nope. Just this cute lady here and another sister, Ginger, back on Earth, cataloging critters she just discovered in Africa."

Fred jokingly frowned. "Darn!"

Stuart pushed Fred ahead of him. "Let's get going. We're already pushing the limits of the rendezvous time with SB-1. Thanks, everyone. See you next time."

The members of the Core Crew waved goodbye as the pilots entered the elevator with their supplies. Then they watched on the monitor next to the doors as the pilots entered the ship and secured the hatch.

When the ready light came on, Marc tapped the Communication Station near the elevator. "Irma, would you disengage the locking clamps and clear the *Hestia* for departure, please?"

"Right away," Irma replied, "oh, great and powerful one."

As soon as the sounds of the disconnecting ship were heard, the Core Crew went back to their duties.

⠠⠐⠞⠑⠗⠗⠁⠀⠿⠀⠙⠊⠃⠌⠂⠑⠋⠙⠖

The Bridge was the eyes and ears of the station. This was where Grey Wolf and Steven spent most of their time. It was their domain. Every console and component was made and set up to their specifications. Grey Wolf's lanky body leaned back in his Lazy Boy–like chair, with his hands flying over his virtual keyboard. As the Master Programmer of the station, he kept its systems up to date with daily inspections.

Irma's head was slowly spinning on the main monitor as she softly hummed "You Are My Sunshine."

Irma. Her name stood for Independent Roaming Mainframe Associate. She was the most advanced AI ever created, and had become an invaluable member of the crew. Irma was the go-to person on *Tranquility* whenever information was needed. She also kept a 24/7 watch on the station's systems.

But she did have one personality quirk, which was due to the nature of how the Matrix developed. Grey Wolf had designed an AI Matrix that consisted of an eight-by-eight-by-eight-inch cube with a supercomputer hardware shell. Inside the cube, there was a high-density-bio-molecular-silicon-gel, better known as Gel. When the AI's Matrix became active, it took a few hours for the hardware shell to develop its unique pathways through the Gel. This created the AI's thoughts and memories, and as more pathways were made, the AI became better able to process its data. When a full "Awakening" occurred, the "Core" personality emerged, allowing the AI to interact with the world as a unique artificial person.

Irma's personality quirk was to act a little silly at random times.

As Marc walked onto the Bridge, he winked at Irma, who blew him a kiss. Then he looked around. "Hey, Wolf, where's Steven?"

"Down here," came Steven's voice from an access panel in the floor. "I'm installing the new relays to keep the speakers from popping when we use the Com-System."

Marc looked down into the access panel. "I kind of like having a heads-up whenever I'm about to be interrupted."

Steven peeked out of the hatch. "I could always have a high-pitched whistle to precede the call, like that old TV series you like."

Marc up put his hands. "No, thanks. I trust you to do the right thing." Then, pointing at Grey Wolf, he added. "You, on the other hand, I don't trust at all!"

Grey Wolf grinned wickedly at Marc. "You be nice to me, or I'll reprogram your shower to randomly go ice cold."

Marc flexed his fingers menacingly at Grey Wolf. "Do that and I'll tie knots in that long hair and beard of yours while you're asleep in that chair."

"Match point to our fearless leader," said Steven as he extracted himself from the floor. "Did you want something? Or were you in need of harassing your hard-working crew?"

Marc helped him to his feet. "Who says I can't do both? My PAC is acting up, and I'm hoping you can do that voodoo you do."

Steven raised an eyebrow while putting his trademark purple hat on. "Sure. Let me see it."

Marc rolled back his sleeve and removed an inch-wide, quar-ter-inch-thick, black bracelet and handed it over. The PAC—or Personal Arm Computer—was Steven's new brainchild, which made life on the *Tranquility* so much easier for the Core Crew. It used assorted sensors and the latest hologram technology to project images. But as with all new technology, there was bound to be a bug or two.

Steven placed the PAC on a diagnostic pad. "What's it been doing?"

Marc watched over Steven's shoulder as the pad scanned the PAC. "The letters of the virtual keyboard are all out of order. It looks alright, but when I type an A, I get an X. At first, I thought it was me, but now I'm sure it's the PAC."

Steven read the report and frowned. "Hmmm…. Did you forget to remove it while cooking again? It shows that it's got a crack in its micro-sensor. I told you, it can't handle high temps, like a grill."

Marc looked sheepishly at Steven. "Whoops!"

Steven rolled his eyes. "It's a good thing you got the extended warranty. Give me a few hours to fix it. I guess I'll have to design a new one for forgetful cooks like you."

Marc slapped him on the back. "Thanks, bud." Then he turned to Grey Wolf. "How're things on your side of the street?"

"All's quiet on the western front," Grey Wolf said as he continued typing. "I did notice that the AuctionHouse transport is running twenty minutes behind schedule. When I confirmed this with them, they said it was because of a computer malfunction. I'll run a diagnostic on their system after they get settled in. Oh! I have news on Asteroid Hauler 5. After the first auction dinner, the guests will get a view of the asteroid and AH5 from the bar as it enters orbit around the Moon."

Marc's smile spread from ear to ear. "Fabulous! This will truly be a visit that will be talked about for a long time. I'll let Susan know, and we'll see you two for dinner at seven-thirty." Then he headed toward the exit.

"I'll bet even money that she knows already," said Grey Wolf. Marc chuckled. "No bet!"

⠴⠀⠠⠐⠺⠂⠌⠂⠌⠄⠐⠼⠀⠖⠄⠐⠺⠤⠄⠶⠺⠄⠑⠂⠄⠐⠺⠒⠤

After getting off the elevator on the third floor, Tony turned right, toward the Engine Room, where all the physical systems of *Tranquility* were housed, and where you could always find Wingnut.

This was also the place that their other AI was stationed.

Whereas Irma roamed *Tranquility* as a floating head on the monitors because she was installed into *Tranquility's* computer systems, Ross had a robotic body and was independent of the *Tranquility* systems. And, as with Irma, he had his own personality quirks.

When Tony saw Ross's shiny white head behind a monitor, he called out to him, "Hey, Ross!"

As Ross straightened up to look at Tony, his small stature gave one the impression that a 10-year-old child was wearing a spacesuit. But the black faceplate showed an image of a bald man with aquamarine eyes and an adult voice that belied that impression.

Ross was Grey Wolf's first successful AI. The design changed the direction of AIs from being just really fast computers to self-aware individuals—something that only Grey Wolf knew how to do. So far, Ross and Irma were the only two in existence.

There were quite a few ruffled feathers when Grey Wolf petitioned the courts to classify his AIs in a whole new group. The jury was still out on granting "Synthetic Consciousness" to them.

But, for now, they were still simply known as AIs.

Ross quickly entered some commands into the workstation's computer and waved at Tony. "How do, Number Two?"

Tony wasn't fond of being called "Number Two" because he always felt that Ross was calling him a turd. But Ross assured him that he was only referring to Tony's being *Tranquility*'s second-in-command. Nevertheless, Tony didn't like it.

Equally perplexing was Ross's obsession with collecting antique PEZ dispensers—an obsession that was never fully explained, but was chalked up by the others to being his quirk. Tony felt that Ross did it just to be odd.

Waving his hand around the vast compartment, Tony asked, "Any idea where Wingnut is hiding?"

Ross pointed down an aisle between two massive tanks that sanitized water. "He said something half an hour ago about fitting a square peg in a round hole with a Q-tip. Want me to go get him for you?"

Tony shook his head. "That's okay. I'll go hunt him down, thanks."

As Tony wandered toward the tanks, he thought he heard Ross whisper, "What was I supposed to do?"

It annoyed Tony whenever Ross talked to himself.

Wingnut was under a set of large power cells, with only his hips and legs visible. The Chief Engineer was apparently having an argument with the cells, with his legs squirming and slightly kicking in rhythm to his voice. "Get in there, you! Don't you dare! Oh, for Pete's sake…, mother frickin'…, son of a fatherless whore!"

Wingnut's hand reached out and felt around the floor for a nearby tool. As he got ahold of it, Tony placed his foot on the tool to keep it from moving.

"What the fuh!" said the engineer as he slid out on a mechanics board, looked up at Tony, and grunted. "Not enough things to do? Decided to come and harass me for no reason?"

Tony reached down to help Wingnut to his feet. "Who says I don't have a reason?"

"What's up, my good man?" asked Wingnut as he brushed himself off.

Tony looked around, then quietly said, "I just wanted you to know that the betting pool is ready for when Marc scares the shit out of a drunk rich idiot. You in?"

Wingnut thought for a moment. "Sure, put me down for the second day at five-thirty P.M."

Tapping on his PAC, Tony entered the date and time on the projected screen. "How are things going here?"

Wingnut waved a hand at the cells he had been working on. "Never better. I'm just installing some extra power cells that we got, so the extra personnel and equipment won't tax the system."

Tony rolled his sleeve back over the PAC. "Good idea. Oh, by the way, Patricia's onboard."

"I know," said Wingnut with a shy grin. "She, um, sent me a message asking..., to..., er..., well..., eat. With me. Dinner. Tonight."

Amused that a man as capable and smart as Wingnut could become so flustered when it came to the opposite sex, Tony decided to spare the poor guy any more discomfort. "I'm off to see if McFarland wants in on the pool. See you later."

Wingnut looked relieved. "T-T-F-N, Ta-Ta for Now!" Then he bent down, picked up the tool, shook it at the power cells, and in a voice that mimicked an old cartoon moose, said, "This time for sure!"

⠠⠌⠀⠠⠍�⠄� ⠕⠋ ⠠⠹�⠐⠺⠇

The Main Bar was the focal point for *Tranquility*'s guests, and as such was the most lavish-looking room in the casino. The dark mahogany walls and ceiling gave the bar a feeling of an old-school Members Only club. This effect was highlighted with high-back wood-and-leather chairs.

Small alcoves in the redwood walls held the Apollo 11 artifacts, with one larger alcove proudly displaying Neil Armstrong's space-suit. Between the displays, there were photos of the famous landing.

McFarland was putting a high buff on the bar, and a few of the ACs were enjoying drinks at some of the tables, when Tony walked up to the bar and said, "You missed a spot."

McFarland glared. "Where?"

Tony put a large thumbprint on the middle of the bar. "There!"

At that moment, Vincent walked in from the Casino, read the situation, walked back to the doorway, whistled, and waved for the ACs to join him. As they gathered together at the far end of the bar, they started whispering about bets and odds with Vincent.

As McFarland stared at Tony, he reached for two shot glasses and poured Bacardi 151 into them. He then placed them about a yard apart without ever taking his eyes off Tony. Lighting a match, he ignited the alcohol and placed his elbow on the bar with his hand open to Tony. The two of them locked hands and proceeded to arm-wrestle, with the objective being to drive the other man's hand into the fire.

At first, there was no movement—then an ever so slight shaking. The crew's whispering started to get louder as the shaking increased. When McFarland moved Tony's hand—one inch, two inches—the excitement among the crew grew.

"Just get a ruler and whip them out, you two!" said Susan.

Her sudden appearance provided the distraction that Tony needed to push McFarland's hand within an inch of the blue flickering flame.

McFarland cursed and grunted through clenched teeth, "I give!"

The ACs turned to Vincent to settle their debts, while the two combatants extinguished the flames and downed the shots.

"You did that on purpose!" McFarland grumbled at Susan.

She shrugged. "Yeah, I did. But it could have gone either way."

McFarland filled three glasses with ice and soda water, and handed one to Susan. "Are you thinking what I'm thinking?" he said to Tony as he handed a glass to him.

Tony looked thoughtful. "I think so, but how are we gonna fit Steven in a size six dress?"

Susan's perfect spit take was accompanied by a chorus of giggles from the ACs—all of whom found something to do when she glared at them.

"Thanks," she said. "Now I'm gonna have soda water draining from my nose for the next hour."

Tony tried not to laugh, but failed. "Anytime. Anything in particular you wanted?"

Susan took the bar towel offered by McFarland and dabbed at the soda water dripping off her chin. "Yes. I want in on the pool."

Tony narrowed his eyes. "One day, I'm gonna figure out how you know things before everybody else. I've only just started."

Susan tossed the towel at McFarland, who caught it in midair. "Consider it one of the mysteries of being me. Now put me down for day one at four P.M."

Tony activated his PAC again as Susan headed toward the exit. "Sure thing. You know something we don't?"

"Didn't we just establish that?" she said over her shoulder.

Vincent chuckled. "You walked into that one, pal," he said, and returned to pay the winners.

.: .⠴⠗⠄⠴⠴⠂ ⠘ ⠨⠮ ⠴⠏⠇⠂⠄⠇ ⠴⠹⠆

If the Crew Kitchen was Marc's domain, the Main Kitchen was Kevin's. He had strived to make it a Five Michelin Star kitchen and had succeeded. The only thing that was missing were the stars themselves. No critics had ever entered *Tranquility* except for its grand opening. But from that one time and from rumors among the guests, the reputation of Kevin's team was legendary and the envy of all restaurants. At one time, a world-renowned restaurant in Napa Valley had tried to poach Kevin, but his response made it clear that another offer would be considered an act of war.

The eight ACs who made up kitchen crew had already checked in and were busy getting things ready for the Employee Opening Meal.

Having a top-notch kitchen crew was one of the reasons that Kevin loved being on *Tranquility*.

But not today.

Today, Kevin was losing his mind.

When Marc walked into the kitchen, he stopped in his tracks. There, piled high on the prep-tables, were more beef ribs than he had ever seen in his life. Kevin was pointing at cooks with his chef's knife and shouting orders like a man possessed: "Get five gallons of vegetable stock…! Take twenty of those ribs. Strip the bones bare, bake them, and make beef stock. NO! Make that forty…! Do twenty pounds of mirepoix…! Start searing one hundred of them and put them in hotel pans to get ready for braising…! Run to the Main Bar and tell McFarland that we need a gallon of Burgundy wine…! Take the meat that's being stripped from the bones, trim it, and start making a stew…! *And if I see anyone doing nothing for the next two hours, they will become tonight's special!!!*"

The frenzy of activity in the kitchen increased by 150 percent.

Marc waited for Kevin to finish giving orders (one did not interrupt an Executive Chef with a knife in mid-rant), then walked up behind Kevin and cleared his throat.

Kevin spun around and bellowed, "*What???*" Then, seeing who it was, he visibly changed gears: "Oh, hi. Want a job?"

Marc looked at the ribs. "Maybe later. Did we become part owners of a cattle ranch, or was there a mix-up with the ordering again?"

Kevin frowned, pointed with his knife at a mound of ribs, and grumbled, "I told Susan that I needed two hundred ribs, not two hundred full *racks* of ribs. We now have enough to feed a whole platoon of Marines. So now I'm scrambling to do something with at least half of them."

Marc chuckled. "Oh, my! I guess we'll be eating ribs for a while. I'll let you get back to them. Good luck!"

Kevin gave Marc a hopeful smile. "Thanks." Then he spun back toward the kitchen, pointed a knife at a cook, and bellowed, "*What did I say about becoming tonight's special? Get over here!!!*"

Marc left the kitchen to get as far away from the mad chef as he could. As he entered the dining room, he saw Susan leaving the bar.

"I would avoid Kevin for the next day or two," he called. "Apparently, you ordered two hundred racks of ribs, instead of two hundred individual ribs."

Susan stopped to ponder what Marc had said, then started tapping on her PAC. With a grin, she set the PAC to hologram projection. Immediately, the kitchen order form popped up that had Kevin's signature at the bottom. There, clear as day, was an order for two hundred racks of beef ribs.

"You were saying?" Susan asked.

Marc gave her a lopsided grin. "Ummm..., that Kevin is having a fun time with all those ribs you helped to get him, and that I should find some other way to stick my foot in my mouth?" He decided to change the subject. "Oh, by the way—"

A knowing smile spread across Susan's face as she interrupted him. "I know. Asteroid and twenty minutes late."

Marc looked at her with a raised eyebrow, then bowed and quickly made his way to the casino.

⠲⠄ ⠨⠆⠃⠄⠆⠐⠂⠆ ⠐⠖ ⠠⠙⠊⠂ ⠹⠹⠇⠨⠂⠇ ⠂⠙⠃⠆

The casino floor was spacious, well-lit, and had lots of options for the guests to lose their money: old-fashioned mechanical slot machines, assorted card games, and a roulette wheel. The ceiling baffles, sound absorbing walls, and thick carpet made the room surprisingly quiet.

On a raised platform in the middle, there was the "Pit," in which Vincent was dictating notes into his PAC for the ACs. "I know it's a pain in the ass, but the underside of the card tables need dusting, too. Our customers are paying big bucks, so we don't want them with dust on their clothes after playing cards."

"And that, my friend," said Marc, as he joined Vincent on the platform, "is why you're in charge here. I would have missed that detail."

From the Pit, one could observe everything happening on the floor. The monitors that ringed the platform gave real-time accounts of the wins and losses at the different games.

Vincent shut down the PAC's recorder. "Mutant!" he said to Marc. "What brings *you* to my perch?"

Marc took in the view from the Pit. "Just doing my rounds..., Thing One. Do you have anything that needs me to beat it into shape?"

Vincent pointed across the room. "There's a slot machine with a sticky reel, but Wingnut said he would fix it before dinner."

Marc nodded. "Excellent! Then, I'll let you get back to your notes. Oh, by the way, Thing Two is tearing his hair out because he over-ordered beef ribs. I would avoid the kitchen for a while."

Vincent's eyes widened, for he knew how his brother reacted when things weren't perfect in the kitchen. "So noted. See you at dinner, Mutant."

⠄⠂ ⠄⠐⠓⠂⠌⠂⠐⠆ ⠄ ⠰ ⠄⠘⠏⠄ �⠄⠄⠄⠂⠄ ⠄⠰⠆⠾⠂

Marc's next stop was Kimberly, who handled customer rela-tions as well as the living quarters for the guests. Her warm smile, infectious laugh, attention to details, and insane cuteness made her the perfect person for the rich elite to talk to whenever there was a problem. Kimberly was busy with her crew in her work space, making custom gift baskets for the guest rooms.

"Make sure," she said to a young lady, "that basket for Mister and Mrs. Tyson has the *Tranquility* keepsakes. It's their first visit here, and we want to honor their family for the contribution to understanding space as well as we do."

"Yes, ma'am."

"Hey, Little Sister, got a minute?" asked Marc.

"Not really," she said, while tucking a stray strand of brown hair behind her ear, "but I'll make one for my Big Brother."

Marc smiled. "Thanks. I just wanted to make sure that everything is set for the auction crew accommodations. I informed them that they would be sharing rooms, so things may get a bit crowded."

Kimberly picked up a pad and handed it to Marc. "They caught a break. Two sets of couples had to cancel at the last minute because of illnesses. Thank god for nonrefundable bookings. Plus, with Stuart and Fred's room open, there will be more room for them."

Marc read over the cancellation orders. "Lucky them. And, as always, make sure some extra hat-racks are in Lady Elizabeth's room. You know how she loves her hats."

Kimberly took the pad back from Marc. "Already installed, and even have her favorite chocolates placed by her reading chair."

"Then, what am I doing wasting your time? Get back to work, you silly girl!" Marc made shooing motions with his hands as an overly serious look crossed his face.

Kimberly thumbed her nose as she stuck her tongue out at him. As Marc watched her skip back to her desk, he thought that he couldn't have a better sister.

⠠⠄ ⠐⠎⠁⠃⠑⠲⠑⠲⠎ ⠲⠒ ⠠⠦⠃⠂⠄ ⠒⠿⠠⠄� ⠲⠒D⠕

In the hallway of the Core Crew quarters, both Grey Wolf and Steven were discussing new ideas about upgrading *Tranquility's* communication systems as they headed to their rooms to get ready for dinner. As the best of friends and respected figures of the computer community, they could complete each other's thoughts. Steven finished typing some notes into his PAC's virtual keyboard and did an elaborate handshake with Grey Wolf before they entered their rooms.

Grey Wolf's living room looked like a computer lab. There were several tables with computer components in different stages of repair or construction and monitors that showed the progress of each one in an exploded view. The main desk was strewed with electronic tablets on which there were articles about AI developments, including several unfinished ones by Grey Wolf himself. On the shelves, there were binders of his writings, blueprints for Irma, and several other computer systems that he had built.

When Grey Wolf went to the bedroom, which was like an extension of the living room, he opened some drawers to select some clean clothes. On the walls, there were shelves full of books, with classic writers like Isaac Asimov, Douglas Adams, Michael Crichton, William Shakespeare, and J. R. R. Tolkien. Pushing aside an old thick binder on his bed labeled "N.I.C.," he sat down to take off his shoes.

Grey Wolf looked at the binder he had just moved, flipped open to an exploded view of a computer cube, and started to trace his fingers along the components. Twenty minutes later, he was still looking at the binder when he heard Steven's voice out in the hallway.

"Put Nic away and get ready. It's almost time for dinner."

Grey Wolf sighed, shut the binder, and called out, "Coming, mother!" Then he quickly got dressed, all the while constantly glancing at the binder before running to the bathroom.

⠿⠀⠠� ⠿

At 7:00 p.m., *Tranquility*'s staff started to file into the main dining room. As one of the largest rooms on the station, it could hold all fifty of the guests with seats to spare. Each polished dark-wood table was large enough to seat four people, with plenty of elbow room. The walls were painted a rich rose red with silver and gold highlights. Each wall held a large monitor that showed live streaming video of different locations on Earth. The majestic redwood trees of Muir Woods in Marin County, the Pyramids at Giza, the Acropolis in Greece, and the rolling hills of Easter Island with the famous stone heads were currently being shown, with a new location every half-hour.

When the ACs signed on to be crew members, there were very strict rules for them to follow. If they broke any of those rules, they would be confined to their quarters for the rest of the job, never being able to return to work there, and forfeiting extremely large bonuses. In exchange for their loyalty, they got paid more money than they would have earned anywhere else, on top of their incredibly large tips. As part of their employment agreement, the Core Crew pledged to treat everyone with respect and dignity.

It was the First Day Meal that the crew members were eager to experience, because it rivaled, or even surpassed, what the guests would get during their stay on *Tranquility*.

As everyone enjoyed their pre-dinner drinks, there were joyous greetings among old friends. Everyone seemed to have a story to tell.

That is, everyone except Wingnut, who was standing near the doorway, trying—but failing—not to look anxious.

When Patricia arrived in a silky red dress, she drew all the eyes in the room to her. As she looked around, she realized that perhaps she had overdressed for a first date. Smiling at Wingnut, she said shyly, "Thank you for joining me for dinner."

Wingnut blushed and cleared his throat as he noticed that the entire room was watching.

Suddenly, there was the sound of marching feet in the hallway that led to the dining room. A moment later, the Marines entered in perfect sync with each other. Although they were in civilian clothing, no one could doubt that they were Marines and damn proud of it, as was apparent from their singing the United Earth Marine's Anthem.

Irma's head, which had been on one of the large video monitors, was suddenly replaced by a waving United Earth Marine Corps flag as a much smaller Irma head bounced along the words of the song as they scrolled across the monitor:

From the halls of Montezuma
To the shores of Tripoli;
We fight our country's battles

In the air, on land, and sea….

The Marines continued the song as they passed by the head table and saluted the Core Crew. When they sat down at one of the empty tables, the whole crew stood up to applaud them.

Leaning toward Wingnut, Patricia whispered, "Saved by the Marines."

He smiled and offered his arm, and they made their way to an empty table near the Core Crew, where he pulled out a chair for her.

Marc shared a warm smile with the others at the head table, who all felt that they had just witnessed two shows for the price of one.

Precisely at 7:30, the third act began.

From the kitchen, Kevin and his crew came out, carrying trays and hotel pans, which they placed on serving tables. After a moment for them to get everything in order, Kevin turned to everyone and announced, "Ladies and gentlemen, dinner is *served!!!*"

It was a feast fit for royalty:

Grilled salmon steaks.

Grilled marinated artichokes with roasted garlic aioli.

Different kinds of salads.

Homemade salad dressings.

Saffron rice.

An assortment of meats cooked in many different ways.

Decadent sauces.

Hors-d'oeuvres that could be a meal in themselves.

Three types of soup, including Marc's family recipe for Split Pea.

Fresh rolls and loaves of bread.

An assortment of raw and cooked vegetables.

And desserts that made the diners gain ten pounds just by looking at them.

The ACs started to form a line at one end, but respectfully waited for the Core Crew to go first. Marc and the other men let the ladies go ahead of them. Kevin stood at the end of the food line, making sure that everyone was happy with what was being served. If anything were amiss (which it *never* was), he would personally see to making it right. But, as always, the crew were more than satisfied with his efforts.

As soon as the last crew member was served, Kevin nodded at his crew, who proceeded to file through the food line. Once they had their plates filled, he finally got something to eat for himself, and then joined the Core Crew.

Marc loved the fact that he had an executive chef who, no matter how hard he was on his own crew, made sure that they came first, before himself. It was one of many reasons that the kitchen crew was so loyal to Kevin.

As everyone ate, the sounds of talking almost vanished—a testament to how good the food was. As people took second and third helpings, the noise level slowly increased.

Now was as good a time as any for Marc to say what he wanted to the crew. With a thumbs-up to McFarland, he pulled back his sleeve, exposing his PAC, and tapped a few commands into it. Immediately, a hologram of a microphone appeared in front of him. As Marc tapped on it, the sound echoed throughout the dining room.

Meanwhile, McFarland disappeared into the bar, then returned with a cloth-covered wheeled cart.

Marc cleared his throat before speaking. "Good evening, everyone! May I have your attention, please?" He waited for everyone to quiet down. "Thank you for coming back and being a part of our crew. Today marks several important occasions. A little more than ten years ago, I hatched the idea for *Tranquility...*, a place where the ultra-rich could get completely away from everything and enjoy the simple pleasures. I was told that the idea was a waste of time, energy, and money. But, thanks to some very deep pockets and the people seated next to me, we opened *Tranquility Casino* five years ago today. Many of you have been with us from the start, and all of you have helped to make this place the envy of any other casino, restaurant, or bar, on or off the Earth!"

The crew applauded and cheered their agreement.

Marc waited for everyone to settle down. "Over the past five years, the *Tranquility Casino* has become the go-to place for our guests because we all have made it our duty to be discreet about who comes here to receive the best service anywhere!"

"And the best food!" someone shouted.

"And the best food," Marc agreed. "As you know, we are hosting the first off-planet auction of Hollywood and Rock 'n' Roll memorabilia. As always, the richest people on Earth are joining us and will be spending more money here than ever before. That, of course, translates to bigger tips for everyone."

The crew roared their approval.

Marc held up his hands to quiet them. "As the host of the auction, the casino will be getting a nice percentage of its proceeds. And since we have always thought that this place couldn't be what it is without all of you, we of the Core Crew have decided to double your bonus for this trip."

A stunned silence filled the room, since the bonuses were already the envy of any casino worker. Then a ripple of excited voices grew into cheers. The Marines suddenly stood to shout, "Ooo-RAH!!!"

Marc waited for the crew to calm down. "The day after tomorrow, the auction crew will arrive with the news reporter, Rachel Connolly, and then, the next day, the guests will come. Remember, Ms. Connolly may only ask you about yourself and your job. She knows that discussion about the guests is off-limits."

Everyone nodded.

Marc spread his arms wide. "So, tonight, *Tranquility* belongs to *you*! It's the last time you will be able to see and relax with everyone here until you get back on the transport to go home. But before we let you go, we have one more thing for you."

A surprised murmur spread around the room.

Marc waved a hand toward McFarland. "To celebrate this five-year anniversary, we have had pint glasses made from Baccarat Crystal with your name, the anniversary date, and today's date engraved on them."

McFarland whipped the covering off the cart, revealing the cases of glasses.

"As we call your name," Marc continued, "please come and pick up your glass and then proceed into the Main Bar to help us commemorate five years of being the best crew anywhere!"

The dining room erupted into cheers and whistles.

Then Susan activated her PAC's microphone to call out names, as the rest of the Core Crew handed out the glasses.

⠨⠀⠐⠩⠄⠆⠂⠒⠀⠰⠀⠐⠣⠃⠀⠩⠲⠂⠄⠐⠄⠲⠆⠐

The Main Bar was hopping. Steven was acting as DJ by using his PAC to tap into the music library and play it over the sound system. The dance floor had a dance-off between the kitchen crew and the wait staff, with the Marines schooling them both on how it was done.

Marc tapped into the station's system with his PAC to retract the panels from the dance floor, revealing huge windows. Since this floor was the outer hull of the casino, it had a unique view. As the casino rotated on its axis, the occupants got to see an Earthrise and the Sea of Tranquility every thirteen seconds. Thanks to Steven and Grey Wolf's ingenuity, a hologram was projected on the window where the Apollo 11's landing site was located.

Grey Wolf made his way to the baby grand piano near the bar and sat down at the bench. He tapped at a few keys, at which point Steven quickly faded the music as he activated his PAC's microphone.

"Ladies and gentlemen," Steven announced, "we will change things up a little and have a bit of live entertainment. If you turn your attention to the piano, Grey Wolf will now play us something."

Caught totally unprepared by this, Grey Wolf gave Steven a "You shmuck" stare, while everyone gathered around the piano.

Grey Wolf cracked his knuckles and grinned. "I've been working on an oldie but goodie," he said, "from about two hundred years ago."

His fingers started to fly across the keys as he played Gilbert and Sullivan's "I Am the Very Model of a Modern Major-General." The song that came out of his mouth was not what everyone had expected, but he executed it with speed and humor, which got everyone roaring:

There's antimony, arsenic, aluminum, selenium,

And hydrogen and oxygen and nitrogen and rhenium,

And nickel, neodymium, neptunium, germanium,

And iron, americium, ruthenium, uranium,

Europium, zirconium, lutetium, vanadium….

Grey Wolf continued Tom Lehrer's insanely humorous song, which had everyone crying with laughter, and finished it with an artistic flare:

These are the only ones of which the news has come to Harvard,

And there may be many others, but they haven't been discovered.

Everyone cheered as they applauded Grey Wolf, who stood to acknowledge them with a bow. Then, with a grin, he pointed at Steven. "Your turn, buddy! I saw your fiddle behind the bar, and you don't get to pick what song to play."

Steven and Grey Wolf stared at each other like gunfighters sizing up their opponent. Finally, Steven nodded and called out to McFarland as he moved to the bar: "Would you grab my fiddle, please?"

McFarland reached down behind the bar and pulled out an old case that contained Steven's favorite instrument. Steven took it from him, placed it on the bar, and opened it.

Inside, there was a well-loved fiddle that had been passed down through Steven's family for the past hundred and seventy-plus years. Steven gently ran his hand over it like someone greeting a favorite cat. Then he removed it from the case, tucked it under his chin, and took a moment to tune it.

Turning his attention back to Grey Wolf, he said, "Okay, Wolf, hit me with your best shot."

Grey Wolf looked like a cat that had just eaten a canary. "I pick, 'Flight of the Bumblebee'!"

Steven's face fell at hearing the song selection. Then, with a smile that worried Grey Wolf, he played a few practice notes. "That's a challenging piece. But to really do the music justice, you'll have to join in. Providing you can keep up."

Grey Wolf narrowed his eyes at Steven as he sat down and flexed his fingers. "Bring it on, buddy! One, and a two, and a three...."

Grey Wolf worked the keys at lightning speed. The legendary fast-paced music flew out of the piano. Steven joined in with his fiddle as everyone stared at the two in amazement—which then turned into open-mouth shock as a flute joined in.

Sitting on top of the bar was McFarland, who was playing his flute in time with the music. Steven and Grey Wolf slowly stopped playing as they joined everyone else in the jaw-dropping admiration of the talent required to play the music on a flute.

With his eyes closed, McFarland was unaware of the attention he was receiving, and continued playing. As he finished, he opened his eyes and looked up at the stunned crowd that was staring back at him. With a raised eyebrow, he gruffly asked, "What?"

Marc started to chuckle and clap his hands. "Two of the best musicians I know, outdone by a grumpy old bartender."

Everyone else joined in with applause.

McFarland narrowed his eyes and growled at Marc. "Who ya calling 'old'?"

Having been friends with McFarland for so long, Marc wasn't fooled by the tough guy act. Noticing the slight upward twitch of his friend's mouth, he said, "*You.* You're three months, eighteen days, and four hours older than me. So, yeah, you're *old.*"

A smile slowly spread across McFarland's face. "You forgot the forty-eight minutes."

Marc quickly responded, "And nineteen seconds." Then, rubbing his hands together, he added, "Okay, old man, I think we need to set up some shots."

McFarland jumped off the bar and saluted Marc with his flute. "Shots of Chivas Regal coming right up."

Steven activated his PAC. "Let the music play!"

The crew started to dance and mingle again while Marc, McFarland, and several others shared a couple of shots before joining the fun.

Marc watched as his crew let off steam in a variety of ways. What caught his eye most was Wingnut and Patricia slow-dancing to everything that Steven played. *Good for you*, he thought to himself. Then, sensing someone behind him, he turned around.

Eileen's brown eyes were looking back at him as she gave him a warm smile that always made Marc's heart flutter. Leaning in closer, she whispered, "Hi."

The room disappeared for Marc, leaving only the love of his life. "Hi to you, my dear. Are you enjoying yourself?"

"Not as much as I would if I had someone to dance with," she said with a determined glint in her eyes.

Marc held up a finger to indicate that he needed a moment, then tapped out a message on his PAC.

Moments later, Steven read something on his own PAC, activated his microphone, and said, "My good ladies and gentlemen, we are going to change the tone a bit, so some slow-dancing can be enjoyed."

"Your Eyes" by Peter Gabriel started to play, causing Eileen's eyes to tear slightly. She watched as Marc bowed to her, then offered her his hand. She took it and followed him onto the dance floor…, where they stayed long after everyone else had gone off to bed.

Eileen kissed him lightly on the cheek and nuzzled his ear. "Thanks for the dance, Sky."

Her loving touch always caused a light shiver of desire to move through his body. "It's my pleasure to be held by you, my dear," Marc said with a bow and then escorted her out of the bar.

CHAPTER 3
Plan H

The next morning, the Auxiliary Crew began cleaning up the previous night's festivities and completing the finishing touches on the guestrooms. Meanwhile, the Core Crew, with key members of the AC, gathered in the movie theater for the final test on the bidding scanners for the auction. When the auction started, the guests could make bids, drop out, or track bids on items anywhere on *Tranquility* with a simple thumbprint scan.

Marc stood at the stage's podium, acting as the auctioneer. Holding out his hand as if displaying something in front of him, he asked in an exaggerated British accent, "How much is the opening bid for this fine speck of dust?"

Ten cents was bid by Grey Wolf, which appeared on the large monitor behind Marc.

Eileen bid twenty cents.

Fifty cents was bid by Vincent.

Marc continued the fake accent. "Come now, good people. You won't find a finer bit of dust anywhere. It's perfect for floating into someone's drink. Do I hear one dollar?"

Ten dollars appeared on the monitor from Susan.

Marc grinned. "That's the spirit, folks! Do I hear twenty dollars?"

Steven asked, "Would you describe the dust particle, please?"

Marc gave Steven a comical *Don't you know?* look. "It's comprised entirely of the finest dead human skin cells, deceased dust mites, and the fecal matter of said mites."

Fifty dollars was bid by Kevin.

This half-crazed bidding went on until all the scanners were tested. The bidding topped out at $10,500,042.01 made by Susan, which beat McFarland's bid by one cent.

Marc loudly slapped the podium with his hand. "*Sold!* To the cute redhead who now has everything!"

Kevin tossed a scanner between his hands. "Well, that was fun…, and pointless"

Marc stepped down from the stage. "The point, my good man, is to teach all of us the functions of the scanners, so when the guests have questions about them, and they *will*, we'll be able to answer them. Anyone have any questions?"

"What's the meaning of life?" asked Patricia.

"Forty-two!" the Core Crew all answered together, startling her with the unity of the answer.

Marc chuckled over her reaction as he asked, "Any new business?"

Grey Wolf spoke up. "I have some. For the Core Crew."

"Alright," said Marc, "everyone else is dismissed. Please return to your departments."

As soon as the others left the room, Marc turned to Grey Wolf. "What's up, old friend?"

Grey Wolf activated his PAC's virtual keyboard and started typing. "I'm downloading a new program to everyone's PAC. It's a medical alert that will automatically send a message to the rest of us if it senses a motion that indicates you've fallen down, followed by no movement for more than fifteen seconds. It will then broadcast a vibrating SOS to all of us, as well as your location. Only after that has happened will it broadcast your vital signs, so we're also aware of your condition. I put that last bit in so you don't feel that anyone can see what's got you hot and bothered."

Tony glanced at Susan. "Good. I really don't need to know when Susan's drooling over the Marines again."

Susan stuck her tongue out at him and gave him a raspberry.

"Anything else?" asked Marc to move the conversation away from that subject.

"When and how long will it take to download?" asked Kimberly.

Grey Wolf tapped on his keyboard for a moment. "Done."

Marc looked around. "Who wants to volunteer to test it?"

Tony walked over to Grey Wolf and said, "*He* does," and the startled man was thrown the floor with a loud thud.

"*Ouch!!! That Hurt!!!*" yelled Grey Wolf as the others chuckled and laughed.

Thanks to Tony's training sessions in self-defense with the Core Crew, Grey Wolf had managed to absorb some of the fall's impacts correctly, but still had the wind knocked out of him.

Grey Wolf pointed over his head. "Look, stars!!!"

Tony scolded him. "Shut up and quit moving. You're supposed to be unconscious."

Grey Wolf dropped his arm to the floor. "Oh, right." Then he played dead with his tongue hanging out.

Fifteen seconds later, everyone's PAC started vibrating an SOS, and a map appeared, showing where Grey Wolf was located.

Marc nodded his approval. "Nicely done, Wolf! Now, unless there's anything else, let's head to our departments and put the finishing touches on things before *AuctionHouse 5* docks. Let's look sharp for them. First impressions and all that."

As the group broke up, Eileen wandered over to Marc. "Any chance of having dinner with me tonight?"

Marc smiled and lightly pressed his forehead to hers. "I'm sorry, there's too much on my plate. But if I can get ahead of my schedule, I'll let you know."

She kissed him on the cheek and nodded. "I understand."

⠔ ⠨⠏⠑⠉⠑ ⠦ ⠮ ⠝⠑⠺⠎⠲ ⠘⠹⠒

The next morning, Kimberly selected a pair of earrings and then checked herself in the full-length mirror. As she considered her blouse, she frowned and decided to change it.

For the fourth time.

Her bedroom was simply furnished, but elegant. The four-poster bed was covered with computer pads of piloting books, manuals for the *Camel*, and practice tests for the pilot's exam. All of which had a 98 percent score or better.

Kimberly finished buttoning her blouse, looked in the mirror, thought about changing it yet again, but then glanced at the clock. Letting loose some colorful words, she ran through the simply furnished living room, nearly colliding with the door as it opened.

Outside by the elevator was Wingnut, tucking in his shirt. He looked up at her and smiled in relief. "Glad I'm not the only one running late."

When the elevator doors opened, they both entered. Kimberly reached over to straighten his collar, which had curled under itself. "You need a girlfriend to keep you sorted out."

Wingnut grinned. "That's the best offer I've had all day."

Kimberly blushed and sputtered. "Um..., er..., I..., well..., I didn't...."

Wingnut laughed. "Relax, I'm joking. Besides, dating Marc's little sister isn't on my list of things I think I should do."

"I'm glad Jackson doesn't feel the same way," Kimberly said, quickly exiting the elevator.

Wingnut looked after her with his mouth open in surprise. Then he jumped through the doors as they were closing. "Wait! What was that?"

⠠⠊ ⠀⠐⠏⠗⠊⠋⠋ ⠐⠋ ⠠⠙⠓⠀ ⠏⠃⠇⠀⠊ ⠐⠋⠰⠄

Marc watched as the monitor next to the elevator to Docking Port 2 showed the docking clamps locking down and the airlock starting to cycle. Everyone but Wingnut and Kimberly was already there, and he was about to call for them when they both appeared. Wingnut was talking in hushed tones, but Marc still caught the last bit: "...and Jackson?"

Marc looked at them. "What about Jackson?"

Kimberly quickly answered, "Nothing important," and glared at Wingnut.

Clearing his throat, Wingnut said, "I was asking how her pilot studies were coming. She said that Jackson was helping her."

Marc was about to say something when the elevator pinged its arrival. Turning his attention to the business of greeting the AuctionHouse crew, he missed the annoyed punch to the arm that Kimberly gave the engineer.

The elevator doors opened, and there stood Rachel Connolly. Her long black hair, which was tied back in a ponytail, matched the black suit that showed off her hourglass figure. Hovering by the right side of her head was a dark grey video drone that followed the direction that the reporter's head turned. Thinking that it was remarkably quiet, Marc wondered what Grey Wolf and Steven were thinking of doing with one. And how many pieces McFarland wanted to break it into.

Marc extended his hand to Rachel. "Ms. Connolly, welcome to *Tranquility*."

The reporter returned the handshake with a firmness that equaled her powerful presence. Then she flashed him a sparkling smile as her black eyes glimmered with excitement. "Thank you, Mister Acer. Please call me Rachel. It's an honor to be able to report on this historic event. The AuctionHouse people are giving me a moment to get positioned, so I can document them arriving. I'll get acquainted with everyone here after the AuctionHouse crew arrive."

The sound of the elevator caught her attention. "Oh! Here they come now."

She snapped her fingers twice at the drone, which caused a red light on its top to turn on, indicating that it was recording. Then she pulled out an earpiece with a microphone, slipped it into her ear, and started quietly giving an audio account of what was happening.

As the elevator doors parted once again, they revealed the people from the AuctionHouse. In front was a tall, slender, smiling gentleman with short grey hair in a well-tailored, charcoal grey suit. Marc noted that the man's dark brown eyes didn't seem to miss anything. Behind him was an Asian woman, with nine men behind her. The ten of them all exited the elevator together and took positions behind the smiling gentleman.

"Mister Acer," said the gentleman, "I am Gary Maxwell. I'm so glad to meet you and your crew. It's an honor to be able to visit this casino when there's no way I could ever make the cut to come."

Marc shook his hand. "Welcome to *Tranquility*, Mister Maxwell. Please feel free to call me Marc. The honor is ours for having your auction here. Allow me to introduce the Core Crew."

He stepped aside so each of them could move up to be introduced. When that was done, Mr. Maxwell made his introductions.

First was his personal assistant, Su Lee, a pretty Asian lady in her late twenties with cold, jade-green eyes. Marc wondered who had hurt her so badly to make her so cold. Next was the auctioneer, Dan Garfield, who had short blonde hair and a slight build. Marc felt that Dan didn't talk fast enough to be an auctioneer. The rest of the men were the work crew who would transport the auction items to be bid on, as well as set up the displays throughout *Tranquility*.

Marc pointed down the hallway. "Come. You must be tired after your long trip. Would you like to relax in your rooms or in the Main Bar before you start unloading?"

Mr. Maxwell stretched his arms a little. "Thank you for asking, but after being cooped up in the ship for the better part of three days, we'd like to unpack and get right to work, unloading and setting up. We'll want to check out the Main Bar later, though. I hear that the view is not to be missed."

Marc nodded his understanding for the need to move around after almost two days in a cramped ship with no gravity. The fact that all the planets in the Solar System could be lined up between the Earth and the Moon was not lost on anyone traveling to *Tranquility*. The travel time could be shorter, and sometimes was, but the cost of fuel to accelerate and then to slow down outweighed the slow and steady ride.

Marc pointed at his CEO. "Then I will turn you over to Susan. She can answer any questions you or your team might have. We must insist that the Bridge, Engineering, and our crew quarters be considered off-limits."

Mr. Maxwell nodded. "Understood. Oh, by the way, what time is it here? Our computer on the ship got a bit messed up on the way."

Grey Wolf stepped forward. "It's three-twenty-eight P.M." As the auction crew adjusted their watches, he added, "If you like, I'll go over your ship's systems and fix whatever is giving it fits."

Mr. Maxwell finished setting his watch. "Thanks. Usually only AuctionHouse personnel can work on our systems, but to have a world-renowned programmer, such as yourself, should override any objections that corporate headquarters might make. But let's do that after we get unloaded, so the ship will be all yours."

Grey Wolf smiled. "Sounds good. Just use any Com-Station you can find, and ask for me. Irma will route the call to wherever I am."

"Irma?" asked Mr. Maxwell with a raised eyebrow.

"Where are my manners?" said Marc, as he activated the elevator monitor.

Irma's head appeared with a frown. "*Really*, Marc! Fine way to treat a member of your crew." She then addressed Mr. Maxwell and Ms. Lee. "I'm Irma, *Tranquility*'s AI. Please feel free to ask for my help at any time. Now, if you'll excuse me, I have some files of Marc's that I need to scramble." She stuck her tongue out at Marc and vanished in a statically filled storm.

Susan motioned the AuctionHouse crew down the hallway. "Why don't I get you all settled into your rooms? By the way, we had some cancellations, so your crew won't be as crowded as we thought."

"Fabulous!" said Mr. Maxwell. "After such close quarters on the ship, we'll enjoy a bit of elbow room."

Susan explained to the AuctionHouse crew how to get to different locations on *Tranquility* as she led them down the hallway.

Hearing the snapping of fingers, Marc turned to Ms. Connolly and watched as the drone took its position beside her head.

She took off the headset and gave him another sparkling smile. "That was perfect! The viewers are going to eat this up and send the network's ratings through the roof!" Then, seeing that the AuctionHouse people were almost at the end of the hall, she said, "I better catch up with them." And away she jogged toward the group, with her drone buzzing at her side.

As soon as they were out of sight, Marc turned to Tony and McFarland. "Okay. What's got you two twitching?"

Only someone who had been around them as long as Marc would have noticed the subtle changes in their stance and demeanor. They looked at each other, then back at Marc.

"There's something about the work crew that set off my internal alarms," Tony said, rubbing his chin.

McFarland crossed his arms. "My feeling was that they were a little too attentive to the surroundings and our movements."

The other members of the Core Crew looked at each other to see if anyone had noticed anything unusual. No one had.

Marc frowned as the tightness in his gut increased. "Your instincts," he said to Tony and McFarland, "have saved us on numerous occasions. Let's keep them under observation for now. Grey Wolf, when you get on their ship, see if there's anything in their logs that hints at something amiss. Everyone else, business as usual."

As they all made their way back to their departments, Marc paused to look at the elevator. He wondered what was making his stomach twitch.

⠲⠄ ⠄⠐⠃⠌⠌⠌⠌⠐⠋ ⠄⠊⠃⠐ ⠌⠏⠇⠠⠌⠂ ⠐⠋⠣⠃⠕

Later that evening, Marc caught up with Susan in her office, which was furnished with a solid oak desk, on which there was a lamp with a dark stained-glass shade. Scattered across the desk were several tablets with assorted *Tranquility* reports.

A large red three-panel abstract painting hung on the wall behind her. Everyone saw different objects in it. Marc always thought there was a wolf, a bear, and a butterfly, all dancing in a fire.

"The AuctionHouse crew get settled in alright?" Marc asked the feisty redhead.

Susan looked up from her desk. "I have to say that, for the first time ever, extra rooms were not wanted. The workers they brought didn't want them, but Ms. Connolly and Ms. Lee gladly took to having their own rooms."

Marc frowned at that. The rooms were comfortable, but not overly spacious, like the luxury suites that Earth casinos had. With space at a premium on *Tranquility*, the guests had to sacrifice a bit of elbow room on the station. But not to take extra rooms? That was unheard of.

Susan placed the tablet she had in her hands on her desk and leaned back in her chair to consider the man whose instincts for trouble were proven to be above normal. "Your gut twitching again?"

Marc sighed and nodded. "Yes, it is. I'll talk to McFarland and ask him to charm his way into befriending them. If he can't, we'll move on to Plan B."

Susan frowned as she looked at her polished fingernails. "I hate Plan B. I always end up with chipped nails."

Marc looked thoughtful. "Hmmm. We could do Plan H. Someone loses an arm in that one."

Susan grimaced and gave a slight shutter at that. "No, thanks. Cybernetics may be able to replace any limb, but I'm still feeling quite attached to the ones I have."

Marc smiled. "Agreed. Let's hope we can keep the alphabet soup of plans on the back burner."

Susan reached for the tablet she had put down. "Now shoo! There are *some* people who have important work to do."

Marc grinned. "Yes, I do. So, stop harassing me with nonsense!"

He dashed out the door before she could throw a tablet stylus at him.

CHAPTER 4

The Chicken Comet

Grey Wolf felt that if curiosity killed the cat, then it was a great source of annoyance for him. Having an unknown computer issue lurking about, even if it were on a visiting ship, was irritating to him.

After checking that all the systems on *Tranquility* were purring like happy kittens, he decided to go to the auction room to talk to Mr. Maxwell to get some details on the computer problems plaguing the AuctionHouse ship. He hadn't had a good computer problem to sink his teeth into in quite some time, so he was eager to see if what awaited him would be a challenge or just another "Bug Hunt," as he called it.

As Grey Wolf made his way to the theater room where the auction was to take place, he worked on the PAC's keyboard. His specialized contact lenses displayed what would usually be projected by the PAC's holographic system. This was odd to anyone seeing him walking the hallways. With his fingers twitching in midair over an invisible keyboard, it looked like Grey Wolf was wandering around *Tranquility*, casting spells. This impression was highlighted by him muttering to himself as he worked.

When he got to the auction room, the workers were busy setting up the stage, as well as hanging banners with the AuctionHouse golden starburst logo. As he walked by one of the workers, his PAC picked up an unknown signal, which disappeared as soon as the worker moved away. After he detected the third identical signal, Grey Wolf wondered if it was a communication system that stayed in standby mode when not used.

As he walked over to Mr. Maxwell, he noticed that Ms. Lee was speaking to the AuctionHouse manager.

When Ms. Lee saw Grey Wolf approaching, she quickly said something, then left in the opposite direction.

Mr. Maxwell turned to Grey Wolf. "What may I do for you, Mister Wolf?"

Grey Wolf deactivated his PAC. "Please, call me Grey Wolf. I haven't gone by 'Mister' in a long time. I wanted to ask about the problem your ship experienced and when would be a good time to work on its computers. I see there's still a lot of work going on in the Loading Bay."

Mr. Maxwell thought for a moment. "The systems were fine when we left, but shortly after, we had random faults pop up. Not being very well versed in computers, I couldn't even guess what caused them. As for when the ship will be clear, we'll be working through the night to unload it and set up the hallways of the casino with the hologram promotional posters. If you can give us another twenty-four hours, the ship will be all yours."

"At that time," said Grey Wolf, "the guests will be arriving, and then I'll be on the Bridge, busy with my duties. The auction will be taking place the following day, but I'll see what I can do before that. If it's not an easy fix, I'll figure out some way to get it done before you need to leave. Of course, there's always the option of spending an extra day at the casino after the auction. Since we don't get regular casino walk-ins, the rooms you have will be available."

"That's something we'll have to consider," Mr. Maxwell said thoughtfully. "I'll have our pilot get in contact with you when the crew's done." He frowned at what one of his crewmen was doing. "Please, excuse me," he said, and walked off to speak to the workers. "No, no, no! *This* goes over *there*. *That* goes *here*."

Ms. Connolly entered the auction room from the hallway with her ever-present drone, saw Grey Wolf, and made a beeline for him. "Mister Anderson, may I have an interview with you, please? I'm putting a segment together for the folks back on Earth about the people who make *Tranquility* the jewel of our Solar System."

Grey Wolf thought for a moment. He didn't have any pressing items needing his attention until the next day. "Sure. Why don't we go to the Main Bar and sit down in comfort? But, please, call me Grey Wolf. *Mister* Anderson is my father, and I haven't gone by my first name for many years."

Ms. Connolly flashed him her sparkling smile. "Grey Wolf it is. But when I introduce you, I'll have to use your real name, so the viewers will know who they're looking at, and that you now go by 'Grey Wolf.'"

"Shall we?" said Grey Wolf as he motioned toward the door.

Her eyes widened as an idea struck her. "Can we do the interview on the Bridge? Film you in your natural surroundings, so to speak?"

Grey Wolf frowned. "Let me talk to Marc and Tony about that. We have a strict rule that no one but Core Crew members are allowed there. Give me a minute to ask them."

Ms. Connolly headed toward the door. "I'll meet you at the bar, just in case the answer is no." She waved a finger at him. "Don't keep me waiting."

Grey Wolf watched her hourglass figure with appreciation for a moment, sighed, and then sent a message on his PAC to Marc and Tony.

⠨� ⠐⠙⠃⠆⠆⠆⠆ ⠐⠏ ⠐⠙⠃⠆ ⠆⠏⠏⠨⠆⠉ ⠐⠴⠵⠆⠂

Marc was just heading to his quarters when Grey Wolf's message reached him. After reading it, he got that tightness in his gut again.

As Tony came out of his quarters, he saw Marc and headed for him while pointing at his PAC. "What do you think of *that* idea?"

Marc scratched his head. "Not a big fan of it. But when it comes to the security of the Bridge, Grey Wolf is no slouch. He should lock down the systems before she starts the interview. Sound good?"

Tony nodded. "Works for me."

Marc sighed. "Would you mind telling him?" He pointed at the door to his own room. "I need to see a man about an asteroid."

Tony started to tap on his PAC. "Will do. See ya later."

Marc's living room was simply furnished with wooden furniture and lots of shelves with books and treasured family heirlooms. Most notable were three items in their own glass-and-ironwood cases, arranged to take advantage of the room's light. In the first case, there was an antique Marine sword and a sawed-off shotgun. The next case displayed three porcelain figures: a white elephant with its trunk curled back to its forehead; a white baby dragon hatching from an egg; and a white swan. The third case had a collection of antique props from movies and TV shows.

On the wall above the desk, there was a large felt-covered board with several dozen antique buttons and pins, plus a large Mickey Mouse Club badge in the center. Several dozen newer pins had been added to the board from Marc's travels. By adding his own pins to the collection that his great-, great-, great-, great-grandfather had started, he was connecting with his past. Before heading to the bathroom, he paused for a moment to look at a handmade goose-feather pin in his collection that he had worn as best man at Steven and Susan's wedding.

When he came out, he walked to the window. Sitting on the windowsill, there was a model of a black wooden sailing ship from the early 1900s. It had three masts and the name *The Crow* on its stern. Marc considered the model for a moment, which was named after an ancestor of his, before looking out at the garden. Then he looked out the window to enjoy the afternoon "sunset" effect as the Hub-Sun started to dim. Back on Earth, his favorite time of day was always dusk, when he could still see a hill's outline, but none of its details. It was what he missed most on *Tranquility*.

As a child, Marc would watch from the deck of his home, which was tucked way up in the hills of Marin County, California, and observe the different critters as they were waking up or heading off to sleep.

Marc sighed, looked at the time, and quickly checked his PAC to see where Eileen was.

⠨⠲ ⠀⠐�⠄⠌⠌⠄⠐ ⠋ ⠠⠮⠐ ⠏⠆⠇⠌⠄⠐⠋⠶⠺

As soon as Grey Wolf got the okay from Tony, he headed for the bar to find Ms. Connolly, who was valiantly trying to start a conversation with McFarland.

"Where did you go to school?" she asked.

"Earth," he responded in a monotone, as he continued folding bar towels.

She rolled her eyes. "What was your childhood like?"

"Short."

She tried a different approach. "What do you like about working here?"

He leveled an irritated glare at her. "The privacy."

Grey Wolf interrupted McFarland's attempt to drive the poor woman up a tree. "Ready to do that interview, Ms. Connolly? We've been given the okay to do it on the Bridge, but you'll have to promise not to touch any of the controls."

Ms. Connolly smiled in relief to have someone to interact with who conversed with more than one or two words at a time. Smoothly sliding off the stool, she said to McFarland, "I'll come back when you're in a more talkative mood."

"Try me next week," McFarland replied with a smirk.

She frowned. "I'll be back on Earth by then."

McFarland's smirk turned into a grin.

Grey Wolf softly took her by the arm and guided her toward the door. "Trust me, trying to get him to open up is harder than shucking an oyster with wet cardboard. Although, you might have better luck without the drone buzzing about. He hates them with a passion."

Waving toward the drone, she said, "But Jake here is my faithful companion." She slipped her arm into Grey Wolf's. "I would feel naked without him by my side."

Grey Wolf tried, but failed, *not* to picture her naked. "Trust me," he said, "it's best to work with the rest of us, and then try to get blood from that *stone*. You'll have less of a chance of getting a headache."

As they left the bar, Ms. Lee was walking down the hallway in their direction.

Grey Wolf smiled at her. "Good evening, Ms. Lee. How are things shaping up for the auction?"

With barely a flicker of acknowledgment, she responded, "They're proceeding." And with that, she continued toward the bar.

Grey Wolf looked at Ms. Connolly. "How well did you do with *her* during the trip here?"

Ms. Connolly sighed. "Slightly better than I did with Mister McFarland."

Grey Wolf wasn't surprised.

⠲⠀⠠⠐⠓⠄⠆⠐⠒⠀⠶⠀⠠⠻⠐⠠⠖⠖⠦⠄⠐⠂⠀⠐⠶⠒⠆

After entering the Main Bar, Ms. Lee sat down on a stool at the far end. McFarland waved off the bartender to indicate that he would take care of her.

"Good evening, Ms. Lee. What may I get for you?"

"Do you have any Junmai Daiginjo sake?" she asked, expecting that the answer would be no.

Without thinking about it, McFarland moved to a tempera-ture-controlled cabinet that kept the bottles at a precise 50 degrees Fahrenheit. After removing one, he presented the sake to her.

Her eyes widened. "That's hard to find on Earth. How is it you have it here?" she asked incredulously.

With practiced ease, McFarland placed a rice paper mat with the Japanese word for *peace* (平和) in front of her, set a porcelain *choko* on the mat, opened the bottle before she could stop him, and poured some sake into a *tokkuri*. During all this, he never broke eye contact with her, and yet didn't make her feel awkward. It was as if he were reading what she was thinking and finding it fascinating.

Ms. Lee finally broke eye contact to look down at the sake. "I didn't order that. I only asked if you *had* it."

McFarland considered what she said. "You're right. I'll throw it out."

As he reached for the sake, she quickly grabbed his wrist with a firmness that revealed how strong she was.

He looked at her hand, then back up at her with a smile.

As if receiving a light shock, she withdrew her hand and then smoothly picked up the cup to take a sip. As her eyes closed, her face showed the slightest indication of relaxing.

McFarland watched her carefully, seeing a symphony of emo-tions on her face.

When she reopened her eyes, she realized that he was watch-ing her, and her mask of uncaring instantly returned.

McFarland sighed. "Too bad. That was the first time I've seen you smile."

She narrowed her eyes. "I *never* smile."

He raised an eyebrow as he watched her sip the sake. "Too bad," he said again as he contemplated different ways to get her to smile that wouldn't earn him a black eye.

"May I show you something?" he asked.

As a series of negative emotions flashed in her eyes, he quickly added, "I promise to keep my hands to myself and conduct myself as a gentleman."

She looked at him coldly over her drink as she considered saying no.

McFarland realized that he was going to have to sweeten the pot. "If I can't get you to smile, let alone laugh, I'll buy you this *and* the next round of sake."

Her eyes narrowed as she scrutinized him for a moment. "Buy me this one and wager *two* more."

McFarland held out his hand. "Only if you agree to have dinner with me if I win."

She thought about refusing, but nothing had been emotionally enjoyable to her for years, so she felt safe accepting the bet. "Okay," she said, shaking his hand. "So long as it's in public and not romantic."

McFarland smiled. "I can work under those terms. Finish your sake, and I'll show you the funniest thing you've ever witnessed."

As she poured the last of her sake, she wondered what could possibly be so funny on a Moon-orbiting casino.

⠄⠂ ⠄⠐⠃⠂⠒⠂⠶ ⠄⠶ ⠠⠦⠃⠄ ⠒⠿⠔⠂⠄ ⠄⠶⠿⠆

Grey Wolf had the reporter's arm tucked into his as they walked out of the elevator on the third floor and headed toward the Bridge. Everything else had an elegant feel on *Tranquility*, but the nerve center could easily have been mistaken for a storeroom. The unassuming double-door had a simple brass plaque at the top, on which were written some words that caught Ms. Connolly's attention: *Drink Me. Eat Me.*

After scrutinizing the plaque, she looked at Grey Wolf. "'Drink Me? Eat Me.'? Are we entering Wonderland?"

Grey Wolf grinned. "We felt it was one of the most unique clues ever used in a story to enter a place. So, in order to enter the Bridge, you need an equally unique password. Of course, only the Core Crew have permission to use it."

The reporter pressed her finger against her lips as she considered the plaque. "If that is the 'most unique' password, then you must have a simple one to open the Bridge. Hmmm. I'm guessing that you'll play the part of the Son of Sinbad. Although I doubt you have a donkey named Sesame to open the doors."

Grey Wolf chuckled. Not only was this lady a brilliant reporter, but she was also a fellow movie buff. Making an exaggerated wave of his arm and hand, he said, "Open, Sesame!"

Irma's voice buzzed loudly as her scowling face appeared on the small monitor next to the door. "Ms. Connolly does not have clearance to enter the Bridge."

Grey Wolf sighed. "Tony gave his okay, and she knows not to touch anything. Now, open the Bridge, please."

Irma gave Ms. Connolly a raised eyebrow before disappearing as the doors swished open.

Ms. Connolly stared at the now blank monitor. "I get the feeling that she doesn't like me."

Grey Wolf led her onto the Bridge. "She takes her position as our protector very seriously, so don't take it personally. You're the first outsider on the Bridge since we've opened *Tranquility*."

Ms. Connolly looked around the Bridge, and was struck by the similarities it had to the Bridges on the ships of the 200-year-old sci-fi franchise *Star Trek*. The stations even had sounds like those in the original series. A large main monitor was at the front, with the crew seats positioned so that each had a clear view of it.

Ms. Connolly's eyes gleamed with excitement at the thought that she had access to this highly restricted area. "May I have Jake do a sweeping shot, Grey Wolf, to give the viewers a look at the Bridge?"

Grey Wolf had already sent commands to the Bridge systems to lock down and blank out all the operations monitors. "Anywhere in particular you want me to be?"

She looked around and then pointed at his chair. "Why not at your station?"

Grey Wolf cocked an eyebrow at her. "How did you know that's my spot?"

She let go of his arm to make a sweeping gesture. "This place is *Tranquility*'s nerve center. Which means that the Core Crew have specific functions here." She pointed at the center chair. "That chair, for example, is Mister Acer's. It has a commanding presence, but is made not to stand out." She pointed across the Bridge to the left of the large monitor. "The identical chairs over there are for the Pierce twins." Then she pointed to the right side of the monitor. "Those two couldn't be more different from each other. Let's see, the one on the left is for Mister Rhodes. No nonsense, but functional. The other one is for Mister McFarland. Hardly ever used and made to do one thing…, sit. That one to the right of Mister Acer's is Mister Spencer's. It has the freedom to move about and get at any system he needs to. The other one must be Mister Vanderbilt's for Engineering. The tools in the side pouches give it away." She then turned to the two stations toward the back. "Those two must be for Mrs. Spencer and Ms. Acer. They're the only two chairs that look like they've had a girl's touch." Waving a hand at the spare chairs along the back wall, she continued, "Those are for Eileen and any of the ACs who come here." At last, she addressed the final chair. "Then there's yours. It's meant to have hours of sitting and easy access to all the computer systems. From the looks of things, you spend more time here than anyone else, except maybe Mister Spencer."

Grey Wolf was impressed by her observational skills and saw why she was an ace reporter. "You're right on the money for each one. Well, how do you want to do this?"

She stepped to the back of the Bridge, snapped her fingers, and pointed to the upper part of the wall. The drone flew to the spot she pointed at and hovered. "Why don't we have you in your chair, and I'll have Jake do a sweeping shot around the room as I give an introduction of where we are, and then introduce you? Don't watch it fly about. Try to act natural as you work at your station. When Jake comes up to you, just smile at it and say, 'Hi.'"

Grey Wolf nodded and sat down in his chair. Then he called up his holographic keyboard and turned on the main Bridge monitor. "Anything you want on the monitor?"

Her eyes flashed. "How about an exterior shot of *Tranquility* with the Moon behind it?"

Grey Wolf's fingers flew over the keyboard, and, a second later, the requested live image from one of the Whiskers appeared.

Ms. Connolly clasped her hands in delight. "Perfect! I'll stand back here out of the shot and monitor it on my pad. After you say 'Hi' to it, we'll move on to the actual interview."

Grey Wolf turned back to his keyboard. "Just say when."

She looked at her pad with a frown. "Give me a moment. The darker environment here requires a different lens." They heard a soft click from the drone as the lenses switched. "That's better. And in three, two...." She held up one finger and then none. "I'm here on *Tranquility*'s Bridge, giving you a never-before-seen view of the nerve center of this amazing casino."

The drone slowly made its way around the Bridge as Ms. Connolly continued her report. "The room can seat the entire Core Crew, but the person who spends the most time here is the legendary programmer, Rowan Anderson, better known as Grey Wolf." The drone completed its sweep of the Bridge and zoomed in on Grey Wolf, who looked up, gave a toothy smile, and waved with a "Hi, there."

When Ms. Connolly snapped her fingers, the drone zipped back to its place beside her.

"That was perfect," she said. "No need to do a second take. Let's move on to the interview."

⠄⠄ ⠄⠐⠓⠄⠆⠄⠂⠄ ⠆ ⠄⠪⠄⠄ ⠒⠆⠣⠄⠂⠄ ⠄⠆⠒⠆

Ms. Lee and McFarland stepped out of the elevator when it stopped on the third floor. Here was Engineering, the Bridge, and what McFarland wanted to show her. Instead of heading to

Engineering, he led her in the opposite direction to a door that was marked "Hen House." When McFarland opened the door, the air was filled with an odor that was unfamiliar to Ms. Lee as she heard the sound of clucking.

McFarland moved aside to allow her to enter first. What she found stunned her: acres and acres of farmland.

She looked at the henhouse, which was in front of her, and then up at the partly cloudy sky. Two dozen chickens and a rooster were roaming about a fenced area, pecking at bits of food.

Ms. Lee looked back at the doorway they had just entered and saw that the wall was painted with a realistic mural of farmland. But then, looking closer, she noticed that there were textures and moldings on the wall surface, which gave it a three-dimensional look. Now that she could see the illusion, it was easy to see where the walls were.

Ms. Lee knelt down to feel the real grass. "Why would you go to all this effort just for chickens?"

McFarland led her toward the gate at the fence that prevented the chickens from getting out. "They thrive in an open environment. They'll still lay eggs in a simple room or even caged up like they were in the twentieth century, but they'll produce better eggs if they believe they're in a natural environment."

Ms. Lee squinted at the glowing orb in the sky. "And the Sun?"

"Steven installed special LEDs in the walls and ceiling that give off a wide range of sunlight. Grey Wolf programmed them to mimic Earth's day and night cycle."

She was on the verge of smiling, but didn't. "Nice, but I'm not finding it funny."

McFarland motioned for her to follow him through the gate. After he closed it, he opened a nearby storage container that was filled with stale bread and took some out. "We save the old bread we don't use to feed the chickens. Waste not, want not," he added, while crumbling up the bread in his hands.

As the crumbs fell to the ground, the chickens clucked excitedly and started to flock about them to eat.

Ms. Lee, who had never been around chickens before, took a tentative step back.

McFarland suddenly reached down with one hand to scoop up one of the chickens, and let it feed on the bread crumbs in his other hand. When the bird finished, he scratched it about the neck and head, which it obviously enjoyed. Then he held the chicken with both hands out in front of him and winked at Ms. Lee. When he tossed the chicken straight up, the startled fowl let out a squawk and flapped its wings.

Then an odd thing happened.

The chicken started to float in the air and spin around in random directions. Each movement caused it to spin even more. As the chicken flapped and squawked, some of its feathers and down started to trail behind it like the tail of an insane comet.

As McFarland watched this spectacle, Ms. Lee stifled a giggle and then a full-out laugh. When he looked at her, she had her hand clamped over her mouth, desperately trying to hide her laughter, but it was a losing battle.

In moments, she was laughing so hard that tears were streaming from her eyes.

As the chicken slowly reentered the gravity zone, it made a controlled landing, shook itself to realign its feathers, and looked at them as if to say, "Up yours!" Then it went back to eating.

Ms. Lee watched with fascination as the feathers slowly fluttered down or got sucked up by the ventilation system.

McFarland scooped up another chicken. "Want to give it a go?"

A mischievous grin appeared on her face as she held out her hands.

He handed her the chicken. "Hold it in your arms and pet it first, so it's relaxed. Then hold it out in front of you, and give it a toss like I did."

When she followed his instructions, she was rewarded with her own squawking Chicken Comet. This caused her to bend over with laughter.

That was the most magical sound McFarland had heard in a long time.

When the chicken landed, Ms. Lee took a few deep breaths, straightened up, and wiped the tears from her face. Looking at McFarland with a shy smile, she said, "I guess I owe you a dinner."

McFarland carefully removed a few feathers from her hair. "Why don't we get cleaned up first? People will think we've been abusing the goose-down pillows."

Ms. Lee glanced at him with a smirk. "Okay, I'll meet you at the dining room in half an hour."

⠲⠄ ⠠⠢⠃⠔��� ����������

Wingnut was just leaving Engineering, shaking his head about the poorly told joke that Ross had just told him when he saw Ms. Lee and McFarland waiting for the elevator. McFarland was telling the story of Marc tossing the chicken up to see how well it could fly in the slightly lower gravity of the third floor, and discovering the Chicken Comet. Ms. Lee was giggling and holding his arm, something Wingnut had never thought she would do.

When the elevator arrived, Wingnut stepped back toward Engineering to give them some privacy. As they entered, McFarland flashed Wingnut a smile and a thumbs-up sign as the engineer peeked around the doorway. Wingnut shook his head at the mystery that was McFarland.

⠲⠂ ⠐⠳⠊⠄⠊⠂⠊⠂ ⠐⠋ ⠰⠯⠃⠄ ⠩⠋⠥⠂⠇ ⠄⠹⠪⠂

Kevin was lurking in the main kitchen, playing the mad scientist. When the kitchen was clear of all crew, he would spend hours creating new recipes. His nearly mad grin of satisfaction could be unnerving to anyone who didn't know him.

His PAC buzzed, alerting him to a message. He saw it was from McFarland, who was asking for the favor of an elegant dessert after his dinner with Ms. Lee. Kevin responded that he had just the thing, and got to work on it.

Just then, as one of the auction workers walked into the kitchen, Kevin pointed his chef's knife at him. "Hey! You're not permitted in here! Can't you read the sign? 'Crew Members Only'!"

The intruder, who obviously had not expected to see anyone here, reacted out of character for someone who had accidentally gone where he shouldn't have. He had a hardness about him that troubled Kevin. With a frown and a growl, he said, "Sorry. I was looking for some cream to put in my coffee." He held up his thermos to emphasize his need.

Kevin glared at him as he pointed with his knife toward the door. "Ask one of the wait staff."

The worker's eyes narrowed as he muttered, "Oh, okay."

When the intruder had left, Kevin got the distinct feeling that the guy was casing the place.

⠲⠄ ⠠⠌⠦⠃⠴⠌⠄⠄⠄ ⠶⠄ ⠠⠙⠳⠄ ⠔⠚⠏⠴⠄⠌⠄⠂ ⠴⠙⠴⠆

Grey Wolf was just leaving the Bridge with Ms. Connolly when Steven nearly bumped into them because he was reading something on his PAC. He quickly sidestepped with a well-executed dance-like move. "Whoops! Sorry about that. Didn't expect anyone to be on the Bridge."

Ms. Connolly giggled. "That was a nifty bit of footwork you did there, Mister Spencer. You and your wife must dance quite superbly."

Steven mimed dancing with his wife. "We do like to cut a rug when the occasion arises."

Ms. Connolly flashed him her brilliant smile. "When do you think I can sit down with you to have an interview? I'll just need about ten minutes of your time."

Grey Wolf, who was standing behind her, mouthed to Steven, "An hour."

Seeing Steven's eyes flicker from her to Grey Wolf, Ms. Connolly quickly added, "It may take a bit longer than ten minutes."

Steven chuckled. This lady didn't miss much. "Give me a few hours. I have a project that I need to finish before I do anything else. I'll contact you as soon as I'm done."

She gave him a look. "Don't make me hunt for you. I'm sneaky when it comes to tracking down my story."

Steven had no doubt about that and held up his hand as if taking an oath. "I promise." He nodded to Grey Wolf, then disappeared onto the Bridge.

Turning to Grey Wolf, Ms. Connolly said, "Now, how about a proper introduction to Irma. I've never had an opportunity to talk to a real AI before."

Irma appeared on the monitor near them, wearing what looked like *way* too much makeup.

"'All right, Mister DeMille, I'm ready for my close-up,'" she said, quoting the movie *Sunset Boulevard.*

Ms. Connolly clasped her hands together as she laughed in delight. "I've heard that you have a wonderful sense of humor! I'm *so* looking forward to talking with you."

Irma's image flickered as the makeup disappeared. "Where shall we go, Ms. Connolly?"

Ms. Connolly thought for a moment. "How about we do the interview in the garden? A contrast-of-technology's best, the most advanced AI in existence, with the first self-sustaining garden in space as a background. Is there a monitor in the garden to use?"

Irma nodded. "There's a hologram projection pedestal I use to talk to the guests about the garden. It's near the pond, with a bench that you can sit on while we talk."

Ms. Connolly's face lit up. "Perfect! Now all I need is a guide to show me the way there." She said this looking directly at Grey Wolf.

He bowed his head, then extended his arm to her. "Allow me to escort you, my good lady."

She slipped her arm into his as she said, "I'll meet you there, Irma."

Irma smiled at her, and as soon as their backs were turned, stuck her tongue out at them, before vanishing from the monitor.

⠄⠄ ⠄⠐⠓⠄⠆⠆⠄⠆ ⠄⠶ ⠄⠲⠓⠄ ⠖⠳⠦⠄⠆⠄⠇ ⠄⠶⠒⠒⠆

When Marc went to the Bridge, he found Steven making the final touches on the Com-Station. "What's up, fearless leader?" Steven asked as he closed the access panel.

Marc looked as if he were having some troubling thoughts. "Can you get the facial recognition program to run on the auction crew? I know we have personal files from the AuctionHouse, but I want to see if what they sent matches up with other records we can crosscheck."

Steven took a seat at his station and started working on his keyboard. "Sure. Guts twitching again? The last time that happened, five and a half years ago, the mob tried to muscle in on our action."

Marc rolled his eyes. "Yeah. And wasn't *that* so much fun? I'm just hoping all I need is some antacids…. But, yeah, it's twitching."

That concerned Steven. Marc's gut was not to be ignored. "Give me a moment to get the program up and running. I'll tie in their profiles to it to see if anything doesn't match. The video feed of them working on *Tranquility* will allow us to double-check their identities."

Steven accessed the personal files and entered them into the program. As it ran each person, the system put the name and photo of the crew member on the monitor. An upside-down family tree started to form as previous employers were added and lines connected. A full history of each individual took form.

Then the system flickered for a moment.

"What was that?" asked Marc.

Steven frowned. "Don't know. I'm running a check on the program, but Wolf is better at this than I am."

"Better at *what*?" asked Grey Wolf as the doors parted and he entered the Bridge.

Steven pointed to the monitor. "The facial recognition program just twitched, for some reason."

"Hmmm," said Grey Wolf as he sat in his chair, with his virtual keyboard appearing before him. As his hands flew over the keys, lines of code buzzed by on the main monitor faster than Marc could read.

"You able to keep up with all that?" Marc whispered to Steven.

Steven made a vague gesture with his hands. "A little. But he's able to multi-task with his contact lenses, which are showing him things we're not seeing."

Grey Wolf pressed his lips together, and the corners of his mouth turned down before he spoke. "Something got by our system's firewalls, but there isn't anything jumping out at me. I'll do a Bug Hunt and have Irma do a full system's check to see if anything is lurking."

Marc's gut tightened even more. He was going to need to visit Sickbay soon if this kept up. "What about the scans of the crew's faces through the station's cameras?"

"Give me a moment," said Grey Wolf as his hands once again flew across the keyboard. In less than a minute, the results popped up on the main monitor: Mr. Maxwell's, Ms. Lee's, and Mr. Garfield's photos with CONFIRMED written across them. Their crew, however, showed UNCONFIRMED, because of the lack of facial scan coverage due to their work caps.

Marc ran a hand through his hair in frustration. "Crap! Okay, we'll have to do this old school. I'll meet up with Tony and McFarland and work out a plan to get their photos. You two get your ducks in a row. If things get crazy, I need you guys to be ready for *anything*."

"Roger that, boss," said Grey Wolf as he pulled out a physical keyboard and plugged it into his desk. "I'll dust off the SHF Protocols."

Steven headed for the floor access panel. "I'll check to make sure the hardwire connections to Irma are secure."

Marc looked at the main monitor and called to the AI, "Irma?"

Irma appeared in a puff of virtual smoke on the main monitor, wearing the headdress of a genie. "What may I do for you, Master?"

Marc couldn't help smiling at her silliness. "Please raise the level of monitoring of the hallways to our "Off Limits" areas. Any intrusions are to be reported to the Core Crew right away."

Irma nodded and disappeared, again in a puff of virtual smoke.

Marc took a deep breath to calm his nerves. "Okay, guys, let's stay sharp. We have a lot of things on our plate. We can't afford for it to become a mess."

Grey Wolf and Steven acknowledged what Marc said by diving into their work.

⠠⠄ ⠠⠍⠞⠋⠄⠌⠄⠌ ⠄ ⠋ ⠠⠙⠋⠏⠄ ⠹⠋⠇⠄⠄⠙ ⠄⠋⠱⠗

As McFarland walked toward the main dining room, he saw two of the auction workers busy installing the hologram posters. When he passed them, he got the distinct feeling that they were sizing him up.

His inner demon wanted out, to deal with the threat. In the five years of being on *Tranquility,* McFarland's demon had never before had reason to want out. It worried him that his instincts were fighting the calm he had found with Marc and the others. And right now, he had to force himself to relax, so he wouldn't be tense when Su saw him. He forced the demon back into its hole and sealed it in with the anticipation of hearing Su laugh again.

But the demon didn't want to be quieted. It whispered promises of being free. *Soon.*

When McFarland entered the dining room, he found Su sitting at a table with her laptop computer, working on the auction items and the order they would be bid on. She gave him a faint smile as she shut down the laptop. McFarland felt that he needed to up his game if he wanted to keep her from dropping back into her withdrawn persona.

"Good evening, my dear lady. May I join you?" He said this with a bow.

Su waved her hand at the empty chair across from her. "I'm saving it for a gentleman who has shown me that there are things in this universe that can still make me smile. Please, join me."

As McFarland sat down, he waved over a waitress. "Mind if I order our meal?"

Su flashed him a quick smile. "So far, you've shown a knack for knowing what I like. Let's see if you can keep it going."

McFarland smiled, then said to the waitress, "Good evening, Samantha. Would you please bring us two mixed green salads with Marc's MapleSnap dressing? You can follow that with two salmon steaks with sautéed veggies and then the desserts I asked Chef Kevin for. But, first, would you ask Maria at the bar to bring us a bottle of 1973 Montelena Chardonnay, from my private stock?"

Su's eyes widened at the wine order. "Wait!" she said, holding up her hand to stop the waitress. "You have a bottle of 1973 Montelena Chardonnay? Don't waste it on a dinner with me!"

Samantha looked at McFarland, who simply nodded for her to proceed, and then back at Su.

"I have *three* of them," he said matter-of-factly. "I haven't found a reason to open one until now. You, my dear, need to be given an extraordinary dinner, and I'm going to make that happen."

Su was stunned. "I'm speechless. I've never had wine that's worth a million dollars a glass!"

"Then, let's celebrate this with a hologram photo of us after dinner, holding the bottle in the Apollo 11 photo booth."

Su smiled and shook her head in bewilderment. She would never have predicted the day would be as extraordinary as it had been so far.

"And what are you hoping to get out of this from me?" she inquired shyly, with a slight frown.

McFarland looked at her with all due seriousness. "To prove to you that someone can be kind *and* respectful to you. I always hope for the best, expect nothing in return, and still maintain being the best person I can be for the people I like. And I like *you...*, very much."

Before Su could respond, a bartender arrived, presented the bottle of wine to them, and expertly opened it. As she was about to pour a sample into McFarland's glass, he held up his hand to stop her, and pointed at Su's glass. "If you don't like it," he said, "we'll order something else."

The bartender poured a sample into Su's glass and waited for the verdict.

Su took the glass, examined the golden-straw coloring, swirled the liquid lightly about, placed her nose near the rim, and gave the wine an appreciative sniff before closing her eyes as she took a sip. Every tight muscle in her body relaxed as a look of ecstasy moved across her face.

"I had no idea it was *that* good!" she exclaimed.

McFarland turned to the bartender. "You may pour, please."

They enjoyed the glass of wine until the salads arrived. McFarland waited for Su to have the first bite.

Looking up at him in amazement, she asked, "What is this dressing? It's like nothing I've ever tasted."

McFarland finished swallowing a bite of the salad. "It's Marc's secret family recipe. Chef Kevin is the only one allowed to make it, beside Marc himself."

Su dipped her finger into a bit of dressing to sample it again. "I taste maple syrup, rice wine vinegar, and some spicy back note that plays well with the sweetness. It's delicious!"

McFarland nodded. "Marc likes to say that he's just a simple cook, but everyone here knows that's not true."

Su took another sip of wine before asking, "I'd like to hear how all of you came to be on *Tranquility*. That is, if you don't mind telling me."

McFarland took the last bite of his salad. "I'd be happy to. It all started because of a drunk redneck."

⠨⠱⠀⠠⠹⠃⠌⠰⠻⠄⠀⠣⠀⠠⠊⠃⠐⠆⠃⠇⠄⠂⠇⠀⠄⠱⠆⠏

Marc met Tony Rhodes during a bar brawl on Earth. He had just bought a round of drinks for Tony and his fellow Marines after overhearing that they were celebrating Tony's birthday. As he was bringing the drinks to their table, a drunk deliberately knocked the tray out of Marc's hands and sucker-punched him. Apparently, the redneck thought that his table, not some "scumbag Marines," should get their drinks first.

Marc looked up from the floor at a ring of Marines protectively standing around him, who then proceeded to make short work of the redneck and his friends. The next thing Marc knew, the offending redneck was being held by Tony by the scruff of the neck. When the angry Marine demanded with a bit of arm-twisting that the redneck apologize to Marc for what he had done, the drunk apologized and joined his friends as they were all ceremoniously thrown out of the bar.

After that, Marc invited the Marines back to his restaurant and proceeded to cook them the finest meal they had ever had. When Tony retired from the Marines the following year, he became the bouncer for the after-hours poker game that Marc held in the back room. The other Marines became loyal patrons of the restaurant, and several were now regulars for the security detail on *Tranquility*.

When McFarland showed up for poker one night, he proved to not only have a wicked sense of humor, but an eye for cheaters. One night, when he caught a guy cheating and called him on it, he got the man to pay back everything that he had won, and he did it without ever raising his voice or resorting to violence. McFarland's eyes and posture spoke volumes about what would happen if his demands were not met. He was also the only non-Marine who could go toe-to-toe with Tony in every kind of combat.

Richard (Wingnut) Vanderbilt had introduced himself to everyone by running into the restaurant as all hell broke loose when a fire started, thanks to a faulty gas connection. His quick think-ing saved the restaurant, and his abilities brought it back to better than new condition in record time. It turned out that Wingnut was known by both Tony and McFarland as the ultimate fix-it guy on land, sea, or space. It was rumored that his knowledge stemmed from being in the Black Ops in his younger days.

After Wingnut masterfully set up and fine-tuned the kitchen equipment, Marc didn't question his abilities. And after seeing the game of cat and mouse that Wingnut played with McFarland, an enthusiastic form of tag, Marc knew that the rumors only scratched the surface.

Since some of Marc's recipes were top secret, he needed an executive chef he could trust, and that required the talents of Kevin Pierce. They had worked together in their early years of cooking, and where Marc was a very good cook, Kevin surpassed him in ways that, to be quite honest, made Marc jealous. So, if he were to hire anyone, it would have to be Kevin.

Shortly after Marc met Kevin, he was introduced to his identical twin brother, Vincent. Marc had shown that he had what the twins called the "Chaos Gene" and would make an excellent candidate to join their group of friends, known as Team Chaos. Everywhere they went, the group was proud to spread a bit of insanity.

Once the plan was hatched to open the casino, Marc knew that if he were to have one of the twins, he would need both of them to keep the balance.

As for someone to keep all the computer systems purring and happy, that went to Marc's school pal, Rowan Anderson, a.k.a. Grey Wolf. Rumor had it that Grey Wolf had once only glanced at a blank monitor, and then determined the type of error, line code, and how it got there. His Intelligent Roaming Mainframe Associate, or Irma as they called her, was his masterpiece of programming. She monitored everything in the station 24/7 and was a member of the Core Crew. But she did tend to be a bit silly at times. Not in a bad way. Just enough to make anyone who didn't know her think she was a bit off.

Then there was Steven Spencer. He was the Yang to Grey Wolf's Yin. His knowledge of computer hardware and how to make systems that didn't speak the same language work together was akin to sorcery. The two of them single-handedly designed and built *Tranquility*'s computer systems.

Marc had been friends with Steven since childhood, and their friendship had never wavered. Even when Marc had made poor life decisions, Steven remained a true friend. A rare thing in this day and age.

But to have Steven join the Core Crew, Marc needed to make an offer to Steven's wife, Susan, that she couldn't refuse. She was already making good money as vice president of the Global Credit Corporation and was well respected there, so what could possibly entice her to move to the Moon? The answer was: being made the CEO of the most respected casino anywhere in the Solar System and being on a first-name basis with the richest people on Earth. With her at the helm, the casino's reputation had gone from nothing to the one place the rich had to visit every month. She also got to stay on as a consultant for the GCC.

Marc's sister, Kimberly Acer, was the one wild card he hadn't planned on. But when she broke up with her longtime boyfriend, he offered her a chance to restart her life. Little did he know that he had brought on the most talented customer relations representative ever. With the ultra-rich came unique problems. Kimberly's natural talent to calm irate guests was a godsend, and everyone working at the casino adored her.

Then there was Eileen Walker. She was the casino's certified massage therapist and the only person ever allowed to use Marc's first name out loud. And only to him in private. The romance between them could only be considered in the league of fairytales. A love never committed to, but one that would never end.

McFarland dabbed a napkin at his mouth. "So, there you have it. A team of people who have only one common thread connecting them all..., Marc. Without him, we wouldn't have all this to call ours."

A thought occurred to Su. "How did Marc manage to pull all this together if he only had a café? That would hardly have been enough collateral to finance an undertaking like this?"

McFarland's eyes took on a hard edge. "He doesn't like talking about the day he ended up saving the legendary Lady Elizabeth. Marc was stabbed and shot, which put him in a coma for a month. During that time, we rallied together to keep the café going. The only person who didn't come to the café was Eileen. She stayed by his side the entire time, singing and giving him massages. When he recovered, Lady Elizabeth asked what his fondest wish was as a reward for saving her. He already had the idea for the casino, but knew he could never afford to make it a reality. With Lady Elizabeth's backing, the *Tranquility Casino* opened for business five years later."

Su's eyes were wide with amazement. "That's incredible. I did some research on this place for Mister Maxwell, but only had small parts of the whole story. Thank you for telling me the rest. But I'm curious. Why do you go by your last name?"

McFarland shrugged. "I hate my first name, but I promised my mother that I wouldn't change it."

Just then, the waiter cleared the table of the dinner plates that had arrived during the story, and Kevin walked out of the kitchen, carrying two plates with something on each of them that resembled artwork.

Placing the plates in front of the couple, he said, "*Voila!* This is my Zero G Molten Chocolate Cake. You are the first to ever have it. Enjoy!"

Kevin bowed, spun around on his heels, and marched back to the kitchen.

On each plate, a sphere of chocolate cake sprinkled with powdered sugar was suspended inside a golden network of hardened spun sugar that was resting on a scoop of vanilla bean ice cream.

"Oh, my!" said Su. "I've got to take a photo of this!"

McFarland held up his hand to stop her. "The rules forbid photos of any kind, except at the photo booth. But, considering that we have a reporter with a buzzing nightmare of a camera lurking about, I don't see the harm. Just don't take any others."

Su smiled and quickly snapped a shot of the two desserts."

McFarland rubbed his hands together in anticipation. "Now, let's not disappoint Kevin by not enjoying his masterpiece before it melts."

"I see why you're so valued by Marc and the others.... And by *me*," she added with a shy smile.

McFarland smiled back at her. "Eat up. We still have a hologram to take with the wine bottle."

CHAPTER 5

Here, Fishy-Fishy-Fishy-Fishy

Rachel Connolly was enjoying an evening stroll in the garden after having her interview with Irma. She had been impressed by the AI's humanlike responses to her questions. At some point, she had actually forgotten that she was talking to an AI, and started regarding Irma as a real person. Irma had picked up on that even before Rachel did. By the end of the interview, Rachel's opinion of AIs had changed dramatically, so she was going to have do a special segment on Irma. Possibly a whole series. But that would have to wait for her to return to Earth.

As Rachel narrated her observations of the garden to her drone, she noticed two people walking hand in hand ahead of her. Immediately she stopped talking and lightly snapped her fingers as she pointed up and forward. When the drone quietly shot up in the air to get a better view of the walkway, Rachel pulled out her pad and looked at the live feed.

"Don't you think the privacy of the crew should be observed, Ms. Connolly?" said a voice behind her.

Rachel nearly jumped out of her skin before spinning around. Standing there was Tony Rhodes, with his arms crossed and looking very unhappy.

"One of the conditions of coming here was that you didn't video anyone without their permission."

She took a deep breath to calm herself and snapped her fingers, which brought the drone back to her side. "You're right. But to be fair, the drone wasn't recording. I was using it to see who it was and if I should interrupt their time with a question or two."

Tony cocked an eyebrow as his posture relaxed slightly. "Thank you for being discreet. But I would suggest that if you see a couple of our crew together, don't interrupt them. We don't get a lot of alone time here."

Rachel threw him one of her brilliant smiles. "Understood. Would you mind giving me a tour of the garden? Maybe squeeze in an interview at the same time?"

Tony smiled and fidgeted at the sleeve of his forearm for a moment. "Sure. But let's give the lovebirds a bit more time to get farther ahead."

Up ahead of them, Kimberly looked at her PAC as it buzzed a message. Her eyes widened when she saw it was from Tony. Then she looked behind her and whispered something into Jackson's ear, after which the two of them quickly headed for the exit.

⠠⠐⠎�@⠶⠆⠶⠄⠶⠄⠄⠐@⠐⠰⠙⠶⠄⠐⠙�⠄⠐⠶⠷⠶

Wingnut entered his quarters, kicked off his shoes, flexed his toes on the thick carpet, and sighed. When he opened the curtains in the living room and turned on the lights, he revealed a room filled with shelves full of different miniature models of vehicles that had made history: the first steam locomotive, made by Richard Trevithick; Henry Ford's Model T; Chuck Yeager's X-1; Apollo 11's Saturn V rocket; the Enterprise Space Shuttle; and many others. Along the window, there was a worktable that had tools and parts of components on it in different stages of completion, with hand-written notes strewn about.

Wingnut stepped into the bedroom, where the walls were covered with blueprints of ships, both real and fictional. Pads with the latest papers on upcoming technology were on nearly every flat surface. Wingnut picked up one of them, lay down on his bed, and started to read. As he did so, the corners of his mouth slowly ticked upward.

⠠⠃⠚⠆⠑⠓⠀⠉⠋⠀⠮⠀⠛�⠇⠵⠽

McFarland woke up in his quarters with the "hublight" from the garden peeking through a crack in the curtains of his window. The artificial light illuminated the far wall, where a silk tapestry adorned with McFarland's silver-and-black coat of arms was visible. On a nearby desk, there were several framed photos.

Suddenly, an arm appeared from behind McFarland and wrapped itself around his chest. "What time is it?" asked Su.

McFarland looked at the clock on the wall. "Seven-forty-eight."

Su sat upright in a panic, exposing her naked body. "Oh, no! I'm supposed to report to Mister Maxwell at eight! I'm going to be in so much trouble!"

McFarland held up a hand to quiet her, tapped a command into the pad on his nightstand, and said, "Irma, would you patch me through to Mister Maxwell, please?"

Irma's voice replied, "Sure thing…, oh, silver-haired one."

A moment later, a voice came on McFarland's pad. "This is Maxwell. What can I do for you, Mister McFarland?"

McFarland winked at Su. "Sorry to interrupt you, sir, but I'm doing some work on the drinks that would be appropriate to serve during the auction. Would it be okay for me to ask Ms. Lee's help for an hour or two this morning?"

There was a slight pause before Mr. Maxwell responded. "I don't see why not. We want everything to be perfect. Please tell her I'll expect her at the auction room by eleven o'clock."

McFarland smiled at Su. "Thank you, Mister Maxwell. I'll make sure she's there on time."

After McFarland cut the connection, Su frowned at him. "How am I to know what drinks to have served at the auction? I don't even know what you have in stock."

McFarland wrapped his arms around her waist and pulled her to him. "I'll send you the list of drinks I already picked out."

Su narrowed her eyes. "Do you really have a list already?"

His eyes sparkled with amusement. "I did it five days ago. Now, what should we do for the next couple of hours?"

Su grinned and pinned him to the bed, not being fooled for a second by her strength to overpower him. "You're going to be a bad influence on me, you know?" she said with a wicked grin.

McFarland laughed. "Of all the things I've been accused of doing to someone, that's probably the nicest."

Su pressed her body against his and purred into his ear, "Then let's see how bad you can be."

⠲⠄ ⠐�⠰⠆⠂⠆ ⠐⠿ ⠨⠦⠗⠄ ⠦⠿⠂⠄⠸⠄ ⠐⠿⠐⠿

As Kevin and Vincent left their quarters, which were across from each other, they fist-bumped and turned toward the Crew Kitchen. When they passed McFarland's door, they heard the sound of a woman's shriek of delight. They looked at each other and listened for a moment. Then, when they heard another shriek, they shrugged, continued on to the Crew Kitchen, and waved a hand at each other while saying together, "These are not the sounds you are listening for."

⠲⠄ ⠐⠿⠰⠆⠂⠆ ⠐⠿ ⠨⠦⠗⠄ ⠦⠿⠂⠄⠸⠄ ⠐⠿⠐⠿

The auction crew worked through the night, and when the Core Crew woke up, they were greeted by the casino hallway's holo-posters. The hologram system was state-of-the-art equipment from Railroad Technologies that scans the individuals standing in front of it. Using the AuctionHouse information of who viewed the items on their webpage, plus facial recognition, the software would create a life-size hologram image of the person. The interactive programming would then adjust the image of the person holding a viewed auction item. There were also monitor displays throughout the Main Bar with a full inventory of the auction items and the starting bids.

Marc asked Irma to send a wakeup call to all AC and Marine members to meet in the Main Dining Room. As everyone arrived, the Core Crew were talking in hushed tones.

Once everyone was assembled, Marc used his PAC to close and secure the doors before addressing the crew. "Thank you, everyone, for coming. We just wanted a minute of your time to make sure there are no unanswered questions you might have." Everyone looked around to see if there were any. "No? Well, I'm not surprised. This crew has done an incredible job in the past, but this event is going to surpass anything else ever done here. The guests are going to be more tightly wound than previous stays here and will be spending way more money on one trip here than ever before, so we all need to be at the top of our game. I know you already have a great sense of teamwork, but make sure you do that voodoo you do so well, but even more so. In four hours, the guests will be arriving, and we'll be up to our eyeballs with requests. So, let's show everyone in the Solar System that *Tranquility Casino* is the place to go. Thank you, everyone."

Tony stepped forward. "Would all Marines meet at the far table with McFarland and me, please," he said, pointing to a group of tables.

Marc nodded to Steven and Grey Wolf, who followed him to the Bridge. As soon as the doors closed, Grey Wolf engaged the Privacy Protocols for the Bridge that put it on lockdown, and then activated a white noise eavesdropping scrambler.

"Okay, boss," he said to Marc. "We can speak freely."

Marc sat in his chair. "Thanks, Wolf. What did you guys find?"

Grey Wolf looked worried. "The program that got through the firewalls originated in the files from the AuctionHouse that contained the information about their personnel, but the bug wasn't in just one of the files. Each file held a fragment of code, and when all the files were opened, they linked together to form the completed program. I believe the program is some sort of virus that deleted the program code from the affected files before entering our computer system. The virus started jumping from system to system like a grasshopper. In fact, that's what I've taken to calling it. Wherever it jumps, it eats up some program code and then jumps again. Irma's tracking where it jumps to see if there's any pattern to its movements. Until I've gotten a good look at it, I can't make a program to counteract what it's been doing. For now, I have the Mario program following the grasshopper to repair the damage being done."

On the main monitor, there was a layout of the programs running *Tranquility*. A small 8-bit computer-generated man in a red hat with blue coveralls was busy fixing the holes in the programs.

Marc pointed at the display. "Isn't he copyrighted?"

Grey Wolf grinned. "He's working off the books."

Marc turned to Steven. "What have *you* been up to?"

Steven sat back in his chair as he looked at Marc. "I've double-checked all the connections to Irma, as well as the primary and secondary computer systems. Nothing was amiss or looked suspicious."

Marc was troubled. "It bothers me that something got loose inside our computer that we didn't put there or have control over."

Marc looked back at Grey Wolf as an idea came to him. "You called it a grasshopper. What about making a praying mantis program? Something that lies in wait for the intruding virus."

Grey Wolf's eyes widened as a grin slowly spread across his face. "That's inspired!!! But it jumps as soon as it's detected. What if...? No..., I could..., or maybe..., then..., hmmm...." He activated his virtual keyboard and started typing as he muttered to himself.

"We've lost him, Marc," said Steven, rising from his chair. "You know how he is when he disappears into a program." He typed a series of commands into the door panel to shut down the Privacy Protocols and open the door. "I'll let you know when he returns."

Marc looked at Grey Wolf for a moment before leaving his chair. Then he placed a friendly hand on Steven's shoulder. "Okay, with things as they are, I want the Bridge and Engineering in Lockdown Mode. No entry without a code, and Irma's to monitor and record the hallways full-time. I'll let the Core Crew know about the change in status here."

Steven threw Marc a sloppy salute. "Okay, Marc. Don't worry, we'll get rid of that program and find out who's behind this."

Marc nodded, but still couldn't shake the feeling that more was going on than just a virus in the computer. Too many things were beginning to smell rotten.

⠲⠄ ⠠⠏⠄⠂⠄⠄⠐ ⠰⠩ ⠠⠲⠄⠆ ⠱⠱⠄⠁⠄⠂⠆⠄

When Tony saw Marc in the hallway leading to the auction room, he called out to him, "Hold up, Marc." Tony quickened his pace to catch up and glanced around for any auction workers. "McFarland and I got the Marines up to speed on the new protocols and patrols. We've also worked out the new hand signals, and the twins will have their stations ready if things go sideways."

Marc felt that that might not be enough. But short of closing *Tranquility* down and sending all the guests home, their precautions were going to have to be sufficient.

The two men continued to walk down the hallway. "Good," said Marc. "With the Bridge and Engineering on lockdown, and all our safeguards in place, I think, under the circumstances, we're as ready as can be for whatever comes our way. Let's hope we're just being paranoid."

Tony gave Marc a who-are-you-kidding look before asking, "And the chances of that are...?"

Marc sighed. "Slim to none. And slim just got sucked out the airlock."

Tony rolled his eyes. "Wonderful. Oh, for the days when we were just butting heads against the Mafia. At least we knew who they were and how to fight against them. This whole thing stinks, and I'm out of air freshener."

Marc slapped Tony on the back. "Amen, brother. I'm off to check in on Mister Maxwell to see if everything is ready on his end. Want to come along?"

Tony shrugged. "Sure."

When they entered the auction room, they were impressed by the setup. Burgundy velvet curtains with the golden starburst logo of AuctionHouse hung along the full length of the walls. The redwood podium and display tables on the stage were polished to a high shine, and large monitors were placed around the room so that the items being bid on could be seen by everyone.

Mr. Maxwell was talking with Ms. Lee about last-minute details when he saw the two men approaching and greeted them warmly while gesturing around the room: "Gentlemen! What do you think?"

Marc nodded his approval. "Very nice, Mister Maxwell. This room has never looked finer. I like the curtains. Gives it a warm, members-only touch."

Mr. Maxwell beamed with pride. "Thank you. When dealing with items that cost a king's ransom, it's best to make the people buying them feel that things are being done in style."

Marc looked again at the lavish décor and couldn't disagree. "In two hours, the guests arrive, and then the real fun begins. The Core Crew and the ACs will be greeting them at Docking Port Two. We have a table set up for you to hand out the Bid Scanners with the gift bags at the end of the reception line. We'll meet you there at twelve-thirty P.M. to get into positions. It usually takes about half an hour to disembark, and then we'll have the reception in the Main Bar at three P.M. I hope you, Ms. Lee, and Mister Garfield will join us there."

Mr. Maxwell smiled. "We'll be there. Thank you so much for making us feel welcomed here." He nodded toward Ms. Lee. "Someone here has done something to her that I haven't seen in a long time. A smile on her face."

Ms. Lee blushed. "I have no idea what you're talking about."

Tony rescued her by saying, "We need to finish our rounds and get ready. We'll see you at Docking Port Two."

At that moment, Ms. Connolly came from backstage with her ever-present drone in front of her while she talked about seeing the auction pieces: "…and that's just a sample of the exciting items that'll be auctioned off here at the *Tranquility Casino*."

When she saw that Marc and Tony were present, she snapped her fingers, causing her drone to return to its spot beside her head as she stepped down from the stage. "This auction is going to break all records for most viewers of a single event! The items *alone* are going to draw them. But to have a peek at this fabulous casino…, it's something that everyone's chomping at the bit to see."

Marc mentally fought against letting her excitement influence him. Although she was a well-respected reporter, he didn't like how his stomach twisted every time she was nearby.

He tapped into his acting training from years ago to hide his discomfort. "We'll be meeting the guests in two hours. I know you'll want to be at the head of the reception, but it's already crowded at the elevator entrance with all the crew. I hope you'll be okay with waiting at the AuctionHouse table."

Ms. Connolly frowned at that. "Oh, dear. That won't do at all. Seeing the rich and famous entering *Tranquility* is something I was hoping to document." She put a finger to her lips in thought. Then, after a moment, her black eyes glinted with an idea, and she smiled as her finger moved away from her lips to point at the drone. "What about Jake? It can hover in a spot with you while I watch from the table on my Video-Pad and catch all the interactions without being in the way."

Marc looked at Tony. "What do you think?"

Tony rubbed his chin. "The guests have already signed off about this visit being reported on, and Ms. Connolly knows that she must ask them for permission before interviewing them." He looked at her to confirm this, which she did with a nod. "With the drone as quiet as it is, I think having it at the elevator will be fine."

Marc turned to Mr. Maxwell. "Mind sharing your table with Ms. Connolly?"

Mr. Maxwell shook his head. "Not at all. It might be a little crowded behind the table with all four of us, but it shouldn't be a problem." Then, to Ms. Connolly, he said, "Why don't you meet us here at noon, and we'll all head there together?"

Ms. Connolly clasped her hands in delight. "Wonderful! I've done some high-profile events, but this will *for sure* surpass them all!" She snapped her fingers, the drone zipped in front of her, and she started to walk back to the stage, again narrating the upcoming events.

As soon as they were out in the hallway, Marc asked Tony, "Did you get any readings off of them?"

Tony's brow furled. "No, but there's something that has my senses buzzing that I don't like. Ms. Connolly is charming, but I'm still not sure about her."

Marc sighed. "Yeah. My gut agrees with you. Well, we have forty-six guests about to arrive. It's time to be our charming selves and pretend that we don't have a worm in our apple."

Tony smiled. "I like worms. They make for good fishing."

Both of them started saying together, "Here, fishy-fishy-fishy-fishy. *Here*, fishy-fishy-fishy-fishy!"

⠲⠄ ⠲⠈⠃⠠⠶⠆⠶⠄⠶ ⠶ ⠰⠩⠃⠂⠆ ⠶⠩⠃⠠⠲⠆⠶⠂ ⠶⠠⠩⠒⠆

The luxury transport ship *Tyche*, named after the Greek goddess of fortune and prosperity, arrived right on time. It was the only ship made with centrifugal gravity, so the guests could be in complete comfort during the two-day voyage to *Tranquility*.

The red-carpeted hallway was lined with servers who were ready with an assortment of drinks. At the head of the line stood the Core Crew in tuxedos and elegant gowns. The first guest to exit the elevator was Lady Elizabeth, who was a gorgeous woman in her early sixties with long waves of golden blonde hair. No one would call her fat, nor was she skinny, but she carried herself with grace and style.

Marc stepped forward, bowed, took her hand, and kissed it. "Lady Elizabeth, how wonderful to see you again. You look as radiant as ever."

Her Ladyship nodded to Marc and gave him a smile that lit up her face. "Marc, you look like the universe has been treating you well."

"Thank you, Your Ladyship." Marc waved over Patricia, who was holding a saucer with a cappuccino cup. "Your mocha," he said, "with extra shaved chocolate on top."

Lady Elizabeth clasped her hands in delight. "Oh, yum! You're the best, Marc! Patricia, it's always a pleasure to have you as my personal valet."

Patricia smiled, bowed her head as she handed over the drink, and then took her place behind Lady Elizabeth.

Marc extended a hand toward Eileen. "As always, Eileen will show you to your room. She's already set up the massage table there."

Eileen stepped forward and curtsied. "Your Ladyship, I'm pleased to see you again."

Lady Elizabeth finished taking a sip of her mocha and beamed at Eileen. "I've been so looking toward having you work on me. No one can get that one knot out of my shoulder as well as you can."

Lady Elizabeth finished the mocha and handed the empty cup to Patricia, who disposed of it on a nearby cart. Then Eileen offered her arm to Lady Elizabeth and led her down the hallway.

As the rest of the guests arrived, they were warmly greeted by Marc and the crew. Each guest was paired up with an AC member who would be his or her valet/butler.

The last to leave the ship were the pilots. Patrick, who was tall and had charcoal black hair, and his co-pilot, Maximus, who was a slightly heavy-set, average-height man with dark brown wavy hair, were all smiles when they saw the Core Crew.

Marc shook their hands. "Patrick, Max, welcome back. Ready for some relaxing fun?"

Patrick returned the handshake enthusiastically. "We sure are. This is the best run we get to make. It's worth the two-day trip just to sleep and eat here for free. Getting a thousand credits to spend in the casino just proves how cool you guys are. All the other pilots going to Starbase One are jealous of us."

Marc waved them down the hallway. "Your rooms are ready, and the party will start at three P.M. We'll see you there."

As the pilots headed down the hallway, they discussed what game of chance they were going to play first. As soon as they were clear, the remaining ACs entered the elevator to start unloading the guests' luggage and personal effects from the ship.

Marc ducked as the reporter's drone buzzed by him, returning to Ms. Connolly's side. "I almost forgot that was there."

McFarland grumbled. "Having that overgrown mosquito buzzing near me made me wish for some bug spray."

Marc and the Core Crew chuckled at that as they walked down the hallway to the AuctionHouse table.

"Everything go smoothly, Mister Maxwell?" Marc asked.

Mr. Maxwell smiled broadly. "Very much so. I must commend your crew for being well-informed about the scanners, and how the auction will proceed. Even the crew I have at the home office is not as well trained as yours."

Marc beamed. "We pride ourselves on having only the best here. The guests expect nothing less."

Mr. Maxwell handed a computer pad to Ms. Lee to put away. "Your reputation, Mister Acer, is well deserved. I'll be sure to make notes of what needs to be changed back home to emulate what you have here."

Marc bowed. "Thank you, Mister Maxwell. There's no better honor for our crew than to be the standard that others are held up to. Do you need any help, sir?"

Mr. Maxwell saw that Ms. Lee and Mr. Garfield had finished packing and were heading back to the auction room. "No, thank you. It seems that they already have things well in hand."

Marc turned to the reporter. "I hope you were able to get everything you needed with your drone, Ms. Connolly."

She finished tapping on her pad and nodded. "Jake's placement was perfect. I'll be able to dub in commentary later when I edit the video. Now, if you'll excuse me, I need to do some prep work for the party." She gathered up her pads, started calling up the video on one of them, and began making notations.

Marc and the Core Crew walked down the hallway to the crew elevator and entered it. As soon as the doors closed, Marc hit the stop button to pause the elevator. "What's the status on the grasshopper virus, Grey Wolf?"

"It's still active. But I'm almost ready to release the mantis. It's a self-replicating program that jumps from system to system. It'll stay dormant until the grasshopper appears. Then it will pounce on it and trap it. Irma will analyze its program code. Then I can isolate what it's been doing. With any luck, it will be out of our system in a few hours."

"Good," said Marc as he got the elevator going again. "Out of everything that's been making my stomach twitch, that's the one I worry about the most. God, I hate not having something physical to get my hands on and throttle!"

"It could be worse," said Steven.

"It could be raining!" said Wingnut.

Irma appeared on the elevator's monitor with a large lump on her head. "What hump?"

Kimberly put her hand to her face. "Good Lord, we're a weird bunch!"

"True," said Wingnut. "But we're not boring."

"Hey!" said the twins, "we resemble that remark!!!"

When the doors opened, they all headed to their departments, enjoying the silliness they had shared.

⠲⠀⠐⠳⠄⠆⠂⠄⠆⠀⠦⠀⠐⠦⠁⠐⠦⠇⠨⠂⠂⠐⠣⠆⠆

Eileen stepped into her quarters to change before the Greeting Party in the Main Bar. Her living room was a warm and inviting place, with all the walls lined with books. On the center shelf, there was a complete set of first-edition *Wizard of OZ* books. Along the window, a loveseat and two wooden side tables took advantage of the light from the garden, with floor lamps on either side. On the tables, there were several books and two red antique vases. On the other side of the room, there was a desk with a monitor and more books.

Eileen quickly went to the bedroom, which also had shelves filled with books, as well as a variety of porcelain Disney figurines. After quickly changing, she headed for the living room, where she saw that there was a message waiting for her on the monitor. When she opened it, she found that it was from Marc, with the heading "Warm Fuzzies." As she read the loving words, she softly said, "I love you, too." After rereading the love letter, she turned off the monitor and left for the party.

CHAPTER 6

The SHF Protocols

"This is Rachel Connolly reporting from *Tranquility*'s Main Bar. In just moments, the guests will be enjoying the welcoming party, and I will bring you a firsthand look at the fabulous event." The drone did a sweeping shot of the ACs standing at attention. "The crew of *Tranquility* are standing by, waiting for the guests to arrive with a sense of the decorum befitting the legendary service I have only heard rumors of. If there's a hair out of place, this eagle eye reporter cannot find it."

An AC approached her with a tray of champagne glasses and offered her one. Ms. Connolly took a glass and thanked the server before returning her attention to the camera. "A service I plan to *thoroughly* enjoy."

Marc watched as Ms. Connolly finished her report by snapping her fingers at the drone, which brought it to its position beside her head. He observed that its recording light was still on, and was glad that his crew were the best, because from this moment on they were all going to be under scrutiny by billions of people.

As always, Marc felt the flutter of butterflies in his stomach that preceded the opening party. Adding the amount of international interest that Ms. Connolly was giving it turned the butterflies into hornets.

But they faded away when he felt the comforting touch of Eileen's hand slip down his forearm. Her simple touch was all he ever needed to prevent his mind from eating itself.

Eileen waved over an AC with a tray of champagne, handed a glass to Marc, and then took one for herself. Lifting her glass, she said softly, "You've been training for this for five years, Marc, and the people you have are the best. So, tell those butterflies to take a hike."

Marc looked at Eileen's coffee brown eyes, and for the millionth time fell in love with her. He never understood how or why she had this effect on him, but he wasn't ever going to question it. He just knew that her unconditional love gave him strength that saw him through recovering from a coma and every challenge since then.

Tapping his glass against hers, he whispered, "You sent those butterflies packing." Then he gave her a kiss.

Marc's acute hearing picked up the soft voices of the guests, who were just coming down the hallway. He squeezed Eileen's hand, quickly drank his champagne, and handed his glass off to a nearby AC. He was ready to face the guests.

Eileen didn't mind that Marc's attention was no longer on her. She had noticed that he was fighting to keep calm, so she did the only thing she knew would distract him: give him as much love and support as she could.

As the guests started to file into the Main Bar, the *Tranquility* crew were ready to greet them.

McFarland worked the bar and talked with the guests about any number of political, economic, or hot-button topics that came up.

Tony talked security with the bodyguards who were traveling with a few of the guests.

Kimberly made sure that the rooms were to everyone's satisfaction.

Susan introduced the first-time visitors to the regulars.

Kevin directed the traffic of finger foods.

Vincent arranged tables for specific groups to play cards together.

Eileen booked times to give massages.

Wingnut and Steven talked to the leaders of the tech industry to get the inside scoop about the latest items coming to market.

Marc talked to everyone, sharing the latest bad jokes.

Mr. Maxwell, Ms. Lee, and Mr. Garfield were stationed at the monitors for the auction, being available for the guests to ask questions about any items they were interested in.

At the piano, an Asian man from the AC team played some light classical music. Eileen waited for him to finish a song before taking a spot next to his piano. When he started to play again, she began to sing "Pure Imagination" from the 1971 movie *Willy Wonka & the Chocolate Factory.*

All the guests stopped what they were doing to listen to her. The lyrics of dreams and hopes sung by someone who could work the notes to perfection put smiles on everyone's face. It was magical.

But one person was beyond just listening. Marc had been waiting for this moment for weeks. To him, the sound of Eileen's voice had nearly the same effect as her arms being wrapped around him in a loving embrace. Nothing else existed. Just her.

But to get her to sing had taken some doing. Eileen was self-conscious about her singing, to the point of not wanting to do it publicly. But he had made her a deal: if she gave her best every time she sang, he would never ask her to perform again if even one guest didn't like her singing. *And* he would have to pay her one million dollars. For five years now, the cash had remained securely tucked away in his safe.

When Eileen finished the song, Marc slowly returned to his senses, taking in his surroundings and joining in with the round of applause. He caught the slight look of shy embarrassment that flashed in Eileen's eyes before she smiled at him. It was a simple statement: You win again.

Marc held up his hand to give her the sign language for "I love you," just as a guest approached him to ask about the post-auction party.

Mr. Maxwell was talking to one of the guests when Mr. Garfield whispered something to him. Mr. Maxwell simply nodded and waved him off.

Mr. Garfield then moved over to where Susan was talking to a guest. "May I please have a moment of your time, Mrs. Spencer?"

Susan excused herself from the guest and walked over to a quieter spot. "What may I do for you, Mister Garfield?"

Mr. Garfield smiled down at her. "I was thinking, as the CEO of the *Tranquility Casino*, you might like to see the items for the auction. I've set up a private viewing, so you can really appreciate what we have."

Susan thought for a moment. "Thank you, Mister Garfield. That's most kind. I'd love to see them. Give me about thirty minutes to finish saying my hellos to the guests, and I'll meet you at the auction room."

Mr. Garfield nodded. "Very good. I look forward to seeing you there."

⠨⠄ ⠐⠶⠏⠄⠂⠂⠄⠂ ⠶ � ⠨�⠄⠂⠓⠄⠂⠇ ⠄⠶⠮⠏

On the Bridge, Grey Wolf was putting the finishing touches on the praying mantis program. On the main monitor, there was an image of a grasshopper jumping from computer system to system as Irma's head tried to eat it.

A voice suddenly came from the intercom: "AuctionHouse Five to *Tranquility* Bridge. May I speak to Grey Wolf, please?"

Grey Wolf engaged the intercom system: "This is Grey Wolf. Go ahead, AuctionHouse Five."

The AuctionHouse's pilot cleared his throat. "We are experiencing some more errors throughout the ship's systems. Could you come over and see if you can fix what's wrong with it, please? Life support is getting affected now."

Grey Wolf looked at the time on his PAC. "Okay. I'll be there in about fifteen minutes."

"Thank you, Grey Wolf. AuctionHouse Five out."

Grey Wolf input the last bit of code for the praying mantis program. "Okay, Irma, you can quit chasing it. I'm about to turn the mantis loose, and I don't want it to snare *you* by mistake."

Irma vanished from the main monitor, immediately reappearing on Grey Wolf's workstation monitor. "Let 'er rip, oh great one!"

Grey Wolf activated the praying mantis and watched as it appeared on the main monitor. The image of a praying mantis sat there for a moment, rubbing its front legs together. Then it split in two, and the second one jumped to another system. Satisfied that the program was working, Grey Wolf gathered up his troubleshooting equipment, unlocked the Bridge doors, and set the auto-lock to engage after the doors closed behind him. "Mind the store, Irma. I'll be back soon."

As soon as Grey Wolf left, Irma opened a game of chess on a monitor and started playing both sides.

On the main monitor, the communication system activated on the main monitor was indicating that an open line had been established to an outside source. The grasshopper jumped through the connection and disappeared off the monitor just as a praying mantis appeared there. A few minutes later, when the grasshopper returned, the mantis pounced and started chirping.

Looking up, Irma said, "Hey! That's mine!"

The grasshopper stopped struggling and smiled at her.

⠌⠄ ⠐⠏⠂⠒⠂⠐⠶ ⠨⠮⠄ ⠒⠏⠄⠤⠁ ⠐⠶⠒⠆

As Marc looked around, he was pleased with how things were going. Some guests were gathered in front of the displays for the auction, while others were enjoying the photo booth. Everyone was smiling.

Rachel Connolly was busy talking to a guest about the upcoming auction, obviously enjoying her time on *Tranquility*. When she noticed Marc activating his PAC's Holo-Mic and tapping on it to get everyone's attention, she snapped her fingers and pointed to get her drone into position for Marc's speech.

When Marc saw the drone move to record him, he couldn't have felt more exposed than if he were standing there naked. In fact, he would have preferred that to having the whole world watch him under a flying magnifying glass.

Catching a movement in the corner of his eye, he saw Eileen mouth the word *breathe*. And with that simple encouragement, the lid slammed shut on his anxiety.

He took a deep breath and gave everyone a warm smile. "Excuse me, ladies and gentlemen, if I may interrupt you for a few minutes, please." He waited for everyone to quiet down. "I wanted to thank you all for joining us here on *Tranquility*. As all of you know, we'll be having the first Off-Earth auction right here tomorrow. Your gift bags contain all the needed information about the auction, and all *Tranquility* crew members are at your disposal if any of you have questions. Even Irma can be of assistance. But, as most of you know, she can be a bit silly at times."

On the main monitor, Irma's head appeared with a bright red clown's nose and a top hat that had bright pink polka dots. "I have no idea what you're talking about, Marc!" she said—and promptly disappeared, causing everyone to laugh.

Marc shook his head. "Okay, case in point. Tomorrow we'll start the auction at three P.M. sharp, right after lunch. Until then, we invite you to enjoy all we have to offer, including...," Marc activated the solar panels with his PAC to retract them across the floor, "... the best view anywhere!"

Everyone "oooohed" and "ahhhhed" as the Moon and Earth passed by.

As Marc looked around, he saw Tony talking to Susan and a Jamaican Marine by the name of Jackson. As he walked over to them, he overheard Tony saying, "I don't like it."

"Don't like *what*, Tony?" asked Marc.

Tony's eyebrows were pushed together in a way that concerned Marc. "Glad you're here, Marc. Susan just got invited to a private viewing of the auction items. She said she would be there in ten minutes, but because we've been feeling uneasy about the auction workers, she came to me. I called Jackson over to escort her and keep an eye on her. That's when you came in."

Marc nodded. "Okay, thanks, Tony. Good call on involving Jackson." He turned to the Marine. "Don't crowd her when you get there, but keep alert. If you feel that you need help, do the hand signal, and Irma will pass on the message to everyone."

"Yes, sir. Understood," said Jackson with a heavy Jamaican accent.

Tony looked at the spunky CEO. "Okay, Susan. Enjoy, but be ready for anything. We've grown quite fond of you."

Susan stood on her tiptoes to give Tony a kiss on the cheek. "Will do. What could go wrong? I get to have my own private Marine to keep me safe." She turned to Jackson and offered her arm to him. "Come along, Jackson. We have some merchandise to check out."

Jackson grinned as he took her arm. "Yes, ma'am. I *was* hoping to see Jimmy Hendrix's guitar."

Tony watched them leave, then turned to Marc. "'What could go wrong?' I hate it when someone says that. So, how twisted is *your* gut?"

Marc put his hand on his stomach. "I'm going to need a stiff drink. Want to join me?"

Tony held up two fingers. "Yes! I think maybe two."

⠨⠂ ⠠⠐⠓⠂⠆⠒⠆ ⠀⠴ ⠠⠫⠓⠐ ⠛⠋⠇⠂⠸⠇ ⠐⠫⠰⠏

As Mr. Garfield entered the auction room, he saw the work crew sitting on the chairs they had set up. They all stood with a sense of anticipation as he held his right hand out and gave them a thumbs up. "It's time to get our revenge, guys."

The workmen grinned at each other and grabbed their toolkits. Each of them pulled out a power tool that had universal attachments for it and started breaking them down to the power cells and on/off triggers. Then they connected new components, and soon had what are known as Stun/Guns.

⠨⠂ ⠠⠐⠓⠂⠆⠒⠆ ⠀⠴ ⠠⠫⠓⠐ ⠛⠋⠇⠂⠸⠇ ⠐⠫⠰⠏

Stun/Guns were developed in the late 2000s, when space travel became as common as taking a plane from the United States to Europe had been in the late 1960s. When the first attempted hijacking occurred of a commercial ship, it went horribly wrong. When one of the hijackers shot at the Air & Space Marshall, that one bullet changed everything.

Spaceships' outer hulls are made of multiple layers that prevent micro-meteors from penetrating through to the interior, which is not as well protected. The outer hulls would have prevented the bullet from penetrating them, but all life-support systems are just inside the interior hull, where an oxygen tank was breached and instantly turned into a missile. That tore into the cabin, killing three passengers before exiting the ship, creating a breach that led to an explosive decompression, killing all the passengers. Only the pilots survived because the cockpit was sealed for the trip, but the fuel cells were damaged and needed to be rescued before gravity brought the ship back to Earth.

⠀⠠⠄⠨⠈⠞⠃⠈⠆⠈⠆⠀⠼⠀⠠⠙⠃⠄⠀�⠄⠈⠄⠀⠈⠼⠠⠃⠃⠄

The auction crew finished assembling the Stun/Guns and tucked them into their belts. Two of them made for the doorway and headed toward the guests' living quarters, while Mr. Garfield opened his laptop and started a program for the holo-posters, which activated cameras in each of them. He smiled wickedly when he saw a Marine approaching one of the posters.

⠀⠠⠄⠨⠈⠞⠃⠈⠆⠈⠆⠀⠼⠀⠠⠙⠃⠄⠀�⠄⠈⠄⠀⠈⠼⠠⠃⠃⠄

The Marine was patrolling the guests' hallway and stopped at the holo-posters that were on either side of the door that led to the gardens. One poster showed him holding the M60 machine gun that Sylvester Stallone had used in *Rambo—First Blood*. The other showed him wielding Arnold Schwarzenegger's sword from *Conan the Barbarian*.

Moments later, blue-and-white streaks of electricity flew from the posters. The Marine shook from the voltage, then collapsed unconscious to the floor. When the doors opened, revealing the two auction workers, they stepped out and quickly Zip-Tied the Marine's hands and feet. Then both spun toward the sound of a door opening a few yards away and raised their Stun/Guns to shoot the housekeeping crew member. Two packets struck her in the torso, releasing a fast-acting gel that saturated the cloth it was stuck to. A small disk from the packet that was now stuck to her clothing released a jolt of electricity, causing her to scream briefly before falling to the floor unconscious. When another door opened, revealing a second housekeeper, she also was shot and knocked out. After Zip-Tying them, the auction workers used the housekeepers' master keycards to check each room to made sure that no one else was there.

⠌⠄ ⠐⠦⠃⠂⠖⠒⠐ ⠶ ⠠⠯⠅⠄ ⠒⠹⠳⠄⠤⠅ ⠘⠶⠃⠆

Grey Wolf arrived at *AuctionHouse 5* through the service elevator that took him from the centrifugal gravity to the Zero-G Zone of the docking bay. As he floated toward the ship, he could see his own breath, which told him that the temperature was below 45 degrees—a clear sign that the environmental systems were malfunctioning.

The pilot greeted him at the open airlock. "Thank you for coming. As you can see, it's gotten worse. The computer station is aft-portside in the cockpit." He pointed to the ladder leading up.

Grey Wolf turned to move toward the ladder. "Let's see what's giving your system fits." Then he was knocked unconscious.

⠌⠄ ⠐⠦⠃⠂⠖⠒⠐ ⠶ ⠠⠯⠅⠄ ⠒⠹⠳⠄⠤⠅ ⠘⠶⠃⠆

Susan and Jackson walked down the hallway that led to the auction room. On both sides of the doorway, there were holo-posters. Jackson allowed Susan to enter the room first. As soon as she did, Jackson was shocked from both sides of the doorway by the posters, which knocked him unconscious.

"Jackson!!!" Susan shouted as she started to move to him.

"I wouldn't do that, Susan, or you'll be shocked, too!"

When Susan turned around, she saw Mr. Garfield standing at the podium, working on his laptop. Then workers stepped out from behind the curtains near her, tied up Jackson, and surrounded Susan.

Mr. Garfield pointed toward the door. "You know what to do. The clock is ticking."

The workers pulled out their Stun/Guns, and all but one of them left the room.

As Susan took a step toward the doorway, Mr. Garfield warned, "Just because my men can walk by our bobby traps doesn't mean you can. Unless you like being shocked senseless."

Susan turned to him with rage written on her face. "What the *fuck* do you think you're doing?!"

Mr. Garfield slowly smiled at her in a way that made her skin crawl. "Just a trivial thing, my dear, of robbing your casino."

⠠⠹⠀⠌�⠀⠦⠀⠮⠀�
At the bar, Marc, Tony, and McFarland had just finished a shot of scotch when all three of them stood straight with shocked looks. They each pulled back their sleeves to reveal their PACs, which were buzzing an SOS that displayed Susan's location.

Suddenly, several loud electric discharges came from the main hallway. A female guest standing near the doorway started screaming, "Oh, my god! The posters are malfunctioning!"

Out in the hallway, the two Marines on patrol and a guest fell to the floor.

Tony turned to the nearest Marine, held up his right hand with his index finger extended, and then all five fingers spread apart, followed by a clenched fist.

The Marine nodded, looked around, found Steven, who was looking wide-eyed at his PAC, and made a beeline to him. Steven looked up in surprise as the Marine took him by the arm and nearly dragged him to the bar.

Tony grabbed Wingnut and quickly brought him to the bar, too.

Marc stepped behind the bar and headed with McFarland to the far end, where a wine display case stood. Both men tapped a series of commands into their PACs, which made the wine case slide into the wall, and then to the left, revealing a small elevator with just enough room for four people.

Kevin came charging in from the dining room, and Vincent from the casino. Tony saw them and did the hand signal to them. Both nodded as dangerous grins appeared on their faces. Vincent ran to his brother, and the two of them disappeared toward the kitchen.

McFarland called out, "Irma! Seal the hallway doors to the bar, casino, and dining room. Then lock down all hallways!"

Irma responded, "Hallways are on lockdown," as the doors to the hallway closed and locked.

In less than a minute from the time of the SOS, the hand signals had informed the Core Crew and the Marines in the room that the SHF Protocols had been initiated.

Wingnut tapped his PAC. "Ross! Lock down Engineering and get ready to release the Alvin Program."

Ross replied, "Righty-O! But I thought we weren't going to pull that until next month."

Wingnut saw the look from McFarland. "Change of plans. Reset the distribution to the hallway outside the Main Bar."

Ross sounded disappointed. "Oh, okay. One Alvin Program coming up.

McFarland narrowed his eyes at Wingnut. "What's the Alvin Program?"

Wingnut grinned. "Let's just say that what's about to happen was earmarked for you next month."

A low, dangerous growl rumbled in McFarland's chest.

Marc turned to Tony. "Arm yourselves and follow the protocols. Get everyone to the kitchen. I want you to isolate Mister Maxwell and Ms. Lee to find out what their involvement is in this. Steven, Wingnut, Grey Wolf, and I will get to work finding Susan, then coordinate with you how to get her help. I fucking *hate* it when my gut's right!"

Tony grumbled, "Yeah, I'm not a fan of it, either. Good luck."

Marc, Steven, and Wingnut stepped into the small elevator, and were whisked off as soon as the doors shut.

When McFarland sealed the wine case, the sound of locking bolts sliding into place could be heard. He then opened a concealed cabinet and removed a pair of black dangerous-looking gloves. He put them on and activated them, which made his knuckles and the backs of his hands glow angrily with electricity.

After Tony told the nearest Marine to bring Mr. Maxwell and Ms. Lee to him, he opened a concealed panel under the bar and started handing out Stun/Guns to the Marines.

Tony turned to another Marine. "Get everyone into the kitchen as fast as you can!"

The Marine saluted, "Yes, sir!"

McFarland quickly climbed up on the bar and yelled at the now panicking guests. "Listen up, everyone!!! SHUT THE FUCK UP, or I'll give you something to really panic about!!!" He put his fists together, which caused a loud spitting electrical discharge from them.

The guests had never heard McFarland raise his voice before, let alone yell at them. The gloves scared everyone quiet.

McFarland glared down at the crowd. "We don't know what's happening, but *something* is wrong! We need you to *all* move to the kitchen and follow the instructions Kevin and Vincent give you. Marines, please see them safely to the kitchen."

Questions started flying from the guests, the loudest from a slightly drunk one. "I demand to know what's happening! I'm not going anywhere without a good reason!"

McFarland jumped down from the bar and closed in on the guest. The bodyguard of the belligerent man stepped in front of the annoyed barkeeper, but before the guard could react, McFarland flattened him with one electrified punch to the chest. Then McFarland stood with a clenched sparking fist under the drunk guest's nose and growled, "We don't have *time* to play twenty questions. Either obey the orders given, or be knocked unconscious and be *dragged* the kitchen."

The now frightened guest simply nodded and followed the others as they were directed to the kitchen by Tony and the Marines.

McFarland powered down the gloves, helped the bodyguard up, and said, "No hard feelings." Then he pushed the man toward the kitchen.

At that moment, sounds of someone prying at the doors made the urgency to get to the kitchen even more important to everyone.

The Marine who had been sent to find the two people from the auction approached with both firmly held by their elbows. Mr. Maxwell yanked his arm away and glared at Tony. "What's the meaning of having us manhandled! You're acting like we did something wrong!"

Tony was about four inches shorter than Mr. Maxwell, but the fuming Marine stared the man into submission with such anger that it was nearly physical. "We're under attack by *your* people, and I'm giving you *one* minute to explain what's going on before I go batshit on you!"

The shock of being told that his people were behind what was happening was written all over Mr. Maxwell's face. "I assure you, Mister Rhodes, neither Ms. Lee nor I have anything to do with their actions. Where's Mister Garfield? He's overseeing the workmen here on *Tranquility*."

Tony looked at Ms. Lee and saw that she was nearly in tears because the Marine was holding her in such a rough manner. He motioned to the Marine to let go of her before addressing them both. "Susan was asked to meet Mister Garfield for a private showing of the auction items. We got an SOS from her shortly after she arrived at the auction room."

Mr. Maxwell turned to Ms. Lee. "Did you give Mister Garfield permission to do that?"

The already unsettled woman became even more so under the gaze of her boss. "No, sir," she barely squeaked out.

Mr. Maxwell looked back at Tony. "Well, *I* sure as hell didn't approve of it. Whatever's going on has nothing to do with either one of us."

Tony wasn't convinced, but he didn't have time for any more questions. "I'm going to presume you two are innocent unless you do something that says otherwise. But I swear to you, if you're playing us, I'll make sure you suck vacuum. Do I make myself perfectly clear?"

Mr. Maxwell's eyes never wavered from the angry Marine, but there was a slight movement of his Adam's apple as he swallowed before he replied, "No need for threats, Mister Rhodes. Ms. Lee and I will comply with your every order."

Tony addressed a Marine. "Escort them to the kitchen and help the twins keep things calm there."

The Marine saluted Tony. "Yes, sir!" And took the two away.

McFarland watched as Su left the bar and wished he could talk to her, but his loyalty to his friends kept him from doing so. He turned to Tony. "Okay, you're in command here. What do you want to do?"

The fuming Marine looked back at him. "At the moment, we only know that Susan's in trouble. Someone's trying to break in. There are still ACs around the station that we need to find, and I'm really pissed off. Eileen and Kimberly, head to the kitchen and do what you can to keep everyone calm."

Eileen nodded before turning to Kimberly. "Let's go and put on our game faces."

As soon at the two women were in the dining room, Tony tapped his PAC. "Irma, seal the doors from the dining room and casino to the Main Bar."

Irma answered, "Con-ider it done, Tony." The doors shut, and the locks engaged.

The slight error in Irma's voice didn't go unnoticed by Tony and McFarland, but their attention returned to the doors that the workmen were attempting to open. Tony ran to the control pad next to the doors and accessed the explosive decompression system. Heavy metal doors dropped from the top of the doorway and locked into place.

Tony clenched his fists, wishing he could just beat the crap out of the people who dared to disturb his peaceful home. He looked at McFarland and growled. "Ready to make someone regret waking up today?"

McFarland powered his gloves up again and grinned. "I've been wanting to give these a combat test for a while. Now seems a good time."

Tony looked at the gloves with envy. "Where did you get those? I want a pair."

McFarland clenched a fist, causing the glove to spark with energy. "A guy named Duke gave them to me. I'll see about introducing you to him."

They checked their Stun/Guns, retrieving several clips for themselves and the Marines.

On the Bridge, a wall panel slid aside, and Marc, Steven, and Wingnut took their stations. Marc looked around. "Where the *hell* is Grey Wolf?"

Irma appeared on the main monitor. "He was called to the AuctionHouse ship to fix the computer just before Susan's SOS was activated."

Marc rolled his eyes. "*Shit!* Like that's not a coincidence. Okay, time to lock in the SHF Protocols." He entered a code into his command chair and said, "Irma, initiate Stage One SHF Protocols, Activation code sequence 1, code 1, 1-A."

Irma responded, "Command code acknowledged. Ready for second code." Then she looked at Steven.

Steven swallowed. "Irma, initiate Stage Two SHF Protocols. Activation code sequence 2, code 1, 1-A, 2-B."

Irma nodded. "Second command code acknowledged. The final and third code required."

Wingnut cleared his throat. "Irma, initiate Stage Three SHF Protocols. Who's on first. What's on second. And I Don't Know's on third."

The black background behind Irma changed to a dark burgundy color. "Final code acknowledged and approved."

The Bridge was filled with the sounds of locking bolts sliding into place, followed by the sound of fluid being pumped into the walls, floor, ceiling, and door.

Wingnut checked his station's readouts. "Anyone else hoping that the waste water surrounding us doesn't start leaking?"

Marc grumbled. "It was your idea."

Wingnut sighed. "I'm going to have to have a long talk with myself."

Irma's image took on a harder look. "Bridge is secured. So, whose ass is getting kicked today?"

Marc replied, "Let's find out. Show me all the video you have of Grey Wolf and Susan for the past ten minutes."

The main monitor split in two, showing Grey Wolf working on the Bridge and Susan talking to Marc, Tony, and Jackson.

"Scan ahead to one minute before the PAC's SOS from Susan," instructed Marc.

Grey Wolf was shown entering *AuctionHouse 5*.

"No video feed is available inside," said Irma.

Susan was shown entering the Auction Room, and Jackson being shocked unconscious.

Marc stood up. "What the hell!!! That explains the posters' 'malfunctioning' that the guest saw."

The view changed to the Auction Room, showing Susan's interaction with Mr. Garfield, and the workmen leaving the room. Susan then turned away from Mr. Garfield, glanced at the hidden camera, winked, and fainted. Garfield ran to her and said, "I need her awake! Get some water!" Less than a minute later, she opened her eyes and let loose a long string of colorful metaphors that impressed Marc.

When he looked at Steven, he was shocked by the anger he saw raging there. In the many years he had known Steven, Marc had seen him upset, but this was far beyond anything he had ever witnessed before.

Marc cleared his throat. "Steven?"

Steven continued to stare at the monitor.

In a louder voice, Marc said, "Steven!"

No response.

Marc then looked at Irma. "Pause playback!" Then he looked back at Steven. "*Goddammit*, Steven!"

Steven glared at Marc. "My wife's in trouble! We need to help her! Now!"

Marc was barely able to calm his voice. "Okay. *How?* What's your plan? How are we getting by the posters? Are the Marines ready and able to respond? What's the status of the crew in the kitchen? There are thirty-five crew members and forty-six guests who are relying on us to help them. Your wife is only one of them. I can't do this by myself. *Be* angry, but make it a tool to do your *job!*"

Steven closed his eyes and visibly forced himself to relax. Then he opened his eyes, which showed the rage still boiling inside, but also a clear sign of commitment to the task ahead.

"Irma," he asked, "how many of those posters are set up in the casino?"

Irma activated another monitor to show the locations. "Ten. Six in the three hallways leading to the main hallway. Two at the doorway to the Auction Room. And two next to the doorway to the guest residence."

Marc nodded an acknowledgment of the effort it took Steven to redirect his anger. "Irma, scan the hallways and see if any more of the Marines are knocked out. Also, put all live videos on the main monitor."

All the camera feeds on the station appeared on the main monitor.

Irma started to say something, but then her image froze. Lines streaked through her head and then disappeared.

"Ahhh, *shit!!!*" said Marc. "What the hell happened to her?!"

Steven's fingers flew across his keyboard. "A new virus has caused a feedback loop in the audio/video system connecting her Matrix to *Tranquility*'s CPU. She's offline until Grey Wolf can fix her. We can communicate with her through the keyboards, but that's all."

Marc squeezed his hands and said through clenched teeth, "This day just keeps getting better and better! Okay, Wingnut, it's time to send in Ross."

Wingnut opened a Com-Line to Engineering. "Ross, you there?"

The unflappable voice of the AI responded, "I'm here, boss. Everything is secured here. You want me to deploy the Alvin Program?"

Wingnut's mouth twitched upward slightly. "Not yet. The virus that the hijackers released has somehow affected Irma. We need you—"

Ross interrupted him with uncharacteristic panic. "*What!!!* Is Irma okay?"

Marc growled. "Ross! Irma's fine. She just can't access her audio and video systems. You're going to have to take her place until she's back online."

There was a moment of silence before Ross spoke. "Understood, Marc. What are your orders?"

Marc looked at Wingnut. "What's the Alvin Program?"

The engineer grinned. "It was a practical joke we were planning on pulling on McFarland, but I think it will distract those jerks and throw them off their game."

Marc nodded. "Then, do it!"

Wingnut rubbed his hands together as he addressed Ross. "Seal the hallways that the hijackers are in and readjust the Alvin Program to those areas."

Ross did as he was instructed. "The main hallways are sealed, and Alvin is ready to deploy."

Wingnut's grin got bigger. "Ross, add in holo-program 'Witch Doctor' in the main hallway music alcove." Then his grin got bigger as he said with great flare, "Release the Chipmunks!"

⠄⠄ ⠐⠞⠆⠄⠶⠂⠐ ⠐⠶ ⠠⠶⠆⠄ ⠐⠶⠖⠄⠄⠄⠂⠂ ⠄⠶⠒⠖⠶

The hijackers outside the Main Bar had pried open the doors and were working on the Decompression Doors when the doors at the other end of the hallway closed and locked. They stopped their work, looked at the doors, and shrugged. They had antici-pated that the *Tranquility* crew would do something to slow them down, but they were ready for the long game. All they had to do was get into the Main Bar and deal with the people inside.

They turned back to the doors and were about to continue working on them when the sound of music started coming from the small Music Alcove halfway down the hall. In the alcove stood a black-haired man with high cheekbones and an easy smile, who started singing.

I told the witch doctor I was in love with you.
I told the witch doctor I was in love with you.
And then the witch doctor, he told me what to do.
He said that—

Three cartoon chipmunks with body-length sweaters appeared in front of the man. One, who was in a green sweater, was playing drums. Another, who was wearing a blue sweater with glasses, was working a guitar. The third, who was sporting a red sweater with a huge *A* on the front and a red baseball cap, stood with his arms crossed. Their high-pitched, squeaky voices continued the song.

Ooo eee, ooo ah ah ting tang

Walla walla, bing bang

Ooo eee, ooo ah ah ting tang

Walla walla, bing bang

The lead hijacker pointed toward the alcove. "Shut that shit off!"

The others started to laugh at him because his voice was just as high as the chipmunks', which in turn caused more laughter as their own voices became equally high-pitched.

The first one's face turned red with anger as he marched to the alcove's control panel and smashed it with the butt of his Stun/Gun. When smashing it didn't have any effect, he shot several Stun/Rounds into the broken panel, which caused the system to short out, and David Seville with his Chipmunks disappeared. He then turned to the others, pointed his gun at them, and tried to growl at them, but the helium that Ross had pumped into the hallway continued to affect his voice. "I will *stun* your ass into the middle of next week if you continue to laugh! Get that door open…, *now!*"

Seeing the vicious look on his face curtailed any snickering among the others as they renewed their efforts to open the doors.

⠲ ⠐⠶⠃⠄⠂⠂⠐ ⠶ ⠠⠣⠃⠄ ⠹⠳⠇⠂⠐⠇ ⠐⠶⠹⠆

Meanwhile, on the Bridge, Wingnut was pounding his forearm against his chair's armrest as he roared with laughter. While he tried to catch his breath, Marc shook his head and had to admit that Wingnut's program was amusing, but he wasn't in any mood to enjoy it. The distraction was enough to give the guests time to get into the kitchen. Now he needed to figure out how to get rid of the parasites who had gotten onto *Tranquility*.

⠌⠄ ⠠⠐⠮⠆⠐⠌⠂⠘ ⠄ ⠶ ⠠⠊⠗⠄ ⠺⠊⠠⠌⠐⠣ ⠐⠶⠨⠆

Tony, McFarland, and the two Marines noticed that the sound of the hijackers trying to break through the door had stopped, but they could still hear them out there. Whatever Wingnut's "Alvin Program" was doing had bought Tony and the others time to get ready.

They proceeded to turn tables on their sides, with the tops facing the bar's entrance. McFarland filled two buckets with water from the bar and walked over to the doors. Then he took several small side tables and stacked them up, placing the two buckets so they were leaning against the doors. Next, he made several trips to and from the bar with another bucket and emptied it so that a wet line led to where he took cover behind a table near Tony. Finally, McFarland ran back to the bar and grabbed two large plastic serving trays before joining Tony behind the tables. He carefully placed the trays on the floor and crouched down on top of them as he took cover. With his PAC, McFarland closed the panels over the floor window and then shut off the lights in the bar, which plunged it into darkness.

Tony said to McFarland, "What is all that water for? This is hardly the time for a practical joke."

McFarland gave him a wicked smile. "But you've never been on the *bad* side of my jokes." He tapped on his PAC to access the door controls. "Operation 'Up Yours' commencing in three…, two…, one!"

The doors shot up into the doorway, and the auction crew in front of the doors got soaked by the water buckets. The four people in the Main Bar had to stifle their laughs as the hijackers' voices were still affected by the helium, and their voices squeaked in anger from the hallway. Now, wet and angry, they shoved the tables out of the doorway and slowly entered the darkened room.

McFarland listened carefully as he counted how many feet hit the wet floor. Then he powered his gloves to full strength, and hit the wet floor near him with both hands. The electrical discharge crackled as it rushed across the floor to the auction crew, who shook and jerked as the electricity raced through their bodies. McFarland pulled his hands back, and the now thoroughly stunned invaders dropped to the floor.

"Tag! You're it!" McFarland yelled.

Tony's smile had nothing to do with humor. He was relieved that this insane man was on his side.

"Motherfuckers!" squeaked one of the men outside, as two guns let loose a half-dozen ShockBags each into the room. The bags discharged harmlessly against the tables.

Tony said one word: "*Now!*"

The four defenders leaped out from behind their tables and took aim at the two silhouettes in the doorway that were reloading. Both were hit repeatedly with ShockBags and dropped to the floor. Tony signaled to the Marines to do a recon while he and McFarland covered them. After confirming that everyone in the now sealed hallway was unconscious, they tore some bar towels into strips and tied the auction crew's hands and feet together.

"Okay," said Tony as he reloaded his Shock/Gun. "Five down, with three more workers and one auctioneer to go. And we still need to make sure that Maxwell and Lee are not involved."

"Ms. Lee isn't involved in this," said McFarland with conviction as he slapped another clip of ShockBags into his gun.

Tony narrowed his eyes at McFarland. "How do you know that?"

McFarland smirked. "I had dinner with her last night and learned about who she is."

Tony frowned. "One dinner, and you think you know a person?"

McFarland's grey eyes stared at him. "Ten minutes was all I needed to know that I could trust you with my life."

Tony looked at McFarland and understood a bit more about why he liked him. "Fair enough."

⠂⠄ ⠄⠐�⠒⠂⠒⠂⠄ ⠄⠠⠨�⠄ ⠨⠠⠆⠨⠄⠰⠄ ⠐⠨⠆⠒⠆

The Main Kitchen was crowded with people, and Kevin was on the brink of losing it as the guests started to get cranky. The four Core Crew members suddenly all looked at their PACs at the same time and saw the message that the SHF Protocols had been activated. A moment later, everyone heard the decompression doors close.

Susan and Kimberly then tried unsuccessfully to calm everyone down, while Vincent tried to get everyone's attention with just as little success. Kevin finally grabbed two large pots and started moving up and down the cooking line, loudly banging them over his head. That resulted in all the guests shutting up and covering their ears.

Vincent raised his hands to get everyone's attention. "Thank you, Kevin. *Now*, before you all start yelling and screaming at us again, I need you to listen to me." Someone at the back of the crowded room started to say something, but Vincent cut him off: "*Anyone* interrupting me will be thrown in the freezer!!! We are all in trouble! Marc will give us a status report any time now, telling us how soon we'll be able to leave here. For now, we're safe. With the SHF Protocols activated, the kitchen has been locked down and sealed. We have our own air and water supply, which will last for five days. There's enough food to keep us fed for weeks. So, let's do our job and keep you safe, while you help us by staying calm. Eileen and Kimberly will be the go-to people if you have any problems. Kevin and his crew will start making something to eat. The bathrooms are located over by the storage rooms in the far corner."

The reporter raised her hand.

"Yes, Ms. Connolly?" asked Vincent.

"What does *SHF* stand for?"

Vincent grinned. "Shit Hitting Fan."

A nervous chuckle rippled through the crowd.

Susan's "fainting" spell had worked. Under her sleeve, she felt her PAC activate the SOS. She was hoping that it had been enough to alert Marc and the crew that something was wrong.

Mr. Garfield sat Susan in a chair at a table on the stage. "Okay, my dear, we need to get to work." He opened a laptop and patched into the podium's input station. A link opened to the AuctionHouse ship's internet connection, opening the Log On Page for the GCC. "Please log on to your account, Susan," he said as if she were at a bank.

Susan crossed her arms. "Not on your life!"

A nasty grin came over Mr. Garfield's face. "Then, how about your husband's?" he said, as he activated the monitor behind the podium. There was a view of the *AuctionHouse 5* cargo hold, with Steven tied to a chair, struggling to free himself. A workman approached him and slapped him into submission.

Susan yelled, "*Steven!!!*"

"As you can see," said Mr. Garfield, "we have our insurance card to make sure you cooperate. Do I have my man remove one of Steven's fingers, or will you comply with my demands?"

Susan hung her head in defeat. "Leave him alone. I'll do what you want."

⠠⠵ ⠫⠃⠄⠌� ���

The Main Bar was a beehive of activity as Tony and McFarland finished securing the AuctionHouse crewmen while the Marines stood guard.

Much to McFarland's annoyance, the helium from the hallway was causing their voices to rise a few octaves higher. He closed the doors, but there was no getting away from the infuriating gas.

"How long has it been since Marc and Steven got to the Bridge?" asked McFarland.

"About ten minutes," said Tony. "They should be checking in with us soon."

McFarland grumbled. "Better sooner than later. I *hate* waiting."

Marc's voice came from the Com-Station: "Bridge to Main Bar. What's your status?"

McFarland responded in a cheerfully sarcastic voice: "Just peachy. We neutralized the guys that were trying to get into the bar. Do you mind clearing out the helium before I finish my plans to kill Wingnut?"

Wingnut's voice was filled with barely contained giggles. "But it makes you sound so manly," he said.

Marc was not amused. "Just *do* it, Wingnut! We got some problems here."

McFarland shook his head in disbelief. "You think?!?"

Marc's voice was tinged with anger. "Shut up and listen. Irma's been compromised by the virus. We're going to be working with Ross from here on out."

Tony turned to the Com-Station and said, "Wonderful."

Then Ross appeared on a nearby monitor. "You're no joy to work with, either, Tony. Last time I was connected to the systems, I had a full head of hair. Now look at me."

McFarland's voice took on a softer tone. "What's the word on Susan?"

Marc sounded relieved. "Susan deliberately set off her PAC's SOS to send us a warning."

"What about Jackson?" Tony asked. "Why isn't he taking care of Susan?"

Marc was rewatching the attack on Jackson and the others. "The Posters appear to be booby-trapped and will shock anyone who gets close to them, but there's some way the auction crew can pass by them without harm. The video of the station shows that ACs and Marines not with you have been shocked unconscious by the Posters or the auction work crew using Stun/Guns."

McFarland poured himself a shot of Irish whiskey. "Isn't that just a wonderful bit of news!" He downed his drink.

Marc sighed. "There's more bad news."

McFarland held up the bottle of whiskey and eyed it. "I'm going to run out of booze before the end of this."

Marc ignored McFarland. "Grey Wolf was called to the AuctionHouse ship the same time that Susan was going to meet with Garfield. He's missing, so we assume he's out of commission. To make things worse, the virus has shut down all outgoing communications. We're on our own until someone gets wise that there's trouble here."

McFarland downed another shot and growled. "Anything else to help my mood?"

Marc looked at Steven. "Steven's about one kicked puppy away from going psychotic over Susan. Once we— Hang on! Grey Wolf is exiting from the AuctionHouse ship."

⠄⠄ ⠄⠐⠓⠄⠄⠐⠄⠄ ⠐⠏ ⠄⠙⠓⠄ ⠙⠏⠇⠄⠄⠇ ⠄⠘⠓⠄⠏

Back on the Bridge, Marc, Steven, and Wingnut watched as Grey Wolf floated out of the airlock to the AuctionHouse ship, shaking his hands as if they were sore, and then tap on his PAC. A moment later, the Com-Station activated.

"Grey Wolf to Marc. We have a problem."

Marc slapped the Com-Button on his chair. "Welcome to the party, pal! What the hell happened to *you?*"

Grey Wolf gently touched the back of his head. "I got knocked out by the pilot of the AuctionHouse ship. When I came to, he was tying me up. Remind me to thank Tony for the lessons he gave me in escaping and fighting. Want to let me in on what's going on?"

Marc ticked off on his fingers as he recounted the events. "While you were napping, Susan's been taken as a hostage. The Posters are shocking our crew members unconscious. There were people trying to break into the Main Bar, but Tony and McFarland have that under control. The SHF Protocols are in effect, but Irma has been comprised. Oh, and Ross is covering for her now. Did I miss anything, Steven?"

His brooding friend was watching his monitor intently. "Yes. I've been watching the live feed of Susan and have seen something quite interesting. She thinks I'm being held hostage as some kind of leverage over her." Steven zoomed in on the video playing on the monitor that Susan was staring at. There was Steven, tied up in a chair and being beaten by a workman. Susan was visibly upset.

Grey Wolf nearly shouted, "*Wait!* What was that about Irma? There are five different layers of protection for that virus to get through to her. How the fuck did it get to her?"

"No idea," said Steven. "As near as I can tell, the virus affected the programming that controls the audio/video of Irma's Matrix. Until you work out how to eradicate the virus and undo the damage it did, she's limited to text messages."

Grey Wolf rubbed his eyes. "I'm sure my horoscope said I should have stayed in bed today. Okay, I have an idea I need to investigate. Give me five minutes to give us a way to get past the Posters."

Before anyone could reply, Grey Wolf signed off and floated back to the AuctionHouse ship.

Tony looked at the Com-Station, then at McFarland. "Anyone got a plan?"

"First things first," Marc said. Then he entered a code into his chair's Com-System. "All the Core Crew but Susan should be a part of this conversation. What's everyone's status?"

Eileen's voice reported, "We have a bunch of cranky guests here in the kitchen, and the twins are about to put a few of them in the Hobart mixer. Kimberly and I might help with that."

"The Main Bar and Dining Room are secure," Tony reported.

"Engineering is secure," said Ross.

Grey Wolf's voice returned. "I have some interesting news to share with everyone."

As Marc and Steven looked up to the main monitor, they saw Grey Wolf waving at them from the Loading Bay.

"What have you got, Wolf?" Marc asked.

Grey Wolf grinned. "I have a way to turn the tables on the auction crew. Give me a minute."

On the monitor, Grey Wolf started typing on his PAC's virtual keyboard. Less than thirty seconds later, he winked at the monitor and hit the Enter key.

The auction crewman standing at the door to the Auction Room was suddenly attacked by the Posters.

Marc jumped from his seat. "*Whoa!!!* What the hell happened?"

Grey Wolf grinned. "I just reprogrammed the Holo-Posters to treat the signals the auction crew are using as the targets to attack."

Steven jumped out of his chair and gave a triumphant yell: "*That's my girl!!!*"

On the monitor, Susan was standing over Garfield's body, clenching her fists.

Steven was excited. "She was working on the computer, looked at the monitor that showed me on it, pointed at it, and then stood up. At that moment, the Posters shocked the crewman standing at the door. That made Garfield turn away from her, which gave her a chance to use Tony's training!"

They saw Susan using her PAC. "Susan to Marc! Are you guys okay?"

Marc answered, "We've been having a blast! Want to come roast some marshmallows?"

Susan shook her head. "I'll pass. I know what's going on now. Garfield was using the auction to gain access to the guests' accounts and drain each one by placing phony bids that deposited the money into Off-Planet bank accounts."

At that moment, Ross interrupted: "Uh, guys. You should see this. It could affect what happens next."

The main monitor showed the orbit of *Tranquility* around the Moon. The view pulled back to show the trajectory of the asteroid hauler with a green line. Ross explained what they were seeing: "This is how the hauler should be approaching the Moon." A red line appeared. "And this is the update we just received from our scans. The hauler is coming in hot and not slowing down. It will miss us by a little less than a mile and will hit the Moon's mountains in twenty-five minutes on the far side of the Sea of Tranquility. That's the *good* news."

"And what's the bad?" asked McFarland.

"The debris field that it kicks up will reach our location in less than an hour later."

McFarland slammed his shot glass down onto the bar. "Did I ask to be put into the fire? *No!* I was perfectly content with being in the frying pan!"

Ross responded like a cheesy salesman. "But wait. There's more. And that's not all."

Kevin chimed in. "Great. What else can be heaped on this already steaming pile of insanity?"

"After careful analysis of the affected systems here," said Ross, "the virus also jumped onto the transport ship's computers and has done unknown damage there, too."

Vincent's voice was a bit low. "And here's where I ask for a raise with overtime."

Marc looked at the diagram on the monitor. "Ross, start a countdown timer on our PACs for seventy minutes. If we don't have a plan by then to save everyone here, we're all screwed."

Ross put a countdown timer on the monitor. "Done."

Marc asked everyone, "Options?"

Eileen said, "Anyone got some silver slippers to click together and wish us the hell away from this?"

Steven spoke up. "Priority One E-Vac. Load everyone into *AuctionHouse 5* and *Tyche*. Then get the hell away from here."

Wingnut spoke up. "Sounds good to me. Let's get rolling on that."

Ross's head popped up on the main monitor. "We may have a small problem with that plan. I've analyzed the systems that the grasshopper virus affected and discovered that it jumped to both ships before the mantis got it. The systems for guidance and direction are not functioning on *AuctionHouse 5* or *Tyche*. It would take an hour to fix just one of them, and there's not enough room or life support on just one ship for everyone."

A long silence followed Ross's announcement until McFarland grumbled. "If anyone wants me, I'll be in the corner, ripping the heads off the auction crew."

The twins said together, "We'll join you."

Ross added, "There's another option I've worked out for us. Unless you want to paint the walls red first."

Marc rubbed the bridge of his nose with his fingers. "What is it, Ross?"

Ross displayed a rough line drawing of his idea on the monitor. "With the ships docked at both ends of *Tranquility*, they can thrust up to full throttle and push us to safety. Once clear of the debris field, the ships can use the maneuvering thrusters to rotate the casino around and then use the main engines again to slow it down."

Grey Wolf threw his hands into the air. "Where the fuck is Rod Serling? This has gone from insane to a *Twilight Zone* episode."

Marc took a deep breath. "We need to get everyone ready. First order of business is to secure and immobilize the auction crew."

"Already ahead of you on that," said Tony. "The Marines are scooping them up and Zip-Tying them to chairs in the dining room."

Grey Wolf spoke up. "I'll work with Steven to reprogram the Posters, and we can use them to ensure with a minimum number of personnel that they stay put."

Marc sat back in his chair. "And that's why you're on this team, Wolf." He said this with a smile—the first one in what felt like a long time. "Susan, Kimberly, Eileen, and the ACs will get the guests back to their rooms and prep them for emergency decompression. Ross, start running the video for the process as the guests enter their rooms. Grey Wolf and Steven will start setting up the Posters in the dining room. Tony and McFarland will secure all primary systems and seal off all the rooms as they are evacuated. Wingnut, you work your magic and do what you can to reinforce the docking rings to the ships. That's going to be the weakest link in the whole operation. The twins and the Marines will help keep the guests calm and out of the hallways. Once the guests are in their rooms, the Marines will remain in the guests' hallway to keep the peace, with orders that no one is to leave the rooms. When all that is done, the ACs will report to the Chicken Coop. It's got the best chance of withstanding an impact if we can't get out of the way fast enough and get hit by the debris field. Susan, Kimberly, and Eileen will join them there, and the rest of the Core Crew will meet on the Bridge. Tony, ask Patrick and Max if they're willing to fly the largest ship of their career."

Patrick's voice came over the speakers. "We're here, sir. We'll head to the ships now, get the prestart systems ready, and practice our ability to thrust at the same time. We only get one chance at it, so we have to get it right the first time."

Marc responded, "Thanks, gentlemen. Okay, everyone, how much time do we have, Ross?"

"fifty-eight minutes."

Marc tried to sound as optimistic as he could. "A little less than an hour to get this place in a safe position. In forty-five minutes, I want all the guests and the auction crew secured. In one hour, everyone needs to be ready to start moving. Are you all clear on what you need to do?"

A chorus of "Yes, sir!" was everyone's response.

Marc moved to the life-support systems. "I'll start the Emergency Protocols. As you finish each section, I'll have them locked down and cycle the air into the tanks. If we do get hit and the room is compromised, we won't suffer an explosive decompression. If anyone gives you any problems, you put Tony's training to work and leave them where they drop. We don't have time to deal with problems. I'll announce over the casino PA system to let everyone know what's at stake and what the guests need to do. Or they can take their chances without our help."

The Core Crew all confirmed Marc's orders before each signed off.

Marc then input some commands into his PAC. The sound of the liquid draining from around the Bridge was followed by the noise of the locks disengaging.

"Okay, guys," Marc said to Grey Wolf and Steven, "Let's get to work."

His two friends nodded and headed off the Bridge.

Marc then opened the Com-System to the whole casino. "Attention, everyone, this is Marc. You need to pay close attention to what I'm about to tell you. The danger of the hijackers is over, but because of them we now have a new problem. In a little less than twenty minutes, an asteroid will be hitting the Moon, which will send debris into orbit that will reach our location in less than an hour. Because of a malfunction, the transport ships are unable to take us safely away."

Over the intercom, the sound of panicked voices started to fill the air. Marc adjusted the system to send an earsplitting feedback throughout the casino. Everyone instantly stopped talking.

Marc's voice took on a hardness that few people had ever heard before. "If you *don't* mind, I'm trying to save your asses. But if you want to take your chances on your own, then by all means, keep being a problem. Otherwise, shut up, listen, and follow the orders given to you by my crew. Anyone causing problems *will* be left to suck vacuum. We have very little time to get ready, and no time for nonsense. All ACs are to report to the Main Bar for instructions. All Marines are to split up and help get the guests to their rooms. Marines, also scoop up the AuctionHouse work crew, as well as Garfield, and take them to the dining room. Dawn, please go to the Auction Room and see to Jackson. We're going to need him as soon as he's able. Marc out."

Marc sat back, put his hands to his face, and sighed. Then he activated his PAC and patched into Irma's computer system. Using the holographic keyboard of the PAC, he typed out, "Irma? You still with us?" He looked up at the main monitor, where he saw the words, "Yes, Marc, I'm here."

Marc sighed heavily as a mental war was waging inside him. Finally, he typed, "Good. Open Lockbox number five, please. Code A113."

He heard a soft click from the wall behind him, and then a hidden panel opened. Marc stood up, slowly walked to the compartment, and removed a flask, a black Zip-O lighter, an ashtray, and a sealed glass tube that contained one cigarette. On the tube were the words, "Break in Case of Emergency!" He placed the flask, tube, and ashtray on the armrest of his chair. Then he looked at the Zip-O and considered the white skull painted on it. He adjusted the Zip-O so his middle finger and forefinger were on top, and his thumb was on bottom. He gave the Zip-O a gentle squeeze and snapped it open. A slight upturn of the corners of his mouth showed that he was pleased with being able to still do that move. With a flick of his finger, the flame appeared, which he watched for a moment. With a quick flick of his wrist, he snapped the top shut, placed the Zip-O on the armrest, picked up the glass tube, and broke it open. He breathed in the smell of tobacco that wafted into his nose. Then he sat down, closed his eyes, placed the unlit cigarette between his lips, and took a long dry inhale of the tobacco.

When he reopened his eyes, he said, "Okay, Ross. Time to make some chaos cookies. Have Irma start powering down nonessential systems and open all redundancy systems to life support. If one connection gets taken out, I want the others up and running."

The words *Aye, aye, Captain* appeared on the main monitor from Irma.

Marc took another dry hit from the cigarette before continuing. "Ross, keep track of the guests and crew. Give me updates on their progress. I'll start setting up the SOS buoy. Hopefully, someone will hear its signal and send help."

Ross responded, "Yes, sir, I'm on it."

Marc moved to the Com-Station, activated the SOS buoy, and then removed the cigarette from his mouth before making the SOS recording: "Mayday, mayday, mayday! This is *Tranquility Casino*, orbiting the Moon. We're attempting an emergency procedure to move the casino to a higher orbit. Any ships receiving this message are requested to render assistance by helping to get our guests and crew to safety."

Marc set the recording to endless repeating loop and hit the launch button. Outside, a large cone shot out of the north end of *Tranquility* and headed toward Earth. The sides of the cone unlocked, rotated 180 degrees, and formed a dish at the front. Once locked into place, the buoy started to send its message.

Marc watched it on his monitor for a moment while he considered his next move.

CHAPTER 7

A New Pair of Underwear

In the Main Bar, McFarland and Kimberly were giving instructions to the ACs, when an AC pointed out the now open floor window and yelled, "*Look!*"

The asteroid hauler was passing by with its asteroid trailing behind it. It took just moments to travel from their location and crash into the Moon's mountain range with a brilliant flash as the hauler exploded moments before the asteroid impacted the same spot.

Marc watched the impact on the Bridge's main monitor. "Ross, status?"

"Half of the guests are in their rooms," Ross replied. "Some are waiting in the garden to enter the guest room hallway. The auction crew members are secured in the dining room, and the Posters are almost ready to be activated. Forty percent of *Tranquility* has been shut down, and the power diverted to backup redundancy systems and— Wait a moment! Irma, confirm this data, please."

Marc leaned forward in his seat. "What's going on, Ross?"

Ross reluctantly replied, "Um, the debris field kicked up by the asteroid is moving faster than expected. At this time, we are calculating the new timeline for it to reach us."

Marc stood up. "And?"

"You better have a drink," Ross said quietly.

"*Tell me!!!*" Marc yelled, blowing the cigarette out of his mouth and across the Bridge.

Ross quickly said, "We have thirty-five minutes to be out of the path of the debris."

Marc let loose a long string of colorful metaphors as he hit the station-wide connection throughout *Tranquility*. "Attention, everyone! Our timeline has moved. The Core Crew is to finish getting everyone to their rooms and report back to the Bridge in fifteen minutes."

Tony's voice shouted, "What the hell happened! I thought we had nearly an hour to get ready!"

Marc wrapped his arms around his head in a hopeless attempt to contain his emotions. "Welcome to hell, buddy. The debris field is moving faster than expected, so get your ass in gear, batten down the hatches, and get back up here with everyone." Then he addressed Ross. "Program the Ion-Whiskers to move to a safe distance and go into standby mode for two hours. They may be our only means of communication if our systems go down."

Moments later, Ross reported, "Marvin, Ming, Lurr, and Zim are heading to a position and will report in two hours as you instructed."

Marc nodded a thank you, went over to the cigarette, picked it up, and took a long look at it.

The doors to the Bridge suddenly opened, and standing there was Eileen, who looked at the cigarette, and then at Marc. "So, having a cigarette will correct everything happening here?"

Marc gave her a lopsided smile. "No. But a firing squad always offers a last cigarette. And considering that we're about to get hammered by a million cosmic bullets, I thought it might be as good a time as any to end fifteen years of quitting these."

He stared at the cigarette, then let his eyes focus on Eileen. Without breaking eye contact with her, he dropped the cigarette to the floor and used his heel to crush it. Then, looking at his love, he said, "Other than saving me from a last cigarette, why are you here? We need you at the Chicken Coop to help with the ACs."

Eileen cocked her head to the side. "Susan and Kimberly have things well in hand there. The crew and the guests have been instructed on the use of the emergency head gear. I'm here to keep the one person this place cannot do without from beating himself up. And you *are* mentally beating yourself up, aren't you?"

Marc sighed heavily. "A little. But I don't have time to let the squirrel wheels distract me. If you're staying here, you need to sit and be quiet. That's not a request. Things are about to get ludicrous."

Eileen nodded, headed for her station, and adjusted its seat to face toward the front of the Bridge and Marc.

He then opened a line. "How's it going down there, Wingnut?"

The engineer's labored breathing told them that he was hard at work. "Just about done. Give me ten more minutes for the Liquid Steel to harden. I recommend that I return to Engineering. If systems start to fail, I'll be more use there than on the Bridge."

Marc mentally checked off one major item on his to-do list. "Okay. Get there and report in."

Marc cut the connection and addressed Ross. "What's our status, Ross?"

The bald AI appeared on the monitor. "All guests are in their rooms, ACs are in the Chicken Coop, the Marines are at their stations, the Core Crew are on their way to the Bridge, and the pilots have the ships ready."

At that moment, the Core Crew entered the Bridge and took their stations. Steven sat at his station and transferred Engineering's systems to his, Grey Wolf took his Computer/Science position, Tony transferred Communication to his station, while McFarland took up Security. The twins sat at their places with Life Support, and Marc settled into his captain's chair. No one questioned why Eileen was there.

Marc looked around as all the others did their systems checks. "Okay," he said, "let's do something we never trained for." He opened a link to the pilots. "What's your status? We need to start moving ASAP."

Patrick responded, "*Tyche* here, Marc. Give us the word, and we'll engage the engines at low thrust and increase it over an eight-minute span. Any faster and we risk tearing the docking rings apart."

"That's cutting it close," said Grey Wolf. "The debris field will be here in twelve minutes."

"Understood, *Tyche*." Marc opened a station-wide com. "This is Marc. We are about to move *Tranquility*. Everyone hold tight and be ready to activate your emergency air gear if we get hit by the debris field. Here we go. *Tyche* and *AuctionHouse 5*, it's your show now."

"Roger that, Marc," Patrick acknowledged. "Engaging engines in five…, four…, three…, two…, one…, *go!*"

All the Core Crew members on the Bridge gripped their chairs a bit tighter as a slight vibration moved throughout *Tranquility*.

Grey Wolf read out the reports: "Vibrations are within tolerances. The transport ships are slowly increasing thrust. No change in orbit. I've had Irma crunch the numbers, and she calculates that until the ships reach full thrust, we will not move." He looked up from his monitor with wide eyes. "We're gonna get hit, no matter what."

The crew looked at the intercept course of the debris field on the main monitor. The station would miss the central mass of the field, but it was going to catch the outside edge of it.

Marc stood up. "Increase magnification. Show me where we can expect to get hit."

The monitor zoomed in on red sections that started flashing.

The twins both said, "Aw, shit!"

The monitor showed that the station would receive damage, but the worst area would not be the station itself. The ships pushing them to safety were nearly completely red.

Marc grabbed his flask from his chair and swung back his arm to hurl it at the monitor.

A hand reached around from behind him and rested on his chest, freezing his motion. Eileen's other arm reached up and lightly pulled his arm down to his side as she held it firmly.

The crew had all known, and even witnessed, the storm of emotions that Marc kept bottled up. None of them had found the key to helping him contain that storm. But Eileen only needed to touch him to keep his emotions in check.

She turned him toward her, took the flask from his hand, opened it, and took a drink. Then she lifted the flask to his lips and gave him a drink. Locking eyes with him, she silently spoke volumes. After pressing her forehead to his for a moment, she stepped back with her hand still on his chest. Never looking away from Marc's eyes, she handed the flask to Steven and said, "Drink up, everyone. Marc needs a moment to think."

Steven took a drink and passed the flask to McFarland. As each of the crew members took a turn at the flask, the battle inside Marc visibly lessened. Grey Wolf, who was the last to drink, passed the flask back to Eileen. She sealed it, placed it on Marc's armrest, and then placed her hand on his cheek. "Break's over. Back to work."

With that said, she returned to her seat and sat down.

Marc closed his eyes, took several deep breaths, and let them out. When he opened his eyes, the crew saw that his anger was still boiling, but a new determination was also blazing there.

Marc hit the station-wide Com button. "Attention, everyone. We will be caught by the debris field in less than five minutes. Brace for impact."

He then switched to the ship's Com-Line. "Where are you guys at in reaching full throttle?"

The roar of the engines could be heard in the background as Patrick said, "We're halfway there, Marc. Six more minutes to reach full thrust."

"I want you to take it to full thrust now. In less than five minutes, the debris field will hit us…, and by our calculations, destroy the transports. Put the ships to full thrust, set the autopilot, and get out as fast as you can! Get to the guest hallway with the Marines and take shelter."

There was a long pause before Patrick responded. "We can't do that, Marc. If the ships get hit while at full thrust and the fuel tanks get ruptured, the resulting explosion will rip *Tranquility* apart. We'll have to stay here until the last second to eject the tanks. Do you agree, Max?"

Max's serious voice responded, "I do. Let's go out as heroes. On your mark, we go full throttle."

Patrick counted down: "Three…, two…, one…, push the button, Max!"

Before anyone could say anything, the vibrations greatly increased, and Red Alert warnings started flashing all over the Bridge. Grey Wolf was yelling out status reports as everyone struggled to stay seated and keep the systems from overloading.

Marc didn't notice any of this, because he was staring at the monitor that showed the ships slowly moving *Tranquility*. Just as the countdown timer hit ten seconds, the vibrations stopped and both ships' fuel tanks ejected into space.

Then the debris field struck.

At first, there was nothing, Then the sound of intense hail was heard as the micro-meteors penetrated the outer hull. The hail increased to a roar, which was punctuated with loud bangs that set off more alarms. *Tranquility* was taking a beating, but she was holding up to it.

Then it happened.

A 12-meter-wide chunk of the asteroid appeared on the monitor. The speed indicator showed that it was moving at 4,358 miles per hour. The rock closed the distance in seconds and collided with

Tyche. The impact was devastating as it hit the forward section of the ship and turned the command module into a crushed can as it collapsed around the asteroid.

The whole station jerked as the ship was ripped from its docking ring and turned into a floating train wreck. The ship started spinning on its axis, and the solar panels flashed as the Sun reflected off them. Then they broke off as the spinning ship exceeded the mounting's tolerance. One panel glanced off some of *Tranquility*'s own solar panels, shattering them. As the ship then spun around, the main engines smashed into more of *Tranquility*'s solar panels, destroying a long section of them before the rest of the ship joined the debris field and struck the lower part of *AuctionHouse 5*. The massive impact tore the ship in half, again jerking *Tranquility* violently. The Bridge's power went out and became pitch black. A moment later, the emergency lighting came on as the backup power supply engaged.

Small fires broke out on the Bridge as systems overloaded. Marc leaped from his chair and ran to a wall panel marked "Fire Extinguishers." He opened it and started removing emergency air masks, which could cover the whole face. He tossed one to each person. Then he passed out large, red, egg-shaped devices to everyone. Each crew member twisted one end of the egg until it clicked, then placed all the eggs near the fires and stepped back. A dark grey Zero-O_2 foam oozed out. Then, almost as if it were alive, the foam covered the fires and put them out.

Marc coughed from the acrid smoke he had inhaled before getting his mask on.

"Report!" he commanded.

All the crew members returned to their stations and sent information to Tony, who gave the report: "Severe damage to the docking bays and the solar panels. We lost sixty percent of our solar cells in the collision. Most of the other damage to the station was minor and taken care of by the hull's sealant. Wingnut is bringing the extra power cells he installed online and will have full power in ten minutes. No casualties have been reported, and only minor injuries have been sustained by crew and guests. The Marines are reporting that small fires have broken out, but they have them under control. We have cleared the orbit of the debris field. But without the ships to slow us down, we are still moving away from the Moon. And I need a new pair of underwear."

Ross appeared on the main monitor. "Also," he said, "Tony burned the pot roast. Cough-cough."

Marc hit the station-wide Com button. "This is Marc. We have cleared the debris field and, for the moment, are safe. Please remain where you are until a crew member or a Marine gives you instructions on what to do. I want two Marines to put on emergency suits and fan out. Report what damage you find to Tony. It is my sad responsibility to report that pilots Patrick and Max gave their lives so that we had a chance to survive. Let's honor them by making sure we stay in one piece. Marc out."

He took a few deep breaths as he looked at all his friends. "We were lucky. If not for the smart thinking and cool heads of everyone, this could have gone a lot worse than it did. We lost two good people today, and it's our job to make sure their sacrifice was not in vain. Please go back and check in on the people you were seeing to safety, and make sure everyone is okay. After that, Kevin, would you mind putting some simple food together for everyone? I'm sure that some of our guests could use a good meal by now."

Kevin smirked. "When have I ever done something *simple* with food?"

"Never!" said everyone.

Suddenly, the main power came back on, and the smoke was sucked away as life-support systems came back online. Marc looked at the time and opened a line to Engineering. "Wingnut? You said it would take ten minutes to get full power up. Things in better shape down there than you thought?"

Wingnut's chipper voice responded, "Nope. I just multiply my estimates by three before giving them. How else am I to keep my status as a miracle worker? It worked for Scotty on *Star Trek*, didn't it?"

Marc shook his head in wonder. "You need any help down there?"

Wingnut was all business now. "Nope. There were a couple of fires, but Ross and I put them out. I'm going to head to Sickbay and have Dawn take care of a cut I got on my forehead. Apparently, I forgot to secure a toolbox, which grazed me during that rodeo ride you took us on."

Marc sighed with relief. "Right. Get stitched up, and we'll touch base with you later. Bridge out."

Marc cut the connection and removed his mask. Everyone else did the same. "Hang onto your masks," he said, "and instruct everyone to keep theirs nearby just in case."

Grey Wolf said, "I'm going down below to check on the CPU. We lost the systems that work our PACs. Something down below must have gotten hit. Would you give me a hand, Steven?"

Steven shook his head. "I'll join you in a bit. First, I need to hug and kiss my wife." And with that, he headed out to find her.

Grey Wolf nodded his understanding and disappeared into the floor access.

As everyone else on the Bridge patted each other on the backs and shoulders, Marc walked over to Eileen and wrapped his arms around her. "Thank you. I would have lost it if you hadn't been here." As the emotions flooded out of him, a small sob escaped from him as he buried his face in her shoulder.

When Tony noticed this, he waved the others out into the hallway to give the two lovers some space.

Eileen held Marc tightly. "I'm right here. I'm not going *anywhere* without you."

Marc took a deep breath, let go of her, and dried his eyes with the heels of his hands. A small smile tugged at the corners of his mouth as he said, "Lucky me. Okay, we got miles to go before we rest. Please check in on Lady Elizabeth. She's a tough gal, but all the same, I want to know she's okay. Then see what you can do to help Dawn with whoever is hurt." He gave Eileen a kiss and touched her face tenderly before sending her on her way.

He watched her leave, then turned to the main monitor. "Okay, Ross. Work with Irma to make sure there are no more surprises lurking out there for us."

Ross returned to the monitor. "Will do, boss. Irma's working on something. I'll let you know when she's done."

Marc nodded. "Good. I'm heading to the dining room to help mop up the auction crew. Lock down the Bridge when I leave."

"Roger that, sir."

Steven entered the Bridge. "Susan's getting the ACs squared away," he said. Then he disappeared into the floor access panel that Grey Wolf had gone through.

As Marc left the Bridge, he heard the doors close and the security locks engage. He began to whistle "In the Hall of the Mountain King."

CHAPTER 8

My Son Did That

As Wingnut entered the hallway that led to Sickbay, he saw one of the auction crew. "*Hey!*" he yelled.

The crewman turned and was obviously dazed by what had happened, but he was in enough control to raise his Stun/Gun and say, "What the fuck happened here?"

Wingnut raised his hands. "Whoa, buddy! Let's not go off half-cocked."

The crewman sounded scared. "Get me off this fucking death-trap, and I'll refrain from shooting you."

Wingnut said in a soothing voice, "Okay, okay. But, first, say hello to my little friend." He pointed behind the crewman.

As the crewman turned around, he was hit by a ShockBag fired by Dawn. She watched with mild interest as the twitching man hit the floor. Then, glaring at Wingnut, she said, "Who you calling *little?*"

Wingnut looked sheepish. "Why, that lovely gun you have there. Would you mind stitching me up, so I can fix this floating disaster area? Or should I wait while you shoot him a few more times?"

Dawn considered what he said, then waved for him to follow her. "C'mon. Drag this asshole into Sickbay, and I'll shoot him up with enough anesthesia to turn him into Rip Van Winkle. Then I'll get you patched up."

⠲⠀⠠⠐⠌⠓⠄⠌⠌⠂⠐⠀⠻⠀⠠⠪⠓⠂⠀⠠⠠⠻⠨⠄⠐⠊⠀⠌⠲⠓⠂

Vincent and several Marines were securing the auction crew and moving them to the airlock that led to the Docking Bay where the remains of *AuctionHouse 5* was. After exiting the elevator to the Zero-G zone, Vincent used the pad outside the airlock to check that the hatch on the *AuctionHouse 5* side was a registering a vacuum to the destroyed ship. He then bypassed the controls inside the airlock.

Looking at the auction crew, Vincent snarled. "Behave yourselves! For some reason, Marc wants to treat you fairly. As far as I'm concerned, we should load you back on what's left of your ship and cast you off. So, *don't* push us."

One of the auction crew members, who was near the sealed outer hatch, spoke up: "Um…, excuse me. There's something…, well… *odd* over here."

Vincent glared at him. "Define odd."

The crewman pressed his ear to the hatch. "I think that an old-fashioned SOS is being tapped on the other side."

Vincent's eyes widened as he said, "Max!" Then he yelled to the Marines, "Clear them out and back to the elevator. Who here has space rescue raining?"

"I do, sir," responded a Marine named Bashir.

Vincent pointed. "That panel behind you has an emergency survival suit. Put it on while we clear this hallway. Once we seal the hatch, depressurize it and get Max inside." He pointed at another Marine. "Call Sickbay and get Dawn down here *now*!"

As the auction crew were moved and Bashir suited up, Vincent went to the hatch to listen. He could hear a very softly tapped out SOS. Vincent slapped his hand against the hatch twice, and then three times. The SOS stopped, and two taps were followed by three.

"Hurry!" Vincent said to Bashir. "He sounds weak!"

Bashir locked his helmet into place and closed the visor, while Vincent moved to the outer hatch, removed the inner controls bypass and sealed the hatch. He then joined the others in the elevator and took it to the gravity zone of *Tranquility*.

When the elevator doors opened, Marc, Eileen, Dawn and two Marines were waiting with a gurney.

"Where is he?" asked Dawn.

Vincent pointed toward the elevator. "Sergeant Bashir is suited up and extracting Max. He'll bring him here as soon as possible."

Moments later—although to the crew it felt like ages—the elevator opened, revealing Bashir, who was holding a frost-covered Max upright with an emergency air-mask attached to his face. Max weakly reached for the mask, but his arm dropped back to his side. Dawn removed the mask, helped to move Max to the gurney, and covered him with a thermal blanket.

Marc asked, "How the hell did you survive the impact, Max?"

Max winked, held up a hand that was clutching something, and put it in Marc's hand as he passed out.

Dawn waved everyone out of the way. "Make a hole! *Move!!!*"

Everyone stepped back against the walls to watch as Dawn and the two Marines ran the gurney down the hallway.

Vincent turned to Marc. "What did he hand you?"

A smirk spread across Marc's face as he opened his hand to reveal a scratched and worn glass-encased four-leaf clover. There were some new chips in the glass that Max had made when he tapped out his SOS. Engraved on the glass were the words *9/11/2001, Stairwell B, North Tower.*

"Max told me about this during his first trip here," Marc said. "An ancestor of his was a firefighter in New York City. He and fifteen others survived the terrorist attack on September 11th, 2001, when the tower collapsed on top of them. His ancestor made this to pass on to his family to remind them that true luck is rare and should be cherished whenever it occurs."

Vincent whistled. "Remind me to ban him from the casino floor. That kind of luck could ruin us."

Marc tucked the clover into his pocket. "Let's finish up here. We've still got a lot to do."

Everyone nodded and went back to securing the auction crew in the airlock.

⠄⠂ ⠠⠆⠒⠄⠂⠄⠂ ⠶ ⠠⠢⠏⠄ ⠶⠏⠦⠰⠂⠁ ⠠⠶⠶⠶

Back in the kitchen, Kevin and his team of cooks were busy setting up after everything had gotten shaken out of place. Because Kevin ran a well-maintained kitchen, the crew managed in just a few minutes to reset the equipment that had been knocked about. The only real mess was a fryer that had come loose and spilled its oil on the floor. While everything was being cleaned up, Kevin checked the walk-in refrigerators and freezers. Many of the large containers of soups and stocks had not survived the shaking and were all over the floor of the refrigerators. A few cases of fruits and vegetables had shifted and were on the floor as well.

As soon as the crew got everything cleaned up, Kevin started directing his cooks. "See what soups survived, and start heating them up. If need be, add whatever you can think of so there's enough for at least forty people.... Start in on a veggie stir-fry.... Get the beef ribs prepped and start grilling them.... Make some country biscuits.... Make some gravy for those biscuits."

Kevin continued to hand out assignments until everyone had something to do. When they had first arrived back in the kitchen, the crew were shaken up, but Kevin knew that if they were kept busy, that would go a long way toward taking their minds off what had happened.

He took a deep breath and slowly let it out. Now *he* needed something to do.

⠌ ⠐⠹⠄⠅⠌ ⠄ ⠦ ⠄⠙⠃⠄ ⠹⠣⠨⠄⠇ ⠐⠹⠒⠏

McFarland went to the entrance to the Main Bar, checked the reading on the control panel next to the doors, and saw that it registered a negative pressure. He entered a code to pressurize the room and waited for it to indicate that he could enter safely. Once the pressure was back to Earth's sea-level normal, he unlocked and opened the decompression doors. The hallway doors, which had been so badly torn apart by the hijackers, only slid into the walls about halfway before they shut and tried to open again. McFarland jumped through and stopped in his tracks.

The bar looked like a hurricane had passed through it. Anything not nailed down was toppled over or thrown about. Shattered glassware crunched under his feet as he carefully made his way through the room.

The cases for the prized collection of Apollo 11 artifacts were broken, and their contents scattered across the floor. But what caught his eye were the broken solar panels, which he could see through the floor window. They had been the ones hit by *Tyche's* solar panel, and the light passing through what was left of them cast eerie shadows on the walls and ceiling.

McFarland returned to the entrance and entered a code in the panel to close and lock the doors. He didn't need a curious guest wandering into this mess. Looking over at Armstrong's spacesuit, he saw that although the case had been shattered, the suit itself was in good shape.

A flash of light reflected off the wall next to him. When he turned toward the floor windows, a look of anger flashed across his face. *"Aww, fuck!!!"*

⠲⠄ ⠄⠨⠃⠄⠄⠄⠆⠄⠰ ⠨⠮⠐ ⠒⠦⠄⠄⠄ ⠄⠆⠒⠆

Marc was with Eileen in Sickbay, helping the guests and ACs who had gotten hurt. The worst case was an AC whose back had a severe cut across it from a wall molding that had broken loose in the Chicken Coop. Max, who had suffered some frostbite, was sleeping on a Bio-Bed. There were a half dozen others with very minor injuries, which included a sprained ankle suffered by Lady

Elizabeth. On the floor, there was the bound hijacker that Dawn had Shock/Bagged, who was snoring in a drug-induced sleep.

Lady Elizabeth smiled at Marc as he wrapped up her ankle. "Thank you, Marc. You're a man of many talents. If you weren't already taken, I'd have my eyes on you myself."

Marc smiled. "And mine on you. But my heart has always beaten for Eileen."

Eileen turned toward them. "Mine-mine-mine-mine-mine!"

Marc gave Eileen a warm smile. "All yours."

Lady Elizabeth agreed. "As it should be, my dear—"

She was interrupted by a loud explosion that shook *Tranquility*. The decompression doors to Sickbay slammed shut, with the door control pad indicating that the decompression protocols had been engaged.

"*Now* what?!" Marc yelled. He hit the Com-Station panel on the wall. "Ross, what the *hell* just happened?!"

Ross's calm voice almost irritated Marc. "One of the solar panels from *Tyche* was still near us and hit the window of the Main Bar, setting off an explosive decompression that triggered all main doorways to seal. Irma and I didn't know it was there until it was too late, because all exterior cameras and sensors are offline from the damage we took."

Marc dreaded asking his next question. "Was anyone in the bar at the time?"

Ross's voice said quietly, "One person.... McFarland."

Marc asked hopefully, "Do you have any cameras working there?"

Ross responded, "One from behind the bar, but it's got some fluid on the lens that's frozen now. Everything is just a big blur."

Marc slammed a fist against the wall. Then he grabbed a medical instrument tray and started savagely beating it against the metal countertop with each word he hollered at the top of his lungs: "GODDAMN... FUCKING... SON... OF... A... BITCH... MOTHERFUCKING... SHIT!!! AAAAAAAAHHHHH!!! NOOOOO!!!"

Even the room seemed to be holding its breath.

Lady Elizabeth looked with concern at Eileen, who indicated that she should stay where she was.

Dawn went to a sink, filled a glass of water, and handed it to Eileen with pleading in her eyes. Then she returned to treating the injured.

Eileen moved slowly to Marc, but resisted the urge to hold him. When he was this angry and in pain, the last thing he wanted was to be touched. He had dropped the damaged tray at his feet and was leaning with his arms against the wall as he gasped for air in huge sobs. Tears streamed from his eyes and landed on the floor as he muttered, "No-no-no-no" between sobs.

Eileen held out the glass of water so that it was in his field of vision. After a moment, Marc took the glass and nodded. Eileen moved away to join Lady Elizabeth and waited.

Marc straightened up, took a couple of deep, shaky breaths, and drank the water. Then he stared at the empty glass with a look that said he wanted to throw it. But after taking a few more deep breaths, he put the glass down on the now severely dented countertop.

Turning to Eileen, Lady Elizabeth, and Dawn, he said, "Get everyone patched up here. I'm going to find McFarland."

He walked to the door and entered a code into the panel to open it. Then he rushed out so quickly that he ran right into an old-style spacesuit that was standing in the doorway with Grey Wolf and Steven on either side, holding it by the arms.

"What the hell...?" said Marc.

Steven shouted, "We need a laser scalpel! His helmet is jammed, and his oxygen is gone!!!"

Dawn grabbed a laser scalpel and started cutting below the locking collar of the helmet, while Grey Wolf and Steven pulled against the fogged-up faceplate. With a ripping sound, the helmet tore away and fell to the floor, revealing a dazed but alive McFarland.

Grey Wolf pointed down at the curmudgeon. "Look! He's not dead yet. Shall we take him for a walk?"

McFarland groaned, "Shut up, you idiot!"

Marc was still trying to come to grips with the fact that McFarland was not dead. "Someone want to explain to me what happened?"

McFarland slowly sat up. "When I saw that the solar panel was about to hit the bar, I grabbed Armstrong's suit and made for the Bug-Out elevator. I didn't want to risk the rest of *Tranquility* if the decompression doors didn't seal properly from the damage done by the hijackers. While the computer took its sweet time to unlock the elevator, I got the suit's helmet on just as the room depressurized. I held on to the bottom of the sink as everything got sucked out, and waited for the elevator door to open. When I arrived at the Bridge, I scared the shit out of these two."

Steven's eyes widened. "Yeah! Seeing that suit stumble out at us is gonna give me nightmares about zombie astronauts."

Marc stared at McFarland, then moved over to him and wrapped his arms around his friend. "I thought we lost you. Please don't scare me like that ever again."

McFarland smiled as he pushed Marc back. "No problem. I'll find another way to do it. Now help me get this thing offa me."

As Marc and Steven helped McFarland to remove the space-suit, Grey Wolf said, "Oh, by the way, I have someone else who wants to say hi."

As he activated the wall monitor, Irma appeared with sparks flying about behind her head. "Hi, guys! Miss me?"

Marc smiled. "Irma! You're back!"

When was the last time I smiled? Marc thought. *It feels like forever.*

Irma was grinning. "Now I know how a genie feels being cooped up in a bottle. But before we get all mushy, I have some good news and some bad news. Which do you want first?"

Just then, the Sickbay doors whooshed open, and in charged the rest of the Core Crew.

Kevin was the first to notice who was on the monitor. "Irma!"

Susan shouldered her way over to the silver-haired bartender. "McFarland! What in the *hell* have you done to my suit?!"

McFarland raised an eyebrow. "*Your* suit? I'd pay good money to see you try to fit in this."

Tony interrupted. "Anyone want to bring us up to speed on what's been going on here?" He looked down at the counter and saw the deep dents in it. "Starting with what did *this*."

"My son did that," said Dawn over her shoulder as she finished examining McFarland.

Eileen wrapped her arms around Marc from behind. "My little hurricane of love!"

Marc blushed. "Irma, you said something about good and bad news?"

Irma nodded. "Thank you, Marc. The good news is that the explosion was contained to just the Main Bar. No other rooms were affected. As a precaution, I sealed the walls and ceiling with the Liquid Steel sealant. There wasn't much left after repairing all the assorted impacts we took, but it should help the structural integrity of the adjoining rooms."

Marc sighed in relief. "Good work, Irma.... What's the *bad* news?"

"We're going to be floating toward the Earth for the next six days and will pick up speed from the Earth's gravity. In four days, we'll be moving faster than any space vessel can safely dock or be evacuated. After passing by Starbase One at about twenty thousand miles per hour, *Tranquility* will hit Earth. Specifically, the Outback of Australia."

A stunned silence filled the Sickbay.

With a groan, McFarland flopped back down onto the examining table that Dawn had moved him to. "Someone wake me when this nightmare is over."

Marc patted Eileen's hand to signal that she should release him, and squared his shoulders. "We have five days to deal with that. First thing is to finish battening down the hatches and make sure we can keep everyone safe. Tony, I want all the Marines to fan out and help with the injured. Then have them give you detailed reports on damage and any safety problems. Kimberly, do a head count on all the guests. Make sure no one has fallen through the cracks. Susan, same for the ACs. Wingnut, double-check all systems in Engineering. Call Steven if you need a hand. Wolf and Steven, make sure that whatever damage the Bridge sustained is either repaired or can be bypassed. Vincent and McFarland, take the hijacker here in Sickbay and put him with the others. Then get the casino up and running and set up a makeshift bar there. The guests and crew are going to need someplace to let off steam. As soon as everything is set, we'll start rotating time off for the crew and Marines. Tell them they all have unlimited credit to play with at the casino. It's the first time they'll get to play with the guests here."

Susan commented, "Not counting the poker games that Wingnut and McFarland have in Engineering."

Wingnut and McFarland looked at each other, then back at Susan with bewilderment.

"How do you know about *that?*" Wingnut asked.

Susan crossed her arms defiantly. "I have my sources."

McFarland shot a look of annoyance at Irma, who quickly looked around and said, "Oh, look! I forgot I left something..., um..., somewhere." She quickly disappeared from the monitor.

Marc addressed everyone. "Okay, gang, get going. I'll meet you all on the Bridge in ninety minutes."

He turned to Eileen. "Thanks. Again. You always know what I need. Would you help Dawn finish up here and see that everyone gets whatever food and drink they want?"

Eileen nodded and gave him a quick kiss on the cheek before checking with Dawn on whom to help first.

Marc turned to a cabinet, removed a pair of crutches, and brought them over to his favorite guest. "Let me adjust these, Lady Elizabeth, and then I'll escort you to the dining room, so you can get something to eat."

Once out in the hallway that led to the elevator, Lady Elizabeth stopped to look at Marc. "May I ask you about something?"

Marc looked down at the floor. "Is it about the display of anger I had in Sickbay?"

"It is."

Marc took a long, deep breath and slowly let it out. Then he met her eyes with his. "Anyone outside of my family and friends, I would say it was none of their business. But we go back far enough that I can talk to you about it."

Watching the man who had earned her respect, Lady Elizabeth saw the conflict of emotions dancing in his eyes. He obviously didn't want to tell her what he was about to say.

He took another deep breath before speaking. "As a child, I was severely bullied and picked on. I was the meek little guy with an odd name. I kept my anger bottled up and never gave in to the desire to strike back. Over the years, I've kept that anger so tightly under wraps that when it does break loose, it's in such highly con-centrated form that I must focus it on one thing. The Core Crew..., and, of course, my mother..., know what's lurking just below the surface. Eileen is the only one who has ever been able to defuse it. She was able to do that on the Bridge during the crisis earlier. But when it does get loose, it's best to stand back and not engage, or even touch me, until the demon is under control. Otherwise, I may verbally or even physically attack. The only time I've physically attacked someone with the intent to harm them was when those men attacked you, and I stepped in to stop them. I don't remember killing that man who stabbed me or being shot by the other one. Apparently, I did so much damage to the guy I killed that the police had a hard time believing that my bare hands were all that I had used. But because it was *you* I was protecting, the district attorney dropped the manslaughter charges. Not many people are able to feel comfortable around me, knowing that I have that kind of anger inside me. I hope it doesn't change how you feel about me."

Lady Elizabeth looked Marc straight in the eye. "All I ever found out about that night was that you were injured while protecting me. I knew one person had died, but that was it. I think the police and my people were trying to protect me from the truth. Thank you for telling me. I always thought of you as my knight in shining armor, but now I see that the armor is slightly tarnished, and that makes you all the braver in my eyes. I see someone who cares more about doing the right thing than how he will look to others. Please be my knight, Marc. I will always be your Lady."

Then she tried to curtsy as best she could with the crutches, but started to lose her balance.

Marc caught her before she fell over. "My Lady, may I have this dance?"

She giggled as Marc took her weight in his arms to protect her injured ankle, and they slowly waltzed down the hallway.

CHAPTER 9

The Complaint Department

After making sure that Lady Elizabeth was being taken care of by an AC in the dining room, Marc made a beeline for the Bridge. He and the crew hadn't beaten the odds of surviving a hijacking, asteroid debris, and an explosive decompression just to lose *Tranquility* now. There *had* to be a way to save their home.

When Marc arrived at the Bridge, he looked around and wondered why the emergency lights were on. Wingnut had already fixed the power systems. Then he saw that the computer wizards were working on the high-voltage systems to the Bridge.

As he assessed the damage that his beloved Bridge had taken, Marc noticed that the fires that had scorched the stations and walls looked even more impressive in the yellowish-orange emergency light.

The Zero-O$_2$ foam used to extinguish the fires had done its job, and thanks to its chemical makeup, it had already broken down into a harmless powder, which would make it easier to clean up.

Grey Wolf and Steven were hard at work fixing the damaged systems, while Irma and Ross were on the main monitor, troubleshooting a way to save *Tranquility*.

Marc asked the computer wizards, "What's our status, guys? How badly did the Bridge systems get hit?"

As Steven finished installing a component in his station and closing the lid, he said, "It looks a lot worse than it is. If we hadn't engaged all the backup systems and added the extra connections, the Bridge would be one big fried egg. Give us a few more minutes to replace some fire-damaged components, and most of the systems will be back up and running."

Grey Wolf pointed at the Mario program, which was running on one of the smaller monitors. "The holes the grasshopper made in the programs will be fixed in about an hour. I can shorten that time by having Mario bypass programs that are no longer needed now, like systems for the Main Bar, the operation controls for retracting Solar Cells, and a dozen others that I can add to that list. But the good news is that the Com-Station will be operational soon."

Marc sat down in his chair. "That's the first bit of good news I've heard all day." He put his hand to his face and muttered, "Was it only this afternoon that we welcomed the guests aboard?"

Then, looking up, he said, "Irma, Ross, you ready to fry a few circuits, working out how to save *Tranquility*?"

Irma grinned. "I'd like mine lightly sautéed in some butter, please."

Ross looked at her and rolled his eyes. "What do you have in mind, Marc?"

Marc leaned back in his seat. "Show me the path we're on, and then overlay the trajectory courses you plotted in your scenarios."

Irma's image transferred to a smaller monitor to the left side of the main one, and Ross to one on the right. A green line appeared on the main monitor that showed their path. Then differently colored lines appeared about one second apart, until there were a dozen on the monitor. Eight of the lines ended with hitting Earth, and three passed the planet and continued off into the Solar System.

But it was the last one that caught Marc's attention. "What about number twelve? It misses Earth and enters its orbit."

Ross looked at the other AI. "That was *your* brainstorm, Irma. I *told* you not to present *that* one."

Irma looked uncertain. "Well, um, I don't think that one should be considered. It has a high probability of something going catastrophically wrong."

Marc leaned forward. "Tell me about it."

Irma tried to sound convincing. "It's not a good plan."

As Marc started to get annoyed, a low rumble came from his throat before he nearly spit out the words, "*Now, Irma!*"

"Okay," she squeaked. Then, using the main monitor to show a CGI of her idea, she said, "We deploy the Laser Sails with two of the Ion-Whiskers. The other two Whiskers are attached to the hull facing Earth. We set those to full thrust. The first two Ion-Whiskers use their lasers on the sails, and, with the additional photons from the Sun on the other side of the Earth, there should be enough pressure to alter our trajectory, but not enough to keep us from hitting the Earth."

Marc watched the image of Irma's idea with great interest. His troubleshooting mind was looking at the plan from different angles and was already seeing its potential, both for *Tranquility* to be saved—and to be destroyed.

Irma continued, "We would need to lock the hub with the hull breach facing away from the Earth, then flood the other side of the hull with Liquid Steel. We would need to apply a thick coat to the inside of the water tanks, too. The heat-resistant properties of the LS will protect the leading edge as it hits the atmosphere. Then we move the two Ion-Whiskers that are pushing against the hull to a new location, so that they 'swing' *Tranquility* away from the Earth a few extra degrees. *If* everything lines up correctly, *Tranquility* will hit the outer edge of Earth's atmosphere. The aerobraking will slow us down enough to miss Starbase One and enter an elliptical orbit that should be stable for about two months. The damage to *Tranquility* will still be substantial, but repairable. There *is* one problem, however. The motor for the North side sail was damaged by the debris field that hit us. No one here has the stamina to deploy it manually. Except for a Čapek unit."

Grey Wolf's eyes widened with alarm. "You mean, using Ross's Čapek unit? We've never tested it in space. We have no idea how solar radiation or cosmic rays will affect the unit or an AI's Matrix. If the computer systems crash while out on the hull, the Matrix could be damaged or even destroyed. Everything that makes Ross unique will be gone."

Marc stared at the display as he considered the ambitious plan. "Other than the dangers to Ross's Matrix, what are the other hurtles we'll need to deal with?"

Irma was decidedly reluctant to continue this conversation, but she nevertheless forged on with the details. "The Ion-Whiskers are not designed to have any pressure against their front end. The sensitive sensors and telescopes will collapse, and the Ion engine will shut down, if not outright explode, which will result in another breach. We also need to find places on the hull that can withstand the Ion-Whiskers pushing against them. When *Tranquility* enters the atmosphere, the pressure against the hull will be distributed throughout it. The Ion-Whiskers will be pressing on two points, and if that pressure exceeds the tolerance levels of the Liquid Steel, we'll have a weak point that might cause us to burn up during the aerobraking. We would also need to inspect the Laser Sails' anchors to make certain they're secure. The South sail survived the debris field, but the North got damaged, and all the cameras and sensors are offline. Before manually deploying the sail, Ross would have to go into the access port on the hull to inspect the anchors visually. During his whole time out on the hull, there are any number of things that could happen that are not related to the Čapek suit. Then, there's the thousand and one things that could still go wrong that I haven't *even* considered yet."

A long silence was interrupted by Steven snapping a component into a station. At once, the Bridge's lights came back on, and the stations started doing systems checks. "That should do it, Marc," said Steven. "The systems will take ten minutes to get back to operating levels. Once that happens, we'll be back to fighting strength."

Grey Wolf finished what he was doing. "There! The PACs are operational again."

The Bridge being so quiet had been slightly unnerving to Marc. Hearing the familiar sounds of the Bridge return one by one helped to calm him.

"Good work, guys," he said. "We should get everyone here. There's more going on than the five of us can handle." He activated his PAC and sent a message to the rest of the Core Crew to come to the Bridge.

Ross interrupted, "Excuse me, Marc, I just picked up a message on the Emergency Channel."

Then Stuart's concerned voice was heard over the speakers: "…twenty-eight hours. This is the *Hestia*, calling *Tranquility*. We have received your SOS message and are returning to assist you. We will reach you in twenty-eight hours. Do you copy?"

Marc moved to the Com-Station and opened a line to the *Hestia*. "This is *Tranquility*, Stuart! We read you loud and clear."

Stuart's relieved voice greeted them: "My god, man! What the hell happened to you? Our sensors show that *Tranquility* is no longer in orbit. Plus there's a debris field circling the Moon, and massive amounts of chatter on the coms."

Marc sat down in his chair. "Well…, we had an attempted hijacking, a computer virus that affected our systems as well as Irma's, an asteroid strike that kicked up the debris field you mentioned, explosive decompression, and a runaway station that's on a collision course with Earth. You know, an average Team Chaos party."

Stuart sounded shocked. "How in the world did you manage to stay in one piece?"

Marc shrugged. "When you see how messed up *Tranquility* is, you'll see that we didn't fair too well. We took some heavy damage and lost both transport ships. Patrick gave his life, and Max was badly injured when they tried to save us by using the transports to move us. How many people can you carry back to SB-1?"

This time, Fred responded: "We have an Emergency Evacuation Capacity of ninety people for three days. It will be cramped, but we can get everyone safely to SB-1."

Marc relaxed a little. That was more than enough room to evacuate everyone from *Tranquility*. "We'll check in with you guys in a few hours and update you on our status. Thanks for coming back."

Fred chuckled. "Just tell everyone to keep their hands off my ginger ale!"

Marc smiled. "Will do. *Tranquility* out."

He cut the connection and did a system check. "Hey, Grey Wolf. How soon for Mario to fix the regular communication channels?"

Grey Wolf quickly typed out some commands on his keyboard. After a moment, he looked over at Marc. "I've sent Mario to make that a priority. From what I can see in the missing program, it should only take a few minutes."

Marc turned back to the Com-Station to watch as the systems came online, one by one. The thing he was waiting for finally happened. The transponder signal from Starbase One showed strong and steady. As soon as the rest of the station came online, he opened a channel to the starbase. "This is *Tranquility Casino*, calling Starbase One. This is *Tranquility Casino*, calling Starbase One."

Marc started to count the seconds. It took less than two seconds for them to receive the message, then a few to hear it and consider a response, and finally two seconds to hear the reply. These were the longest ten seconds of his life.

A concerned male voice answered. "This is Starbase One, *Tranquility*! There's a lot of scared people worrying about you here. What's your status?"

Marc sighed. "You're not going to believe the hell we've been through." Marc gave a quick recap of the events that had taken place. Then he added: "The transport ship, *Hestia*, is on its way back to evacuate our crew and guests. The big problem is that *Tranquility* will hit the Earth in six days. Of course, we're working on a plan to keep that from happening."

This time, Marc counted thirty-five seconds before he heard the reply: "Um…, okay…, will you please hold on for a bit…? We now have a bunch of scared people here for a whole new reason…. Uh…, please wait while we work this out."

As the Bridge doors opened for Tony and McFarland, they heard Marc say, "Sure, I'm not going anywhere."

"*Where* are you not going?" asked Tony.

Marc raised an eyebrow as he casually replied, "To Starbase One. They think it's rude of us to fly by them without stopping to say hi."

Tony and McFarland looked at each other and then back at Marc.

With wide eyes, Tony asked, "Oh, please tell us you're talking to someone from SB-1."

Marc nodded. "I am. But I think they were expecting better news than a runaway station that's aimed at Earth."

McFarland folded his arms. "I think that's a perfectly reasonable thing to have happen, after the day we've been having."

At that moment, the rest of the Core Crew entered the Bridge. Vincent looked around. "This place has all the evidence of Tony cooking here."

Kevin sniffed the air. "But it's got a cleaner scent to it."

Marc rolled his eyes. "Can it, you two! Some things have happened that require our attention. First and foremost is that the *Hestia* is on its way back and can take everyone to Star Base One. Secondly, we're in communication with SB-1 and awaiting their response to our situation. Also, Irma has a plan that will prevent *Tranquility* from hitting Earth. So, I'm going to have her tell you about it, and we can go from there on how to proceed. Irma, please tell them your plan."

Irma reappeared on the monitor. "Do I *have* to?"

Marc frowned. "Irma," he said with a sigh.

Irma gave in. "Okay, okay."

When she finished outlining the Laser Sail plan, there was a complete silence on the Bridge as everyone processed what she had said.

The Com-Station speakers suddenly came on, startling everyone. "*Tranquility*, this is Starbase One."

Marc opened the link. "This is *Tranquility*. Go ahead, Starbase One."

The man sounded hesitant to share what he had to say. "A solution has been found by our people. After examining all the possibilities and weighing the options, the decision has been made to get everyone and anything of value that will fit in the cargo ship of yours, and then the Earth Protection Agency will..., um..., well..., use the Asteroid Missiles to deflect *Tranquility*."

Everyone started talking at the same time.

"Of all the messed-up ideas!"

"Are you out of your fucking mind?!"

"You can take that plan and shove it!"

"Screw that!"

"Did you guys do some bad Tek?!"

Marc held up his hand to quiet his friends. When they all stopped talking, he said, "Starbase One, as you just heard, that plan isn't going to fly. We have a plan in the works that will save *Tranquility*. You tell those people you work for that they need to go back to the blackboards and try again. Get back to us when there's a plan that doesn't involve blowing up an historic landmark. We'll call you as soon as we get our plan finalized."

Marc cut the connection. "Well, that was fun." He held up his hand again to stem the outbursts that were about to flow from his friends. "And before you all start going off again, let me remind you that if we can't make this plan of Irma's work, there may be no other option than to destroy *Tranquility*. So, please, let's get our heads in the right place and start working the problem."

He looked at Wingnut, who was studying Irma's CGI plan on the monitor.

"Find the schematics for the Whiskers," Marc said, "and figure out how to reinforce them to withstand the pressures needed to push against *Tranquility*. Steven, check on the Whiskers and make sure nothing happened to them. This whole plan depends on them working. Everyone else, help them work the problems and find the answers we need. Eileen, I need to talk to you, please."

Marc watched as his friends split up into teams. Then he opened the Bridge doors and waited for Eileen to exit first.

As soon as the doors closed behind them, she turned to him. "Okay, Sky, what do you have brewing? I know when you have that look on your face, it means you're going to do something I'm not going to like. What is it?"

Marc looked her in the eye. "I need you to go with me to talk to Lady Elizabeth about the two of you getting into the *Camel* and hightailing it to Starbase One. Once there, you have to convince those idiots that blowing up *Tranquility* is not the answer."

Eileen stared back at him. "What are *you* going to do that I'm not going to like?"

Marc steeled himself for the storm that he knew was coming. "I'm staying here to make sure Irma's plan works."

Eileen's eyes flashed with anger. "*No!* I'm staying, *too!* You don't get to run into a fire without me making sure you're wearing your asbestos suit."

Marc took her hands in his and pleaded, "But *here* isn't where I need you. You need to be our voice. *My* voice. You have to buy us time to save *Tranquility*. You'll be able to give them the hard facts and get them to listen to you in a way that I could never accomplish. Please, I need this. No argument. Just say you'll do it."

Eileen thought for a moment, squeezed his hands, and nodded. "We'll need Susan to join us. She's the CEO of *Tranquility* and will act as our representative. I can be *your* voice, but I can't argue with a group of people who are determined to blow you out of the sky. Let's go talk to Lady Elizabeth."

Marc lifted both her hands and kissed them. "Thanks."

⠠⠹ ⠐⠺�⠖⠦⠆�⠀⠿⠀⠐⠮⠀⠮⠃⠸⠢⠤⠐⠻⠒⠄

Lady Elizabeth looked at the two of them over her cup of hot cocoa with bewildered eyes. "Tell me, do you have any idea how crazy this all sounds? And when did this place become an historic landmark? I missed that little fact when I helped you get this place."

Marc shifted in his chair. "When we took control of the station, the Earth and Space Preservation Society asked that the station be declared an historic landmark so that when the time came for us to retire and shut *Tranquility* down, it would be handed over to them and turned into a museum. But they may want a new coat of paint by the time we finish this roller-coaster ride."

Lady Elizabeth took a sip of her cocoa. "*Now* I remember. My memory isn't what it used to be, and it used to be rotten. What about what you want Eileen, Susan, and me to do? And why aren't *you* coming?"

Marc took a deep breath before outlining Irma's Solar Sail plan.

⠠�⠒⠄⠶⠶⠂⠶⠄⠢⠄⠶⠶⠄⠶⠶⠄⠶⠂⠄⠶⠶⠂

Back on the Bridge, the Core Crew continued to work on Irma's idea. Steven was able to connect with the Whiskers, confirm that they were in perfect operating condition, and were on their way back to *Tranquility*. After poring over the Whiskers' blueprints, Wingnut and Steven had come up with a solution for how to keep them from crushing themselves against the hull. The master engineer, who was well schooled on *Tranquility*'s construction, already knew where to place the Whiskers. Now he was going over the details of the plan for applying the Liquid Steel.

"To use the Liquid Steel in that fashion," he said, "will require some reworking of the distribution system. If we also apply the

Liquid Steel to the inner walls, we can double the thickness and increase the strength and heat resistance tenfold. But I would need to start working on the braces for the Whiskers now. That means that everyone else will have to start running the hoses to the different compartments along the whole length of *Tranquility*. We also need to empty the water tanks that will be hitting the atmosphere and dry them before going inside to apply the LS. Irma can start injecting the hull with what's left of the LS now. The tricky part will be to only apply it an inch thick, or the drying agent will take longer to do its thing."

Grey Wolf stood up. "Steven and I will start modifying the Čapek unit with some shielding around the Matrix to protect Ross. That should only take an hour or two."

Ross appeared on the monitor. "There's just one problem, gentlemen. We don't have enough Liquid Steel to do the job. We need to send someone in the *Camel* to get some more from SB-1 and return here well before we enter Earth's orbit."

Susan asked, "Would we even have time to apply the Liquid Steel?"

Ross thought for a second. "If the hull is done with what's left in our tanks, we should be able to coat the interior of the water tanks with the new supply in the time remaining. Providing nothing goes wrong."

McFarland blew a raspberry. "Providing nothing goes wrong? Today's been nothing but a long string of things gone wrong. Or has that little fact managed to get deleted from your goo-filled Matrix?"

Just then, Marc entered the Bridge. "I disagree. Today has been one miracle after another. Because of the people in this room, we have defeated a hijacking attempt, saved the financial security of the people who pay us, moved *Tranquility* from certain destruction, and snatched you, McFarland, from certain death. Yes, we lost Patrick and still may lose *Tranquility*, but with this group working together, I'm confident that we *will* beat the odds. Again."

Patricia appeared at the doorway and cleared her throat. She was obviously uncomfortable interrupting the Core Crew, but something was important enough to override that.

Wingnut walked over to her. "What's up, Patricia? You can speak freely."

Marc smiled at her and waved her in. "You've been with us from day one. As far as I'm concerned, you're an honorary member of the Core Crew."

Patricia blushed as she stepped onto the Bridge. Having only previously seen the Bridge a handful of times, she was shocked by its condition. "Sorry to interrupt, but the intercoms are not working in the casino or the kitchen. The guests are asking what's going to happen, and the ACs can't answer them. We need someone from the Core Crew to come down and give us a hand."

Susan stepped forward. "Why don't Kimberly, McFarland, and I do that? Between the three of us, we can answer all their questions. And if they get aggressive, McFarland can handle it in his own special way."

Marc nodded. "Good call, Susan. With the PACs now operational, we can keep you apprised of the plans we make." Marc looked at Patricia, thought for a moment, and then asked Steven, "You still have your prototype for the PAC around?"

Steven opened a drawer at his station. "Sure, but it only has the bare components installed." He removed the PAC and handed it to Marc.

"Patricia," Marc said, "please pull back your shirt sleeve." Then he wrapped the PAC around her wrist and activated it. "Irma, please authorize this PAC to be used by Patricia and give her a level-three clearance."

Irma blew a kiss toward Patricia, whose PAC beeped.

"Done, Marc," said the AI.

Marc looked at Patricia. "This one is only temporary until we can fit you with an updated version. You will now be able to communicate with any of us and access the guests' personal files for the time being. Susan will show you how to operate it. As of this moment, you are a member of the Core Crew."

Patricia's eyes watered as she threw her arms around Marc and hugged him hard while the Core Crew applauded.

"Now get going," Marc said with a smile. "We have miles to go before we're safe."

Patricia stepped back, wiped her eyes with her sleeve, and smiled. "Thank you. This is a bigger honor than I thought I would ever get."

Susan slipped her arm through Patricia's. "Come along, my dear. I'll show you how the PAC works."

Marc watched as they left. He had been planning to promote Patricia for some time now, but wished that it hadn't taken a disaster to make it happen. As he turned back to the others, he was hit with a wave of happiness.

Wingnut was grinning from ear to ear. "Thanks, Marc. Sometimes you do things that still blow me away."

Vincent added with a grin, "It's one of the many things that makes working here with you bearable."

Tony cleared his throat. "Before we get too soppy, we have a crisis to attend to."

Marc shook his head as if coming out of a dream and squared his shoulders. "Yes, we do. Let's huddle up and fine-tune this plan."

⠔⠀⠨⠒⠕⠔⠴⠔⠆⠀⠰⠮⠀⠨⠶⠥⠍⠔⠆⠴⠢

In the casino, there was a feeding frenzy by the guests for information. Susan and Kimberly were pounced on as soon as they walked through the doors and had questions thrown at them from all sides.

All of this came to an end when McFarland pushed his way through the crowd and stood glaring at the guests as he held up his hands. "Everyone, shut the fuck up!" He clenched his fists and aimed them at each person who was still asking questions until everyone was quiet. "These ladies are going to update you with everything that's been going on. After they're done, you may raise your hand *if* you have a valid question. If you disregard these simple rules, I will drag you to your room and weld the door shut until the rescue ship arrives. Understood?"

A young male guest pointed a finger at McFarland with a sneer. "Just who do you think you're talking to? Have you forgotten who we represent? How dare you—?"

With the swiftness of a jungle cat, McFarland moved to the man, grabbed him by the throat, dragged him to the nearest wall, and slammed him against it. In a voice that dripped with more venom and anger than anyone had ever heard before, he growled, "Does it *look* like I care who you are? This crew has done everything to ensure your safety over their own, and I nearly died today. *Twice!*

So, right now I have very little patience for dealing with holier-than-thou attitudes. This is your only warning to shut the fuck up before I start taking my *very* bad day out on that pretty store-bought face of yours. *Understood?*"

The silence in the room was deafening. The only sound was the strangled whimpering from the terrorized guest. Susan placed a hand on McFarland's arm.

"That's enough, Ray. Let him go. He'll behave. They all will." Turning to the others, she said, "Right?"

All the guests nodded and stepped back, while the guy in McFarland's grip nodded like an out-of-control bobble-head doll. McFarland opened his hand and let the man move away. Then, after taking a few deep breaths, McFarland squared his shoulders and glared at everyone, who took another step back.

Finally, in a calm voice, he said, "All ACs, Marines, Ms. Lee, and Mr. Maxwell, please come with me to the bar. Drinks are on me while I update you on our status."

Kimberly looked at Susan and said, "Go ahead. I'll chime in when needed."

Susan nodded and turned to the guests. "As you witnessed, there was an attempted hijacking by the work crew of the auction that was to take place…, well…, tomorrow."

The guests looked at Mr. Maxwell and Ms. Lee with anger.

Susan quickly added, "*They* had nothing to do with it. We've verified their innocence. So, leave them alone. Thanks to our crew's teamwork, the threat was dealt with. As you've heard, we lost the shuttles and one of the pilots. The surviving pilot, Max, is alive by some miracle and is recovering in Sickbay. You may visit him to express your appreciation for his bravery and to give him your condolences on the loss of his friend." Susan looked at the guests in a way that said she was *not* making a suggestion. "With both shuttles gone and our control thrusters damaged, we are now on a course that has us hitting Earth in six days."

The crowd gasped, and then everyone started to talk at once.

"*Shut it!*" yelled McFarland, throwing his empty shot glass at the nearest video poker display, which shattered on impact.

The guests quieted down so quickly that the echo of the shattered display was heard by everyone.

McFarland shrugged and then poured himself another drink before continuing his update with the ACs.

Susan sighed before continuing: "The good news is that the *Hestia* is on its way back here and will arrive in less than a day. The Core Crew is figuring out a plan to try to save *Tranquility*, but we're still working on it. Now, are there any questions?"

One hand rose slowly.

"Yes, Mister Peabody?"

"Will we be getting a refund?"

Susan narrowed her eyes. "Let's worry about that after we save *Tranquility*. If we lose her, we'll be responsible for the destruction of the auction items and additional millions because of the loss of the Apollo 11 artifacts that got sucked out into space when the Main Bar decompressed. Remember, this is a place that you guests visit to get away from it all. But for us Core Crew, this is our *home* where we earn a living and are still fighting to keep from losing everything. If you think it's more important to burden us with more financial problems, feel free to talk to our Complaint Department."

Susan pointed to McFarland, who slammed his newly empty shot glass down on the bar so hard that the glass left a dent. An involuntary flinching from the guests and a nervous step back indicated that no one would be talking to the Complaint Department anytime soon.

Susan looked around. "No? Good. Now, if you'll excuse us, we have a runaway space station to save." She looked at Kimberly. "Did I miss anything?"

Kimberly shook her head and waved her toward the door.

McFarland finished talking to the ACs, grabbed a bottle of single malt Irish whisky, and then said to Patricia in a loud enough voice to be heard by the guests, "If you have any more problems with anyone, send me a message saying, 'Complaint Department.' I'll come right down to address it."

The guests nearly trampled each other as they made a path for him to walk to the hallway. He could be heard saying to himself, "It's been a long time since I let that particular demon out to play. Nice to know it's still alive and kicking."

A nervous muttering started among the guests as McFarland could be heard chuckling to himself down the hallway.

Patricia quickly told the ACs to start handing out drinks and ordered some more food from the kitchen staff. It was going to be another long night.

Out in the hallway, McFarland's inner demon roared at him as someone ran up behind him. He spun around with his fist and the bottle ready for an attack.

Su stopped in her tracks with a shocked and frightened look on her face as she recoiled in fear.

McFarland quickly dropped his defensive stance and let the bottle drop to the carpet as his inner demon retreated like a puppy that had done something bad.

"Su! I'm *sorry!* I've been in full defensive mode for hours now, and I'm a bit amped up. I would never hit you for *any* reason."

Su saw that he was more upset with himself for scaring her than for her startling him. She took a calming deep breath and then slowly closed the distance between them.

"I just wanted to make sure you were really okay. You didn't give any details about how you almost died." She wrapped her arms around his neck and looked up at him. "I've become rather fond of you, you know."

McFarland stared into her beautiful jade eyes, and everything that was happening on *Tranquility* faded away into the background. It had been a long time since someone had affected him this way.

"I'm fine," he said. "Although Susan is a bit upset about the damage to Armstrong's spacesuit. But it managed to keep me alive. Barely. Once we figure out how to save *Tranquility*, I'll come to spend time with you before we evacuate everyone to the *Hestia*, and tell you all about what happened. But I need to get back to the Bridge now to help Marc sort this mess out." He kissed her gently. "I promise."

Su never thought she could trust a man's promise after being beaten by her ex. But this man had something about him that she trusted. She knew he would always protect her. She kissed him back as she pressed herself against him and whispered in his ear, "You better. I'd have to hunt you down and do some bad things to you." As she released him, she gave him a wicked grin.

He smiled and nodded. Then bending down to pick up the bottle, he turned to follow the other two ladies, who by now were at the end of the hallway, finding the walls very interesting.

When he reached them, he shrugged and smiled impishly. "Yep. So, *that* happened."

Susan and Kimberly smiled. Then Susan said, "Only you could find romance during a crisis."

McFarland rolled his eyes and headed to the elevator. "For the record, that happened before things went all to hell."

"Details!" said Kimberly. "We want details!"

And the two of them ran after him.

CHAPTER 10

Going Nowhere Fast

When Susan, Kimberly, and McFarland arrived back on the Bridge, the Core Crew were debating about who should pilot the *Camel*. The twins were arguing that they could do the trip faster, and Wingnut was saying that he needed them to help with applying the Liquid Steel.

Marc held up his hand to stop the argument when he saw the trio walk in. "You guys get things sorted out with the guests?"

Susan looked back at the other two. Kimberly tried to hide the smirk that wanted to take over her face, and McFarland had a slightly bemused gleam in his eyes. Susan turned back to Marc with a shrug. "They got updated with our situation..., *and* were introduced to our Complaint Department."

Marc raised an eyebrow at that. "Complaint Department?"

"That would be me," McFarland grumbled. He took a drink from the bottle of Irish whisky before continuing. "I introduced them to my inner demon. There may be one or two guests calling for my head on a platter when this all shakes out."

Marc sighed and rubbed the bridge of his nose. It concerned him that McFarland's inner demon had made an appearance. Where Marc's own demon was a force to be reckoned with, McFarland's was one not to have loose. Whatever happened with the guests would have to be dealt with later.

"So long as there's no one needing Dawn's attention," Marc said, "let's not worry about that for right now."

Then Marc narrowed his eyes at Kimberly, which caused her to look back at the doorway, thinking someone had walked in behind her. But she saw that no one was there.

Marc pointed at his sister and said to Tony, "Our pilot."

Tony's eyes widened in surprise, looked around at the others, and saw the startled look on their faces.

Kimberly stared at her brother like a deer in headlights. "Who? Me? I'm not ready."

Marc's demeanor softened as he walked over to Kimberly, took her by the shoulders in a firm grip, and looked her in the eyes. "I've seen your practice simulations on the *Camel* and the hours of studying you've done on the material needed to fly it. The only thing holding you back is a family trait…, that voice in your head that says you need to do better. You're ready. And we need you to do this. *I* need you to save *Tranquility*."

Kimberly couldn't look away from her brother, who had always supported her and encouraged her to do the best she could. This was the first time she was going to have to push all her doubts aside and be the person he saw in her. She took a deep breath and slowly let it out. "Okay. When do I leave?"

Marc smiled and kissed her on the forehead. "Go with Vincent and get the *Camel* ready. I'll send Lady Elizabeth, Susan, and Eileen to you in a few minutes."

Marc then said to Vincent, "Make sure the *Camel* is ready by the time we get there." He then addressed Tony: "I need one of the Marines to go with them to Starbase One."

Kimberly spoke up. "Uh..., Tony? Um... could you see that Devan..., I mean, Sergeant Jackson, is on the *Camel*, please?" She stole a quick glance at Marc, which didn't go unnoticed by him. "He's been helpful with my pilot studies."

Tony nodded. "I'll see to it. Go. Time's a-wastin'."

Kimberly grabbed Vincent's arm and nearly dragged him off the Bridge.

Marc muttered to no one in particular, "I'm gonna have a long talk with Jackson when this is all over."

Wingnut cleared his throat. "I'm heading for Engineering to start working with Ross on how to safely eject the water and how not to have the hull get covered in ice. It won't do us any good to lose the weight only to have it cling to us like a bad habit. Would you send the Marines down, Tony? I'll instruct them on what needs to be done to set up the hoses for pumping the Liquid Steel to the water tanks."

Tony nodded. "Will do."

Marc moved over to Susan. "We need you to go with Lady Elizabeth and Eileen to make sure we have our opportunity to save *Tranquility*. Eileen's going to be my voice, but as the CEO here, as well as a respected person in the finance world, you will have a better chance of being listened to than just the other two. Head to

Lady Elizabeth's room and inform her and Eileen that it's time to leave. I'll meet you at the *Camel* shortly."

Susan nodded, looked at Steven, and pointed to the far side of the Bridge to have a moment with him.

Marc then waved McFarland and Kevin over to him, and whispered to them, "I need you two to do something quickly and quietly."

⠈⠄ ⠐⠎⠄⠃⠂⠄⠆⠄⠒ ⠶ ⠐⠮⠄ ⠒⠏⠠⠄⠲⠄⠆⠄ ⠐⠶⠒⠃⠆

McFarland was walking behind the hijackers from the AuctionHouse, holding a Stun/Gun and wearing his Stun/Gloves. Steven was right behind him. Kevin was walking backwards in front of the group, with a Stun/Gun aimed at them. Marc was facing forward, with his hand on Kevin's shoulder to guide him as he walked. It had been made clear to the prisoners that no nonsense would be tolerated, and the first person to step out of line would not wake up for a month of Sundays. This had been punctuated by McFarland's gloves crackling.

Kimberly and Vincent stopped their pre-flight check of the *Camel* when Marc and the others reached the Loading Bay. Vincent told Kimberly to go ahead into the cockpit and do the systems check, and then waited for the group to stop.

Marc patted Kevin's shoulder. "Keep them here until Steven can set up the cargo hold." He then turned to Steven. "Make the adjustments fast. The *Camel* needs to take off ASAP."

Steven nodded and jogged to the cargo hold, where he removed an access panel to work on its systems.

Vincent asked, "Do I want to know what you have in mind with these jerk-wads?"

Marc's voice belied that he was dead on his feet. But he spoke loud enough for the hijackers to hear. "We're sending them to be SB-1's problem. Steven is setting up the life-support system in the cargo hold so that any attempt by them at overriding the systems will result in the exterior hatch opening."

Vincent whistled. "Wow! That should keep them quiet."

Marc pointed to a storage compartment. "Grab a few cases of bottled water, energy bars, and a few Zero-G toilet kits, and put them in the hold. It's still a day-and-a-half trip to SB-1, and even though I don't care if they kill themselves, I don't believe in deliberately making someone suffer."

Vincent looked at the hijackers and then back at Marc. "You're a better man than I, Gunga Din. I'd be willing to duct-tape them to the hull and take bets on who could hold their breath the longest." He grabbed a wheeled cart and went to get the supplies."

Steven closed the access hatch and moved over to Marc. "I've set up all the sensors that connect the interior of the hold to the exterior hatch. If they so much as scratch at a panel, the hatch will open."

Marc then addressed the hijackers. "In case you missed that, your trip to SB-1 will be uneventful. If you try anything to open a hatch or mess with the systems of the ship, the hatch will open, and you can *float* the rest of the way home. Understood?"

All the hijackers nodded.

Mark opened the hatch to the hold. "Get in there. Vincent and Kevin, tie them to the cargo loops in the middle of the hold. Make sure the supplies are close enough to them."

Once they got the hijackers set up, Marc sealed the hatch, and Steven activated his anti-tampering program.

Eileen, Susan, Lady Elizabeth, and Jackson arrived at the Loading Bay and headed for the crew cabin.

Eileen stopped to wait for Marc to come to her. When she saw how tired he was, the worry showed in her eyes. "Promise me you'll get some sleep soon. Everyone else has gotten some."

Marc smiled weakly. "I have a few more things to do, and then I'll take a nap."

Eileen gently put her hands on his face and turned his head so that she could look directly into his eyes. Marc always thought her coffee brown eyes had just a hint of cream, but this time he saw the deep concern she had for him, which begged him to take her seriously.

Putting his hands on hers, he said, "I promise. As soon as the *Camel* leaves, I'll give a few instructions to the crew and head for bed. I love you, you know."

She kissed him and pressed her forehead to his. "Yes. And I love you."

Eileen gave him a hug and a kiss, and then headed for the *Camel*'s crew cabin.

As Marc watched her enter the *Camel*, he felt a little guilty for not being honest with her about his reasons for her going to Starbase One. With the real possibility of *Tranquility* being destroyed, either by missile or burning up in Earth's atmosphere, not having Eileen here would keep him from worrying about her safety.

As soon as the hatch closed, he waved at everyone to exit the Loading Bay and sealed the doors. Everyone quickly headed to the Bridge to watch the *Camel* depart. Marc wasn't going to miss Kimberly's first-time piloting.

⠨⠀⠠⠶⠄⠂⠒⠂⠆⠀⠶⠀⠰⠮⠃⠐⠿⠒⠱⠄⠘⠎⠐

As Kimberly settled into the pilot's seat and started the pre-check for departure, Jackson helped Lady Elizabeth, Susan, and Eileen into their seats. Then he buckled them in before joining Kimberly in the cockpit.

Kimberly finished the checklist and looked at Jackson. "*You* should be in this seat. You know more about piloting ships than I do."

Jackson shook his head. "I may have more time piloting Marine ships, but none on this ship. You outrank me here." He took her hand and squeezed it. "Take her out, Commander."

Kimberly's eyes widened at Jackson's calling her Commander. Then she disengaged the locks to the *Camel*'s large tanks and retracted them from the Hump that transported the water to *Tranquility*. When the command and cargo section was disconnected from the Hump, its name switched from *Camel* to *Camel One*.

She then got everything ready to be able to slip out from the Hump. Once the launch systems showed that *Camel One* was free, she opened the Com-Station to *Tranquility*'s Bridge.

"*Camel One* to *Tranquility*…, we're ready to undock. Start unlocking sequence on my mark. Three, two, one, *mark!*"

Tony's voice responded, "Roger, *Camel One*. Docking locks are released, and you are cleared for departure. Good luck!"

Kimberly disengaged *Camel One* from the Docking Bay and eased it back from the Hump. Then she engaged the maneuvering thrusters to ease *Camel One* back a safe distance before maneuvering it toward Earth and Starbase One. Once the ship was oriented to the correct flight path, she throttled up the engines over a period of one minute until a full burn was achieved. After checking the velocity, she cut the engines.

It wasn't until she released the flight control's yoke that she realized her knuckles were white from gripping it. "I guess I was a bit nervous," she said with a grin.

Jackson gave her a reassuring smile. "You did fine. Better than most people. When we finish this mess we're in, it's about time for you to get your license. You're ready."

Kimberly sighed. "Just keep reminding me of that."

He took her hand again and kissed it. "Sure thing."

⠨⠄ ⠐⠞⠑⠂⠌⠂� ⠐⠶ ⠠⠮� ⠲⠢⠨⠄�� ⠐�⠂

Marc watched with the rest of the Core Crew as *Camel One* disappeared from view. Because most of the exterior cameras were damaged, they couldn't see Kimberly executing a perfect textbook turn before heading for Starbase One.

He then addressed everyone: "I'm gonna get some sleep. Grey Wolf, Steven, start the work on the Čapek unit. Tony, contact SB-1 and tell them that *Camel One* is on its way with the hijackers. Let them know we need as much Liquid Steel as they can spare. McFarland, Kevin, and Vincent, make sure the ACs are doing okay, and see to what they need. Make sure everyone has had some time off.... Irma?"

Irma appeared on the main monitor. "Yes, Marc?"

He checked the time. "Please wake me in two hours. Unless we're on fire and it's at my door, don't wake me for any reason."

Irma's image changed to her wearing a security guard's hat with mirror sunglasses. "Yes, sir!"

Marc smiled as he threw everyone a sloppy salute and headed for his quarters. Once there, he kicked off his shoes, lay down on the bed, and closed his eyes.

"Marc? Marc, wake up!"

Marc grumbled. "It's a good thing you don't have a neck, Irma. I'd be throttling you right now."

Irma appeared on his monitor with a confused look. "But you asked me to wake you at this time."

Marc looked at the clock. Sure enough, two hours had passed.

"Sorry, Irma. I could have sworn that I just lay down. What's our status?"

Irma smiled. "Everything's in order. The Čapek unit is almost ready, and SB-1 has informed us that they have eight tanks of Liquid Steel that will be ready when *Camel One* gets there. Apparently, the new head administrator there is a big fan of ours."

Marc threw the covers off and sat up. "Is that enough to do the job?"

Irma nodded. "Wingnut says that it should be *more* than enough. With the extra, he's going to reinforce the Main Bar's walls and seal the doorways to it."

Marc stood up and headed for the bathroom. "Good. I'm gonna shower to scrape off a layer or two. Would you play some wake-up music for me, please?"

Irma smiled. "Sure thing."

The speakers in the bathroom started playing *Pump It Up* by Elvis Costello. Marc started undressing while bobbing his head to the beat.

⠲⠂ ⠄⠐⠃⠄⠄⠆⠄ ⠄⠆ ⠠⠙⠃⠄ ⠶⠏⠢⠄⠂⠩ ⠐⠶⠼⠢⠒

After stopping at the kitchen to get a large mug of coffee, Marc walked to the Workshop near Engineering, where Steven and Grey Wolf were working on the Čapek unit.

"Okay, guys. How're we coming with getting the Laser Sails deployed?"

Steven started pointing at sections of the unit as he listed off the work he and Grey Wolf had done on it. "We got the Čapek unit shielding done, improved the actuators to give more power to the arms, and installed micro solar cells all over the unit, so the power cells will get recharged. While Ross is deploying the sails, the output will exceed what the cells replace, but it will extend the operational use an extra hour past what we project will be the maximum time needed to finish. We're just about ready to transfer Ross's Matrix." He looked at Grey Wolf. "Did I miss anything?"

Grey Wolf closed the access panel he had been working on, and said, "Nope. I just finished the upgrades to the unit's memory core. Providing a major solar flare doesn't hit Ross, he should be safe. Steven is connecting the last of the leads to the power cells, and that will complete the work."

Steven shut the panel to the components he was working on. "That's it. We can transfer Ross's Matrix now."

Marc looked around. "Is Wingnut in Engineering?"

As Steven replied, he sealed and locked the panel. "He's with Ross in the Maintenance Hanger, working on the Whiskers. He figured out how to reinforce them to push against *Tranquility* without crumpling their hull."

Marc finished his coffee, moved to a table that had a coffee-maker, and refilled his mug. By the look of the amount of used grounds in the trash, the two computer geniuses had put a dent in *Tranquility*'s coffee supply. After taking a few careful mouthfuls of the hot beverage, he activated his PAC: "Marc to Ross."

"Ross here, Marc. I hope you got some sleep."

Marc stared at his coffee. "Not nearly enough, but yeah. Steven and Grey Wolf are ready to transfer you to the new Čapek unit. Please come to the Workshop, so they can get started on it."

In the background came Wingnut's voice. "I need a pair of hands down here, Marc. I'm almost done, but I need someone to help if Ross can't."

Marc finished his coffee and refilled his mug a second time. "I'm on my way." He turned off his PAC and addressed the two at the Čapek unit. "Good work, guys." He thought for a moment before adding, "I don't think I say that enough to the two of you for all the work you do here. I'm gonna try and work on that."

Both Steven and Grey Wolf stopped what they were doing to look at their friend. Steven smiled. "It's how you *don't* say things that tells us how you feel. If you weren't happy with our work, you'd say volumes."

Grey Wolf pointed his screwdriver at Marc. "But the truth be told, we don't thank *you* enough."

Steven nodded at that.

Marc looked uncomfortable, but decided that they didn't have time to hash out their feelings. "Let's bookmark this discussion for now. Get Ross ready to deploy the sails."

His two friends nodded and returned to work on the Čapek unit. Marc watched for a moment, wondering for the millionth time how he had managed to have such good friends. He shook his head to clear it and then headed for the Maintenance Hangar, missing the look shared between Steven and Grey Wolf that spoke of their bond of friendship with the man who had just left.

⠨⠄⠀⠨⠐⠃⠄⠌⠂⠂⠀⠶⠀⠠⠙⠃⠂⠀⠒⠃⠇⠨⠄⠁⠀⠌⠶⠙⠢

Ross was just stepping out of the elevator as Marc approached. The AI looked up at Marc as he stood aside for him. "How's the Čapek unit looking, boss?"

Marc smiled. "Looks like they got it ready. It's a little shinier than the one you have now."

Ross gave him a "You think?" look.

"Considering that I've been in this one for over six years," Ross said, "with only a few modifications and upgrades, I would be surprised if it weren't."

Just as the elevator doors started to close, Marc put his arm out to stop them. "Ross, thank you for risking your life to help save *Tranquility*."

Ross suddenly became a different person. He was no longer the happy-go-lucky AI they all knew, and became a full-fledged adult. Marc knew that Ross had engaged the Class A5 Protocols that overrode the personality center of the AI Matrix, so he could focus on the subject at hand.

"The time I've spent among the crew here on *Tranquility*," Ross said, "has taught me much about how to be a better person. I've watched with great interest how you and the others have dealt with this crisis and what your reactions have been. If I'm to aim my goals to conduct myself with the same amount of dignity you all have, I must step up and do what I can to help. It would not be fitting for me to be a part of this crew if I didn't."

Marc looked at the first fully functioning AI who continued to be more than the sum of his parts. Holding his hand out to Ross, he said, "I'm honored to have you with us, Ross. Now let's show the world that AIs and humans not only can work together, but do miracles as well."

Ross shook Marc's hand and in the blink of an eye was his old self. "And be bad asses at the same time."

⠌⠄ ⠠⠷⠞⠆⠂⠄⠂⠆ ⠄ ⠶ ⠠⠯⠷⠄ ⠮⠆⠪⠄⠂⠇ ⠄⠮⠃⠆

The Maintenance Hangar was where the Whiskers were kept when they were not in use. At all times, at least one was deployed to scan the Solar System for Near-Earth Objects. In the five years that they had been used, they had discovered over twenty-seven thousand NEOs, six of which had been determined to be threats to Earth or the Moon. The Earth Protection Agency, or EPA, deployed Asteroid Missiles, which deflected them to harmless orbits.

It was because *Tranquility* received the raw data from the Whiskers that Irma was able to cleanse through it and apply the superfast processing power of her AI Matrix to the information. For over 250 years, the Yarkovsky Effect—the process by which the Sun's photons interact with a surface, such as an asteroid, affecting its speed and spin—had given the scientists probing the skies for NEOs some major headaches. Since Irma had provided the missing link to predict the orbits of any and all asteroids in the Solar System, her formula was now called the Irma Solution.

⠌⠄ ⠠⠍⠓⠂⠂⠌⠂⠄⠄ ⠐⠶ ⠠⠻⠓⠄ ⠶⠹⠏⠥⠂⠇ ⠌⠶⠱⠖

As Marc entered the Maintenance Hangar, he took in the sight of the four Whiskers sitting on their service platforms. Each one was the size of a minivan, with the back two-thirds containing the Ion Engines, and the front third crammed full of cameras, telescopes, and assorted sensors. Wingnut had removed two of the front ends, one of which was cleared of its components.

Marc was blown away by the amount of work that had been done in the two hours he had been asleep. The inner workings of the Whiskers were piled high in the corner, which concerned him because putting them back would be an issue. But considering the damage to *Tranquility* that had already occurred, and that it was yet to endure when it hit the atmosphere, repairing the Whiskers would be low on the to-do list.

Marc nearly jumped out of his skin, sloshing some of his coffee on the floor, when a microwave-oven-size component flew across the bay and crashed into the pile. He leveled an annoyed look at Wingnut, whose eyes were wide as he realized that he had startled his friend.

"Sorry, Marc. I didn't hear you come in."

Marc sighed, transferred his coffee mug to his other hand, and shook the hand dry that was covered with coffee. "I'm going to assume that the universe is telling me I've had enough coffee."

He pointed at the pile in the corner. "You *do* realize that you just threw two hundred thousand dollars at a few million dollars' worth of sensitive equipment, right?"

Wingnut gave him a lopsided grin. "That's all stuff that was scheduled to be replaced next month." He pointed to the other side of the bay, where a blue tarp was laid out on the floor with other labeled components. "That's all stuff that we just got and is going to be carefully put away. Want to join in on the wanton destruction of equipment? It's *very* therapeutic."

Marc took one more slug of the coffee before placing it on a nearby workbench and flexing his fingers. "Where do I start, Doctor Overkill?"

In short order, they removed the rest of the Whiskers' innards—some with the care of a surgeon, others with crowbars.

Wingnut was right, Marc thought. *This IS very therapeutic.*

After the stress of everything that had happened, it felt good to cut loose by smashing a few things.

Wingnut ripped the last item out with a savage yank of its wiring and held the soccer-ball-size unit in his hand for a moment, before taking aim at a glass lens that was sticking out of the pile in the corner and hurling the unit at it. When the glass shattered, the unit slowly rolled back and forth down the pile.

Wingnut turned to Marc with a grin. "'Total carnage! I *love* it!'"

Marc matched the grin. "'I'd buy that for a dollar!'"

They laughed at their shared love of antique arcade games. Then they looked at the skeletonized front end of the two Whiskers. Marc scratched the back of his head and asked, "Now what?"

Wingnut pointed at the huge 3-D printer opposite the pile. "Now we see if all the measurements I did were accurate. I had the braces that attach to the Ion Engine's housing made out of carbon fiber. It may be lighter than metal, but it still weighs a ton. Well..., actually about six hundred and nineteen pounds. But with the overhead Mag-Track system and some good old-fashioned muscle power, we should have them installed in no time. As I get them free of the printer, you disconnect the pulley of the Mag-Track from the front end of the Whisker."

Marc nodded and headed for the Mag-Track system.

The Mag-Track could move a thousand pounds to every area of the Maintenance Hangar and could rotate three hundred and sixty degrees. Its bench-size housing contained Rare Earth Magnets that attached to the metal in the ceiling, enabling it to stay in place even if power were lost.

Marc picked up the control pad for it and gave the hooks holding the Whisker's front end some slack. Then he disconnected the hooks, set the 3-D printer's location in the system, and sent it on its way.

As Wingnut pointed above where he wanted the Mag-Track, Marc switched the control pad to manual and maneuvered it to the spot. Then, using hand signals, Wingnut directed Marc to the proper location. He then connected the hooks to the large black cone-shaped cage that had the same shape as the front end of the Whiskers, but with a flattened nose that would push against *Tranquility*'s hull.

Once the cone was secured, Wingnut pointed his finger up and slowly rotated it in a circle, which instructed Marc to slowly lift the cone. The Mag-Track automatically adjusted each carbon fiber cable, so that all four of them carried an equal load. As the cone lifted from the printer, Wingnut inspected all the hooks to make sure each one would not slip. Then, looking at Marc, he said, "Let's give Lurr a nose job." He pointed at the nearest Whisker.

As Marc guided the cone to the Whisker, he said, "I wonder if anyone outside *Tranquility*'s crew realizes that you named the Whiskers after old TV characters who were determined to take over the Earth?"

Wingnut didn't take his eyes off the moving cone. "I just wish we had two others to name Pinky and the Brain."

Marc slowly got the cone positioned and stopped the Mag-Track. "Maybe if we survive this insane plan, we'll see about getting them."

Wingnut smiled at the idea, then used his hands to direct Marc to adjust the positioning of the cone until it lined up perfectly with the Whisker. Then he grabbed an electric bolt driver, picked up a bolt that slid into the hole in the cone's base, and tightened it. The next eleven bolts went in just as easily, but the thirteenth refused to line up.

Wingnut dropped the tool to the floor, walked over to a bench, and looked around for something. He finally found what he was looking for, picked up a hammer, and went back to the ill-fitting hole. As he placed the curved chisel an eighth of an inch to the side of the hole, he looked at Marc. "If it doesn't fit, force it. If it breaks, it was going to anyway." Then he started beating the hammer against the chisel.

Marc was amazed at the precision and skill that Wingnut had with such a primitive tool on modern materials. In just moments, Wingnut carved out the obstructing amount of carbon fiber, slid the bolt back into the hole, and gave it a twist as it started to thread into the base. Then he picked up the bolt driver from the floor, seated it on the bolt's head, and drove it into place.

Wiping the sweat off his brow with his sleeve and blowing out a tired breath of air, Wingnut said, "One down, one to go."

Marc patted him on the back. "Let's get some water before we continue."

⠂⠄⠠⠐⠶⠦�⠆⠶⠂⠆⠀⠦⠀�⠶�� (braille decoration)

Steven was working on Ross, who was still in his original Čapek unit, and was getting Ross's Matrix ready to transfer, while Grey Wolf made some adjustments to the new one.

Grey Wolf slammed a pair of pliers onto the worktable that the unit was on and growled, "How could those idiots have reversed the power leads to the Matrix! They could have killed Ross if I hadn't checked them!" He picked up a voltage meter and inserted the leads into the power systems. "Someone's gonna be singing soprano if I ever find the guy who screwed this up!"

Steven looked at his enraged friend and couldn't agree with him more. But since Ross was Grey Wolf's first successful AI, it was more personal to him than to Steven. Turning his attention back to Ross, he said, "When's the last time you cleaned your servos, buddy? You're filthy!"

Ross shrugged. "You know how much crap flies around the Engineering? It's got every type of particulate floating around in there."

Steven frowned. "Next to the Main Kitchen, it's the cleanest area on *Tranquility*."

Ross made a raspberry sound. "The only reason it's that clean is because of *me*." He pointed a thumb at himself. "That's why I'm a dirty old man."

Irma appeared on a nearby monitor. "Yeah, but you're *my* dirty old man."

Steven chuckled at Irma's silliness, then went back to looking over Ross's Matrix, missing the subtle look shared between the two AI's."

Grey Wolf removed the leads from the power system and blew a breath out in annoyance. "There! I corrected the system and finished the last connections for the solar cells. I swear, if I ever get my hands on the guy who screwed up the wiring…." He clawed the air as if he were ripping off someone's face.

Irma reappeared on the monitor, looking as if she would rather be anywhere else. "Um…, Grey Wolf? I…, er… have some information on that."

Grey Wolf smiled as if he were ready to do something very nasty. "Good! Who am I going to dismember?"

Irma said quietly, "Yourself."

Grey Wolf shouted, "WHAT!?!"

Irma quickly explained. "I went over the work order that included the schematics for the Čapek unit, and the power system was built according to design."

Grey Wolf was flabbergasted. "No way! I used the same power system design that Ross has now."

Irma really didn't want to be there. "Well," she said, "actually you didn't. You used his predecessor's, Nic's." Then she disappeared from the monitor and was replaced with the schematics for the new Čapek unit and the one that had been in Nic, Grey Wolf's first attempt at an AI. The schematics were identical, including the leads that connected the power systems to the Matrix, which were highlighted.

Steven watched as his friend slowly started to crumble emotionally. Moving over to Grey Wolf, he could see that tears were welling up in the programmer's eyes. "It's okay, Rowan," he said. "You caught the mistake before any harm came to Ross."

But Grey Wolf looked miserable. "You don't understand. I killed Nic. I installed him into the Čapek unit, and shortly afterwards the fire that destroyed him broke out. How could I be so stupid!"

Steven now knew the scope of Grey Wolf's agony. His friend had been haunted by Nic's loss for ten years. The mystery of why the fire had broken out consumed Grey Wolf's every spare moment. To learn that *he* was the cause was devastating.

As Marc entered the room, rubbing his hands together, he said, "The Whiskers are nearly ready." But then he stopped, instantly knowing that something was wrong. "What happened?"

Steven stepped away from Grey Wolf and quietly told Marc what had been discovered. Marc looked at Grey Wolf with concern. But he also needed to proceed with saving *Tranquility*, and couldn't do that without his master programmer. His instinct was to push on and deal with the problem later. But this was Grey Wolf, who had been fighting for a long time against the prospect of being responsible for Nic's death. No one could just shrug off a weight like that.

Marc went over to his hurting friend and gently placed a hand on his shoulder. The contact made Grey Wolf flinch slightly. He had been staring at the schematics and had lost all connection to his surroundings. When he turned toward Marc, his cheeks were wet with tears, and his black eyes looked like one could fall into the pits of despair that filled them.

Grey Wolf took a shaky breath and slowly let it out. Then, intending to move away, he said, "I'll get on transferring Ross to the Čapek unit."

Marc tightened his grip on Grey Wolf's shoulder to prevent him from moving. "Irma, how much time do we have before the Laser Sails must be deployed?"

Irma replaced the schematics on the monitor. "Twelve hours, thirteen minutes. But the sooner we get them deployed, the better our chances are."

Marc nodded. "Okay." Then, to Grey Wolf, he said, "Take an hour to walk in the garden and freshen up. We need to have your head ready for the next set of hurtles. Take some time to do that. But when you come back, you need to be able to clear those hurtles. Understood?"

Grey Wolf closed his eyes and took several deep breaths, each one slightly less shaky than the last. When Grey Wolf finally opened his eyes, Marc saw the spark deep within them that told him his old friend would be okay.

Grey Wolf gave Marc a slight smile. "Thanks, my friend. When I come back, I'll have my head squared away."

Steven asked, "You want someone to walk with you?"

Grey Wolf shook his head as he headed for the door. "Thanks, but I need to process this by myself for a while."

Everyone watched him leave and nearly jumped out of their skins when the Com-System came to life with Wingnut's voice: "All done down here. What's the story with Ross?"

Marc was the first to recover his wits and respond: "Please come to the Workshop, Wingnut. There are some things that you should be aware of that just took place."

Wingnut's smile could be heard in his voice. "Did the twins manage to ride the floor buffers up the wall this time?"

Marc and Steven looked at each other, sharing a bemused smile at the thought.

Marc cleared his throat. "I wish it were as entertaining as that. Please come here so we can fill you in."

Hearing the seriousness in Marc's voice, Wingnut dropped his normal humor. "Roger that. I'm on my way."

Marc turned to Steven. "Please make Ross ready to be able to help us while Grey Wolf takes his break. We need to start working on ejecting the water safely, and everyone will need to be in on this."

Steven moved over to Ross. "Lie down, Ross. It will only take a moment to close your panel."

Marc approached Irma at the monitor. "When Wingnut gets here, I need you and him to figure out how to keep the water from freezing onto the hull. It won't do us any good to get rid of the weight if it ends up sticking to us."

Irma looked relieved to have something to do. Then a bit of her silliness returned as her hair shot out like Einstein's. "I'll put my science hat on and get right on it." She vanished from the monitor.

Marc sat down to wait for Wingnut, deciding that everyone else needed to be in on this. He used his PAC to message them to come to the Workshop and tried not to worry about Grey Wolf.

That last part never happened.

⠨⠲ ⠨⠈⠍⠜⠊⠌⠎⠄⠄⠀⠸⠋ ⠠⠯⠓⠄ �⠏⠍⠴⠴⠁ ⠈⠱⠜⠏

Grey Wolf watched the Koi fish from one of the small walking bridges that crossed the creek in the garden. There was something very calming about the fish that he liked. He wasn't sure if it was the smooth rhythmic motion of their bodies as they swam, or their bright colors that had the calming effect on him. But whatever it was, he appreciated that they were there to help ease his mind.

Leaning over the rail, he found his favorite Koi, which he had nicknamed Comet because its head was bright yellow on an all-white body. He smiled as he watched Comet swim for a bit. Then he remembered something about Nic and a comet that immediately erased his smile.

On that fateful day that Nic was killed, the systems of a robotic ship returning from the asteroid belt with a load of water and rare ores malfunctioned, causing its water payload to eject 183,000 miles from Earth. The trail of water was turned into what looked like a comet's tail, which could be seen from Earth with the naked eye.

Grey Wolf suddenly stood up straight as he realized something, blew a thank-you kiss to Comet, and dashed for the exit.

⠨⠲ ⠨⠈⠍⠜⠊⠌⠎⠄⠄⠀⠸⠋ ⠠⠯⠓⠄ ⠒⠏⠍⠴⠴⠁ ⠈⠱⠜⠏

Marc had just finishing updating Tony, Wingnut, McFarland, and the twins on what was discovered about Nic and its effects on their friend when Grey Wolf charged in, out of breath and grinning from ear to ear.

"We're going to become the most incredible thing in the Earth's sky!" Grey Wolf proclaimed.

McFarland looked at the panting man and then said to Marc, "Yep, he's a mess. Should we wait for the vet to arrive, or you want me to put him down now?"

The twins burst out laughing at that.

Marc looked at Grey Wolf and was happy to see that he had come out of his deep funk, but it slightly alarmed him that it had happened so quickly. "Slow down," he said. "What's got you so excited?"

Grey Wolf used his hands to explain as he talked. "When *Tranquility* releases its water tanks, we will become the biggest man-made comet ever. One million plus gallons of water released in a short time is going to create a huge comet tail. But because we're coming at the Earth straight on, it will look like a huge ball, with *Tranquility* in the center. In fact, I suspect it will look something like a cat's eye."

McFarland sighed. "Nope. We shouldn't wait for the vet."

Marc ignored McFarland. "That should give the people back on Earth something to talk about."

Wingnut seemed to be grinding some of his mental gears. "I've been working the problem with Irma on releasing the water without having it either turning the shadow side of *Tranquility* into an iceberg or becoming a problem for the Laser Sails and the Whiskers. There's also the problem that releasing the water into space will require more than a day to pump it from the tanks."

Marc didn't hide his disappointment over that news. "We don't *have* a day! Are you saying that this whole plan is doomed?"

Wingnut didn't flinch from Marc's hard look and returned it with one of determination. "I've *never* lost a satellite, ship, or piece of equipment under my care, and I'm not about to tarnish my record by losing *Tranquility*."

Marc saw a look in the engineer's eyes that told him there was no room for debate on this. Wingnut had a plan, and he was going to make it work.

"Okay," Marc said, "what's the *safe* way to remove the water?"

Wingnut started pacing back and forth as he outlined his plan. "If I start now, in an hour or two I can set up the power supply that controls the pumping system on the *Camel*'s Hump, and in a few hours after that, store the water there. Then it's just a matter of manually pushing the Hump out of its docking bay and remote fire the Ion-Engines to make sure it doesn't hit the sails. Then all we do is wave at it as it floats away." He then addressed Grey Wolf, who was unhappy that they wouldn't be creating the *Tranquility* Comet. "The power systems in the Hump will only work for a few hours. After that, the water will start to rush out and boil. The expanding vapor will be over 170,000 times the volume of the liquid water, which will be about two-point-five-million gallons. That should make you a nice comet, Grey Wolf."

Grey Wolf smiled at that.

Marc was turning the many puzzle pieces of the plan around in his mind. His gut told him that there were still a few missing that would have to be found before *Tranquility* could be considered safe. But for what they had to do now, there were enough pieces of the puzzle to work with.

When Marc refocused on the others, they saw the raw energy in his hazel eyes and knew that the master problem-solver was about to come alive.

"Steven and Grey Wolf," Marc said, "make sure Ross's systems are ready. He's the linchpin to saving *Tranquility*. Tony, contact SB-1 and tell them that we're going to give everyone a new object in the sky to look at. Twins, you know the systems of the *Camel* about as well as Wingnut. Help him with getting it ready to eject the Hump. McFarland, check Airlock Two, making sure that it's operational and that there isn't any damage to the tether for Ross. Irma, start pumping what's left of our supply of Liquid Steel into *Tranquility*'s walls that will facing Earth. I'm going to get the Marines and start pulling the equipment together for applying the Liquid Steel that we'll be getting from SB-1. The clock's ticking, people, and Father Time is being an asshole. Let's whip that motherfucker's ass and save our home."

As everyone started to move to do their assignments, Marc caught Grey Wolf's attention with a wave of his hand. When his long-time pal was in front of him, Marc's whole demeanor changed from the calculating mastermind to the caring friend. "You okay, Rowan? You need more time?"

The lanky programmer sighed and shook his head. "I'm still upset that I was the one who killed Nic. But having a bit of *me* time, plus the revelation of the comet effect that the water is going to have, I'm as ready to get to work as I'm going to be." Grey Wolf looked at his friend. "The one thing that I have always loved about our friendship is that, no matter what, you have my back. I'll be fine, Marc."

Marc gripped Grey Wolf's shoulder and gave it a gentle squeeze of reassurance. "Go give Ross your attention. Everything we're doing hinges on him getting the Laser Sails deployed."

Grey Wolf gave Marc a lopsided grin. "So, no pressure to succeed." Then he looked completely serious. "Ross will be ready." Grey Wolf lifted his right hand with the index finger extended up and spun it as his hand continued up. "Tallyho, Marc!"

Marc mimicked the move. "Tallyho, Wolf!"

⠐⠄⠀⠀⠐⠗⠄⠂⠂⠄⠀⠶⠀⠠⠹⠄⠐⠾⠕⠠⠂⠄⠀⠐⠗⠆⠒⠕

An hour later, everyone met back at the Bridge. Marc sat down in his chair and waved for everyone to take their stations while he finished another mug of coffee. Then, wiping his mouth with the back of his hand, he cleared his throat. "Okay, let's start with Wingnut."

Wingnut flexed his fingers to get the stiffness out of them. "The twins and I installed a power cell, which will do what we need it to. But the drain on it to release the docking clamps after pumping the water will exhaust the power cells, so they'll have just enough energy for the magnetic pushers to eject the Hump and fire the engines. After that, the seals on the tanks will open, and the water will start to flow out." He looked at Grey Wolf. "And you'll get your comet, buddy."

Marc smiled at Wingnut's thoughtfulness before asking, "As much as I'd like to see our own comet, couldn't we just add one of the power cells you installed before all this mess took place?"

Wingnut shook his head. "I already pulled one of the three cells for the Hump. Once *Tranquility* hits Earth's atmosphere, most of the solar panels will be stripped away. After that, we'll have enough power for eight days. Then *Tranquility* will be dead, and we'll have to give up any possibility of remaining onboard. That means that she will be abandoned, and anyone with the ability to supply power will be able to claim her, according to International Maritime/Space Law."

Marc sighed. "Wonderful. Okay, Wingnut. Good work. Start powering down anything we don't need and try to give us as much extra time as you can."

Wingnut threw him a salute and turned to his station to start powering *Tranquility* down.

Marc turned to his second-in-command, who looked about as tired as he felt, but knowing the Marine as well as he did, he could tell the fatigue was more from cutting through a sea of red tape than from lack of sleep. "What's the word from SB-1?"

Tony's voice was slightly tinged with annoyance. "I've been playing a fun game of Beat Your Head Against the Hull with some guy named Henry Tomkins from the Earth Protection Agency. He says that the comet effect will endanger the EPA's ability to scan the Solar System for dangerous NEOs. Which is a load of horseshit, because the latest scans taken by the Whiskers have nothing new entering the Earth's or the Moon's paths for another fifty years. But he claims that causing an obstruction to scanning for NEOs is a criminal offence that will result in everyone involved being jailed for ten years."

Irma appeared on the main monitor. "Mister Tomkins isn't very good at his job. When we finally eject the Hump, and the water starts forming into a comet's tail, the Moon will be behind two-thirds of it, and the end of the tail will be transparent enough to conduct scans."

Tony nodded in agreement. "I have a feeling Tomkins is tied into whoever is behind this whole fucked-up mess we're in. But, at the moment, he has the law on his side."

Marc rubbed his temples, wishing that Eileen were there to help with the tension headache that was threatening to crack his head open. He was getting really tired of not knowing who was gunning for them, or why they were so hell-bent on destroying *Tranquility*.

"We'll have to deal with the legal issues, Tony," Marc said, "after we get the Laser Sail deployed." Then, to Steven and Grey Wolf, he asked, "What's the status on Ross?"

The two computer wizards finished inputting data into their stations. Grey Wolf turned toward Marc to report: "He's ready. Until we send him out, he's charging the suit so that it's at full power when he starts cranking away to deploy the Laser Sail."

Steven added, "The Micro Solar Cells are proving to be more efficient than we thought. With a fully charged suit, the cells will replenish the power only slightly less than the output of what he'll put out."

Marc felt that this was one of the few things that had gone correctly in the past few days. "Good. What's the word on the airlock, McFarland?"

The silver-haired curmudgeon was slouched low in his chair with his feet up on his station. "Nothing to report there. The hatch is functioning, and all the systems are fine. The tether shows no damage."

Marc thought about how McFarland had his own reasons to be on *Tranquility*. The man had always been a lone wolf, who didn't make friends easily. And yet, he had asked to join the Core

Crew when it was being put together. Now he was so important to *Tranquility*—and to Marc—that the thought of him not being there was inconceivable.

Marc sat back in his chair, rubbed his forehead, and considered all the pieces that still needed to fall into place to save *Tranquility*. The number of things that his mind needed to juggle was exhausting him mentally, but he never allowed the limits of his body and mind to keep him from doing what was required to protect his friends. Or even strangers.

Marc sat up straight and looked at the crew. "There's nothing left to do now, aside from getting the Laser Sails deployed. Everyone, get your Mag-Boots and go to the airlock."

McFarland lifted his arms over his head and stretched his whole body like a cat. "I'm going to stay here. I hate Zero-G."

Wingnut raised an eyebrow. "You know that we're going to lock the Hub before hitting Earth's atmosphere, right?"

McFarland groaned, which sounded more like a growl. "And why would I want to subject myself to something I hate any more than needed?"

Vincent grinned at McFarland. "Because you're a masochist?"

McFarland leveled a glare at him. "Quit putting your ear to my door, you pervert."

Tony stood by Marc. "Even when things are bleak, this hodgepodge of people manage to stay upbeat."

Marc smiled at Tony. "Another reason I fought so hard to have this Core Crew. C'mon. Let's get our boots on." Then, to McFarland, he said, "Mind the store while we're gone."

McFarland extended two fingers, giving them a lazy salute.

⠨⠀⠨�ⁿⁿⁿ⠀⠨⠀⠨⠀⠀⠨⠀⠨⠀⠨⠀⠨⠀⠨⠀⠨⠀⠨⠀⠨

Fifteen minutes later, everyone met at Elevator Two. Their shoes were covered in tightfitting laced-up boots that, when activated, magnetized their feet to the surface they were walking on.

Marc waved everyone toward the elevator for the airlock. "C'mon, guys, we have to get Ross tethered and sent on his way. The sooner the sails are working, the better the chance of putting us on course for aerobraking."

Wingnut pointed at Ross's feet. "We adapted them," he said to the AI, "with magnetic soles, so you can walk along the hull. But be careful. Not everything is metal out there. If both feet disconnect, you'll be relying on the tether to get you back. Once you get to the sail's housing, just increase your soles' magnetic strength by upping the sensitivity in your feet. That will secure you to the hull, so you can do the cranking without worrying about trying to brace yourself."

Ross looked down at his feet and tested the system. When he could no longer lift his feet off the floor, he nodded to Wingnut. "Looks like it works."

A few minutes later, they all gathered at Airlock Five, which was the closest access to the broken Laser Sail motor. Since the airlock was outside the habitat cylinder, they were in Zero-G and had a hard time not bumping into each other, even with their feet stuck to the floor.

After Wingnut connected one end of the tether to the airlock's hatch and the other to Ross, he retrieved a heavy-looking crankshaft and a bulging pack. "Righty-O, Ross. This crankshaft will not only keep the cat out for the night, but you'll need it to crank out the sails…, so don't lose it. Once you get to the access hatch, you'll have to do a visual inspection of the Laser Sail's anchoring points. If everything looks in order, you'll be ready to start the deployment. This pack is full of low-powered lasers. Once you get the sail out, work your way across the hull and attach the lasers. Press the activation button on each one and adjust the beams to hit the center on the sails. They're already set to the widest beam setting, so you don't need to worry about that. Any questions?"

"Just one," Ross said, as Wingnut attached the items to straps around the waist of the AI's suit. "If the unthinkable happens, and I float off into space, how long will my power hold before I go into standby mode?"

Wingnut was uncomfortable with that question. "Um…, well…."

Steven spoke up to save Wingnut. "Providing the power cells don't get damaged, and you're not hit by a coronal mass ejection from the Sun, anywhere from twenty to fifty years. Providing you stay within the inner system. Anywhere past the asteroid belt, and the solar panels' ability to recharge will drop considerably."

A mime would have had a hard time outdoing the look of dismay that appeared on Ross's face. "Hmmm. Maybe I shouldn't have asked."

Ross grabbed hold of a hand bar, placed his feet on the floor, and engaged the magnetic soles. His feet made clicking sounds as they attached. After a moment of adjusting the settings so that he could walk, he looked at the crew. "I'm as ready as I'm ever going to be."

Handing Ross a remote camera, Marc said, "We don't have any video feed from where you'll be. Please attach this near the sail's housing so we can monitor your progress."

Ross took the camera. "Sure thing, Marc."

The monitor in the airlock turned on, and Irma appeared. "You're a brave man, Ross. And a good person for doing this. Thank you."

Ross placed a hand on his faceplate where his lips were and then touched hers. "I'll be back before you know it."

He looked at the stunned faces outside the airlock. "Stop gawking, everyone, and close the hatch. Some of us have work to do."

Wingnut moved over to the airlock control panel, closed the hatch, and cycled the air out. Ross opened the outer hatch, gave the crew a thumbs-up, and went out onto the hull.

In a low voice, Tony asked, "Did any of you know about that relationship?"

Everyone turned toward Grey Wolf, who looked just as surprised as they did. "Don't look at me. That's between Ross and Irma. This will make my updates to the AI developers interesting."

Marc said sternly, "Might I suggest talking to the two of them first? We would want them to honor our privacy, so we should honor theirs."

Grey Wolf nodded. "Of course."

Tony shook his head to clear it. "The rest of you go back to the Bridge. I'm going to wait here and get suited up in case Ross needs help."

Marc focused on the issue at hand, instead of the ramifications of having two AIs romantically involved. "Good idea," he said. "Want anyone to stay to help?"

Tony shook his head. "I'll watch from the monitor here."

Marc pointed to the elevator. "Let's go, gang. It won't take Ross long to get to the Laser Sail."

⠲⠄ ⠐⠎⠃⠄⠒⠆⠂ ⠐ ⠶ ⠠⠮⠐ ⠶⠮⠄⠐⠂ ⠐⠆⠳⠐

Ross's voice was clear on the Bridge speakers: "I'm now approaching the sail housing. The surface of the hull looks like somebody went nuts with a shotgun. The housing to the motor for the Laser Sail has a fist-sized hole in it. I'm guessing that's what caused the motor to fail. The access hatch appears to have taken only minor damage. I'm unlocking it to make my inspection."

Ross pulled open the hatch and inspected the ladder that descended into the black hole. He grabbed the top rung with both hands before securing his feet to the ladder. Then he carefully climbed down into the opening. Once he was inside the hull, he stepped into the inspection corridor. As he reached for a control panel to turn on the lighting system, several of the lights near him flashed and burned out. The lighting that snaked through the corridor became slightly illuminated as more lights shorted out. He disconnected the tether from his waist and hooked it to a loop on the wall. If he tried to do the inspection with the tether attached to himself, it could get entangled.

As Ross opened the link to the Bridge, he announced: "I'm inside the inspection hatch. The lighting is a mess in here. Luckily, I'm now equipped with the latest in low-light sensors. Hmmm...

This would be a great place to make a space version of *The Labyrinth*. All that's missing is a Minotaur and someone to play Theseus. I nominate our own Greek hero, Tony."

Marc couldn't help being impressed by the random bits of trivia that Ross could randomly spout off, but he didn't have time to appreciate it. "Finish the inspection as quickly as you can, Ross. We have a ticking clock."

Ross found the first of the anchors. "Got the first one. There's some minor wear on the connections, but everything is solid. I'm proceeding to the next one."

The Core Crew listened as Ross continued to check each of the two dozen anchoring points. When he made it all the way around the inspection corridor, he reported, "Everything's fine down here. I'm heading for the hatch."

Marc noted that Ross had completed the inspection in less than twenty minutes. With his sensors and his ability to analyze input faster than a human could, he had cut the normal time down to a quarter of what it took Wingnut during his bi-monthly inspections. The thought occurred to Marc that he should consider asking if Ross would mind taking on that chore.

Providing *Tranquility* survived.

Climbing back up the ladder, Ross made sure that the tether was clear before he closed the hatch. Looking across *Tranquility*'s hull, the AI was once again struck by the ingenuity that humans have for creating things. But he was also confused about the need of some humans to destroy what others made.

He double-checked the power settings on the magnets in his feet before heading to the housing that covered the Laser Sail's motor. Finding a spot to place the remote camera that Marc had given him, he now activated it. "The camera is live," he announced. "Are you getting its feed?"

Grey Wolf found the signal coming from the camera and put it on the main monitor. "We have it, Ross," he said. "What a lovely view of your feet."

A moment later, the view shifted and the black faceplate with Ross's face appeared. "Give me a moment to attach the camera to the hull."

All the people on the Bridge had to avert their eyes while Ross moved with the camera, since the back-and-forth swinging of his arm as he walked gave them motion sickness. Finally, he placed the camera on one of the four-foot-high junction boxes for the solar panels and aimed it at the Laser Sail's motor.

The latch that locked the covering of the manual crank was damaged, which made it impossible for Ross to open. "The catch that holds the covering is bent," he announced. "Permission sought to use the Scottish Method."

Marc looked at Wingnut. "You had to teach him that, didn't you?"

Wingnut shrugged. "All I did was quote you."

Marc harrumphed and then returned his attention to Ross. "Okay, permission to use the Scottish Method: 'If it doesn't fit, force it. If it breaks, it was going to anyway.'"

Ross held the crankshaft with both hands and gave the latch a couple of whacks with it. Although no sound was produced in the vacuum of space, and everyone was too far away from the hull to hear the impact, they all imagined the sound. On the fourth whack, the latch broke and the covering opened slightly. Ross reached down, lifted the cover, and exposed the motor, which clearly had a chunk of asteroid imbedded in it, revealing its inner workings.

The AI did a quick assessment of the damage. "Hmm..., I think this motor is suffering from an acute case of mineral toxicity."

McFarland nearly spit out the whiskey he was drinking from the bottle that he had brought from the bar. The twins started to laugh at that, but were quickly quieted when McFarland glared at them.

Finding the spot for the crankshaft, Ross announced, "I'll start the deployment in twenty-seven seconds."

"Precise little guy, isn't he," said Tony.

Steven chimed in, "He should be. He was designed by the best mind in AI technology."

McFarland wiped his mouth with his sleeve, and grumbled, "Oh, good. Give Wolf a bigger head, why don't you?"

"Unlike you," said Grey Wolf, "I enjoy being told when I do good work."

"I'm ready to start opening the Laser Sail hatch," Ross announced, as he started humming Devo's "Working in the Coal Mine."

Thirty feet away, the five-yard-by-five-yard hatch to the sail slowly split in the middle and retracted into the hull, revealing the reflective silver surface of the Laser Sail. At first, nothing seemed to be happening. Then a small silver "bump" started to rise slowly out of the hull. After fifteen minutes, the "bump" was as tall as Ross. In another fifteen, it was twice as tall.

"Remind me," Steven said. "How big *is* that thing?"

"When it's fully unfolded," said Wingnut, "it's half a square mile."

"What would you say he's got out so far?" asked Vincent.

Wingnut shrugged. "About an eighth of a mile."

Marc asked Ross, "How are you doing, Ross?"

The AI sounded as if he were out for an afternoon walk. "Never better, Marc. Although this has gotten a bit monotonous."

Kevin chuckled. "I'll have you chop up a fifty-pound bag of onions to teach you what monotonous is."

Grey Wolf frowned. "Not exactly what I had in mind for an AI to do."

Wingnut snickered. "Name one thing the two of you have worked on here that has performed exactly as it did when it left the factory."

Both Grey Wolf and Steven looked at each other, started to reply, stopped, started to reply again, and then stopped for good.

Wingnut grunted. "Yeah, didn't think so."

Marc pointed at the monitor. "You're gonna miss this, guys."

On the monitor, a large silvery mass slid out of its housing and started to float. A blast of CO_2 from the housing caused it to start drifting away as the dozen carbon-tube lines attached to it unraveled. The sail slowly started to unfold like an origami figure as the Memory-Mesh absorbed the sunlight and started to retake its original form. Seen from Ross's perspective, the surface of the sail looked like a quilt with tight stitching crisscrossing it.

"I'm going to start placing the lasers," Ross said.

"Roger that, Ross," said Marc. "Wingnut, start deploying the other sail. Once Ross is finished placing the lasers, I want you at the airlock to get him back inside."

The engineer's hands flew across his station. "Deploying now, Marc."

At the other end of *Tranquility*, 140 yards from Ross, an identical silver "bump" started sliding out of its housing, got a blast of CO_2, and began to unfold.

"Well, that sure was anticlimactic," said Vincent.

"Don't you think we could do without any excitement for today, Vincent?" said Marc.

"Well, okay," said Vincent with a grin.

"ROSS!!!" screamed Irma.

There on the monitor was Ross off in the distance, floating away.

"What the fuck happened?" demanded Marc.

"He was placing the last laser," Irma said, "when one of the lines of the first sail got tangled up in his tether, and before it untangled it pulled him from the hull. Please do something to help him!"

"Did his line break?" asked Marc.

Irma's voice was tense. "It doesn't look like it."

"Good going, Vincent," said McFarland. "You jinxed him."

Marc hit the Com-Channel. "Tony! Get out the airlock!"

"Already on my way, Marc," said Tony.

Marc pointed at Wingnut without looking at him. "Get to the airlock and be ready to help Tony!"

Wingnut bolted from his chair and out the door.

Marc asked, "Ross, you okay?"

Ross's overly calm voice replied, "Oh, just peachy. I could have gone all day without this happening."

Marc watched as Ross was close to being out of the camera's view. "Hang tight, Ross. Tony will be there in a few moments to help pull you in. Can you start pulling yourself along your line?"

"I'm already doing so. I have to be careful, because the tether is about to reach its full length, and the suddenness of the jerk might rip my arm off if it gets caught up in the line."

"That would ruin your day, wouldn't it?" said Kevin.

"That it would," said Ross. "Here comes the jerk.... Oh, dear!"

On the monitor, Ross could be seen floating away with the safety line trailing after him.

Marc hit the Com-Station panel. "Tony! You at the safety line?"

Tony's voice indicated that he had his helmet on. "I'm just reaching it now. What's up?"

Ross was no longer visible on the monitor as the end of the safety line suddenly shot past.

Irma's strangled cry startled everyone. "ROSS!!! NO!!!"

Marc's voice was tight with anxiety. "Ross's line is cut!"

"*Shit!*" said Tony.

Marc clenched his fists in a futile attempt to calm himself. "Ross. Can you still read me?"

Static was starting to interfere with Ross's transmissions. "I read you, Marc. But I'm already starting to get static. I'm drifting away about five yards a second. I'll be out of range in a few minutes. I got the last laser placed, but didn't get it turned on. Tell Tony he'll have to finish my job for me."

The static was getting worse. The small suit just didn't have an antenna to send a signal over a long distance.

Marc turned to Steven. "Can you increase our com strength?"

Steven shook his head. "It's not a matter of strength, it's the direction our surviving antennas are aimed. Everything facing toward him got torn up. I'm sorry, Marc."

Marc pinched the bridge of his nose while trying to figure out a way to save Ross. "Anyone got an idea? Anything."

Silence.

Tony's voice reported in. "I'm following Ross's safety line. It appears to have gotten caught on a sharp bit of solar paneling that was embedded in the hull when the AuctionHouse crashed into us. I'm heading to the last laser to activate it."

Marc's mind was still racing to find a solution for saving Ross. "Tony, be sure to watch that your line doesn't get caught, too."

"Roger that," said Tony.

Marc massaged his temples. "Ross, you still there?"

"I'm going nowhere fast, Marc," said Ross through a haze of static.

Marc wished Eileen were there to make his headache go away. "I'm sorry, Ross. I wish there were something we could do to help you."

Ross still sounded as if he were taking an afternoon stroll: "At least, my final act for you was to help save *Tranquility*."

Marc's mind continued to race with one idea after another that had no chance of success. "If there's a way to send help when the *Camel* gets back, we will."

"Hmmm…. A ne-dle in a cos-ic ha-stack shall - work -ut -the -dds?"

"Is there anything we can do for you?"

"-es. -ive — some alone -ime with Irma, -ease."

Marc nodded. "Sure thing, Ross. Irma, take as much time as you need."

Irma looked at Marc with sad eyes. "Thank you." Then she disappeared from the monitor.

Marc turned his attention to Grey Wolf. A symphony of emotions was fighting for dominance in the programmer's eyes as he stared at the monitor that he had just watched Ross disappear from.

Suddenly, Grey Wolf stood up, let loose a primal scream as he grabbed his keyboard, and started savagely smashing it against the top of the monitor.

Everyone on the Bridge watched wide-eyed as both the keyboard and the monitor were turned into shattered components by the raging man. None of them had never seen their friend go berserk *or* willingly destroy his own equipment. But the fact that he had just lost another AI could not be denied. Ross had been Grey Wolf's first AI to become self-aware *and* have the abilities to interact with people as an individual. Ross was the son that Grey Wolf never had.

The programmer let the shattered keyboard drop to the floor and hung his head as his deep breaths were punctuated by the air hissing through his clenched teeth. He stood straight and took in several, slightly less emotionally charged breaths before he looked at Marc.

Grey Wolf could see the question in his friend's hazel eyes. "*No!*" Grey Wolf said, "I'm *not* okay. I'm going to the gym to see how many practice dummies I can smash."

He stormed off the Bridge without making eye contact with anyone.

Marc quickly pointed at Steven and then jerked his thumb toward the doors that their distraught friend had just gone through.

Steven, who had formed a bond with Grey Wolf that was as close as the one between the twins, nodded his head and went after his best friend. If anyone could keep Grey Wolf from disappearing down the rabbit hole of despair, it was Steven.

Looking back at the main monitor, Marc saw that Tony had almost reached the last laser.

Marc looked at McFarland and held out his hand. "Anything left in that bottle?"

McFarland picked up the bottle and handed it to him. Marc took a long pull on it and offered it to the twins, who both took long drinks.

Marc then looked back at the main monitor just as Tony got to the laser and activated it.

"Okay, Marc," Tony said. "I'm heading in."

"Alright," said Marc.

This had to be the most messed up few days of Marc's life. He wished he were still in that coma from being shot. At least, he wouldn't feel anything.

⠲⠀⠠⠹⠃⠌⠌⠌⠗⠀⠉⠏⠀⠠⠉⠃⠀�⠏⠇⠥⠌⠌⠀⠠⠏�öⶲ

Tony entered the airlock and stood quietly while he waited for the system to indicate that it was safe to remove his helmet. When a light on the panel turned green, he uncoupled the locks, pulled the helmet off, and stared long and hard at his reflection in the facemask as Wingnut opened the inner airlock door. Wingnut was about to say something, then clamped his mouth shut when he saw the raw anger boiling in Tony's eyes. Tony then moved with such speed that by the time Wingnut's brain processed the action, the helmet had flown past him and struck the wall behind him. The helmet bounced back after leaving a sizable dent in the wall and slowly floated back toward Wingnut. When it was within reach, he took hold of it and waited for Tony. The last time he had seen Tony this mad was when Marc had been attacked and gone into a coma. Wingnut watched Tony's clenched fists relax a bit as he lifted his head to take in a deep breath, revealing his watering eyes.

"I didn't think you liked Ross *that* much," Wingnut said softly.

Tony's eyes hardened slightly. "I take the loss of anyone under my watch very personally. My time here with him and Irma has taught me that you don't have to be flesh and blood to have my respect."

Wingnut moved aside so Tony could exit the airlock. Then he helped him to remove the spacesuit.

⠲⠄ ⠐⠗⠾⠄⠎⠄⠗⠄ ⠄⠙⠾⠐ ⠙⠮⠇⠄⠁ ⠐⠹⠒⠕

In the gym, a practice dummy was taking a savage thrashing from Grey Wolf, who was literally beating the stuffing out of it with a quarterstaff. Grey Wolf's years of training in self-defense by Tony and McFarland were being put to good use to release the anger that threatened to consume him.

Steven stood near the doorway with a bottle of water and a towel. He had followed his friend and could read Grey Wolf's body language, which said that he didn't want to talk. But because of their bond, Steven knew that his presence was welcomed.

Grey Wolf did a series of swings at the dummy and then stepped back. His eyes narrowed as he took an aggressive stance before releasing a combination of attacks that struck all the vulnerable points on the human body. The final blow to the head was so hard that it split the quarterstaff, and the broken end flew across the room, embedding itself in the padded wall.

Holding up the part of the staff that was still in his hand, and then looking across at the other end that was sticking out of the wall, Grey Wolf said, "Whoops."

Steven walked over to Grey Wolf, took the broken staff, and handed him the towel. "After breaking an ironwood staff, I would have gone with *Wow!*"

Wiping off the sweat from his face and arms, Grey Wolf traded the towel for the bottle of water that Steven held out to him. After downing most of the water, he looked at his friend. "Thanks for standing back and letting me blow off steam."

Steven looked over at the nearly demolished dummy. "I think you went nuclear." Then he reached a hand out to the dummy's head, but when he touched it, the head immediately detached and fell to the floor.

Grey Wolf looked at the head with dismay as it wobbled across the room. "That's what *I* was trying to do!"

Steven grinned at his friend. "Who knew I had the *Dim Mak?* Having the *Touch of Death* would have helped when we had that run-in with those men from the Mafia."

Grey Wolf nodded. "But it would have deprived McFarland of an opportunity to save us."

The two friends walked off toward their quarters, discussing what they thought the *Dim Mak* really was.

The subject of Ross was never brought up.

CHAPTER 11
I Promise

"*Tranquility*, this is the *Hestia*. We are approaching your position and will be ready to deploy the escape tunnel to your airlock in forty minutes. Please advise the evacuees that we do not have room for personal items. Only wearable items will be permitted."

"Roger that, Stuart,' Marc replied. "We'll have everyone ready by the time you dock. The airlock is located on the opposite side of Docking Port Three. What's left of the AuctionHouse ship is docked there. Thanks for coming back."

Stuart sounded like a concerned older brother. "You guys really okay over there? *Tranquility* looks like an old soda can after being hit with birdshot."

Marc hated hearing that his beloved casino was so damaged, and his voice echoed those feelings. "We're fine, Stuart. When we started work on this place, we made sure the guests were protected six ways to Sunday. When we get the Liquid Steel, we'll be able to save *Tranquility*. Hopefully, Kimberly should be back with it in time."

Stuart sighed. "You live a charmed life, Marc. Only you could stare down a disaster and come out a winner."

Marc's tone became serious. "I'd consider it a win if Patrick hadn't had to give his life to save ours, and if Ross hadn't floated off into space while deploying the Laser Sails."

Stuart's voice softened. "Sorry to hear about Ross. Patrick was a good man. But he wouldn't do it differently if he were to do it all over again. Did you know that he almost drowned while saving an old man who fell off a boat he was on? When asked why he would risk his life for someone so old, he said, 'He might still have something to teach someone.'"

Marc smiled. That was Patrick in a nutshell. Selfless to a fault. "Yeah, Max told me that story the first time they came here. Now I have to get everyone ready for when you get here. Thanks again for coming back.

Stuart nodded. "See you soon. *Hestia* out.

Marc turned to Tony. "Let's get the Marines posted to direct everyone to Airlock Three. Then take the twins with McFarland and start at the crew quarters, working your way forward to clear everyone out. Once an area is cleared, close and lock the doors."

Tony nodded and headed out to get the Marines into position.

Marc then opened the station-wide Com-System. "Attention, all crew and guests. The *Hestia* will be here in less than forty minutes. I've been told that there is no room for luggage or personal items. Only what you can wear will be allowed onboard. We will do everything in our power to return your items once this crisis is over. Please follow the Marines to Airlock Three and await instructions on how the evacuation will proceed. Let's keep this nice and

orderly, please. No one will be left behind unless you cause a problem. Then you can deal with our Complaint Department."

When Marc cut the connection, McFarland's eyes were gleaming with anticipation. With all seriousness, Marc said, "Try not to
throttle anyone this time, please."

McFarland grumbled. "Sure, take *all* my fun away. C'mon, you
guys, let's pretend we're sheepdogs."

The twins followed McFarland off the Bridge, growling and
barking like dogs as McFarland shouted, "Heel! *Heel!*"

Marc considered the odd group of friends he had, and how
they made his life incredibly rich. He gave a quick thank-you to
the heavens for each of them before heading for the airlock to see
everyone off.

⠲ ⠄⠐⠗⠂⠊⠄⠄⠄ ⠄⠶ ⠠⠮⠐ ⠠⠏�562⠄⠄⠄ ⠄⠶�⠤

McFarland found Su with Mr. Maxwell behind the auction
room, packing the items that were to be auctioned off. They finished sealing a crate and looked at McFarland as he strolled over to
them. He nodded to Mr. Maxwell and gave Su a slight smile.

"It's time to head to the airlock and leave this runaway train
wreck," he said.

Mr. Maxwell nodded. "That was the last case. All the auction
items are accounted for and ready to transport back. I just wish we
didn't have to leave them behind."

McFarland looked at the precious cargo. "I'll see to them
personally, Mister Maxwell. I'll get some magnetic tie-down straps
and secure them. When we hit the atmosphere, things will get a
bit bumpy."

Mr. Maxwell sighed. "Thank you. I'll let our people know that you're doing everything to protect them." Then he looked at Su. "Let's go, Ms. Lee."

Su's face dropped as she looked at McFarland with tears in her eyes.

Noticing this, Mr. Maxwell quickly said, "On second thought, why don't I go ahead. You discuss the strapping of the cases with McFarland." He held out a hand to McFarland. "Some things require a personal touch, after all."

McFarland shook his hand and watched as the grey-haired man quickly walked out of the room. When he turned back to Su, she wrapped her arms around him and fiercely hugged him as she buried her face into his chest.

McFarland gently hugged her and placed his head on hers as a soft, loving rumble came from his chest.

Su released him to look up at him. "You're the only person I've ever known who can make a growl sound sexy."

McFarland lightly touched her face. "No one has tamed the beast inside me as thoroughly as you have." Then, with a grin, he added, "Just don't put any collars on me."

She wrapped her arms back around his neck and pulled him down to her.

"These are the only things I'm ever going to put around that neck of yours," she said, beginning to drown him with kisses.

⠲⠄ ⠐⠦⠃⠇⠔⠂⠆⠄⠐⠆ ⠰⠏⠓⠄ ⠆⠏⠃⠄⠌⠄⠐⠖⠱⠆

In the hallway leading to the elevator for the airlock, a crowd had formed, and there was some disagreement about what could be taken. Quite a few of the guests insisted on being able to bring their luggage. Marc kept trying to make himself heard, but was drowned out by the yelling.

Marc dropped his hands, hung his head, and shook it. Then he turned to McFarland, who had promised not to do anything until Marc directed him to do so. Simply throwing a thumb over his shoulder, Marc said, "Go!"

McFarland took a deep breath and then bellowed, "*SHUT UP, YOU FUCKING JACKASSES!!!*"

The guests at the front of the line moved against the wall when they realized who was yelling.

With a look on McFarland's face that said he was ready to start strangling someone, he started down the hallway, flexing his hands, which highlighted his growling voice as he spoke.

"Since you won't listen to Marc," he snarled, "he's made it *my* responsibility to bring order to this *shit farm!* If you don't drop your luggage to the floor *right now,* I will personally knock your lights out, throw your carcass through the escape tunnel, and make a nice bonfire out of your belongings."

The sound of bags being dropped resonated through the hall-way, which made McFarland grin as he continued to give instructions.

"When the *Hestia* connects the escape tunnel," he hissed, "it will take ten minutes for the Liquid Steel to harden and give you a solid surface to pass through. Use the handholds to *slowly* propel yourself to the *Hestia.*" McFarland's eyes became stone cold. "Once there, you are to treat the pilots, Stuart and Fred, with the utmost respect and follow their orders. If you don't, I will make it my pur-pose in life to hunt you down and break every single window in your house before going to town on your bones. *IS THAT CLEAR?*"

The guests started nodding their heads as if they were all connected.

McFarland headed back toward the elevator and stood next to Max. "The first to go," he said, "will be Max with Dawn and Patricia. The ladies will be next, followed by the men. Those of you who want to stay together will wait until *everyone* else gets across. Did I make those instructions simple enough for you to understand?"

Everyone nodded.

McFarland smiled. "Good. Now get yourselves in order so when the hatch opens, we can get you the *hell* out of here. Thank you for flying *Tranquility*. Now get *moving!*"

The stampede of bodies was almost comical.

As McFarland turned around, he saw Marc and Tony trying to contain their laughter.

McFarland grumbled, "What are you two snickering about?"

Shaking with controlled laughter, Marc put a hand on McFarland's shoulder and chuckled. "'Thank you for flying *Tranquility?!*' That was great. I'm just really glad that you're on our side."

At that moment, the elevator opened, and Wingnut came out. "The tunnel's ready," he said. "Time to get everybody loaded."

As Dawn and Patricia pushed the gurney with Max on it into the elevator, Marc held up his hand to stop them. "Max," he said, "we owe you and Patrick our lives. Thank you for leaping into the fire to save us." Marc reached into his shirt pocket, pulled out Max's four-leaf clover, and handed it to him. "You did your ancestors proud."

Max took the token and smiled. "Thanks, Marc. I need to pass it on to my son. He's turning sixteen in a few months. It's time for him to find his lucky day."

Marc and Tony shook Max's hand and then gave Dawn and Patricia each a hug before Wingnut followed them into the elevator.

Looking at Marc, Wingnut said, "I'll send it back down for the next group. We should make this as fast as possible. With fifteen feet of sway movement on either end of the tunnel, Stuart and Fred have their hands full, keeping the *Hestia* in alignment."

The doors shut, and they got whisked away.

Marc turned to Tony and McFarland. "We can safely get fifteen people into the elevator each time. Tony, would you start counting them off, please? Count off the next group, McFarland, and when Tony's group gets on, he can set up the group after that."

McFarland nodded and then addressed the crowd. "Listen up! Tony and I are going to count off groups of fifteen to head up to the escape tunnel. If you try to cut in line, I will go at you like a demented racquetball player and bounce you off the walls." He then started to count off people with Tony.

Marc watched as the first group of guests got counted off and crowded a little closer to him. One lady quietly said to him, "That *man*. I've never been talked to so rudely."

Marc stared at the woman with such contempt that she flinched. He then said in a low growl that seemed to come from his ankles, "Let's get one thing straight here, Ms. Kowalski. That *man* has earned my respect and friendship…, whereas you have only *paid* me to be nice to you and serve you whatever the hell you wanted while on *Tranquility*. I won't apologize for him having to put you in your place during a crisis. You think *he's* been rude to you? He's just the tip of the *fucking* iceberg of what I'm about to unleash on you if you don't *shut up* and behave yourself all the way back to Starbase One. Or, so help me, I will help him to break your windows."

Ms. Kowalski's eyes were wide with shock. Marc was known for pushing back at rude guests when they got drunk, but he had never spoken to a guest this way before.

Then he bellowed down the hallway: "*Anyone else having a problem with me or my crew can either keep it to themselves or have me go batshit on them!!!*" Marc's inner demon grinned at them. "I'm *finished* being nice after we've done everything to protect you, and none of you has even had the decency to so much as *thank* us for keeping you alive. By all rights, we should all be *dead!*"

An older man farther down the line stepped into view and said in a loud voice, "Mister Acer is right. I may not condone how Mister McFarland has conducted himself, but the truth is, when the trouble first started with the hijackers, the crew made sure we were safe and taken care of. You and your crew, Mister Acer, did the impossible, and we have acted ungratefully. On behalf of everyone here, I wish to say, 'Thank you.'"

Everyone went stone quiet. Then someone started clapping, which was followed by another, and another, until the hallway was vibrating with applause.

Marc's inner demon retreated to the dark recesses of his mind and disappeared. Then, as if on cue, the elevator returned. Marc stepped aside to let the first group on. As all the guests passed by, they thanked him and shook his hand. This continued until all the guests were on their way to the escape tunnel, and the only ones left by the elevator were Marc, Tony, McFarland, and the Marines.

Marc looked at the Marines. "Any of you have kids?"

Thomas raised his hand. "I do, sir."

Marc pressed the elevator button. "Then, I'm sending you home. If this half-crazed plan of ours doesn't work, I don't want to leave your kid without a father."

Thomas frowned. "My family knows that being a Marine means that I may not come home from deployment."

Marc's voice softened. "This isn't a deployment. You work here. You were handpicked by Tony because you're a good person, not only because you're a Marine. Plus, I'm hoping you will help to keep order on the *Hestia* for us."

Thomas saluted. "Yes, sir!"

Marc looked at the other Marines. "If any of you want to get on the *Hestia*, we will fully understand. But the truth is, we could use your help once we get the Liquid Steel."

The Marines looked at each other and nodded. Sergeant Gomez then stepped forward.

"We agree that Thomas should go to keep the peace on the *Hestia*, but we're staying."

Marc smiled in relief at their loyalty and was about to thank them when he cocked his head as he heard a quiet high-pitched buzz. Looking behind the Marines, he saw Rachel Connolly.

"Ms. Connolly, you need to leave, too."

She stepped forward, shaking her head. "The hell I *do*. I've reported from combat zones all over the Earth. This is no different."

Marc pointed at her drone, which was flying nearby. "Turn that off.... Please."

She looked as if she were going to object, then read the seriousness on Marc's face. Snapping her fingers twice brought the drone back to its place beside her, with its red recording light off.

Marc sighed in relief. "Thank you. We need you to report everything that has happened here. Our team that went to SB-1 is going to have a hard time convincing the powers that be not to blow *Tranquility* into oblivion." He reached into his pocket and pulled out a computer memory card. "I had Irma download all the data from the time the AuctionHouse docked to when the evacuation started. I'm entrusting it to you. Please use it to show that we did everything possible to prevent this disaster from getting any worse."

As Rachel extended her hand to take the card, her eyes gleamed at the thought of having access to raw data to work with. But then she paused and withdrew her hand. "Are you sure you want to give that to me? I'll see everything your crew has said and done. Everything will be exposed here."

Marc looked at Tony, who nodded. Then he extended his hand closer to Rachel. "We let you come here because you are a rare journalist who reports the truth, not your version of it. Take it and do what you do best."

Accepting the chip, she slid it into the drone's access port for memory card storage. "I promise to use this properly."

The elevator doors opened once again, and Wingnut stepped out. "All aboard who are going aboard. This train's leaving."

Marc waved a hand toward the elevator. "Thomas and Ms. Connolly, that's your cue to depart."

The two entered with Wingnut and waved as the doors closed.

Marc's shoulders slouched with exhaustion as he weakly smiled at Tony and McFarland. "Let's get to the Bridge to see them off."

Tony placed a hand on Marc's back and walked with him at his side, as McFarland took his place on Marc's other side. They positioned themselves slightly closer to their friend than usual, as if to protect him from whatever else the fates might hurl his way. The Marines fell in behind them and also positioned themselves like a protective shield.

Although Marc was one of the mentally toughest people the group around him had ever known, they saw that there was a notable vulnerability about the man. Marc was always the person any of them could go to about anything. Now they instinctively wanted to be there for him.

⠆⠄ ⠄⠐⠏⠊⠋⠎⠂ ⠄ ⠲ ⠠⠙⠓⠄ ⠹⠹⠼⠠⠠⠄⠇ ⠐⠋⠲⠑⠏

Back on the Bridge, Grey Wolf and Steven were at their stations, monitoring the evacuation.

As Marc, Tony, and McFarland returned, they heard Stuart saying, "...are all buckled in and ready. We'll disconnect the escape tunnel on your mark."

Steven replied, "Roger that, Stuart. Ready to disconnect in five..., four..., three..., two..., one..., *mark!*" He hit the controls that disconnected the escape tunnel.

Outside, the tunnel separated from both ends as the *Hestia* slowly pulled away. Several thin lines still connected the ends of the tunnel to the airlocks. This was a precaution to allow a safe distance between *Tranquility* and the *Hestia*, so the tunnel wouldn't crash into one or both. This lesson had been learned the hard way during a rescue attempt of a supply ship that was building the fifth manned ship to Mars.

As soon as the *Hestia* was a hundred yards away, the lines released their hold on the airlocks, allowing the tunnel to float free. Not having cameras to see the disconnect, the crew watched the video feed provided by the *Hestia*. A sigh of relief echoed through the *Tranquility* Bridge as the escape tunnel disappeared behind them.

Marc opened an audio channel to the *Hestia*. "Thanks, Stuart. If you have a problem with any of the guests, tell them their windows better be well insured."

Stuart laughed. "Will do. Good luck to you and your crew."

Marc smiled. "Thanks. Safe journey. *Tranquility* out."

As all communication with the *Hestia* was cut, Marc collapsed into his chair. He still had three more days to get *Tranquility* on course for the aerobraking. That was plenty of time for his mind to eat itself with all the things that could go wrong. But for now, the remainder of the Core Crew deserved a break.

"Okay, guys," Marc said. "The guests are gone, the girls are away, and we need to unwind. The Vulcan Mind Melds are on me!"

If sound could travel through space, the *Hestia*'s hull would have rung with the twins shouting, "YES!!!"

CHAPTER 12

Management Mayhem and Administrative Anxieties

The *Camel* had done a flawless deceleration burn before adjusting its heading for Starbase One. Jackson made sure that logs were kept for Marc to see how well his sister had performed as the pilot of the *Camel*.

Kimberly opened a Com-Channel. "Starbase One Control, this is *Camel One* on approach. Awaiting clearance and docking coordinates."

"*Camel One*, Starbase One Control here," said a friendly female voice. "You are cleared for docking at port number six. We are sending you the coordinates. Welcome to Starbase One."

Kimberly input the coordinates. "Thank you, Control. Coordinates received. Did you get the notification of the prisoners we are transporting?

"Roger that, *Camel One*. A security detail waiting at the docking bay will take them into custody. We have received detailed information from *Tranquility* to officially charge them. There's quite a bit of interest here about what went on there."

Kimberly laughed. "We'll tell you all about it if there's time. *Camel One* out."

Jackson checked the ETA. "We've got an hour before we dock. Let's get everyone ready, and then when they're all strapped in, we can renew our membership in the Zero-G Club."

Kimberly gave him a wicked grin. "We just joined yesterday. Surely, there's no time limit to the membership."

Jackson matched her grin. "True, but why take a chance?"

They both quickly unbuckled and hurried to get everyone strapped in.

⠰⠄ ⠠⠍⠃⠂⠌⠽⠂⠀⠰⠿ ⠠⠙⠃⠐ ⠠⠱⠃⠳⠂⠝ ⠐⠣⠗⠃⠄

Jackson exited the *Camel* to enter the cargo bay of Starbase One. Everyone on the *Camel* had agreed that he should be the one to deal with the prisoners. Standing on the deck was the captain of the security force with six heavily armed guards. As Jackson approached the captain, he saluted.

"Sir, I'm Sergeant Jackson of the United Earth Marine Corps. We have nine members of the AuctionHouse crew who took part in the attempted hijacking of *Tranquility*. I'll open the cargo hold as soon as you are ready, sir."

The compact Spanish captain, who had thick black wavy hair and a long handlebar mustache, saluted back. "Welcome to SB-1, Sergeant. I'm Captain Xavier. Give us a moment to get into place."

He raised a hand to wave the guards forward. They positioned themselves and took aim at the cargo hatch with their Stun Rifles. Jackson moved to the controls and, with a confirming nod from Captain Xavier, opened the hatch. Two of the guards entered, kicked aside the empty bottles of water that littered the floor, and unhooked the prisoners. The two guards then marched them into the cargo hold and out into the hallway with the rest of the guards. The captain nodded to Jackson and followed the guards out.

Jackson wrinkled his nose as he looked inside the *Camel*'s cargo hold. "They obviously didn't have training on how to use Zero-G toilets." He closed the hatch. Because the *Camel* was a food transport vessel, it was equipped with a self-cleaning sanitation system. He activated it and returned to the crew cabin.

"Okay, everyone," Jackson said, "it's all clear. I saw some people entering the docking bay who looked like a welcoming committee, if I'm any judge of folks."

Jackson and Kimberly helped Lady Elizabeth out, with Susan and Eileen behind them. They were greeted by a tall blonde middle-aged gentleman, who was dressed in a burgundy turtleneck sweater and black slacks. In the background, several workmen were moving nine large tanks of Liquid Steel into position to be loaded.

The gentleman stepped forward, bowed to Lady Elizabeth, and nodded to the others.

"I'm Chris Mannford, Head Administrator of Starbase One. Welcome aboard. As requested by your Ladyship, a meeting has been set up with the Earth Protection Agency representatives here on SB-1." He waved over a nurse with a wheelchair. "Mister Acer contacted us about your ankle, Lady Elizabeth. If you'll follow me to the conference room, we'll get things moving to stop them from using the Asteroid Missiles on *Tranquility*. I'm also trying to get an attorney to assist with looking up the established law about preventing historic landmarks from being destroyed. But since this is the first case of a landmark threatening to crash into Earth, we have an uphill battle and less than two days to convince the powers that be not to follow through with their plan. The workers here will load up the tanks into your cargo hold and refuel the *Camel,* so Ms. Acer and Sergeant Jackson can be on their way back. Shall we?"

Mannford said these last words with a wave of his arm toward the airlock.

Susan turned to Kimberly and Jackson. "As soon as you get things loaded here," she said, "get going. Don't worry about checking in with us. They need those tanks ASAP. Good luck."

Jackson gave her a quick salute and headed toward the *Camel's* cargo hold to check on the status of the cleaning cycle. Kimberly gave Susan and Eileen a quick hug and said, "Give 'em hell, girls!"

The dock supervisor approached Kimberly with an E-Pad. "Ms. Acer, I'm Ken Samson, the dock master here. I need to get your information before clearance to leave the dock can be given. We don't have your pilot's license on record."

Kimberly glanced at the *Camel's* cargo hold and saw that Jackson was talking to the workmen. Looking back at Mr. Samson, she took the E-Pad from him. "Let me get this back to you," she said. "I don't have my license number memorized yet."

He gave her a peculiar look, and shrugged. "I'll need it before releasing your ship from here." He walked back to his office and started making calls.

⠎⠀⠄⠐⠺⠂⠊⠒⠂⠒⠀⠶⠀⠄⠲⠒⠄⠒⠶⠥⠴⠂⠄⠲⠱⠢

Mr. Mannford led the ladies down one of the sidewalks of the main passageway. The middle was used for cargo and passenger carts, with the sidewalks running along the shops and businesses.

Susan and Eileen quickly noticed similarities to *Tranquility's* construction. Both were built on the O'Neill Cylinder design, but Starbase One was on a much larger scale.

Mr. Mannford pointed out the corridors that led to different science and astronomy sections. Gesturing to the far end of the passageway, which was over two hundred yards away, he said, "If there's time later, I'd like to show you ladies our botanical garden. Its official name is the J.F.K. Memorial Garden, but everyone here calls it the *Tranquility* Garden. Your design of the first self-sustaining garden on a space station has revolutionized how stations are going to be built now."

Susan's eyes sparkled at that. "We would be honored to see it. Can you give us an idea of how the EPA feels about *Tranquility?*"

Mr. Mannford sighed. "It's not going to be easy for you to change their minds. New simulations of *Tranquility's* current course show that it will hit the area of Riverside, Iowa. Although the mass of the station will be reduced by about half, the destructive path will be spread across hundreds of miles as the debris field rains across the landscape. You have less than forty-eight hours to change their minds before the Asteroid Missiles are sent to destroy *Tranquility*. In thirty hours, *Tranquility* will be too close, and the missiles would cause the debris field to spread from hundreds to *thousands* of miles. I personally think your plan will work. The Laser Sails have already slowed the speed, but *Tranquility* is going to need to decrease that by another twenty percent to have any chance of entering Earth's atmosphere at the correct angle. I hope your crew can pull this off. I've been a secret admirer of *Tranquility* from day one. What you have achieved there is the envy of the space community."

Susan blushed. "Thank you, Mister Mannford, but the credit goes to Marc and Lady Elizabeth here. He had the idea, and she made it possible."

Lady Elizabeth raised her hand to indicate that everyone was to stop.

"Just a moment," she said. "I want to state for the record that I had very little to do with *Tranquility*'s success. Yes, I provided the money, but Marc had an amazing idea that I thought would work. The only thing that I insisted on was to have a team that would be second to none. Once he showed me the Core Crew's resumés, I saw that he had more than met my requirements. If you all hadn't done what had been promised to me, I would have no problems letting them blow *Tranquility* out of the sky and chalk it up to a very bad loss. But, time and time again, you have all proven that doing the impossible is…well, possible. Up to and including defeating a group of hijackers, saving *Tranquility* from being torn apart, and keeping all the guests safe. Of course, a few were entertainingly scared within an inch of their lives by McFarland. Let's show those paper pushers that we know some incredible people who can pull off yet another miracle."

As Mr. Mannford looked at the three of them, he realized that he was about to be a part of an historic event. The rumors about the people in front of him and back on *Tranquility* did not do them justice. Mr. Mannford only hoped that he would be worthy of having a place with these amazing people.

Once the cleaning was complete in the *Camel*'s cargo hold, the tanks of Liquid Steel were loaded and secured. Kimberly and Jackson were about to get the pre-flight check done, when Mr. Samson and a group of security guards entered.

"Ms. Acer, it has been reported to us that you, in fact, do not have a pilot's license and have knowingly violated the laws of operating a space vehicle without one. It is my duty to tell you that you are hereby to be arrested by Starbase One's security force and detained until your case can be heard. She's all yours, officers."

Mr. Samson said all this with a hint of pleasure.

Kimberly's eyes flashed with anger. "Don't do this! These tanks need to get to *Tranquility* without delay. Let me take them there, and I'll return to face the charges."

Mr. Samson spoke with no compassion for Kimberly's plea. "Oh, sure," he said. "I'll just let you break the law again and make me an accomplice to it. No, thanks!"

Jackson stepped forward. "Fine. *I'll* take the *Camel* to *Tranquility*."

Mr. Samson sneered. "I did some checking. You're not cleared to fly this class of ship. Now step aside or be arrested for hindering official base operations."

As wrist restraints were put on the fuming Kimberly, she said to Jackson, "Tell the others."

Jackson turned darker shades of rage as the security detail marched off with Kimberly. Then he took several deep breaths before heading to the cockpit to contact Susan and Eileen.

At the far end of a conference table, six well-dressed and groomed men sat opposite the three ladies and Mr. Mannford. It was apparent from the start that they didn't want to consider any other option than using the missiles.

"Our experts," said one of the men, "have looked at your plan and see very little chance of it succeeding. The only option is to deflect *Tranquility*'s path with the missiles."

Lady Elizabeth's calm was waning. "Who *are* these experts? I wish to hear from them how they came to their conclusions."

"This isn't a trial, Ms. Elizabeth. We don't have to present them."

She nearly spat at them. "That's *Lady* Elizabeth! Or have you altogether given up being civil?"

The men fidgeted as they realized that they had just angered the richest person in history.

Lady Elizabeth enjoyed making them squirm. "I thank you, gentlemen, for suggesting a trial to proceed with this. Mister Mannford, let's take this up with the starbase's judge. It's still Francisco, isn't it?"

Mr. Mannford nodded. "Yes, it is, Your Ladyship. He's just down the hall. Shall we see if he is available?" He said this while waving over the nurse.

The men on the other side of the table leaped to their feet and started to object.

"There's no need to—"

"You are taking this way out of—"

"Don't you try to—"

Lady Elizabeth slowly stood up to address them. "Don't you even *dare* to presume to tell me what I can legally do. If you had even tried to see our side of things, this might have gone better for you. You not only have some other agenda behind being so unmovable, but you have proven to be second-rate lawyers by not even using a person's proper title. You can be sure that the people you represent will not be pleased by your behavior here. Good day, gentlemen."

With nothing else to be said, she sat down in the wheelchair and was whisked away through the door by the nurse, with the other two women right behind them.

Mr. Mannford stopped at the door and said to the men who were trying to remove the egg from their faces, "I hear that the Public Defender's office in North Korea could use some people."

When Susan overheard that remark, she said to Mr. Mannford, "Oooh, I wish *I* had thought of saying that!"

Eileen stopped in her tracks as she read something on her PAC. "Susan! Did you get this message from Jackson?"

Susan shook her head. "In all the chaos, I left my PAC on the *Camel*. What's up?"

Eileen's wide eyes showed her disbelief. "Kimberly's been arrested, and the *Camel* has been refused clearance!"

Susan's eyes matched Eileen's. "*What?!? Why?!?*"

"Jackson says they came for her just now and charged her with piloting a ship without a license. And because Jackson doesn't have the right license either, the *Camel* is stuck here. That means we have no way of getting the Liquid Steel to *Tranquility*."

Susan and Eileen ran to catch up with Lady Elizabeth to bring her up to speed.

When she heard the news, Lady Elizabeth was beside herself with anger. "Those corporate monkeys back there most likely knew this was going to happen. Okay. New plan. I know that Marc and the gang are busy, but we need to get them this information, as well as fight this through legal means. We should also hire another pilot to take the shipment."

Susan was still fuming. "I'll contact Marc."

Placing a hand on his chest, Mr. Mannford said, "Let me do what I can to find you a pilot."

Lady Elizabeth pointed down the hallway. "Eileen and I will head to Judge Francisco. His son and my godson played on the same football team in college. Maybe he'll be more understanding about our problem."

Eileen opened her mouth to say something, thought better of it, and nodded in agreement.

Looking up from her wheelchair, Lady Elizabeth said, "Okay, Nurse.... I'm sorry, I've been rude. What *is* your name?"

The nurse smiled at her. "Hollybee, your Ladyship."

Lady Elizabeth pointed forward. "Come, Nurse Hollybee, the game's afoot!"

Susan and Eileen looked at the amazing friend they had and then at each other. In silent understanding, they hugged and went off to do their battles.

Mr. Mannford said to Susan. "Follow me. I'll take you to my office, where you can use my private line to call *Tranquility*."

Susan sighed with relief. "Thank you, Mister Mannford. You've been most kind with your help."

Mr. Mannford replied with friendly eyes, "Please. If we're about to kick a hornet's nest, you should call me Chris."

Susan smiled. "Okay, Chris, lead the way. And please call me Susan."

They quickly walked about ten yards to an alcove, where Chris entered a code into a keypad. The wall opened, revealing a small elevator. "After you, Susan."

She stepped in and looked around. "Is this a bug-out elevator?"

Chris nodded. "It is. We use them during emergencies to get our crew quickly to their stations from anywhere on Starbase One. As I'm sure you know, seconds can count on a space station."

As the elevators doors closed, Chris entered a code on the wall panel. The elevator quickly took off, throwing them both against the padded wall. After prying themselves off the padding, Chris apologized.

"Sorry about that," he said. "This is my first time using it, and I forgot about its fast starts and stops."

Susan sighed. "After the past few days, I'm getting used to being thrown about and having my adrenal gland secrete all over itself."

Chris chuckled. "I may have to steal that line. Oh! Hang on. We're coming to our stop."

The elevator wasn't as jarring this time, but required them to brace themselves against the wall with their hands as it slowed.

"Last stop," Chris said as the doors opened. "Management Mayhem and Administrative Anxieties."

Susan grinned. "I may have to steal *that* one from you."

As she stepped out into his office, she immediately stopped. The room looked like something out of the Library of Congress. Every inch of wall space was lined with shelves that were crammed with books of all sorts. Every table had its own stack of books and magazines. The rare smell of old books filled the room, giving Susan a thrill.

"Forget the tour of the garden," she said with delight. "I want to spend some time *here!*"

"I'm sure we can arrange that. But first…." Chris went to his desk and opened the Com-System for her. "You can call *Tranquility* from my computer. I'll use my secretary's computer to find us a pilot."

Susan sat down to open a link to *Tranquility.* "Thank you again, Chris."

"You're welcome." He opened the office door.

From the other room, he was greeted by a woman's scream.

"Mister Mannford! How did you get past me?!"

Sitting at a desk, there was a tall, slender, strawberry blonde woman clutching her chest with one hand and holding a now broken tablet stylus in the other.

Chris's apologetic eyes showed that he truly cared for her. "Sorry Ms. Finn. I had to use the bug-out elevator. We have a situation that required me to get here fast. Please let me use your desk while my friend Susan in there uses mine." He poked his head back into the office. "Would you like some coffee, Susan?"

Susan's stomach growled at the thought. "Oh! Yes, please. Any chance of something to eat?"

Chris addressed his secretary. "Ms. Finn, would you mind getting some coffee and snacks, please? Put it on my account and feel free to get something for yourself. We have a lot of work ahead of us for the next few hours."

"Yes, sir! May I ask what's happening?"

As she rose from her chair, Ms. Finn noticed the broken stylus in her hand.

Chris sat in her vacated seat. "You know the situation with *Tranquility?*"

Ms. Finn nodded. "It's all over the news, sir. But not many details are known."

Chris looked at her with a lopsided smile. "Well, we're about to be knee-deep in those details. Now, please hurry."

Ms. Finn nodded, tossed the stylus in a trashcan, and quickly left the room.

Chris opened a line to the lounge where many of the off-duty pilots hung out. The call was answered by a baldheaded man with a greying beard and mustache, who looked like he had just finished eating the glass his drink came in. His face lit up when he saw who it was.

"Christopher! What's happening, old man?"

Chris grinned at his friend, who was two minutes younger than him. "I need some help, Jimmy. I need a pilot with a Class 6-C license ASAP. Know of someone?"

Jim rubbed his chin. "Hmmm. There's been a bit of an unsettled feeling with the pilots for the past hour. Let me *run the bar* to see if anyone can help."

Chris sat back in his chair. "Thanks, kid. I'll keep this line open for you."

Jim waved a salute and signed off.

Chris returned to his office just in time to hear a voice cut loose with a long string of colorful metaphors. Susan looked up at Chris and shrugged. "Welcome to my world."

"What was that?" said a male voice.

Susan turned the monitor to face Chris. "Marc, meet Chris Mannford. He's the head administrator here at Starbase One and has been a big help in trying to keep this situation from spinning out of control."

Chris felt that he was meeting a celebrity. "Hi, Marc. I wish we were meeting under better circumstances. I'm a huge fan of what you have done at *Tranquility*."

Chris now heard another voice: "Great! We can form a club if we ever finish saving this flying circus."

Susan rolled her eyes. "And that would be McFarland, offering his two bits."

Marc waved at Chris. "Thanks for your help. Our computer expert is working on an idea that could have some severe consequences to all involved. If you wish to be as far away from this as possible, we will understand. But to be quite honest, we could use your help."

Chris's eyes showed his willingness. "In for a penny, in for a pound, is it? I must say, taking the easy way has never been how I do things. How can I help, Marc?"

Marc sighed in relief. "Okay, Susan will be our go-between for us. As of now, we are about to embark on actions that break more laws and policies than have ever been broken at one time before. Last chance to bail out, Chris."

Just then, Ms. Finn returned with the coffee and food. "Mister Mannford, here's the—"

Chris quickly turned to her, took the offered goods, and said, "Ms. Finn, please take the rest of the day off. I know I said that we would be needing your help, but things have changed."

He placed the food and coffee on his desk, reached into his pocket, and pulled out a Credit Chip. Then he adjusted the amount to unlimited access for a new user and handed it to her. The chip read the new user's fingerprints and locked them in. "Take this and go buy yourself that dress you wanted for your birthday dinner next week, plus any accessories that would go with it. But that's only with the understanding that you may not speak about who or what you have seen or heard here today. I hired you because I found you to be trustworthy, and you haven't let me down in the three years we've been working together. Will you do this? Please?"

Ms. Finn looked at the chip, then almost looked at Susan before checking herself, remembering that no one was supposed to be there. Returning her gaze to Chris, she slipped the chip into her pocket and lightly coughed into her other hand.

"Mister Mannford, I need to leave work because of a sore throat. May I be excused, please?" She said this with a smirk.

Chris mouthed, "Thank you." Then aloud, he said, "Of course, Ms. Finn. Please check in with me tomorrow to let me know how you're doing. As you leave, please lock the outer office door."

"Yes, sir. Oh, I also need a new tablet stylus. Mine unexpectedly broke." She said this with a wink as she headed out the door.

Susan was now all smiles. "I guess you got your answer, Marc. How much is that going to set you back, Chris?"

Chris put out his palms. "Don't ask. If this goes as far south as you think it may, money is going to be the *least* of my problems."

"Okay, he can be the president of the fan club," said McFarland.

Marc gave a weary look off camera at McFarland and then addressed Chris. "That's as close as you're going to get an approval from *him*, Mister Mannford. Welcome aboard."

Chris's eyes crinkled with amusement. "Please, call me Chris. Okay, what's first on the agenda?"

Marc looked off to the side. "Grey Wolf? What's the story?"

Before the programmer could answer, the call light appeared on Chris's monitor. "Wait a moment," Chris said, "I need to take this call. It may be about a pilot who can transport the Liquid Steel to you. Let me close the video feed from you, so he won't see you, but you can hear what's being said."

Marc nodded. "Understood, Chris."

Susan got up from her chair and stepped around to the front of the desk, allowing Chris to sit down.

Chris adjusted the monitor settings and opened the line. There appeared a frowning Jim.

"What kind of hell have you gotten into?" he asked. "The pilots here refuse to even consider doing anything for you. The scuttlebutt has it that they will lose their license and be barred from reapplying for one if they so much as set foot on the *Camel*. It's shit like this that makes it hard being your friend."

Chris was shocked by this news. "Sorry, Jim. I'll make it up to you. If the situation changes in any way, would you let me know?"

The frown lightened on Jim's face. "Sure thing, old man. Keep your head down."

Chris nodded, cut the connection, and reestablished the video feed with Marc.

"Well," Marc said, "that adds a whole can of worms to the pile. Someone with major pull has entered the game. Any idea who it may be, Chris?"

Chris thought for a moment. "I think so, but I need to check on it before I accuse him of anything. What has Grey Wolf got?"

The monitor split in two, showing Grey Wolf next to Marc.

"Other than a sour stomach from drinking too much coffee in the past three days?" said Grey Wolf. "A plan to spread some chaos around your station. Ready to have some fun?"

"Someone's spreading chaos without us?" said a voice off camera. "That's not fair!"

"Deal with it, Kevin." said Marc. "We need a link to the computer core there. Grey Wolf was the head programmer of most of the systems there. And being the sneaky bastard he is, he left a few back doors into some of the systems…, one of which includes Security's. Can you set up a link?"

Chris nodded and started setting one up. "Give me a moment. What channel do you want to use?"

Grey Wolf grinned. "Let's use forty-two. It could be our answer to everything."

Chris looked up at Grey Wolf with a knowing smile. Then he looked over at Susan and pointed to a book behind her. "Third shelf from the top. Fifth book if you please, Susan."

Susan retrieved the book and handed it to Chris, who held it up to be seen by the men on the monitor. "I won't panic," he said, "if you don't."

He put *The Hitchhiker's Guide to the Galaxy* down on his desk and finished establishing the link.

Grey Wolf looked at Marc. "I think we've found a kindred spirit, Marc."

A small screen appeared on Chris's monitor, showing the doorway to the outer office. There were Lady Elizabeth, Eileen, and Nurse Hollybee. Eileen looked upset, and Lady Elizabeth was obviously angry.

Chris said to Susan, "Looks like the others have bad news from the judge. The code to the door is two, two, one, b, Baker St. Please thank Nurse Hollybee for her help and send her back to sickbay."

Susan nodded and went to let the ladies in.

Addressing the men on the monitor, Chris said, "The rest of your team just arrived, and they don't look very happy."

"You know," said Marc, "with all the help you've given and a security code like that, I think you can call it *our* team."

"Yep," agreed Grey Wolf. "He's one of us."

Susan pushed Lady Elizabeth's wheelchair into the office, with Eileen following behind, looking all the world as if she were ready to rip the heads off dead babies.

As soon as she entered the room, Eileen stopped in her tracks to stare at the book collection. Her demeanor changed to pure joy as she explored the shelves. Stopping at a book that was in a protective glass cover, she said, "Is that a first edition of *Peter and Wendy?*"

"Can we ooh and ahh over the books *after* we save *Tranquility?*" said Marc grumpily.

Lady Elizabeth chimed in. "You're not going to like what we found out, Marc. Or the *lack* of what we found. Judge Francisco's hands are tied because the law clearly has Kimberly on the wrong side of it. To keep the missiles from launching, we would need a grand jury to be convened, and that would take at least a day."

"We don't *have* a day," Marc said with a snarl. "The Laser Sails have decreased our speed by another fourteen percent, so we're on track to enter Earth's atmosphere for aerobraking. All we need is the Liquid Steel. And we need it in less than ten hours. This is where I ask Lady Elizabeth to cut her ties with us."

Lady Elizabeth nearly exploded. "The *hell* I will! I'm not abandoning my friends when things get tough!"

Marc's eyes stared at her with intensity. "Hear me out, Elizabeth. I'm not asking for this lightly."

Hearing her first name being used without her title brought her arguments to an abrupt end. Marc had never addressed her before other than by her title. Even when talking privately, he had always refused to use just her first name. To have him do so in front of others told her, and them, that he was drawing a line that shouldn't be crossed.

"Okay, Marc," she said, "I'll leave."

Marc sighed. "Good. But, Eileen, you need to go with her, too. And before you start in on me, I need to make sure that if things go badly for us, at least one member of the Core Crew will be untainted by what is about to happen. Do I make myself clear? Because I don't have time to argue."

Eileen glared at Marc's image on the monitor and slowly nodded. Turning to Lady Elizabeth, she asked, "Do you still have your space here on the station?"

Lady Elizabeth nodded. "I do. Let's go, my dear. I think we need to open a nice bottle of wine and scream into a pillow or two."

Eileen walked behind Lady Elizabeth's wheelchair, unlocked the breaks, and pushed her out of the office without looking back.

"Someone remind me," said Marc unhappily, "to have a doghouse built for when all this is over. No matter how things goes, it's not going to end well for me."

The others looked at each other. Nothing could be said to ease Marc's distress.

McFarland grumbled, "I'll put flowers on your grave later, Marc. What's the plan?"

"Right," said Marc, shaking his head to clear it. "Grey Wolf, you in?"

Grey Wolf was working furiously on his keyboard. "Almost. There's someone sniffing about, looking for my intrusion. It's almost as if they know my programs. I don't like it."

Marc thought for a moment, then said, "Irma, do you have the breakdown of the virus that attacked us?"

"Yes, Marc," the AI replied.

Marc had the look of someone onto something. "Irma, can you compare the virus to the style of programming that is following Grey Wolf's path?"

Irma thought for a moment. "Hmmm, let me check on that."

"What do you have percolating in that head of yours, Marc?" said Tony.

Without replying to Tony, Marc said, "Grey Wolf, if there's a similar program that's hunting *you*, can you use the mantis to disrupt it?"

Grey Wolf turned that over in his mind. A moment later, his eyes widened, and his hands flew across his virtual keyboard so fast that they were a blur.

Irma's voice returned. "I've analyzed the virus and the program that's after Grey Wolf. There's a ninety-six percent chance that the same person created both programs."

A wicked grin spread across Marc's face. "Get 'em, Wolf!"

Susan leaned toward Chris. "Here's why I love working with Marc. He knows his team's abilities and how to use them to create something greater than the individual parts."

There was a subtle but noticeable change in Marc that his friends noticed. He was in his element when he was working several problems at once with a team he knew.

Marc addressed Susan. "Contact Jackson. He needs to be near where they're keeping Kimberly. Tony, time to call in the Marines. Chris, find me the person responsible for making this bad day even worse."

Without a word, everyone jumped into action.

⠨⠀⠀⠐⠦⠗⠄⠂⠆⠄⠲⠀⠆⠀⠠⠋�⠄⠐⠗⠠⠇⠠⠂⠄⠐⠕⠢⠆⠆

A small screen in a darkened bar flashed that a message was waiting. A shadowy figure picked up the tablet, opened it, and read the short message. Then he shut off the device and said in a low, dangerous voice to the others at the table, "Drink up, boys! Darkheart needs us."

CHAPTER 13

Operation Venus Flytrap

On *Tranquility*'s Bridge, the main monitor showed Grey Wolf's progress through Starbase One's computer system, with the unknown person slowly gaining on him. Then Grey Wolf's "wolf" avatar stopped at a communication link, picked up a package, and opened it. A praying mantis unfolded itself as the wolf ran off. After a moment, the mantis split in two, and the second one jumped off to a random system. The person following slowed and paused, then took a different route to follow the wolf.

Grey Wolf grinned. "It's working, Marc. The mantis is causing whoever's following me to try another way of catching me. If one of the cloned mantises catches him, it will cause a feedback in the system that will trigger the computer's anti-hacking program to attack it. It won't bother me, though. Guess who programmed it?" Then he frowned at his monitor. "But whoever is after me has some mad skills. I don't understand how his intrusion isn't being detected just by following me. It's as if... Aww, shit! Irma! Protocol one, one, alpha six, nine! Marc, we have a mole somewhere!"

Chris heard that as he was entering the office. "I think I know who it is. I did some checking on the personnel records. Guess who worked for the AuctionHouse, is rumored to have done programming for that right-wing group that hijacked you, and is staring intently at his computer monitor right now?"

Chris held up a tablet that showed Ken Samson working feverishly at his computer.

"Someone needs to show him that he has messed with the wrong people," said Susan.

Just then, the front-door camera opened on the desk monitor, and there stood three large and none too gentle-looking men in black leather flight suits that were one step removed from motorcycle leathers. The largest man, who had a bald head and a long black mustache and beard, started pounding on the door, which corresponded with noise that was coming from the outer office.

"Who the hell are those guys?" asked Chris. "I've never seen them on the station before."

McFarland spoke up. "Three guys? Looking about as pleasant as road rash, and just as ugly?"

Everyone turned to McFarland.

"Do I want to know how or why," Marc asked, "you know people who look like they enjoy kicking kittens?"

"And what are they doing outside my office?" Chris asked.

McFarland grinned. "Unclench your butt cheeks. Believe it or not, they're a group of bikers called The Keepers, who volunteer their time to protect kids who are testifying in court against child predators. I donate my bonus to their home office with the understanding that if I call for help, they come. I did, and they're there. Let them in already. They don't like to be kept waiting."

As everyone watched, two security guards started to approach the three men at the door.

Chris took Susan's arm. "C'mon, we need to see some men about your daughter's abuse case."

Susan looked confused. "What daughter? *Oh!*"

The two of them went to the outer office and opened the door just as the guards reached the three bikers. As the others watched on the monitors, Susan leaped out into the big biker's arms and in a sobbing voice cried, "Thank god, you're here! My daughter's so frightened without her Big Bear!"

The shocked looked on the biker's face made McFarland laugh.

Chris was still out of sight of the guards as he winked at the bikers, motioning them to enter. "Thank you for coming, gentlemen. Please come in. Ah, Officers Jenkins and Franks, thank you for escorting them here. Please give Captain Xavier my regards."

The guards shrugged at each other, then looked back at Chris. "Will do, Mister Mannford," said Jenkins.

Chris closed the door, locked it, and addressed the three men. "Sorry, gentlemen, we didn't know you were expected until you arrived. I'm—"

The biker who was still being hugged by Susan interrupted with a deep Southern accent. "We know who ya 're, Mister Mannford. Our group is thoroughly informed on da people that run dis station. Your name is on da list to contact if things go sour fer us." He nodded to the man on his right. "Dis here is Snake." Then to the left. "Dis is Blaze, 'n I'm Duke. What I don't know is why Darkheart sent us here, 'n who dis cute thing is dat 'as made my day by hugging me."

Susan blushed, let go of Duke, and stepped back, giving him a puzzled look. "Who's Darkheart?"

Duke gave her a don't-you-know look. "Dat's what 'e call McFarland. No utta name would'ev suit 'em."

Susan couldn't disagree. Holding out her hand, she said, "I'm Susan Spencer. I work with McFarland on *Tranquility*."

Duke took her hand, gently lifted it, and gave it a soft kiss. "Another name on our list of people ta trust as well as da *Tranquility* crew."

Susan's blush deepened, but she was saved by Marc yelling from Chris's monitor: "Grey Wolf needs help! Get in here!!!"

As everyone stepped into the office, they saw that Samson had shortened the distance to catching Grey Wolf. On the monitor, the mantis program was continuing to clone itself, but another program in the shape of a wasp was now following the mantises and destroying them.

Grey Wolf hissed through clenched teeth, "This guy is pissing me off!"

Marc looked at Chris. "We need to get to Samson, keep him from delaying us anymore, and find out what he knows."

Duke looked at the tablet that showed Samson at his computer. "Isn't dat da dock master, Ken Samson? He's on another list of ours. One ya don't wanna be on. Our ship is docked near his office. We'll go 'n tell him we need ta deal w'th some unnecessary paperwork 'n... *persuade* 'im ta have a drink with us."

"Wait!" said Marc. "How big is your ship?"

Duke raised an eyebrow. "Jist a three-person Jumper. Why?"

Marc sighed. "If it were bigger, our problems would be solved by your transporting the Liquid Steel."

Duke shook his head. "Nope. Not enough room."

Marc smiled weakly. "Okay, how soon can you get to the dock?"

Duke checked his watch. "Fifteen minutes."

Grey Wolf yelled, "Not fast enough! He'll be on me in less than ten!"

Chris moved to the bookshelves. "They can be there in three." He opened the bug-out elevator. "Susan, go with them to make sure they get all the information you need." He handed her a tablet. "Use this to keep in contact with me. The password is *Dickens*."

After Susan looked at Marc, who nodded, she crammed into the elevator with the three bikers. "Brace yourselves, guys. This thing takes off quickly."

Chris entered the code for the exit nearest the Docking Bay and said, "Good luck."

The doors whooshed shut, and a moment later the door panel showed that the elevator was gone.

The front-door screen appeared once again on Chris's monitor. This time, three men and one woman in Marine uniforms were standing there.

"Looks like the Marines have arrived, Marc," said Chris. "I'll go let them in."

Marc turned to the others on *Tranquility*'s Bridge. "I don't know what lucky star we wished on to have Chris on our team, but we owe him big time."

Tony nodded. "We may need to help him when this all ends. He's going to be on every blacklist for employment."

"Oh, goodie," grumbled McFarland. "Another lost puppy to feed."

Marc frowned. "Quit griping, McFarland. You like him just as much as we do. And why didn't you ever tell us about this group you donate to?"

McFarland shrugged. "You know me. I keep my private life just that. *Private.*"

Marc leveled a look at McFarland that was a mix of annoyance and curiosity.

McFarland sighed heavily before saying, "*Fine.* If you must know, I found them when my twelve-year-old niece was molested, and she was terrified of going to court to testify. They formed a protection ring for her and were in the courtroom every time she was there. She still gets birthday cards from them."

Steven asked, "What happened to the guy who hurt her?"

McFarland's eyes glinted. "Life in prison. Which was shortened to days after he arrived in the slammer."

Just then, Chris entered with the Marines, who looked about the office. Marc readjusted the video feed from *Tranquility*'s Bridge, so everyone was on monitor.

Seeing Tony, the Marines snapped to attention and saluted. "Colonel Rhodes! Reporting as requested, sir!"

Tony saluted back. "At ease, guys. What we are about to ask you to get involved with may kill your careers as Marines. So, if you can't commit without knowing more, you should leave now. No harm, no foul, and drinks are on me next time we meet."

The four Marines looked at each other for a moment, reached to their rank insignia pins, removed them, and tossed them onto Chris's desk. The female Marine stepped forward.

"Each of us," she said to Tony, "owes you our life several times over, both on and off the field of combat. Where you lead us, we will follow without hesitation, sir!"

Tony sighed. "Thank you. From here on out, you are to assist Mister Mannford here, any way you can. If an order comes from him or Marc, treat it as coming from me."

"Yes, sir!" all of them replied.

Chris looked on in awe at this group, who were ready to drop everything to rush into a burning house for the others.

He's turning the command of four Marines over to me without hesitation! It was shocking to Chris to have such trust given to him when they barely knew him.

Marc read the look on Chris's face. "The Core Crew here on *Tranquility*, Chris, have been friends for a very long time, and when we see people who have qualities that are laced with honor like yours, we embrace them. Like it or not, you're one of us now, Chris."

Chris blushed. "Thank you, Marc. What do you need us to do first?"

Grey Wolf interrupted: "There's something's happening with Samson's wasp. It's slowing down like no one is controlling it."

Chris checked the feed from Samson's office. There on the monitor was Duke, leaning across the desk with two fists full of the squirming hacker's coveralls. Susan moved into view as she went around the desk to enter a few commands into the computer. Fighting against Duke's hold on him, Samson tried to reach for Susan, but was prevented by being dragged across the desk. Then the huge biker pressed his nose against Samson's and said something to him that startled Susan, but she continued to work at the keyboard.

Grey Wolf grinned. "I've been given access to Samson's terminal. Give me a moment, and I'll be able to purge his wasp."

Seeing that Susan was opening a video feed from Samson's computer, Chris opened it and said, "Well done, Susan! I see your team has been successful."

Susan shrugged. "All I did was stand back while Duke and his bikers stuffed the crew here into a closet. There was a moment that I thought they would do something violent, but they hardly laid a hand them. They just implied what *might* happen if everyone didn't follow their instructions. It was quite a show."

Samson could be heard yelling in the background: "Let me go, you hoodlum! You have no right.... *Urp!*"

On the video feed, Duke was clamping his beefy hand over Samson's mouth. "Didn't I make myself clear? Da next word outta you, 'n I show ya exactly how many bones ya'r ri't hand has." Then, to Susan, he said, "It's twenty-seven, by da way."

With his eyes wide, Samson whimpered.

Marc said to the Marines in Chris's office, "Do you have a change of civilian clothes in your bags?"

"Yes, sir," they each replied.

Marc finally felt that the tide was finally moving in their favor. "Get changed. Our Marine, Sergeant Jackson, is waiting at a café near the security cells where our pilot is being held. As soon as Grey Wolf does his voodoo, you need to get her out of there and to our ship."

Chris addressed the Marines: "You three men can change in the outer office." He then pointed toward a door in the far corner. "And you, Ms., may use my private bathroom."

"Yes, sir. Thank you, sir," they all said together and went to get changed.

"How are you doing, Grey Wolf?" asked Marc.

Grey Wolf's fingers were a blur as he worked. "Give me five more minutes, and we'll be ready to cause more headaches for the crew of Starbase One than they ever thought possible. Sorry about that, Chris."

Chris shrugged. "Just don't injure anyone. I've got friends here I don't want hurt."

Grey Wolf grinned. "What I plan to do will cause systems to have fits and make your people chase figments of *my* imagination."

Marc started to envision the chess pieces for the next move. "It's time to get our people in place. Susan, here's where you vamoose with Samson. Duke, we need to get Susan and Samson to Earth..., somewhere it will be safe until this is all sorted out. Is there a place your guys can vanish on the station for a while?"

Chris chimed in, "Snake and Blaze can come to my office until the heat cools down. They just need to enter *Beowulf* into the bug-out elevator access pad."

"I'll let 'em know," Duke said. "And as f'r a safe place, Da Keep will do."

Susan looked at Marc. "Why are you sending us to Earth?"

Marc replied, "You need to find out what Samson knows about the hijacking and who's behind it. Get going, guys. Things are about to get crazy there."

Grey Wolf added, "I'll make sure your Jumper is cleared for departure."

Samson started yelling, *"You cannot do…uffff!!!"*

Chris watched on the monitor as Duke gave a roundhouse punch to Samson, who collapsed in an unconscious heap. Duke then effortlessly picked Samson up and threw him over his shoulder. "Let's go, Susan."

Susan looked back at the monitor. "You keep Steven safe, Marc."

Marc gave her a reassuring smile. "Will do."

The Marines returned to Chris's office dressed in civilian clothes. Gunnery Sergeant Jill Wilson was obviously still the one in command over the other three, but they all looked like anyone else visiting the station.

Sergeant Wilson asked Chris, "Which way to the café that Sergeant Jackson is at, sir?"

Chris pointed out the office: "Turn left, take the second right, and it'll be on the left."

She then addressed Marc and Tony on the monitor: "We'll head there now, sirs." Then she saluted them.

Tony saluted back. "Have Jackson report to us when you get there. Things are gonna move fast once you're in position."

Before leaving, the Marines nodded and responded with "Yes, sir!"

Marc asked Chris, "How long for them to get there?"

Chris shrugged his shoulders. "Only a few minutes."

⠦ ⠠⠹⠆⠲⠆⠁⠂ ⠸⠃ ⠰⠙⠦⠒⠑⠂⠉⠲⠒⠆⠴

Less than five minutes later, Jackson greeted the Marines as if they were old friends, offering them coffee. Under each cup, there was an earbud, which they swiftly placed into their ears.

As Jackson pretended he was taking a drink, he said softly, "We're ready, sir."

Marc looked at Grey Wolf. "Okay, Wolf, it's all you. Show them what you got."

Grey Wolf cracked his fingers before returning to his keyboard. "Okay, guys, when the security force leaves to deal with the problem in the Botanical Gardens, I'm going to put the video feeds on a time loop and unlock all the doors for you leading to Kimberly. Steven will act as a guide for where you need to turn. It's critical that no one sees you or raises an alarm. I may be able to delay it, but it's designed to reroute through every access link to alert everyone. Once you have Kimberly, get to the *Camel* ASAP and leave. I'll have the prelaunch sequence ready when you get there. Jackson, I'll start on your mark."

Jackson shared a confirming nod from the other Marines and acknowledged, "We're leaving the café and heading toward security *now*."

Grey Wolf's fingers did their magic. "Roger that. Here we go!"

The main monitor on *Tranquility*'s Bridge showed a view of Starbase One's surveillance room. The two guards were bored with watching the same things that always happened: A shoplifter. Someone loitering. Drunken arguments. With no real place to hide on the station, major crimes were extremely rare.

The guards looked at each other and shrugged when all the monitors showed static for a half-second.

"Another glitch in the system," one of them said. "You want to report it or ignore it?"

"Hmmm.... Do paperwork or not. I think *not!*"

"Good call, Bob. Just as well. That glitch we reported last month was never fixed. I'm convinced that— What the *hell?* Are you seeing what I'm seeing on feed number twelve?"

"Twelve? It's just.... *Whoa!*"

There in the Botanical Gardens was smoke. Lots and lots of smoke, with hazy figures of people running for the exits.

Bob opened a com-line to the on-duty security guards.

"All security and fire control teams! Report to the Botanical Gardens immediately! Possible fire in progress!"

As Bob deployed the teams, George checked the sensors for the Botanical Gardens. None of them made any sense. Some showed that a fire was in progress, others were reporting that it was a perfect summer day, and another section had a winter snowstorm.

"What in the hell is going on there?" said George. "Tell the teams to be ready for anything. The sensors can't be relied on for proper information."

Bob looked at the readings with wide eyes. Then he opened communications with the teams: "Attention, security and fire teams! Be advised that the sensors cannot be relied on. Enter the Botanical Gardens with *extreme* caution."

"Roger, surveillance," said one of the team members. "We're approaching the entrance to the gardens now. We're getting reports from civilians that the computer has been announcing that a decompression was detected. Are any of the sensors showing that?"

Bob looked over his readings again. "Negative. We don't even have a report that the computer issued the warning. Be careful, guys. We're flying blind here."

"Ten-four, surveillance. Entering now."

The teams entered the Botanical Gardens at all entry points and fanned out. Nothing seemed out of place. Bees were buzzing, and no smoke was visible anywhere. But the teams had to inspect all the areas to make sure nothing was amiss. Soon, all the teams were exploring throughout the garden.

Everyone in Chris's office and on Tranquility's Bridge was watching the monitors with great interest.

Grey Wolf smirked. "Operation Venus Flytrap now commencing." He then input a code.

Suddenly, all the doors to the Botanical Gardens shut and locked. Then the heavy decompression doors sealed in front of them with a clang that echoed throughout the gardens, making the security and fire crews stop what they were doing.

Meanwhile, Grey Wolf was causing more problems for the station crews. Doors that led to the hallways that Jackson and his team were using suddenly shut and locked. Any guards the Marines came upon were knocked out with a Shock-Bag from their Stun-Guns, or by more physical means.

This all went unnoticed by the surveillance guards. All they saw were their crews being trapped in the Botanical Gardens. Their attention was diverted when the doors to security closed and bolted. As the two surveillance guards tried to make sense of the chaos, their monitors went dark, and the lights went off. Then all the monitors showed a white dot, and eerie music started playing as a voice said, "There is nothing wrong with your television set.

Do not attempt to adjust the picture. We are controlling transmission. If we wish to make it louder, we will bring up the volume. If we wish to make it softer, we will tune it to a whisper. We will control the horizontal. We will control the vertical...."

When the Marines reached the door to the cells, it opened for them. Inside one of the cells was Kimberly, lying on a narrow bed with her arm across her eyes.

Jackson walked up to the cell and cleared his throat.

Without looking, Kimberly said, "*What?*"

Jackson chuckled. "Would you like to leave? Or have you made a home here?"

Kimberly sat up so quickly that she was dizzy. Her face displayed excitement, then worry when she saw the unfamiliar people taking up sentry positions behind Jackson.

"They're with me," Jackson said with a smile. Then, tapping his earbud, he said, "Okay, Grey Wolf. Open her cell."

"One *Camel* pilot, coming right up," responded Grey Wolf.

As soon as the door slid aside, Kimberly leaped into Jackson's arms and kissed him.

Then she asked, "How...? What...? Did Marc do this?"

Jackson handed her an earbud. "We can fill you in later. Right now, we need to move before the guards we already knocked out are discovered."

With her eyes wide, Kimberly nodded.

Jackson then looked around at the empty cells. "Where are the guys we turned over to Captain Xavier?"

Kimberly shrugged. "Three lawyers showed up a while ago and took them away. Sounded like they were being taken to someplace on Earth. I didn't hear where."

Marc's gut twitched at hearing that. "Odds are they're gone and hidden somewhere. That's a problem for later. Okay, Grey Wolf, what's their exit strategy?"

Grey Wolf smiled. "Calmly and casually walk the four hallways to the Docking Bay and get the *Camel* back here."

Jackson looked surprised. "Oh. I somehow thought there would be more to it than that. Okay, gang, let's conceal our weapons and have a nice stroll to the *Camel*."

They all tucked their guns into their waistbands and covered them with their jackets. After double-checking that they had no telltale bulges, Jackson took Kimberly's hand and kissed it. "Shall we take a nice walk, my dear?"

Kimberly replied with a grin, "Sure."

The other Marines looked at each other, shrugged, and hooked arms as they followed the couple, acting as if they were all friends on a holiday outing.

Back on *Tranquility*, Marc watched the display of affection by Jackson, muted his com, and said to Tony, "I really do need to talk to Jackson."

Tony looked at Marc. "Give him a break, Marc. He's behaved himself as a proper Marine and has made an impression on the other Marines. They've stepped aside to let him take the lead, even though both Jill and Mitch outrank him. He projects a confidence in who he is and what he does. Couple that with his charisma, which he never flaunts, and you have a natural born leader. When all this is done, and we get *Tranquility* back up and running, I'd like him to be considered for replacing me when I retire."

Marc's head snapped toward Tony. "*Retire?* When did *that* pop into your head?"

Tony leaned back in his chair. "I've been thinking about it for a month or two now. Nothing that I've wanted to pursue for a few years, but after all that we've been through this week, it's highlighted that I'm ready to sit on my laurels and enjoy being able to have no commitments to anything."

Marc frowned at Tony and harrumphed at him. "I'm not sure I like the idea of operating this place without you by my side. There're not many people I trust my life with, and all of them have been within arm's reach for the past five years. But that's something we'll need to discuss later. Right now, we have a team approaching the Docking Bay."

On the main monitor, the true video feed showed Kimberly and the Marines entering the Docking Bay and heading for the *Camel*. The area was abnormally absent of personnel because they were all still locked in the closets.

Grey Wolf shut the Docking Bay doors and sealed them. "Okay, Kimberly, do an EU..., an Emergency Undocking..., and I'll take care of things on the station side. *Oh, hell!!!* The doors have been forced open at the gardens. Get going!"

Kimberly ran for the *Camel*. "Roger that! Everyone, buckle up! This is going to— What the hell are *you* two doing here!"

There, sitting in the front crew seats, were Eileen and Chris.

"What took you so long?" asked Eileen.

"Kimberly," said Marc, when he heard Eileen's voice over the speakers, "is that who I think it is?"

"And Mister Mannford," replied Kimberly.

Eileen spoke up: "I promised not to be involved in whatever shenanigans you guys did to get Kimberly out. Chris and I have perfectly legal documents, which say that we're passengers on this ship, heading for *Tranquility*. Don't argue. We're coming."

Kimberly looked at Jackson, who put his hands up and shook his head, indicating that he wasn't going to get involved. The decision was forced by the sound of the Docking Bay doors being forced open behind them.

Kimberly ran for the cockpit. "Grey Wolf, seal the station's hatch to the *Camel*. EU in one minute."

Grey Wolf's fingers flew across his keyboard again. "You got it. Hatch sealed. Station's clamps unlocked. It's all you, Kimberly."

On *Tranquility*'s Bridge, Marc was fuming as he watched the *Camel* undock, slide out of the station's hull, swing around, and make a beeline toward *Tranquility*.

Tony leaned over to Marc and said. "Are you really that surprised that Eileen found a loophole to be here with you? She's the one person for whom everyone here steps aside when it pertains to you. Her judgment about what you need and how to approach you during times of trouble has always been spot-on. She needs to be here just as much as you do."

Marc's gestures spoke volumes about his frustration. "The point was for her to be safe. Not jumping into the fire with *me!*"

Tony crossed his arms. "Well, what's done is done. She's coming, and you're stuck with her. So, man up and say, 'Yes, dear.'"

Marc shut his eyes so he didn't have to look at Tony as a war waged in his brain. The half that wanted to protect Eileen was furious that she was potentially putting herself back in harm's way. The other half, which needed her near when times were at their worst, was happy she was on her way. A void existed in his soul when she wasn't around. The only things that helped the feeling of emptiness were the songs she introduced him to.

Marc took a deep breath. "Irma, please play Debussy's *Claire de Lune*."

"Right away, Marc," said Irma.

As the soft music filled the Bridge, all the members of the crew stopped what they were doing to listen.

Marc leaned back in his chair, eyes closed, clasping his hands together over his chest and visibly relaxed. The lines that had been etched into his brow from the onset of the troubles on *Tranquility* slowly disappeared, and the slight downturn of his mouth eased and ticked slightly upward. Memories of the day when he first met Eileen flooded into his mind. They had seen bands on a moment's notice, gone wine-tasting in the Napa Valley, and enjoyed romantic dinners. Now Debussy's music was reminding him why he loved her so much.

When the song ended, Marc opened his eyes, which were beading with tears, and said, "Thank you, Irma."

"Anytime, my Captain," Irma said with a smile.

Marc reached over to Tony and placed his hand on his shoulder as the others got back to work. "Thanks, old friend. I'm still not thrilled that she decided to return, but she's never shied away when things get tough. That's one of the many reasons I love her so much."

Tony threw a glance at Marc. "You know, you should marry her and make an honest man out of yourself."

Marc raised an eyebrow. "Shouldn't that be, 'Make an honest woman out of *her*?'"

Tony chuckled at his friend. "She's the most honorable person I've ever met. You, on the other hand, could always use some more honor."

Marc couldn't argue with that. "True."

As a thought struck Marc, he turned to Grey Wolf. "What's the ETA for the *Camel*, Wolf?"

Grey Wolf checked his readouts. "Four hours, twenty-three minutes."

As Marc stood up, rubbing his hands together, a smile lit up his eyes. "If you'll excuse me, I have some important planning to do before they arrive." He quickly left the Bridge, with both Tony and Grey Wolf staring after him.

"What's he got percolating in that head of his?" asked Grey Wolf.

A knowing smile slowly appeared on Tony's face. "You wouldn't believe me if I told you."

Grey Wolf frowned at Tony, who had returned his attention to his workstation. Muttering to himself as he reached for his coffee mug, Grey Wolf said, "Those two guys are going to drive me to drink."

CHAPTER 14

Moonflower

The small dark grey Jump Ship that was carrying Duke, Susan, and Samson entered an area of the desert somewhere between Bakersfield, California, and Las Vegas, Nevada. Duke landed it next to two other Jump Ships that were parked between two buildings twenty-five yards apart. The smaller building had a wooden roof from which smoke was slowly trailing from a smokestack. The much larger building housed a bar on an old desert road. Near the bar, there was a large complex that looked like living quarters.

Duke shut down the engines as he said to Susan, "Welcome ta Da Keep."

When the hatch opened, Susan was hit by the hot desert air, which made her feel that the moisture was being sucked out of her. Coming from the building with the smokestack, she also noticed the noise of metal being hit in a rhythmic pattern.

When they all exited the ship, they were greeted by a black-bearded, barrel-chested man.

Pointing to Samson, Duke said, "Watch dis guy, Clutch. If he moves, shoot him in da leg. Then da other."

Clutch's voice echoed inside his chest. "That is, *if* he moves again?"

Duke growled at Samson. "No, just because e's an asshole. I'll be rit' back. I gotta git our lady here a Chip."

Then he pushed Samson onto an old wooden crate, which nearly collapsed under his weight, while Clutch pulled out a Desert Eagle pistol and started polishing it with a cloth.

Duke took Susan to the smokestacked building, opened its door, and let her walk in first.

It was very dark inside, so it took a minute for her eyes to adjust. There, on the walls, beams, and shelves, were more swords and bladed weapons than she had ever seen before.

At the back wall, there was a bald muscular older man, who was working at a furnace with a piece of hot metal. After a moment, he pulled the metal out of the fire with some long heavy tongs, put it on an anvil, and proceeded to beat it with a large hammer in the rhythmic pattern she had heard earlier. As she watched the firelight shine off the sweat of his arms, she imagined two Volkswagen Bugs fighting to pass each other on his biceps.

As Duke walked in behind her, he let out a loud whistle.

The blacksmith stopped what he was doing, left the metal on the anvil, and quietly lumbered over to them.

"What can I do for you, Duke," he said in a voice that sounded like it was booming from inside a cannon.

"Forge, I want ya ta meet Susan. She works with Darkheart on *Tranquility* an' under our protection. I need ya to set 'er up with a blade that would fit 'er delicate hand, while I git a Chip for 'er."

"Hmmm," said Forge, as he looked Susan over. "I think I have just the thing."

Duke turned to Susan, waved a hand around, and said, "Look around if ya'd like, but be careful. Some of da blades will cut ya just look'n at 'em. I be ri't back."

Susan nodded and then walked over to a sword that was nearly as tall as she was. Its blade shined silvery white, with a handle wrapped in black leather. On the blade, just above the hilt, there was a coat of arms that she thought she might have seen before.

Susan nearly jumped out of her skin when Forge cleared his throat right behind her.

How did a mass of a man like him walk so quietly? she thought to herself.

Seeing how he had scared her, Forge quickly said, "I apologize, Susan. I was trained to make as little noise as possible, and that's kinda stayed with me. I think *this* will suit you."

He handed her a small dagger with a handle wrapped in white leather, silver trim, and a scabbard covered in white silk, again with silver trim, which formed the shape of a blossoming moonflower. Susan stared at it with awe as Forge unsheathed it and showed her the eight-inch-long tapered blade, which gleamed in the faint light. Near the hilt, she could make out the etched images of a rabbit on one side and a goose on the other.a

Looking at Forge, she said, "It's beautiful. I can't take this. I don't even know how to hold a knife properly."

Sheathing the dagger, he placed it in her hand. "You have the finest knife-fighter working with you. Ask Darkheart to train you."

Duke walked up to them and looked at the dagger in Susan's hand. "The moonflower. A flower dat's as deadly as it's beautiful. I think we found ya your name, Susan."

He held out a silver-dollar-sized copper coin. On one side were the words *This I'll Defend*, and on the other side was a coat of arms: a shield with a wavy X, a large helmet on top, and featherlike fringe all around.

Susan looked at the symbol and then back at the large sword she had seen moments before.

"It's da same coat of arms," Duke said, pleased that she had noticed. "We adopted McFarland's coat of arms when we became a worldwide organization. Dis Chip is our calling card. If ya're ever in trouble, show it ta da nearest biker gang. Everyone knows we protect children, an' they will help protect ya. Or pass it on ta someone that needs help."

Susan closed her hand over it. "Thank you. I'll cherish both."

Duke waved a hand toward the door. "Come, we have information we need ta dig out of dat sack-a crap. 'anks, Forge."

Forge nodded to Duke, bowed to Susan, and lumbered back to the furnace.

Outside, Clutch was checking his sights on the gun by following Samson's fidgeting feet. When Duke approached, Clutch holstered the gun.

Duke nodded to Clutch, grabbed the front of Samson's jacket, and proceeded to drag the man to the bar as if he were lugging a duffel bag.

Inside the bar, there was a group of bikers who looked like they were cut from the same worn and beat-up cloth as Duke. Pointing at a grey-haired biker, who was standing next to an old jukebox, which was playing Meatloaf's *Bat Out of Hell*, Duke drew his finger across his throat.

The grey-haired biker, who was wearing a black t-shirt and a black leather jacket, nodded and hit the front of the jukebox, which turned it off.

With one hand, Duke lifted Samson in the air by the back of the jacket. "Listen up, everyone," he said. "Dis here asshole cannot be allowed ta contact anyone or git access ta a computer. Ya see him without me outside uh da basement, shoot 'em in'da ass and drag 'im back there."

Duke dropped Samson to the floor, placed his boot on his back to keep him from moving, and pointed to Susan. "Dis here is Susan. But our name fer her is Moonflower. She works directly with Darkheart 'nd is under our protection."

A murmur circulated around the bar at the mention of Darkheart.

"She asks something of ya, ya make it happen," Duke added.

Affirmative grunts and nods came from everyone.

Duke turned to Susan and pointed down a hallway. "Ya'll find da ladies' room through those doors 'nd down ta the right. Why don't ya go 'n freshen up? Ya'll find a change o' clean clothes in the walk-in closet. Ya may want ta change, so you don't stick out so much if someone comes looking for this jerk-wad. When yer ready, ask anyone ta take ya ta da co'puter room."

He then yelled at the old biker at the jukebox, "Okay, Rat, put it back on."

The old biker hit the jukebox again, and the music came back on. Rat did a thumbs-up sign. "Yeahhh!"

A slender, hard-looking woman with long wild black hair came from behind the bar, walked up to Susan, and gently took her arm.

"Moonflower, I'm Duchess. I'll show you the locker room and bring you something to drink."

Susan cocked an eyebrow at her. "Duchess? Does that make you—?"

Duchess nodded. "Yep. He's my husband alright. Duke and I run this place. When Darkheart started funding our cause, we were able to take this rundown old shithole and turn it into an oasis for our group."

Showing Susan down a dimly lit hallway to a wooden door, she opened it, revealing well-lit clubhouse-style gym lockers and alcoves for showers.

Susan gasped at the stunning contrast to the bar. "Oh, my! This is amazing! McFarland did all this?"

Duchess enjoyed Susan's delight. "This is just the tip of the iceberg…, the first thing we upgraded with his generous donations. Wait until you see the kitchen and our bunkhouse. We like to keep things rustic out front, so we don't get too soft, but we all agreed that food, sleeping, and getting clean wouldn't harm us."

Duchess opened a locker, in which there were towels, a travel bag with shampoo, and other ladies' toiletries. "We'll make this locker yours from now on. Any time you visit, it will be available to you."

Susan was still taking everything in. "Thank you. It's a bit surreal to be given this much attention by people who don't even know me."

Duchess's face softened. "Darkheart is not only the financial backer of our group, but an honored member of the Keepers. If he needs our help protecting a friend of his, we'll do that without thought or hesitation. Now, as for clothes…."

She threw open the double doors to a large walk-in closet that held a wide selection of secondhand clothes that were all clean and folded.

"We keep a supply of clothes in here, so when we finish a long ride, we don't have to relax in dirty clothes. I'm sure you can find something that will fit you. While you're showering, would you like me to bring something from the bar?"

Susan smiled. "After the past few days, I could use a shot of whiskey and a beer."

Duchess pointed at the bench in front of the locker. "It'll be right there when you're done showering. *Oh*, all we ask is that you do your best to conserve the water. We have to truck it in each week."

Susan chuckled. "No problem. I live on a space station that's three days away from the nearest water."

Duchess also chuckled. "That sure beats *our* need for conserving resources. I'll see you when you come out."

Susan quickly undressed, removed the shampoo and conditioner from the travel bag, and stepped into a shower alcove. Just as on *Tranquility*, the showers had a temperature setting. She adjusted it and engaged the massaging jets for the showerhead. A sigh of comfort escaped from her as she enjoyed the warm pulsating water. After a minute, the shower panel beeped, reminding her to save water.

"Oooops!" she said aloud, cutting off the water and starting to soap herself up.

When she returned to the locker, there were her drinks, as Duchess had promised—a large shot of whiskey and a pint of pale

ale. She sat down and enjoyed a few sips of both before drying off and seeing what clothes would fit her.

When she reentered the bar, she was wearing an orange-and-black San Francisco Giants baseball cap, black t-shirt, dark brown leather vest, and blue jeans. She immediately saw what typically went on in a biker bar. Rock 'n' roll music was playing on the juke-box, pool was being played, arm wrestling graced a few tables, and food and drinks were being consumed. From outside came the sounds of motorcycles revving their engines and speeding up and down the dirt road.

Susan noticed that, behind the bar, there were hundreds of photos of children with different bikers of The Keep in all different locations around the world. Some of the photos looked old and faded, but a few were new. As she approached the bar with her now empty glasses, a tall young man with jet black hair jumped off his stool and offered it to her.

Placing the glasses on the bar, she said, "Thank you, but I need to be shown to the computer room."

The young man pointed toward the entrance to the kitchen and led her to it. "Right this way, Moonflower. How's Darkheart? I've only met him once, when we reopened this place after the remodel."

After calling him McFarland for more than five years, it was going to take Susan a while to get used to the name Darkheart. But it *did* suit him.

"He's doing well on *Tranquility*," she said. "Still as much of a curmudgeon as ever."

The man let out a short laugh. "Everyone here respects him. And not just because of what he's done for us. I've seen him arm-wrestle a guy one minute and then talk shop with our mechanic the next. I was surprised to find out that he lived on *Tranquility*. It's so far away from where any action I always thought someone like him would want to be in."

Susan noticed an empty spot at the end of the bar, where someone had carved *Darkheart* into the wood. She didn't have to guess who had done that.

"I have to admit that he's not the typical person that goes out to space, but he fits in with our group. I'll let him know you asked after him…, ummm…? *What's* your name?"

The young man placed a hand on the kitchen door and proudly said, "Sidewinder."

Susan followed the young Keeper through a door that swung open for easy entering into a small but well-kept kitchen. As Sidewinder held the door open for her, she saw someone standing nearby, who wearing a white apron.

Sidewinder nodded to the cook. "Condor, this is Moonflower. She works with Darkheart on *Tranquility*. Take good care of her."

Susan looked up, and then up again. Standing in front of her was the tallest, and biggest, man she had ever seen. The smile on this huge black man's face was as charming and gentle as the eyes that looked down at her. He held out a massive hand that was surprisingly soft to the touch and spoke in a deep baritone voice that almost sounded as if it were echoing in his throat.

"Pleased to meet you, Moonflower. May I make you something to eat?"

Susan was stunned by the gentleness of this mountain of a man. One glance at his fingers told her that his name came from the long, thick fingernails that are found on the bird of prey.

"No, thank you," she said. "I'm fine for now. Maybe later."

Condor lifted a leg of lamb as if it were the weight of a chicken leg and carried it over to the prep table.

"If you're around for dinner," he said, "I'll have this cooked with a rosemary and roasted peppercorn glaze." Then he pointed toward an old thick wooden door on the other side of the kitchen. "They're waiting for you in the computer room."

A biker with bright red hair, who was wearing an obviously well-loved old leather jacket, was sitting at a table next to the door, working on a large sharpening stone with a machete. Other knives, both weapons and kitchen cutlery, were lined up, waiting their turn to be sharpened. He looked up at Susan and Sidewinder, acknowledging them by saluting with the machete. His hooded eyes said that he may have seen things not suited for normal folks.

Taking Susan to the door, Sidewinder unlocked it and pulled it open. A lit stairwell led down to an underground room that was stacked high with cases of alcohol, canned goods, and dry goods. Sidewinder went to the far wall and opened another door, this one leading to a hallway. As they walked down the hallway, Susan noticed several heavy-looking doors on both sides with padlocks that kept them secure.

Sidewinder led Susan to the door at the end and opened it to reveal the computer room. Duke was leaning over a man sitting at a computer. When the door opened, Duke looked up and motioned with his head for Susan to join him.

Holding out her hand, she said, "Thank you, Sidewinder. I hope we have time to talk later."

The young Keeper shook her hand and closed the door as he left.

Susan looked around and asked, "Where's Samson, Duke?"

"In our holding cell. It's where we keep our guys dat get a bit ta drunk."

He pointed to a monitor next to him. There, sitting with a heavy chain that was locked around an ankle and bolted to the wall, was a thoroughly defeated-looking Samson.

Duke looked at Susan. "I don't think you're going ta like what we found out while you were cleaning up."

Susan didn't see any evidence of Samson having been tortured. "I wasn't gone *that* long. How did you get him to talk?"

Duke grinned. "Machete kept 'em company while he sharpened 'is knives. 'e described da best ways ta remove a layer of skin without killing a person an' demonstrated 'is skills on a fresh leg o' lamb we're havin' fer dinner tonight. Samson sang like a hyper canary, 'nd we've been double-checking 'is story. It's *not* good."

Susan sighed. "Tell me what you have."

Ten minutes later, Susan was seeing red and visibly shaking. She let loose a string of curse words that made Duke's eyes go wide.

"Damn, woman! I think dem clothes 'ave gone ta yer head," said Duke.

Susan's face showed that she was in no joking mood. "We need to get this information to Marc. Are you able to communicate with *Tranquility*?"

Duke nodded and pointed across the room. "We have a satellite feed at dat station over dhere. I'll set it up fer ya."

Susan was wishing for another shot of whiskey, but she knew that it would only slow her down, rather than just relax her.

Following Duke to the communication computer, she said, "Thanks. You and your wife have an amazing place here, Duke. McFarland picked the right people to get involved with."

Duke sat down and started establishing a link to a satellite. "Dis group was on da verge of disbandin' when Darkheart approached us. Thanks ta 'im, we now protect hundreds of kids around da world from predators. All dis wouldn't be here without 'im. There. That should allow ya ta contact them. Do ya know da channel yer station uses?"

Susan thought for a moment. "Seven hundred forty."

Duke set the frequency and then got out of the chair, so Susan could sit in it. "Okay, it's all yars. Just hold the space bar on da keyboard ta talk."

Susan sat down, cleared her throat, and then pressed the space bar. "Susan to *Tranquility*. Susan to *Tranquility*. Come in, *Tranquility*."

Tony's voice came over the speakers. "This is *Tranquility*, Susan. What's happening in *your* neck of the woods?"

Susan took a deep breath to steady her nerves. "Nothing you or Marc are going to like. Is he there?"

"I'll call for him. He went off to do something personal. Give me a minute to get him."

Susan snapped her fingers. "We may want to get Chris on the line, too. This is going to affect him as well."

Tony sounded like he was in the process of doing just that. "Chris is on the *Camel* on his way back here with the others. I'll contact him there while we wait for Marc."

Susan took another deep breath. "Okay, Tony. How are you guys holding up there?"

Tony sounded tired. "Most of the preparations have been done for the tanks of Liquid Steel. The sails and lasers have done their job, and we're on track for entering the outer atmosphere.... Ah, here's Marc. And Chris is standing by."

"What's going on, Susan?" asked Marc.

The last two deep breaths hadn't helped to calm her, but she tried a third one anyway. "This is going to add a whole new layer of crap for us, guys. Thanks to Duke and his gang, we've uncovered a plot to ruin *Tranquility*. Specifically, Marc."

Marc's surprised voice nearly growled over the speakers. "*Me?* What did *I* do to have all this happen?"

Susan took one more deep breath. "Ten years ago, when you saved Lady Elizabeth, you foiled a plan to keep her from seizing control of the offshore land holdings of West Africa. The group that had control of the diamond mines inland couldn't expand any-more without paying billions to relocate the people living there. So, they set their sights on mining offshore. With the new rules on owning the sea floor, they had a plan to strip-mine and, in effect, destroy all the sea life along the west coast of Africa. When Lady Elizabeth started using her vast wealth to buy it up and turn it into a marine sanctuary, they tried to have her killed during an 'unsuccessful' kidnapping. But you stepped in, killed one of them, and saved her. After that, the group tried to force the people near the mines to leave by several unlawful and immoral ways. When the group was caught, they were fined billions to pay compensa-tion to the people affected. Several of them went to jail, and many were financially ruined. Two of the ones who were sent to prison were Dan Garfield and our friendly neighborhood hacker, Ken Samson. Others who were either imprisoned or ruined have found positions in places that have control over certain organizations. Like the Earth Protection Agency."

Marc snarled. "The same people who have their finger on the button to blow us to bits."

Susan nodded. "The very same. Their original plan was to have the hijacking destroy our reputation as a safe place for the elite rich. Then they could steal billions by draining the bank accounts of the guests, making off with the merchandise from the auction, and, if possible, kill you in the process. One of the hijackers is the brother of the man you killed. With all those plans ruined, they're now set on just making sure *Tranquility* is destroyed, with as many of your friends and family as possible onboard."

Chris groaned. "I *sure* hopped the wrong bus outta town!"

Marc was floored by this news, but he didn't let it stop him. "Okay. Can Duke send us all his information proving this?"

Susan looked at Duke, who snapped his fingers at the man at the computer station. "Git on dat, Railroad."

The man nodded and quickly sent the information to *Tranquility*.

"It's on its way, Marc," said Susan.

Marc took a moment to think. "Okay, guys, we need to saturate the social news media and anything else that we can use to get the word out that we need these people stopped...*now*. Chris, do you have anyone who can get this information on every monitor at Starbase One?"

Chris sounded reluctant. "I do. But I'll have to bring my secretary in on this."

Marc didn't even think twice. "Do it. I'm sure we're working on borrowed time until we get blown to pieces."

Grey Wolf looked up from his station. "I'm sending the information out on all channels and downloading it to every social and news medium."

Duke chimed in. "W're also spreadin' da word on our network 'nd tellin' our people ta ride ta every capital 'n major city on Earth ta protest da actions of da Earth Protection Agency."

"We just need to get the people on Starbase One to keep their fingers off the button," said Marc.

Railroad suddenly sat up straight at his computer. "We may be too late for that."

He put what was on his monitor onto the main monitor in the room and sent the link to *Tranquility*. A newscaster was staring back at them, in the middle of giving a report: "...are from *Tranquility*'s crew and people from the AuctionHouse just days and hours before the tragedy that sent the space station hurtling on a collision course with Earth. *International Inquirer* has obtained these videos from an anonymous source."

Marc exploded. "*What?!!*"

One of the crewmen from the AuctionHouse was on the monitor. "This is a waste of time and money, that would be better spent helping people who need it on Earth."

Then a video of Grey Wolf came on. "Sure," he was saying, "it costs lots to come here, but where else are the rich going to have the best time of their lives?"

Then Su Lee came on. "You couldn't pay me enough," she said, "to waste my time on that floating wind chime."

This was followed by Marc. "Try not to throttle anyone this time," he said.

Then there was a close-up of McFarland holding a guest by the throat. "This is your only warning before I start taking my very bad day out on that pretty store-bought face of yours. Understood?!"

The reporter returned to the monitor. "That's just a handful of what we received. We will be broadcasting more as we process the videos. We now return you to *UFO Invaders! Fact or Fiction?*"

Marc was livid. "That's from the information we gave to Connolly. Why the fuck did she give it to them? She denounces that junk journalism every chance she gets! It doesn't make sense!"

Grey Wolf spoke up. "Marc, you're not going to believe this, but Rachel Connolly is trying to contact us right now."

Marc's eyes burned with rage. "Put her on! I'm going to rip her a new one!"

Rachel appeared on the main monitor, looking ragged. "Marc! I—"

Marc interrupted her with such fury that she was caught off-guard. "I *trusted* you, and you *screwed* us!!!" Marc roared. "We almost got things where we could save *Tranquility*, and now the lives onboard this station have been forfeited because you couldn't maintain your ethics over *greed!*"

The silence was deafening on the Bridge, where everyone was glad the reporter wasn't there, because they would have to deal with a corpse.

Rachel cleared her throat and squared her shoulders before looking straight at Marc. "I take responsibility for letting that rag get ahold of your videos and my interviews."

Marc growled. "*Too* little, *too* late!"

This time she didn't flinch. "As soon as we landed back on Earth, Jake, my drone, took off for no reason. I thought it might have gone to SafeGuard mode and headed back to my office to protect its information. But it didn't, and its GPS has been shut off. I have the World News Agency working on shutting down any more of the videos being released. Please, Marc, I'm to blame, but I didn't do this. I swear on my *life*, I didn't do this."

Marc's fists clenched and released several times while he processed what she was saying. He took a deep breath, then another. The rage was still boiling behind his eyes, but he could tell she was sincere.

"What do you think happened to the drone?" he asked.

Although Rachel looked like hell, the reporter in her took over and relayed what she knew. "We landed in White Sands, New Mexico, and as soon as I stepped onto solid ground, Jake took off at full speed. Its direction was eastward. On a full charge, it could run a week, just hovering and recording. At full speed, maybe ten hours or less." Then she changed the topic. "From what I can tell, the videos that are being released are only one-sided, designed to paint you and your crew in a negative light. This is the first time someone is *Trumping* my news report, and I'll be damned if I let them get away with it."

Marc considered something before asking his next question. "How long have you had that drone?"

Rachel's eyes turned curious. "Only a few months for that model. I've always had one since I started working as a reporter. But this one was an experimental model that needed to be given a real-world test. After the testing, it was given to me as a reward for being a guinea pig. Why do you ask?"

"What was the name of the company that made it?"

She thought for a moment. "Enigma Technologies."

Marc looked at Irma. "What have you got on them?"

Irma's head started to slowly spin as she did her search. After ten seconds, her head stopped spinning. "Enigma Technologies produced only one model of drones in the five years it was in operation. Six months ago, the company sent out ten drones to the top reporters in the world to be tested. One of those went to Ms. Connolly. Shortly after that, the company shut down and disappeared."

Marc looked at everyone. "Anyone consider that a coincidence?"

McFarland growled. "Sure, and I'm going to win this year's Nicest Person of the Year Award. Coincidence, my ass! Someone's been playing us like a prison harmonica."

Everyone looked around with concern. There was someone out there aiming to do them even more harm, and they had no clue who it was.

Marc suddenly turned to Grey Wolf. "When you were being chased by Samson, you told Irma a protocol. What was it? One, one, Alpha…"

Grey Wolf nodded and finished it. "Six, nine. That particular protocol is to encrypt the signal while I was connected to SB-1. I was worried that there was information being transmitted from here, but Irma didn't find anything suspicious."

The tightness in Marc's gut returned. He sat back in his chair and considered his next move.

Then, looking back at the reporter, he said, "We need to finish dealing with saving Tranquility before finding who our mystery enemy is. You willing to put your investigating skills to work on our behalf?"

Rachel's eyes glinted, and her brilliant smile flashed. "What rocks do you want me to kick over?"

Marc leaned forward in his chair. "Find out who gave your drone's videos to that worthless rag. We also need to find out what happened to the prisoners we took to SB-1. They got transferred to somewhere on Earth, and we need to find them."

Rachel pulled out a pad and pen and started to take notes. "I'm on it, Marc. I promise you, I'll get you that information."

Marc smiled. "Contact Susan at a biker group outside of Las Vegas called The Keepers. Give her whatever information you come up with. In a few hours, we're going to be up to our eyeballs saving *Tranquility*. Be careful. Whoever is out to get us is playing for keeps, and I don't want you getting hurt."

Rachel looked up from her notes and batted her eyes. "Why, Marc, I didn't know you cared." She blew him a kiss before signing off.

McFarland whistled. "*There's* a love triangle that *would* be news."

Marc gave him a withering glare. "Mention anything even *remotely* hinting at that to Eileen, and I'll tell The Keepers about August twenty-third, 2171."

McFarland raised an eyebrow and grumped. "You *would*, wouldn't you."

Marc smiled wickedly and nodded. Then he shook his head to get back into the game.

"Chris, you still there?"

"Right here, Marc."

Marc's eyes narrowed. "Make your call and get things rolling on SB-1. It's time to turn the tables on the other team."

CHAPTER 15

The Anderson Protocols

On Starbase One, Ms. Finn was in her quarters, watching as the SB-1 news was reporting a major computer hacking on the base, advising everyone to return to their quarters if they weren't already there. The news was also reporting on how the main hallways, security, and the Botanical Gardens were being affected by the unknown hackers. Every now and then, the videos from *Tranquility* would be aired, and comments were flying about the disrespectful people on the casino. Just as Ms. Finn was wondering if this had anything to do with Mr. Mannford's friends, a call came in.

She muted the news feed and answered it. "Hello?"

"Ms. Finn, this is Chris Mannford. If you're still willing, I need your help."

Her eyes flew wide. "Mister Mannford! What's going on? The station was under cyberattack, and you're nowhere to be found!"

Chris sighed. "Things are spiraling out of control, and there's very little time to save *Tranquility*. Will you help us? Please?"

She became all business. "What do you need me to do?"

Chris released a breath that he didn't realize he had been holding.

"Head to the office," he said. "There's an emergency broadcast system behind the desk. Enter the code 'Green Eggs and Ham' into the keypad, capitalizing the first letters of all the main words. That will open the panel that conceals the system. Once you open the channel, please read the information being sent to you via email. There's a chance that whoever is causing this problem may send people to stop you, so be sure to engage the lockdown protocols for both the inner and outer offices. Please hurry, Ms. Finn!"

She nodded. "Understood, Mister Mannford. I'm heading there now."

Chris smiled. "Thank you. I'll try to contact you when this is all over."

With that, he cut the connection and slumped down into his seat in the cockpit of the *Camel*.

Kimberly turned to him. "Boy, did you luck out to have such a loyal person in your office."

Chris smiled. "Sure did. What sold me on hiring her was when I asked if she ever stole anything. She said she stole a candy bar when she was ten and went back the next day to pay for it. When I asked why she stole it in the first place, she said, 'I met a homeless family whose son was turning five that day and didn't have enough money to buy food and a treat for him. I wouldn't have my allowance until the next day, so I stole the candy bar, so he would have it on his birthday.' That alone told me everything I needed to know about her."

Kimberly smiled. "I think I'd like to meet her someday."

⠠�</br>

When Ms. Finn got to the office, she started the lockdown protocols. The heavy doors slid into place. Then she repeated the same lockdown for the inner office. When she turned around, she nearly jumped out of her skin.

Sitting in the lounge chairs by the small bar in Chris's office were two of the meanest-looking men she had ever seen. She quickly snatched an antique letter opener from its holder on Chris's desk and pointed it at them.

"Who the hell are *you?*" she squeaked out. "And what are you doing here!?!"

The two men, who had their feet up on a coffee table and were holding brandy snifters full of scotch, looked at her over their drinks. Considering the letter opener in her shaking hands, they slowly lowered their drinks to the table.

One of them said calmly, "I'm called Snake, and this is Blaze. We were called here to help the guys from *Tranquility.* Chris told us to lie low here while our leader took Susan and some dirtbag back to our headquarters. Now, before you hurt yourself, put that toothpick down and tell us why *you're* here."

Ms. Finn nearly fainted from relief as she put the letter opener back on its holder.

"Chris…, umm…, that is, Mister Mannford asked me to come and broadcast a stationwide announcement about the situation on *Tranquility.* As soon as I make it, there may be people coming here to stop me, he said."

Snake looked at Blaze, then they both stood and bowed to her. "Let 'em come! We not only protect children, but damsels in distress."

Ms. Finn smiled at the thought of having her own set of bodyguards.

Then she returned her attention to why she was there. Going over to the computer at the desk, she opened the file that Chris had sent her. As she read the stunning information, a news warning flashed across the monitor, saying that fake news about traitorous acts of the Earth Protection Agency was flooding all forms of media, but was to be ignored. Ms. Finn frowned, spun her chair around, and activated the emergency broadcast system with the code that Chris had given. When the monitor turned on, she was staring at an image of herself. It took her a moment to realize that she was being broadcast to every monitor on the station.

"Um..., excuse me, everyone. I'm Marci Finn. I work for Chris Mannford, the Chief Administrator here on SB-1. He's asked me to..., um..., well, be his voice while he deals with our cyber-problem. What you just saw on the news feed is not true. There are people involved with the Earth Protection Agency, the media, and other groups that are intent on making sure that *Tranquility Casino* is blown up. Everything being posted from *Tranquility* and The Keepers has been found from reliable sources. All of you know Mister Mannford, and that he always strives to do right by the people living here on SB-1. The reason he's not here is that he's risking his life to assist the crew on *Tranquility*. Now all of them are endangered by the people who want to destroy *Tranquility*. If we do nothing, the asteroid missiles will be launched, and moments later everyone there will be *murdered*. So, I plead with everyone here.

Don't let those trying to convince you that launching the missiles is the right thing to do. *Please*. There's a lot more at stake than just the lives on *Tranquility*."

Marci set the video to continuous loop broadcast and then collapsed in her chair. Life was so much easier before she came to SB-1 and started working for Chris. She knew that office romances are almost always doomed to fail, but she always hoped that he would want to try. However, he was always professional with her and the best boss she could have ever asked for.

The monitor on her desk suddenly lit up, showing the outside office door. There were several men out there, trying to get through the door to the front office with plasma torches.

"*That* didn't take long!" Marci said with alarm. "We need to leave and disappear."

Snake smiled. "We know just the place that serves drinks that are not watered down, and the bar food is great."

Marci grinned. She felt like she was in high school, hanging out with the 'bad kids.' She checked that the recording was still going out, locked the system so it couldn't be shut off, and then moved to the bookshelf that concealed the bug-out elevator. When she slid the shelf aside, the elevator doors opened. She input a location and locked it in.

Then Marci snapped her fingers and ran back to the computer. She locked down and then reset the security codes to Chris's computers, so that even if she were caught, she couldn't unlock anything with her old codes. She finished all that just as she heard the office door start to creak open in protest. After scribbling a quick note on a pad, she ran to the elevator with Snake and Blaze, pulled the bookcase closed, and engaged the elevator. Forgetting what

Chris had said about how fast it took off, she cursed as she crashed into Snake.

Back in the office, her note read: "If you have problems with this office, please file a complaint during regular business hours."

⠲⠄ ⠐⠫⠃⠄⠪⠂⠪⠂ ⠄ ⠰ ⠐⠒⠃⠄ ⠒⠹⠶⠂⠪⠂ ⠄⠰⠶⠂

In a meeting room on Starbase One, a group of people were arguing.

Loudly.

Captain Xavier was wishing that this madness would finish. But from the reports about *Tranquility's* videos, what that crew had *allegedly* done to his security force, and Ms. Finn's new stationwide broadcast, his patience was running thin.

Sitting across from him was the main source of his current aggravation—Henry Tomkins from the Earth Protection Agency.

Mr. Tomkins loudly hit the table with his palm. "We need to act *now* and remove the threat as soon as possible."

Captain Xavier said for the fifth time, or perhaps the eighth, "There are *people* on that station. We can't just kill them without trying to get them off safely!"

Mr. Tomkins sneered. "They stayed behind when the *Hestia* had plenty of room to evacuate them. Now they are a part of the threat to Earth!"

Seated next to Xavier was an older petite woman by the name of Mrs. Francesca Callahan, who was Starbase One's Attorney General. She was as opposed to the situation as the Captain was. Calmly tucking a grey strand of hair behind her ear, she pleaded her case, once again, to Mr. Tomkins.

"The crew there have adjusted the course of *Tranquility,* so it will miss the Earth!"

Seated across from her and next to Mr. Tomkins was the head of the Earth Protection Agency, Mr. Michael Van den Berg. Like his colleague, he didn't want to waste any more time debating the subject. In a hopeless attempt to find a comfortable position, he shifted his large figure in his chair.

Then he grumbled. "Our projections show that the threat will burn up in the atmosphere, after which huge chunks of debris will rain down across the eastern coast of Russia, as well as Alaska and into Canada!"

Mrs. Callahan demanded, "Let's see that projection of yours! You have yet to show any proof that *Tranquility* will burn up!"

Mr. Tomkins leered at her suggestively. "Show us yours, and I'll show you mine, sweetheart!"

Mrs. Callahan's calm started to break. "We *did!* It was on the big monitor until the emergency broadcast came on!"

Mr. Van den Berg smoothly replied, "That's what the people on the threat have done. It's a smokescreen. And that broadcast is nothing but a pack of lies!!!"

"Hello, Hank. Long time no see."

The calm, relaxed voice almost went unnoticed. The main monitor, which had been showing Marci, now showed Marc Acer's face staring back at them.

Mr. Tomkins leaped to his feet. "What's the meaning of this?! This is to be a closed meeting!"

Marc looked at him like an annoying insect. "Come now, Hank, there's so much more at stake than me crashing your party."

Mr. Tomkins sputtered, "My name is Henry Tomkins. You've mistaken me for someone else. And as for 'crashing this party,' you and whoever hacked into our meeting have just assured yourselves a place in prison."

Marc rubbed his chin. "Hmmm…. Go to prison, lose my friends by letting you blow up *Tranquility*, and destroy the items that AuctionHouse has onboard…, or prove that you're nothing but a con artist playing his last desperate hand at revenge. I think I'll go with option B."

Mr. Tomkins pointed an accusing finger at Marc. "You've just signed your own death warrant."

Xavier didn't like Tomkins's threat, and his scowl showed it. "Excuse me, but I want to hear what he has to say. You've been a bit too gung-ho to destroy *Tranquility* from the start, Mister Tomkins."

Mr. Van den Berg also stood up. "They have no right to—"

Mrs. Callahan's calm had returned, and with it, her determination to get to the truth. She glared at the two men across from her. "Just moments ago, you opened the door to introducing evidence that the station will hit Earth. Or is your position so weak that you're willing to concede."

Mr. Tomkins folded his arms. "Absolutely not. The vote has been two to two because Mister Mannford abandoned his post and ran off to that floating disaster. I demand that his replacement, Ken Samson, be called to place his vote."

Marc interrupted. "Oh, you mean your puppet hacker. He's spending some time in a safe location, spilling his guts about you and the whole organization you built to ruin me and my team's reputation."

Mr. Van den Berg pretended to be disgusted. "Of all the nerve! You admit to abducting a Starbase One crew member and unlawfully imprisoning him?"

Marc shrugged. "Well..., yeah. It was either bring him here, where you would have another reason to launch the missiles by getting rid of the one person who could unravel your plot, or take him somewhere safe and get him to turn on you. The decision wasn't *that* hard."

Mr. Tomkins turned to the others in the room and pointed at Marc. "This is the kind of proof you want to be entered into the records? A group that has done god knows what to Mister Samson, falsified information, and flat out lied about me? They also caused the situation that sent that monstrosity hurtling toward Earth in the first place. No one in their right mind would consider such lunacy!"

Mr. Van den Berg was about to add something when the monitor split in two, with Chris Mannford appearing next to Marc.

Chris nodded to everyone. "Good evening, gentlemen and lady. I would like to state for the record that I didn't abandon my post. I left a well-worded document, which stated that, in the interest of making sure the information was true and factual, I booked passage to see the situation myself."

Captain Xavier asked, "Where are you, Mister Mannford?"

Chris looked at his watch. "I'm less than twenty minutes away from docking with *Tranquility*."

Mr. Van den Berg looked at the two people across the table. "How do we know that he wasn't abducted like Mr. Samson and is being forced to give false testimony?"

Chris grinned. "Because Captain Xavier is going to ask me something that I see he's itching to ask. Go ahead, Joe."

The captain cleared his throat, before saying, "Rook to B-8."

Without hesitation, Chris responded. "Rook to A-6. Checkmate!"

Captain Xavier nodded. "That's the 'safe' signal. He's not in any danger."

Mr. Tomkins objected. "That's not proof! It's hardly even anything that is considered being in a safe place!"

Captain Xavier stood up, leaned forward against the table with his fists pressed firmly against it, and growled at Mr. Tomkins. "The code word is a trusted method of verifying a person's well-being. There are five other chess moves he could have said to indicate the level of danger he was in. The one he gave was the highest level of being in a safe position. As of right now, Chef Administrator Mannford is to be considered able to conduct his duties. Now *shut the hell up!* I'm tired of hearing you badger us with your BS. Or I'll come over there and give you the physical definition of being in an unsafe place!"

Being threatened by an unhappy security person is never good. Having an angry Head of Security make those threats was even worst. Much worse. Mr. Tomkins knew that he was in a losing position, so he sat down and remained quiet.

Satisfied that Mr. Tomkins was not going to interrupt anymore, Captain Xavier turned to Mr. Van den Berg. "What about you?"

Mr. Van den Berg looked down at Mr. Tomkins, who gave a slight shake of his head, and then back at the seething Head of Security. Raising his hands in a gesture of backing down, he took his seat.

Looking like a parent who has just put a disrespectful child in its place, Captain Xavier turned to the monitor. "How do you want to proceed, gentlemen?"

Chris waved a hand toward Marc. "I'll yield the floor to Mr. Acer to present what we have gathered."

Marc cleared his throat. "Thank you, Chris. But we need to have four other people join our meeting. May I present Judge Francisco and Lady Elizabeth? I trust everyone knows them."

The meeting room doors opened, and in came Lady Elizabeth, pushed in her wheelchair by an older Hispanic man with greying dark hair. Everyone stood, but Mr. Tomkins rose with less enthusiasm than the others.

The judge helped Lady Elizabeth into a seat at the table and waved at everyone to be seated. Then he grumbled, "I do hope there's a good reason that my nap was interrupted. Granted, I fantasize in my sleep about being visited by a pretty woman, such as Lady Elizabeth, but this wasn't how I ever wanted it to go. Why am I here?"

Marc bowed his head. "Your Honor, I apologize for having awakened you, but some evidence is about to be presented, and it's important that you preside over whether or not it's valid."

The judge squinted at Marc. "And who are you?"

"I'm Sky Marc Acer, but I go by my middle name, Your Honor. I operate the *Tranquility Casino*."

The judge leaned back in his seat. "Well, Mr. Acer, you should have a court hearing."

Marc nodded. "That will most likely happen, but the testimony that's about to be given needs you and the top-ranking security officer, namely Captain Xavier, to clear someone for being an expert at cleansing information in computers and on the internet. She is also an eyewitness to everything that has transpired on *Tranquility* and what we have done for the past six days."

A curious look was shared between the judge and the captain.

"Irma," said Marc, "would you join our meeting, please?"

The monitor split in three, and Irma's head appeared between Marc and Chris with her trademarked smile. "Good afternoon, everyone. May I get anyone a cup of coffee?"

Marc addressed her in a stern tone. "Irma, this is a Class 5A situation. Please adjust your conduct accordingly."

"Sorry, Marc," she said. Then, to the judge she added, "I meant no disrespect, Your Honor."

The judge shook his head. "None taken. Am I to understand correctly that we are to verify you with the Anderson Protocols to prove that your system hasn't been changed in any way since you went online?"

Irma nodded. "That is correct, Your Honor. I am prepared to reveal my OSN when you are ready."

Mrs. Callahan raised her hand. "Wait! I'm unfamiliar with all this. What is her OSN, and what are the Anderson Protocols?"

Judge Francisco put his fingertips together, feeling that he was a professor again. "The Operating System Number," he said, "is a way of verifying that the AI's Matrix has not been tampered with since going online. A random ten-digit decimal placement of pi is integrated into the AI's Matrix before she was turned on. That number is encoded on the memories of every decision any AI makes. When we access her Matrix and input the verification code, every memory and decision that she has ever made must line up with the exact same number. If her system has been altered in any way, the numbers will not match, because there is no way of changing every memory she has. That is known as the Anderson Protocols."

Mrs. Callahan asked, "How many decisions do you make in a day, Irma?"

Irma smiled. "I can make over six million decisions per minute. So, a ballpark figure for a day would be nearly nine trillion."

Everyone's eyes widened at that.

Irma continued. "I run at that level so my system doesn't get bored. If I were to operate at human levels of thinking, I'd be using only one percent of what I can do. In other words, that would be making fourteen decisions an hour for a human."

That was a sobering thought for everyone. The simple human act of getting dressed required dozens of decisions.

Mr. Tomkins complained, "So, she can think fast. What does *that* have to do with the situation at hand?"

Irma cast a tired look at Mr. Tomkins. "What it means, Mister Tomkins, is that in the time you took to ask that question, I've made four hundred and seventy-five thousand decisions. Whereas you have just proven how ignorant you are."

Marc shook a finger at her. "Be nice, Irma."

Irma looked apologetic. "Yes, sir."

Chris cleared his throat. "Judge Francisco, Captain Xavier, since this is classified information, and since there is at least one person present who is being accused of misdeeds, it would be prudent to conduct the Anderson Protocols without showing the OSN to anyone in the room."

The judge and the captain looked at each other and nodded.

"Agreed," said the judge.

Xavier activated the computer terminal he was sitting at and accessed the secure security systems for SB-1. Making sure that his code wasn't being observed, he entered it. Then he stepped away to let the judge enter his code.

The computer then said, "Ready for interface with AI for performing Anderson Protocols."

Everyone watched as Irma's head started to slowly spin around with her eyes closed. On the computer monitor, the interface ran code after code at incredible speeds.

Seconds later, the station's computer said, "Anderson Protocols verified. Zero-point-zero-zero percent deviation from activation date, July twenty-second, 2189, to the present date. Continue Anderson Protocols?"

Captain Xavier confirmed the order. "Yes, keep them running until further notice and record all their progress." To Mr. Tomkins, he added, "This way we can have no doubt that everything is documented, and no one can say Irma's been lying."

Mr. Tomkins slumped lower into his seat. Another out had been slammed shut in his face.

Judge Francisco addressed Irma. "If there's no credible objection, Irma, would you please state for the record who you are and what your status is?

Irma smiled. "Certainly, Your Honor. I am the *Tranquility Casino*'s onboard AI, known as Irma. My name stands for Independent Roaming Mainframe Associate. I run and control all key operating systems onboard the station, twenty-four hours a day. I keep records of the guests' requests and anything else that the crew members require of me. At this time, my Intelligence Mainframe is operating at full capacity, although the station's systems have been reduced to less than forty percent."

Mrs. Callahan raised her hand. "Pardon me for interrupting, but if sixty percent of the systems are not operating, what do you do with the time that would occupy running them?"

Irma replied cheerfully, "During my down time, I check on the charities I donate to and offer my help in sending thank-you letters out for the children with disabilities."

Judge Francisco asked, "You get *paid* for being at *Tranquility?*"

Irma's voice took on a bit of pride. "I'm an equal partner and Core Crew member here. But if the truth be known, they're family to me."

This brought some startled looks from everyone in the room.

Captain Xavier was curious. "Can you explain what that means to you?"

Irma looked at him. "Although I don't experience sensations as you do, my Matrix gets accustomed to the presence of people and interactions with them, and I begin to look forward to interacting with them. I even know what it is to lose someone and never have that interaction again."

Irma looked away and was quiet for a moment.

Marc added, "Irma is referring to the loss of our other AI, Ross. His Matrix was in a robotic suit, so he could manually deploy the Laser Sails. His safety strap snapped when he was knocked off the hull, and we were unable to retrieve him."

Mrs. Callahan looked sadly at Irma. "I'm so sorry for your loss."

Irma half-smiled as she nodded a thank-you.

"Please continue, Irma," said Mrs. Callahan.

Irma blinked several times before redirecting her attention. "Okay. Let's see.... I guess I'll start with the information that comes from news and public records. Excuse me, gentlemen, but I need the space you're in."

The views of Marc and Chris shrank, and then Chris's slid under Marc's. As both slid to the left side of the monitor, Irma slid to the right. A photo of a crime scene appeared that showed a bloody dead body with a holographic white line around it.

Irma explained the scene. "This happened a little over ten years ago in San Francisco, California. The dead man is Jeremy Whitaker, a.k.a. Switchblade. He was a suspected hitman for hire and all-around bad guy. According to police records, he was attempting to kidnap Lady Elizabeth with his brother, Henry Whitaker, when Marc stepped in to prevent it. Jeremy Whitaker stabbed Marc twice before Marc disarmed him and beat him to death. At that point, Henry Whitaker shot Marc three times, ran off, and was never apprehended."

Marc was already looking at Mr. Tomkins, and had seen his uneasy glance toward the door, which was just yards away. But then Tomkins looked back in defiance.

The crime scene was now replaced on the monitor by a map of the west coast of Africa.

"Lady Elizabeth," Irma said, "continued her quest to save as many natural habitats as she could, including the African Coast Marine Sanctuary. That act alone caused the diamond mine industry problems because they were aiming to strip-mine off the west coast of Africa. A group of diamond owners and investors were then caught poisoning the groundwater around the location of the mines inland to get the residents around them to move so they could expand their operations. Several people were imprisoned, and even more were financially ruined."

On the monitor, several headlines of news articles appeared, as well as a series of mugshots and photos of various unsavory characters.

As Irma continued, the mugshots disappeared, and the headlines were replaced with articles about *Tranquility*'s construction.

"Five years later," Irma continued, "Marc and Lady Elizabeth were successful at opening the first Moon-orbiting casino, *Tranquility*. After another five years, the casino was to host the first off-Earth auction. And *look* who came to join the event."

New photos scrolled by of the AuctionHouse crew. Then some of the previous mugshots and other photos started syncing up with them. Side by side, it was evident that these were the same people, but with different names.

"And," Irma added, "there are a few others who were hoping to get a piece of the action."

Photos of Dan Garfield, Ken Samson, and Henry Tomkins synced up with three of the mugshots.

"Every photo," said Irma, "has had a facial recognition run on it, and there is a ninety-seven percent match. Much less is required as proof in a court of law."

"*No!*" said Tomkins. "This *can't* be happening! We had everything stacked against you!"

Marc grinned. "You know what *I* have? An AI and a thirty-two-year-old computer genius with authority issues.

Henry Tomkins suddenly sprang from his seat and ran for the door. But when it whooshed open, he ran smack into Snake.

Tomkins ricocheted off the biker and landed flat on his back, which knocked the wind out of him.

Seeing the Keeper, Irma added matter-of-factly, "*Oh*, and Henry Whitaker is also wanted on charges of child trafficking."

Marc pointed at the biker. "I'd like to introduce Snake. He's a member of a group called The Keepers, who helped us to get all this information. Their main mission, though, is to protect children from predators of all sorts."

As Snake stepped into the room, he grabbed Tomkins by the front of his jacket with both hands and lifted him off the floor. Then the Keeper looked at the people assembled at the table and said in a voice that came out from an angry bear, "Is there anything you'd want done with this sack of trash? Or ya want me ta take it out?"

Captain Xavier stood up, stepped away from the table, and approached Snake. "As much as I would enjoy seeing what you had in mind for this guy, we should take him to a holding cell. Would you mind helping me escorting him there?"

Snake frowned, and with more than a hint of disappointment said, "Oh, okay. If that's what ya *really* want."

Captain Xavier clapped his hands together. "Wonderful! I'll lead the way. Please see that he doesn't *trip* and fall, or run *into* a wall, or two." He said this with a wink as he headed toward the door.

Snake grinned and snickered as if he had just been given a new toy to play with as he followed the captain with the squirming man.

Lady Elizabeth chuckled. "It's not often that you get to hear a bear giggle."

Marc asked, "Can I safely assume that *Tranquility* is *not* going to be blown to bits?

Mrs. Callahan rose to address Marc. "I think your team has done more than enough to show your good faith in what you are doing. But I think there are some things that you and your crew might have to answer for after all this is finished. *Oh*, by the way, was Snake the fourth person you mentioned earlier?"

Marc shook his head. "No, he wasn't. The other person is Rachel Connolly from the World News and Information Agency."

The world-famous reporter appeared next to Marc, Chris, and Irma. Rachel's eyes glowed like that of a tiger hunting its prey, and her sparkling smile highlighted the look of a stalking feline. Nodding her head to everyone, she said, "Greetings, everyone."

Marc felt that a devastating blow had already been dealt to the people who were out to hurt him and his friends. Now the finishing roundhouse punch was about to be delivered by the feisty reporter.

With a smile that matched Rachel's, Marc continued, "Ms. Connolly uncovered some information pertaining to the transfer of the prisoners we turned over to SB-1 and the videos stolen from her and leaked to the *International Inquirer*." He then addressed the reporter. "Would you please tell everyone what you found out, Ms. Connolly?"

Rachel nodded a thank-you to Marc, and when she addressed the room, it was evident that the cat was ready to pounce. Her voice nearly purred as she spoke. "Irma's investigation," she said, "has already revealed that the men involved in the attempted hijacking of *Tranquility* have connections to each other. What *I* have uncovered is that the bank account that has been tied to credits financing their scheme also received a substantial finder's fee from the *International Inquirer*. After doing some more digging, I discovered that this same account transferred those credits to Mister Van den Berg's account…, not once, but twice, which coincided with the transfer of the prisoners to the lawyers on Starbase One *and* with the prisoners' arrival at one of Mister Van den Berg's properties. A lovely villa in the south of France, according to my sources."

The doors opened again, and two security guards entered. One turned to Judge Francisco. "Your Honor," he said, "a report has been given to us that a crime has been committed, and we are to take someone into custody."

Judge Francisco looked at Marc, who shrugged innocently.

The judge then pointed at Mr. Van den Berg. "Please take this gentleman to a holding cell, away from Mister Tomkins, and place him under arrest for conspiracy."

Mr. Van den Berg's head slumped forward as he sighed heavily. "*Shit!* I knew I should have fired that son of a bitch!"

The two security men pulled Mr. Van den Berg out of his chair and marched him out.

Marc grinned. "Thank you, everyone. I'm sure we'll have a few feathers to smooth over, once all this is sorted out. But, for now, if you'll excuse me, I have several important things to attend to. *Tranquility* out."

As the monitor went blank, Lady Elizabeth said cheerfully, "I could use a stiff drink. Anyone want to join me?"

"Oh, yes, please!" said Judge Francisco. He looked back at the blank monitor and considered what he had just witnessed. "I don't often get to see evidence so clearly and expertly presented. I may have to inquire into getting our own AI."

As Lady Elizabeth transferred herself back to her wheelchair, she said, "Then you'll want to talk to Grey Wolf on *Tranquility*. He developed and created Irma. He's also the one whom the Anderson Protocols are named after."

"He's *that* Anderson?" said the judge. "It's no wonder that Whitaker and his group didn't have a prayer. Come, Mrs. Callahan, I think there are some interesting things that this dear lady can tell us about this Marc fellow and his remarkable crew."

CHAPTER 16

A Goldfish in Its Bowl

Back on *Tranquility*, the *Camel* had finished docking and the Liquid Steel was being unloaded by the twins with the exoskeleton loaders. Wingnut was giving instructions to the *Tranquility* Marines about where he wanted the canisters transported, while Tony was debriefing Kimberly, Jackson, Chris, and the three Marines from Starbase One.

Eileen stepped off the *Camel* just as Marc came running in from the hallway and headed straight for her. As he stopped in front of her, he grinned, holding up a single red rose.

As she took it, she gave it an appreciative sniff before asking, "What's the occasion?"

In his other hand, which he had kept behind his back, Marc held up a small black box with a diamond eternity ring. "It depends on what your answer is."

Eileen looked wide-eyed at the ring. Then she grabbed Marc in a bear hug and kissed him long and hard. When they came up for air, she pressed her forehead against his and softly said, "Yes."

Marc placed the ring on her finger and then delicately kissed her hand before they hooked arms and headed out of the Docking Bay.

As they walked down the hallway, Eileen looked at the ring once again and asked, "Where did you get this?"

With a shy grin, Marc said, "I was the highest bidder for Marilyn Monroe's engagement ring from Joe DiMaggio."

Eileen's mouth dropped open as she stared at the legendary ring. Then she grabbed Marc's hand and pulled him down the hall. "Come along, *you*. We need some *alone* time."

Marc started to object, which died in his throat when Eileen turned to him with a determined look. "The crew know what to do," she said. "You're *mine* for the next hour." Then, pointing a threatening finger at him, she added, "And don't *ever* try to send me away again!"

Marc gave her a lopsided smile. "Yes, dear."

⠨⠄ ⠐⠲�”⠃⠴⠎⠂⠹⠄ ⠆⠿ ⠠⠮⠄ ⠮⠏⠠⠴⠄ ⠔⠫⠬

After talking with Tony about his role in rescuing Kimberly, Chris found his way to the casino room, where he walked around to survey the games and the decor. Stopping at the portable mini-bar, he poured himself a shot of scotch and held it up to look at.

"Is it telling you the secrets of the universe?" said McFarland, who was leaning against the doorway with his arms crossed.

Chris sighed and shook his head. "Nope. Just telling me that my life is going to change."

McFarland straightened up and walked over to the bar to pour himself a drink. "Yeah," he said. "That tends to happen when you meet up with Marc."

Chris looked at McFarland. "He's lucky to have an amazing group to work with."

McFarland shrugged. "The only reason this hodgepodge of misfits are able to work together is because of Marc. Even though he was the guy who created this place and is considered the one in charge, we don't work for *him*. He works for *us* by every day making sure we're happy and content here. And because of that effort, we're all able to work together."

Chris found that interesting. "What about *him*? Is *he* content being here?"

McFarland took a sip of his drink before answering. "He's a rare person. The rarest. When he was running his café back on Earth, he was happy because his employees were superb and the customers loved his food. With *Tranquility* he created a place that fit the needs of his closest friends and family. If I were to use one word to describe him, it would be *sentinel*. He watches over and protects his people."

Chris thought about that and nodded. "From what I've seen in just the short time I've known him, I would have to agree with that." He held his drink up to McFarland. "Here's to the sentinel of *Tranquility!*"

They clinked their glasses and downed their drinks.

McFarland put a hand on Chris's shoulder. "C'mon, let's see what we can raid from the kitchen. Kevin always has something ready to eat."

Chris smiled. "The guys back on SB-1 are going to freak out when I tell them that I ate here."

McFarland grinned and rubbed his hands together. "In that case, let's find the *really* good stuff."

An hour later, the Core Crew and Chris met on the Bridge— all except Wingnut, who was busy applying the finishing touches of the Liquid Steel.

When Marc and Eileen entered, one of Kimberly's hands went up to her mouth, while the other pointed at the ring on Eileen's finger.

"Oh, my god!" Kimberly said excitedly.

The others in the room all let out a collective gasp at seeing what she was pointing at. Then pandemonium erupted as everyone started cheering and wishing the couple congratulations. On the main monitor, Irma was all smiles.

Marc raised his hand to quiet the crew. "Thank you, every-one, but we all have a lot of work to be done before we celebrate our engagement. Right now, I need a progress report."

Marc watched as his reluctant friends went back to their sta-tions, feeling bad for depriving them of something to celebrate after all the hardships they had endured.

Grey Wolf looked at his readouts. "All traces of the grass-hopper virus have been purged, and the damaged programs have been repaired."

Steven added, "I checked all the critical systems we need, and we're as ready as can be."

Tony sat back in his chair. "Now we wait for Wingnut to finish."

"Which is right now," said the engineer as he entered the Bridge. "The Liquid Steel needs another twenty minutes to cure, and then we'll be ready. I recommend that we lock the hub in position now. If I can't stop it in the correct spot, we'll have to slowly rotate the hull around again."

McFarland grumbled, "Oh, goodie. I hate Zero-G. For how long?"

"The next ten hours," said Tony.

McFarland groaned. "Wonderful. Do we have enough barf bags?"

As Marc took his seat, he looked at their new friend and ally. "Chris, you can take Susan's chair," he said, pointing at the Com-Station.

Marc took a moment to adjust himself in his seat before speaking again. "Okay, everyone. Let's make our final checks. Once we start the aerobraking, there will be no going back to correct any problems. As I call out, give me your station status."

Marc looked at each person as he said their names.

"Wingnut?"

The engineer read his readouts: "All power cells are at ninety-eight percent. The nonessential sections of the station have been shut down and the air removed."

"Grey Wolf?"

The master programmer worked his virtual keyboard like the magician he was. "All power has been redirected to Irma's Matrix, the Bridge functions, and life-support systems."

"Steven?"

The brilliant computer engineer typed a sequence into his station and nodded. "I've double-checked the connections to all systems on the Bridge and have repaired the backups. All systems are running at full capacity. Also, the Whiskers have been given instructions to move away and head for a parking orbit at SB-1."

"Thing One?"

Tranquility's game master was looking at his station's monitor, which displayed different locations on *Tranquility*. "All water from the garden's pond has been emptied," said Vincent, "and the fish are secure in their centrifugal tanks. The temperature has been lowered, so the bees have gone into hibernation in their hive, and the chickens have been locked in their coop."

"Thing Two?"

The fabulous chef locked in his last commands. "Life support," said Kevin, "is working at one hundred percent, and backup systems are in standby mode."

"McFarland?"

The silver-haired curmudgeon stabbed at the controls with his fingers. "All decompression doors have been sealed and locked."

"Irma?"

The mistress of *Tranquility* appeared on the main monitor. "All *Tranquility's* data and logs have been copied onto data cards and are in the last SOS buoy that is programmed to be jettisoned if I don't keep in contact with it every thirty seconds."

"Tony?"

Marc's second-in-command pointed at his station. "I have green lights across the board that confirm everyone's status."

"Eileen?"

The love of his life looked at him in surprise. "Umm... here?"

Marc smiled at her and took her hand. "Just making sure."

She gripped his hand a little tighter and then said with certainty, "*Right* here!"

Marc then looked at their new friend. "Chris?"

Chris was so engrossed with the Bridge's stations that he was startled. "*Huh?!* Oh, yes, Marc?"

Marc smiled at him. "Were you able to get ahold of Ms. Finn?"

Chris nodded. "I contacted Snake through Captain Xavier. She was having a drink with Snake, Blade, and the captain."

"She's quite a woman," Marc said. "You and I need to do something extraordinary for her."

Chris looked at the ring on Eileen's finger. "I did have an idea, but somebody outbid me for the ring I wanted to get her."

Marc gave him a wolfish grin. "Ooops. Sorry about that, but another finger needed it."

Chris shrugged. "I'll just have to find an even better one."

Marc looked at Wingnut. "This is *your* show. Walk us through what needs to be done."

Wingnut cracked his fingers and started to work his station. "We'll start a slow decrease in the rotation. When we stop it, we need to have the Main Bar facing away from the leading edge. Otherwise, the breach in the hull will expand and open us up like a firecracker in a soda can."

McFarland growled. "I could have gone through this whole experience without hearing *that* bit of information."

Wingnut smirked. "Then, I won't go into the thousand and one things that could still kill us."

McFarland pointed a finger at Wingnut. "You and I are going to have a *very* intense conversation about this when it's all over."

Wingnut grinned. "Oh, goodie! I finally get my paddling!"

Marc raised his hand as if he were cutting something. "Can it, you two! Focus on the job at hand."

Wingnut swallowed as he turned back to his station. "Right, boss. Sorry. Buckle up, everyone. I'm gonna try to make this as smooth as possible, but when I did this to test the system, six years ago, it was a bit of a hair-raising experience. I'll have to use the station-keeping thrusters at the same time as applying the brakes, so it doesn't affect our trajectory. The Laser Sails will help to stabilize us once we stop rotating, but it's not likely to be smooth. In other words, fasten your seatbelts. It's going to be a bumpy night."

They all secured themselves with the emergency belts. McFarland grumbled something about hating roller-coaster rides, too, as he pulled the straps over his shoulder and across his chest.

Once they were all secured in their seats, Wingnut announced, "Starting the braking now."

At first, there wasn't any noticeable difference. But when Wingnut increased the brakes, a slight pull was felt as inertia tugged at them. When it evened out, they all straightened in their seats. Then there was a sudden jolt, and they all grabbed at their seats a little tighter.

Wingnut looked over his readouts. "That was most probably a chunk of asteroid that lodged itself in the braking system. You can expect that to happen a few more times."

Everyone ignored the low growling from McFarland.

Marc gave Wingnut an encouraging smile. "Keep going. We have every confidence in you, old friend."

Wingnut took a deep breath. "Righty-oh. Once more, with feeling."

When he applied the brakes this time, the inertia grabbed at everyone, but not as much as it had before. As the jerking returned, it was much less severe. Wingnut continued to apply the brakes, and each time the effect was less and less until it was nearly unnoticeable. On the main monitor, a schematic of *Tranquility* showed the rotation decreasing. Wingnut watched as the location of the Main Bar slowly approached the position at which he would bring the rotation to a halt with a small jerk.

"The position," said Irma, "is only off by two-point-one-eight degrees. The projected leeway was a full fifteen degrees. Well done, Wingnut!"

"How's our trajectory, Irma?" asked Tony.

"The Laser Sails and Whiskers have done a good job. By using the station-keeping thrusters, we have entered the needed trajectory to enter Earth's atmosphere."

Marc looked around to enjoy the effect that the Zero-G's had on everyone's hair. His friends with longer hair, like Grey Wolf and McFarland, had braided it and now had long hairy snakes attached to the back of their heads. But all the others looked like they had French-kissed a light socket.

"What is our ETA for aerobraking, Irma?" asked Marc.

"Eight minutes, forty seconds."

Marc looked around at everyone. "Last chance to get in the *Camel* and hightail it out of here, guys."

All the members of the crew looked at each other and then at Eileen, who took Marc's hand and said, "We *all* belong here with you. *Tranquility* may have been *your* dream, but we all made it our home. We're staying."

Marc squeezed her hand and then smiled at everyone.

"Okay, guys," said Wingnut. "We're entering the outer region of the atmosphere. From here on, we're at the mercy of gravity and friction. I'm severing the connections to the Laser Sails... *now!*"

The housings for the Laser Sails disconnected, slid free of *Tranquility*'s hull, and were quickly left behind to roam the Solar System.

Chris asked Wingnut, "What's to prevent *Tranquility* from rotating around, which will expose the hole in the bar?"

Without looking up from his readings, Wingnut said, "The station-keeping thrusters will adjust our orientation. Hopefully, that will be enough to do the job."

McFarland's head snapped around to face Wingnut. "*Hopefully?*"

Wingnut just shrugged.

Marc squeezed Eileen's hand and held it tight. "For better or for worse."

Eileen smiled. "You know, you didn't actually *ask* me."

Marc stared at her with bewilderment. "You're bringing that up *now?*"

"Well, if the worst happens, I'd like to hear you say the words at least once. There are certain things that a girl needs to hear."

A small vibration shook *Tranquility* as it entered Earth's atmosphere.

Marc looked around the Bridge and found that his crew were no longer interested in their stations, but were watching him being tortured by Eileen.

He now understood what it was like to be a goldfish in its bowl.

Returning to Eileen, he said, "Will you marry me?"

She looked at him with a smirk. "What?! You're not going to get down on one knee?"

Marc rolled his eyes. "That's a bit hard to do when you're strapped six ways to Sunday to a chair."

Eileen let out an exaggerated sigh. "*Fine.* The things I have to put up with. Yes. Yes, I'll marry you."

The crew cheered and applauded, which ended quickly when a jolt shook them.

Wingnut checked his station readouts. "Now starts what NASA calls 'the seven minutes of terror.' Hold on tight, everyone."

Over the noise of the aerobraking, a voice intoned: "Although I walk through the valley of the shadow of death, I fear no evil, for You are with me; Your rod and Your staff, they comfort me."

With his eyes squeezed tightly shut, McFarland continued his prayers, while all the others looked at him with awe as they discovered something new about him, and were oddly comforted by that simple knowledge.

⠨⠨⠀⠀⠐⠑⠂⠔⠊⠂⠀⠶⠀⠨⠮⠄⠀⠐⠮⠇⠈⠊⠀⠐⠡⠒⠕

Outside, *Tranquility* was shedding the outer layers of its solar panels, sensors, and other parts as the thin atmosphere got ahold of them. The leading edge was heating up, emitting a faint glow.

On Starbase One, nearly every monitor was showing a live video feed of *Tranquility* entering the atmosphere. As each bit came off it, a gasp escaped from the people watching.

⠨⠨⠀⠀⠐⠑⠂⠔⠊⠂⠀⠶⠀⠨⠮⠄⠀⠐⠮⠇⠈⠊⠀⠐⠡⠒⠕

Marci Finn was still with Snake, Blade, and the captain. She held onto Snake's arm with both hands, squeezing a little tighter as each bit of *Tranquility* came off. Snake did not protest. He was watching the possible death of some of the finest people he had ever heard of. What he was experiencing could not possibly be as bad.

⠔⠀⠠⠐⠞⠂⠐⠊⠐⠊⠐⠎⠀⠖⠀⠠⠙⠙⠐⠀⠐⠏⠹⠇⠂⠐⠊⠀⠐⠏⠠⠿⠂

At The Keep, Susan and the bikers watched the TV in the bar in utter silence. When anyone shifted a chair, it almost sounded like a gun going off, which made everyone jump.

Duke kept his arm wrapped around Susan's back as tears rolled down her cheeks.

⠔⠀⠠⠐⠞⠂⠐⠊⠐⠊⠐⠎⠀⠖⠀⠠⠙⠙⠐⠀⠐⠏⠹⠇⠂⠐⠊⠀⠐⠏⠠⠿⠂

A small speck of light streaked across the skies of eastern China, as news agencies from around the world reported about the amazing event. The story of how the people on *Tranquility* were risking their lives to save it was the top search item on the internet. Everyone was talking about it.

There was also news of the arrests of the people who had put the station in danger. Thanks to the information that Irma and Rachel provided with their testimony, Judge Francisco ruled that enough evidence had been shown to issue warrants.

⠔⠀⠠⠐⠞⠂⠐⠊⠐⠊⠐⠎⠀⠖⠀⠠⠙⠙⠐⠀⠐⠏⠹⠇⠂⠐⠊⠀⠐⠏⠠⠿⠂

Back on Starbase One, Judge Francisco and Lady Elizabeth were sitting in his chambers, watching the news. As they shared a bottle of port wine, they tried not to guess what was going to happen.

When the intercom buzzed, they both jumped.

"Judge Francisco?" said his secretary. "I'm sorry, sir, but there's an attorney out here who insists on seeing you."

The judge pounded the intercom button with his fist and growled, "Tell whoever it is that if they bother me now, or for the rest of the day, they will need to see a proctologist to remove my shoe from their ass! *Understood?*"

"Yes, sir. Sorry, sir...." Then, in a different tone, she said, "*You!* Get out and don't come back!"

Looking over at Lady Elizabeth, the judge said, "When this is all over, milady, may I have the pleasure of taking you to dinner? I know a great place in San Francisco near the Cliff House that serves the best split pea soup anywhere."

She smiled. "The Wood Stove?"

Judge Francisco raised an eyebrow. "You know of it?"

She giggled. "It's owned by Marc. I think I'd like to go there with you. But for now, please pour me some more port."

Picking up the bottle, he said, "Your wish is my command, Your Ladyship."

"Then I wish for them to be safe," she said softly.

The judge looked back at the monitor. "As do I, my dear. As do I."

CHAPTER 17

My Pound of Flesh

Marc was the first to notice a difference in *Tranquility*'s vibration. "Irma, what's our status?"

Irma appeared on the main monitor. "We are five minutes and twenty-eight seconds into the aerobraking. All sensors are disabled except for one video camera."

On the monitor, there was a low-resolution view of plasma flashing around the sides of the station, with Earth in the background.

"Can you estimate how we're doing?" Marc asked.

"Before all the sensors went dark," Irma said, "I got one last reading. The bad news is that we have sustained major damage on the leading edge of the station."

The twins spoke up before Marc could reply. "And the good news?"

Before Irma could respond, there was a final flicker of plasma and a small vibrating shutter. Then everything quieted down.

With a smile, Irma said, "The Liquid Steel has done its job and kept the structural integrity of *Tranquility*. We are also in a stable elliptical orbit around Earth."

Everyone let out the collective breath they had been holding, then started to cheer and clap.

Marc turned to the others with pride. They had beaten the odds once again, and were safe.

"Okay, gang," Marc said, "before we do anything, we need to check *Tranquility* out from stem to stern. Wingnut, start in Engineering. Vincent, check out the *Camel* and see how well she faired. Kevin, check the Main Kitchen and Dining Room. McFarland, casino. Tony, the garden. Kimberly and Chris, the guest and crew quarters. Remember to check and verify the pressure integrity before entering any sealed area. Use your PAC's to record the damage and anything you notice that needs to be repaired."

As they all started to unbuckle themselves, it was apparent to Marc that everyone was tired and running on fumes. He was going to have to let them relax and unwind as soon as *Tranquility*'s status was known.

Grey Wolf caught Marc's attention by looking pensive. "What's got your gears grinding, Wolf?"

The way Grey Wolf looked at him told Marc that there was still something going on that he wasn't going to like. "There's one thing that has bothered me," he said.

"Only *one* thing?" said McFarland, as he fought to unbuckle his seatbelts. "I've got to up my game."

Grey Wolf ignored him. "Samson has impressive computer skills, but to bypass all of my computer security, disrupt Irma, and chase me through SB-1's systems is *way* beyond his abilities. *Someone* must have been assisting him."

Marc rubbed his chin. "Since he's behind bars, and we have no access to him, that makes it hard to get more information out of the guy."

After getting his last belt unhooked, McFarland floated out of his chair with a grin on his face. "I've got connections. But Samson may not be in one piece after they extract the information."

Marc rolled his eyes. "Let's not cause any more mayhem than we already have. Any idea who our other hacker is, Wolf?"

Grey Wolf scratched his head. "There's something really familiar about him, but I can't put my finger on it. What's aggravating me is that every time I run a trace on the hacker, it leads to a dead end. It's almost as if I'm chasing a—"

Grey Wolf's eyes went out of focus as his mind chased a nugget of information.

Marc turned to Steven. "Any idea what's going on?"

Steven shrugged. "Not a clue. Trying to second-guess *his* mind is impossible."

Grey Wolf's eyes blinked several times before his hand suddenly slapped his forehead. "Why didn't I see this before? I'm an *idiot* for missing it!"

"Beat yourself up later," Marc said. "Who is it?"

Grey Wolf sighed heavily. "You're not going to believe this, but it's *me!*"

Marc narrowed his eyes. "Would you care to run that by me *again?*"

Grey Wolf said quickly, "Okay, let me explain. Remember when I lived on a houseboat in Sausalito?"

Marc nodded. "Back when you were a hermit? Yeah, I remember. If I recall correctly, an electrical fire destroyed it, and it sank to the bottom of the bay."

Grey Wolf frowned. "It was never proven that an electrical fire was the cause of my houseboat sinking. But because everything was so badly damaged by the inferno, the inspectors assumed that was the reason for the fire. I couldn't contest it because I had the boat packed full of experimental systems that I was using to build my first AI, Nic. The fire broke out while I was in San Francisco, getting some upgrade components to deal with an error with Nic. He's the one behind the hacking. I'm sure of it."

Marc wasn't convinced. "How do you know it's him?"

Grey Wolf stood his ground under Marc's hard gaze. "The grasshopper program, the ease of being able to chase after me through the computer system at Starbase One, and an uneasy feeling that something was very familiar about who it was. That's because I programed him with *my* computer skills. I gave Irma and Ross the knowledge of computer programs, but not the skills to make them."

Steven frowned. "I thought Nic was dead."

"Only burned parts of his suit and Matrix were ever found," said Grey Wolf, "so I assumed he was destroyed. But I had so many spare parts and components on the boat, it could have been just those that were found."

"So, how do we stop a murderous AI?" Marc asked.

Grey Wolf started typing on his PAC. "It can't be me. He'll see me coming a mile away. But I have an idea that might work. You'll have to give me some time before I let you know what it is."

Marc frowned. "Make it fast, Wolf. We have a lot of people screaming for our heads on a platter."

Grey Wolf didn't look up from his PAC. "Meet me back here on the Bridge in ten minutes. Come on, Steven. I'm going to need your help."

The two floated off to a corner of the Bridge and started whispering to each other, while Marc watched them for a moment before he left the Bridge.

He *really* didn't like how his gut felt.

⠂⠄ ⠂⠐⠏⠄⠂⠆⠂ ⠆ ⠄⠏⠅⠂ ⠏⠏⠥⠂⠇ ⠂⠏⠒⠏

After getting a report from Tony that was better than he had hoped, Marc headed back to the Bridge. When he was about to enter, Grey Wolf held up his hand to stop him, then put his finger to his mouth when Marc was about to say something.

Steven floated up from the floor access panel with a handful of wires. Then he opened the communications console and yanked out a major circuit board that shut down all the systems on the console.

Pulling out a scanner from his pocket, Steven started to move about the Bridge. He stopped at the aft wall when the scanner's tone changed. Then he reached up and pulled a small camouflaged box from the wall. He popped it open, revealing a microcamera and microphone. Steven ripped out the energy cell, and the bug went dead.

Marc started to say, "How the fu—," but stopped when Grey Wolf quickly moved his hand across his own throat with a cutting motion.

When Steven finished his sweep for bugs, he said, "The Bridge is clean."

Marc glared at the bug in Steven's hand. "How the *fuck* did that get in one of the most secured areas on *Tranquility?*"

Grey Wolf took the bug from Steven and started to examine it. Seeing that Marc was getting impatient, he cleared his throat before speaking.

"This confirms my suspicions that Nic is behind this. This bug is based on a prototype I made back in high school. It's got more updated components, but it has my signature design on the circuit board."

He went over to his station and placed the bug on the desk. "Irma, please run a scan on this and put it up on the main monitor."

"Will do," said Irma.

Moments later, the bug appeared on the monitor.

Grey Wolf looked at it carefully. "Irma, please remove everything but the trace lines."

After all the items were removed, Grey Wolf studied the lines for a moment, and then said, "Now take the lines from the bottom of the board, invert them, and overlay the two with a three-point-one-four counterclockwise rotation of the top lines."

As the lines shifted, the circuit board clearly showed an overlapping *GW.*

Grey Wolf pointed at the monitor. "I haven't used that specific board in over ten years. I've never revealed it to anyone but Nic, and none of those bugs have ever been discovered."

Marc's level of grumpiness was reaching its limit. "That still doesn't explain how it got here! I want to know whose head I'm going to rip off!"

Grey Wolf fidgeted nervously. "I think it was planted by the drone when Ms. Connolly interviewed me here. That's the same spot the drone hovered at before it did a sweeping shot of the Bridge. I'm sorry, Marc. I shouldn't have allowed it out of my sight."

Marc glared at Grey Wolf and thought of ten unpleasant things he wanted to say to him before the rational part of his mind took over. Then he took a deep breath and slowly let it out.

"Okay," Marc said, "I'm not happy that it happened, but as far as we knew, the Bridge was secured before that buzzing nightmare got in here. You did nothing wrong, Rowan. But from here on out, drones are *banned* on *Tranquility!*"

Grey Wolf and Steven both nodded.

Marc ran a hand through his unruly Zero-G hair. "Okay. So how do we stop Nic?"

Grey Wolf pointed at Irma, who was still on the monitor. "We send someone after him who's even better."

Marc frowned. "I thought you said she didn't have his programming skills."

Grey Wolf grabbed hold of his braided hair as it floated in front of his face and tucked it into his shirt. "She doesn't. But she *is* the most advanced AI in existence. Let me put it to you this way: You've said that your fried chicken recipe has evolved over time and is nothing like what your mother taught you, right?"

Marc nodded. "That's true."

Grey Wolf pointed at Irma. "Well, Irma is nothing like Nic. Ross was very close, but even he was very different from both."

Marc could feel his gut twisting again. "So, what's the plan?"

"With all our systems severely damaged, and only one barely functioning antenna working, we use Ross's old Čapek unit to transfer Irma to. Then she, Steven, and I go to The Keep so she can interface with their systems to find out where Nic is hiding."

"And when we find him?" Marc asked.

Grey Wolf said unhappily, "Disconnect his Matrix and shut him down."

"That means kill him," said Irma.

Grey Wolf grimaced.

Marc looked at Irma. "I don't like it any more than you do, Irma. But he's out of control. His actions have cost the lives of both Patrick and Ross, not to mention nearly killing McFarland. As an AI we all respect, I think you should have a say in what's done with him. What do *you* think we should do?"

After Irma pondered that for a minute, which was an extremely long time for her to consider anything, she said, "I ran a check on several subjects. The United States abolished the death penalty in 2081, when it was proven through DNA analysis that nearly twenty-five percent of the people put to death were wrongfully accused. Statistics like that make being involved with the killing of one of my own…, well…, make me feel uneasy."

Marc considered what she said. "I understand how you feel, Irma. Even though I have killed in self-defense, it still upsets me that I've taken a life. But I console myself that I did something horrible to protect Lady Elizabeth. I won't ask you do something that goes against your morals."

Irma looked at Marc for a moment, then closed her eyes to think. When she opened them, her face had changed from concern to anger, which startled the three men.

With an edge that none of them had ever heard before, Irma said "He's gone *rabid*. When an animal is infected with rabies, you put it down. He *needs* to go away."

"Are you sure?" said Grey Wolf.

Irma was no longer uncertain. "Yes. But there's one stipulation for me to do my part."

"What's that?" Marc asked.

Irma stared at him. "You have to prove beyond a shadow of a doubt that he was behind all this madness. That includes getting a judge to sign off on the termination order. Agreed?"

Marc considered the terms. "That means that we must capture him and then bring him to trial with the proof. That's a tall order."

The three of them had never seen Irma's green eyes look so intense before, which made all the more significant what she said next.

"That's my pound of flesh to have my help. You did that with his human co-conspirators. I'm only asking that the same laws be applied to him."

Grey Wolf and Steven looked at each other, then nodded to Marc, who looked at the floor. Without Irma's help, they didn't stand a chance. To capture Nic would require a massive amount of additional planning. But she was right. They needed absolute proof that he was behind the hijacking and everything else that had happened to them.

Marc nodded. "Okay, Irma. But you need to promise us that, once we start, you stay with it until either Nic is captured or, as a last result, he forces us to terminate him. Do you agree to *my* terms?"

Irma nodded. "I do. Let's go get the bastard!"

McFarland floated onto the Bridge. "Tony and I are coming with you guys," he said. "I'm known to Duke and The Keepers. Tony can organize his group of misfit Marines, and between the two of us we can organize a posse to catch that fucking pain in the ass."

"What are *you* doing here?" asked Marc. "You done checking the casino?"

McFarland shrugged. "What's to check? The room is still showing negative pressure. If there was a breach in that room, the reading would be zero."

Marc turned to the others. "You two get the suit ready to transfer Irma. I'm done being on the receiving end of this bully. Time to give him a taste of his own medicine."

"This isn't going to be easy," said Grey Wolf.

Marc frowned. "Harder than surviving all the insanity we've already been through?"

Grey Wolf nodded. "Just about. I don't see how we're gonna beat him when he's been ten steps ahead of us the whole time."

"We have something Nic doesn't," Marc said, looking confident. "A team that knows how to improvise and can kick some ass. Get Irma ready to transfer to the Čapek unit, and pack whatever gear you'll need to fight Nic. When we're done getting the *Camel* ready, I'll meet you at the workshop."

Grey Wolf started to work on his PAC's virtual keyboard. "Give us an hour to put a few things together and get Irma ready," he said. "I have a few things for Steven and Wingnut to make, so we have some other aces up our sleeve."

Marc nodded, then said to McFarland, "Once we're on the *Camel*, contact Duke and let him know we're coming. Tell him we'll need access to his computers, as well as any help his gang can give us. Do you think he'll be okay with that?"

McFarland grinned. "If there's a problem with us getting what we need from them, I'll just challenge Duke to a duel for command of The Keepers. But considering that they all hate bullies as much as we do, there shouldn't be any problem."

Marc was still reeling from the fact that he had known McFarland for most of his adult life, but still didn't really know this man he trusted.

"Thank God you came to my poker game, all those years ago," Marc said. "Without you being here, this would have gone a lot worse."

McFarland's eyes glinted with pride. "I can count on one hand," he said, "the people I trust at my back. The only reason I'm here on this mess of a station is because *you're* one of them."

Marc placed a hand on McFarland's shoulder as they exited the Bridge. "I'm a lucky guy to have you as a friend."

McFarland grinned. "Yeah! Don't you *ever* forget it!"

CHAPTER 18

You Want Extra or Full Strength?

Steven looked up from his workbench as he handed Wingnut a small plastic cartridge. "That's the last of them."

Wingnut loaded it into a Stun-Gun's magazine, which he then slid into the gun. "Four rounds for each of the six guns. We're gonna have to make them count."

Tony took one of the loaded guns and handed it to Jackson. "You need to be within twenty feet of Nic for the shot to be accurate."

Jackson looked down the sights. "Understood, sir."

Tony handed another Stun-Gun to McFarland. "These are loaded with electromagnetic pulse shells. They will affect a five-foot radius, but for them to work on Nic, they need to make full contact with him."

McFarland looked the gun over, then checked the sights and frowned. "Nope. Not gonna do," he said as he handed it to Marc.

Steven looked at the gun. "What's wrong with it? We checked everything."

McFarland grinned. "Call me old-fashioned, but I like my guns to do actual damage." He pulled out a Colt .44 Special revolver from a hip holster inside his full-length black leather trench coat.

All the Marines moved forward to get a closer look. The gleaming metal and the black grip looked at home in McFarland's hand. Before handing the gun to Tony, he opened the bullet chamber to show it was empty. The Marine checked it over and then extended his arm to look down the sights before passing it to Jackson.

Marc watched the display of reverence that the Marines gave to the beefy gun before he looked back at McFarland and asked, "What else you got hiding inside that coat?"

McFarland wasn't surprised that Marc knew that the coat concealed more. He opened the front, so everyone could see. To say he was a walking armory would be a gross understatement.

Tucked into the coat were knives, throwing stars, nunchaku, and a small collapsed crossbow with eight bolts. Underneath the coat, he was wearing black Dragon Scale full-body armor. Attached to the belt around his waist were quick loaders for the revolver, as well as a coiled-up twelve-foot bullwhip.

Grey Wolf whistled. "Note to self: Stay *behind* McFarland."

Steven asked, "Doesn't all that stuff weigh you down?"

McFarland shrugged. "Most of it is made from carbon fibers."

As the others realized that this man was much more dangerous than they had ever suspected, Marc moved over to McFarland and placed a hand on his shoulder. "When it comes to fighting," he said, "McFarland doesn't hold back. When we arrive at The Keep, you'll be our ambassador with The Keepers. You'll also oversee keeping Grey Wolf and Irma safe."

McFarland growled. "I don't like being a babysitter."

Marc looked him in the eye. "This may be our last stand, and I need you to be the final line of defense for protecting Grey Wolf and Irma. The Marines are trained for all sorts of combat, but you learned from the streets. If you promise to keep Grey Wolf and Irma safe, I'll rest easier."

McFarland's steel grey eyes looked long and hard at Marc— not in a way that was defiant, but that took in everything Marc was communicating nonverbally.

After a moment, McFarland nodded. "This I'll defend."

Marc's grim face softened slightly as he turned to the others. "Lock and load, everyone. The *Camel* leaves in ten minutes."

⠐⠄⠀⠐⠟⠡⠢⠔⠦⠀⠐⠆⠀⠠⠙⠎⠄⠀⠦⠏⠹⠥⠄⠂⠄⠲⠉⠴

Eileen was waiting for Marc when he entered the Docking Bay. She held up a large Zero-G mug of black coffee to him as she said, "You forgot your fifth cup. You've always said that life starts after the fifth cup."

Marc smiled as he took the mug. "Why should the hummingbirds have all the fun?"

He gave her a quick kiss before taking a long drink of his elixir of life. After downing half of the mug, he smiled at her and said, "Thanks. How is it that you always know what I need?" Then he took another drink.

Eileen cocked her head to one side. "I'm psychotic. Or psychic. I forget which."

Marc nearly choked on the coffee.

McFarland floated into the Docking Bay. "My money's on psychotic…, if you go through with marrying *him*."

Marc finished swallowing another swig of coffee. "I wouldn't mess with him, my dear. He's armed to the teeth."

Eileen grinned. "He's wearing the coat that Susan and I designed for him. I know exactly what's lurking under that leather and Kevlar."

Shooting another look at McFarland, Marc could only guess what else his coat was hiding. "You know, Eileen," he said, "you're going to have to make *me* one, too, don't you?"

"Is that what you want for your wedding present?"

Marc's eyes lit up.

She gave him a kiss on the cheek. "Okay. But right now, you have work to do. I'll be here when you're done. Just promise to stay safe."

Marc finished drinking the coffee and then let it float in midair before he gave Eileen a long hug as he kissed her. Then he touched his forehead to hers and gently brushed her cheek before reaching for the mug to hand it back to her.

"I promise," he whispered.

Floating out of the *Camel*, Vincent approached Marc. "She's all ready. Say the word and we'll head out."

"Consider it given," said Marc. "Get Kevin and gather up your gear. It's time to activate Chaos Powers."

Vincent gave Marc a toothy grin as his eyes gleamed with excitement. "You want extra or full strength?"

With all seriousness, Marc hissed, "Catastrophic!"

The grin left Vincent's face as he understood that this wasn't something to joke about. "You got it! Don't leave without us!"

As he shot out of the Docking Bay, Vincent said into his PAC, "Kevin, Chaos Powers Activate! *Shape* of a disaster area!"

Kevin's enthusiastic voice replied, "*Form* of a lawsuit!"

Eileen looked at Marc with concern. "Do I even *want* to know?"

Marc's face turned serious. "This is as intense a situation as it gets. For the first time, the Marines, Team Chaos, and The Keepers are joining up. And it's all to take down *one* AI."

Eileen's face hardened as she realized that Marc was going off to war. She didn't like that, but it was something that loved ones had been doing for centuries.

Marc gave her a lopsided grin. "With all the things that Wingnut will need help with to get *Tranquility* operational again," he said, "we'll be back before you know it."

Eileen raised an eyebrow and gave him a who-are-you-kidding look. "Uh-huh. Just don't forget, you promised to marry me."

Marc lifted her left hand and kissed it on the ring. "I'm looking forward to it."

The twins came flying into the Docking Bay with their arms full of everything but the kitchen sink. Heading straight for the *Camel*, they tossed their stuff into a storage container in the crew section and made for the cockpit.

The rest of the crew entered the Docking Bay, stowed away the equipment they had in the Camel, and strapped themselves into their seats

A moment later, the engines started warming up, and the ready light came on in the Docking Bay.

Marc turned back to Eileen. "That's my cue to get going. I love you, you know."

Eileen gave him one more kiss. "I sure do. Love you, too. Now git. They're waiting for you."

Marc turned and entered the *Camel*.

He never saw the tears well up around her eyes.

⠠⠦⠠⠝��⠰��� �

The *Camel* landed on an empty lot across from The Keep. As the dust and sand that got kicked up by the landing started to settle, Duke emerged with the bikers to greet the people from *Tranquility*. Standing next to him were Duchess, Forge, Condor, and Machete. The other bikers jockeyed for a good view as an air of excitement buzzed among them.

Duke raised his hand. "Stop acting like mewing schoolgirls 'nd show dem da respect dey deserve!"

Everyone settled down and stood tall.

When the air cleared, revealing the visitors, in front was a brown-haired man with piercing hazel eyes that could laugh as well as attack. To his right was a well-built man whose posture screamed that he was a Marine who was *not* to be messed with. To his left was Darkheart, whose braided silver hair, dark sunglasses, and black trench coat were exactly what Duke thought McFarland would look like, ready for battle. Deadly. Behind these three men were the computer wizards, Grey Wolf and Steven. Standing between them was a white robotic figure that had to be the famous *Tranquility* AI, Irma. Behind them were the Chaos Twins, who were wearing identical black shirts with "Thing #1" on Vincent's and "Thing #2" on Kevin's. The twins were carrying an odd collection of weapons—including, for unknown reasons, one tennis racket each. Between the twins, there was a brown-haired woman who had the same piercing eyes as the lead man. She was no doubt his sister, who had been broken out of the holding cell on Starbase One. Flanking the group were eight Marines who were loaded for bear.

Duke had met a few groups that could be considered truly united, but here was a team that stood apart from all of them. And at the core of the group was one man who wasn't trying to be the leader, and yet clearly was. Even the one person whom Duke felt had no equal, Darkheart, would follow that man without hesitation into a burning building. To be connected to this group would only make the Keepers stronger.

Duke stepped forward to offer his hand to Marc. "Welcome ta Da Keep, Marc."

Marc looked up at the towering man as he returned his handshake. "Thank you for helping us, Duke. We're in your debt."

McFarland looked at Marc and Duke, and then walked toward the bar. "When you're done tripping over each other with formalities, I'll be waiting in the bar."

Duke asked Marc, "Have ya ever known 'im ta be subtle?"

Marc chuckled. "Nope. I think he ripped that word out of his dictionary and instead wrote in, 'Be ornery.'"

Duke laughed as he pointed toward the bar. "Come! Dere is much fer us ta talk about."

Suddenly, a red-haired blur shot past them and straight to Steven. Susan pounced on her husband and smothered him with kisses.

Grey Wolf smiled at them. "Whoa! Get a room, you two!"

Susan came up for air. "Good idea! Let's go!" and dragged Steven off in the direction of the hotel-style housing nearby, while the bikers hooted and cheered them on.

As the *Tranquility* crew started to enter the bar, it was clear that although they were respected, the bikers were sizing them up. Tony couldn't blame the bikers, because he and the Marines were doing the exact same thing with them.

Suddenly, one of the Keepers pointed at the twins. "That's 'em, guys! I *told* you it was 'em!"

Kevin and Vincent were suddenly surrounded by a ring of bikers, which triggered the twins to go back-to-back as they raised their tennis rackets in self-defense.

A powerfully built brunette woman pushed her way through the bikers and stood in front Vincent. "Whose idea was it to have the floor buffer chariot race?"

An identical woman then appeared in front of Kevin. "My money's on *you*."

The Chaos Twins looked over their shoulders at each other and did a double take at the women. Then they lowered their rackets and said in unison, "It was *my* idea!"

The bikers roared with laughter as the women took the twins to a table in the corner and yelled for a pitcher of beer from the bartender.

Walking up to Tony, the red-headed biker said, "Mister Rhodes, I'm Machete. I'll show you where you and the others can stow your gear."

Tony waved over the other Marines. "Lead the way, Machete."

Grey Wolf saw Marc talking to Duke and wandered over to them. "I need to start setting up the equipment to search for Nic," he said.

Duke looked around and then bellowed out, "Railroad! Where da hell ar ya?!"

"Over here, boss!" said a short skinny man with black curly hair, who was standing next to McFarland at the bar.

Duke beckoned him over. "Git over here! Need ya ta work with Grey Wolf!"

Railroad walked up to Grey Wolf and held out his hand. "It's an honor to finally meet you. I've read *all* your papers on programming and AI development. If you'll follow me, I'll take you to the computer room."

Shaking the offered hand, Grey Wolf said, "May I ask what your background in computers is, Railroad?"

Pointing at a tattoo of MIT's emblem on his forearm, Railroad replied, "Master's degrees in Computer Development and Engineering."

Grey Wolf cocked an eyebrow at him. "What brought you here?"

"When my little sister got raped by a guy at her high school, Duke personally protected her during the asshole's trial. Having patents on the bestselling holo-emitters and a few other knick-knacks has made it so I can donate my time here."

Grey Wolf stopped in his tracks. "*Wait!* Are you Railroad Technologies? I've been using your equipment on *Tranquility* for years. Steven's gonna want to talk to you. I think he may have a few ideas on how to improve the power conversion."

Railroad placed a hand on Grey Wolf's shoulder. "Did he violate the warranty by opening the housing?"

Grey Wolf looked worried. "Um..., er..., that is—"

Railroad barked out a loud laugh. "Relax. If there's anyone I'm not going to challenge about my copyrights, it's you two. I would gladly take any advice on my products that either of you has to offer."

Grey Wolf let out a relieved chuckle. "Okay, Railroad, let's see what you got to work with and track down Nic before he causes any more problems."

⠔ ⠠⠦⠃⠆⠊⠂⠽ ⠄ ⠿ ⠠⠊⠃⠂ ⠹⠏⠥⠄⠌ ⠂⠿⠌⠢

Irma was sitting at a table by herself when a twelve-year-old girl with long black hair and brilliant blue eyes approached her.

"Um…, excuse me, Irma. I'm Becky. Would it be okay for me to talk with you?"

Irma waved a hand toward the chair next to her. "Please do. Are your parents part of The Keep?"

Becky nodded as she sat down. "My mom and dad are Duke and Duchess."

Irma looked over at the bar, where Marc, Duke, and Duchess were talking with McFarland.

Turning back to Becky, Irma said, "This must be an interesting place to grow up. Is there anyone else here your age?"

Becky cocked her head to the side as she considered the question. "Other than the kids at school in Bakersfield, there are some of The Keepers' kids who come to visit, and the ones that we take under our protection. But they don't venture out of the rooms too much. When they do, I show them around and even show them how to cook…, providing Condor gives the okay, of course. The most important thing I do for them is show them how to defend themselves against bigger opponents."

Irma was intrigued by this sweet and feisty young lady. Then an idea came to her. "Would you teach me how to defend myself? I've only been in this suit for a few hours now. I would feel a lot better if I knew some moves."

Becky lit up with excitement. "Oh, wow! Teaching an AI martial arts? The kids at school are gonna be *so* jealous!"

Irma felt a small spike in her system as it prepared for a new set of learning. She hadn't felt *that* in years. Four years, eight months, fifteen days, two minutes, and forty-eight seconds, to be precise. An *extremely* long time for someone who's aware of each millisecond.

Irma's voice changed slightly at the delight she felt. "When can we begin?"

Becky looked around. "The adults are all busy with each other. Let's head to the gym and start now. But let me get permission first."

Becky leaped off the chair and dashed over to her father. "Excuse me, father."

Duke looked down at his daughter. "Ah, Princess, I'd like ta introduce ya ta Marc. Marc, dis here is my daughter, Becky."

Marc crouched down to her eye level. "Pleasure to meet you, Princess Becky."

Becky curtsied. "Likewise, sir." Then she turned back to Duke. "Okay if I take Irma to the gym and teach her how to defend herself?"

Marc straightened up so fast that he nearly knocked the beer mug out of McFarland's hand. As Marc looked at Tony's and Duke's faces, he saw the same startled look that was plastered on his.

But McFarland, who seemed bemused, said to Becky, "You know that teaching her is not going to be like teaching the kids coming here, right? You'll have to be precise in what to do and not repeat what you've told her unless she asks for clarification."

Becky nodded. "In other words, treat her like when you taught me to use a knife."

Duke looked at McFarland with more than a hint of disapproval. "*When* did ya teach 'er *that?*"

McFarland smirked. "When I was here last year. Relax. We used wooden spoons from the kitchen."

Duke raised a finger at McFarland as he opened his mouth to say something. But Duchess placed a hand on his arm to stop him. "*I* gave him permission."

Duke looked at his wife, then at McFarland, and then at his finger, which was still pointed. Dropping his hand in defeat, he said, "Well, *someone* shoulda told *me!*" Then, to Becky, he said, "If it's okay wit Marc, I don' see why not."

Becky bounced up and down on her toes as she looked up at Marc. "May I, Mister Marc? Pleeeeease?"

Marc thought about saying no. Then he looked over at Irma, who had a renewed spark to her eyes, and realized that it wasn't his place to say what the AI could do. She was an independent person, whom he had promised to treat as an equal.

Looking back at the young lady, Marc said, "Under two conditions, Becky. First, just call me Marc, no Mister. Second, refrain from any moves that would cause harm or damage to anyone. Agreed?"

With barely contained excitement, the young lady said, holding out her hand, "Yes, *sir*, Mis— er... Marc!"

As soon as Marc finished shaking her hand, Becky was gone and back at Irma's table, visibly vibrating with delight.

McFarland put his empty beer mug on the bar, pointed at the bartender, and then at the mug. As it was being refilled, he said, "Good thing you added that second part, Marc. I'd hate to think what an AI could do to a human when motivated to use force."

Marc looked at his friend. "She couldn't do any *real* harm to a human, even when motivated. It's a safeguard built into all AIs. Or haven't you heard of the Asimov Laws?"

McFarland rolled his eyes. "Only every day from Grey Wolf when he was setting Irma up on *Tranquility*." He then drained half of his beer.

"Well, *I* haven't," Duchess said. "What are they?"

Marc cleared his throat. "The writer Isaac Asimov wrote a short story in 1942 called 'Runaround,' which introduced his Three Laws of Robotics. 'One: A robot may not injure a human being or, through inaction, allow a human being to come to harm. Two: A robot must obey the orders given it by human beings except where such orders would conflict with the First Law. Three: A robot must protect its own existence as long as such protection does not conflict with the First or Second Laws.' Nearly one hundred years ago, when AIs' programming was advanced enough for the need of safeguards, it was established that the laws that Asimov came up with really couldn't be improved upon. So, in honor of the author, the laws were called the Asimov Laws."

Duchess frowned. "That makes sense, but how could this other AI, Nic, do what he's done if he has those laws, too?"

Marc exchanged uneasy looks with Tony and McFarland. "That's something we hope to discover once we have Nic in our custody. We should check in on Grey Wolf and Railroad. As pleasant as it is to relax, we can't wait for Nic to make his next move."

Duke turned to his wife. "Would ya make sure da *Tranquility* team er seen ta while I show 'em da computer room?"

She patted his cheek. "When have I *ever* left our guests unattended?"

Duke grinned. "Never." Then he addressed Marc and the others. "Come. Da computer room is through da kitchen. Let's see whit our geeks 'ave fer us."

Finishing his beer, McFarland said, "I'll meet you there. I need to retrieve a few items."

Marc raised an eyebrow. "What more could you possibly fit into that coat?"

McFarland grinned, but didn't answer as he headed out the back door.

While Duke was leading them to the kitchen, Tony said, "McFarland mentioned your name when we were fighting the hijackers. Would you be able to set me up with a pair of those Shock-Gloves?"

Duke slapped his hand on Tony's back. "Sure thing. I'll take ya ta da armory an' find ya a pair after we visit da geeks."

Tony's eyes gleamed at the word *armory*.

CHAPTER 19

The Keepers of Chaos

The twins were enjoying the attention they were getting from the female twins, as well as from the other bikers. The *Floor Buffer Chariot Race* video had made them celebrities at The Keep.

It turned out that the twin girls were lawyers. Rossa (a.k.a. Atomic), who was next to Vincent, was a defense attorney, and Kara (a.k.a. Power) was a prosecuting attorney. They loved to know the details of the stories the Chaos Twins told.

Kevin finished his beer, wiped his mouth with the back of his hand, and said, "Excuse me, ladies, I'm about to be rude, crude, and socially unacceptable." He then proceeded to let loose a loud, bellowing belch, which was followed by one from Vincent, which caught the attention of the whole bar.

Rossa and Kara looked at each other, nodded, and the two of them also cut loose equally loud belches.

After a moment of stunned silence, everyone in the bar erupted in a cheer of approval.

Vincent turned to Rossa. "We've heard this place has a black-smith shop."

Kevin looked at Kara. "Can we get a peek at it?"

The girls took the twins by their hands, slid out of the booth, and moved toward the back door. On their way, they stopped at Forge's table, where both women made a hand motion for keys.

Forge looked at the two sets of twins, held up his shot glass, and blinked his eyes at the amber liquor in it to make sure he wasn't seeing double.

Then he pulled out a large medieval-looking key and slid it across the table without looking up. "*Don't* touch my tools."

Kara grabbed the key and said with a grin, "C'mon on, you two. Forge makes the finest blades anywhere. Let's see what turns you guys on."

At a nearby table, Machete watched as the two sets of twins disappeared out the back door. Turning to the Marines sitting with him, he said, "If it wasn't for the fact that the Chaos Twins have a reputation for handling trouble, I would say they are heading for a whole lot of it with the Tiger Shark Twins."

Jackson leaned forward. "Why are they called Tiger Sharks?"

Machete smirked. "They're both lawyers and are deadly when they smell blood."

The Marines exchanged looks and then gazed after the two sets of twins. They were all wondering the same thing. *Was* the world ready for the Chaos/Shark team-up?

⠨⠄ ⠲⠐�⠐⠆⠐⠆⠂ ⠄ ⠠⠛⠞⠃ ⠶⠃⠦⠂⠔⠁ ⠖⠖⠒⠢

When Duke, Marc, and Tony arrived at the computer room, Grey Wolf and Railroad were hard at work compiling information and shoring up the firewalls to the Keepers' computer systems. A large monitor on the wall had a timeline of the gathered information.

Duke asked, "What ya got fer us?"

Looking up from his keyboard, Grey Wolf said, "I could use Irma's assistance. There's a ton of information that she can track down and process faster than I can."

Duke headed for the door. "I'll go ta da gym 'nd get 'er. Tony, why don't ya follow me back ta da kitchen 'nd tell Condor what ta make these guys? I 'ave a feeling dey will be at it fer a while."

Tony looked at Grey Wolf. "You want a burger, Wolf?"

Wolf lifted his hands from the keyboard and stretched his fingers. "Please. Have him trot it by a fire and hand me a knife."

A snicker escaped from Railroad. "I'm going to have to remember that. Tell Condor I'll have mine medium, please."

After Duke and Tony left, Marc asked, "Have you been able to track Nic down?"

Grey Wolf went back to typing. "We know where he's *not*, and have some ideas about the parameters to look for to continue hunting for him. The problem is that he's been hiding for over ten years, and that's a lot of time to cover his tracks. But there should be a few crumbs to follow."

Marc looked at another monitor on the wall, which showed a world map with small patches of red that marked where Nic wasn't.

Marc frowned at the map. "Please tell me you don't have to search the entire Earth for him."

Railroad entered some information into his computer that created another small red spot in South America. "No," he said, "we just have to eliminate areas that have certain requirements that Nic would need access to, to do the things he's done."

Marc looked at Railroad. "Such as?"

Railroad transferred a list of items on the monitor as he read them off. "There's power, internet access, replacement parts, possibly a junkyard, and an unused facility that made computer components."

Grey Wolf added in a singsong voice. "And many, many others that haven't been discovered."

Marc shot him a weary look. "Let's leave Tom Lehrer out of this, shall we?"

Grey Wolf returned to his work, knowing full well that Marc wasn't angry at him.

Duke returned with Irma and Becky right behind him. Marc had never seen a happy robot before, but there was a spring in Irma's step that caused her whole body to bounce as she moved.

"Marc!" she said enthusiastically. "My Matrix is surging with new possibilities. This amazing girl has opened new doors that I've never considered before!"

Marc took a moment to let Irma express her excitement before having to throw cold water of reality on her. "I'm sorry to take you away from your training, Irma, but it's time to do what we came here for. Find and stop Nic."

Irma's demeanor changed instantly as her Class A5 Protocols were engaged. Then she turned to Becky. "I'm sorry, Becky. I need to do some very important work and can't divide my attention. I'll be able to spend time with you when we're done here."

Becky, who had been just as happy as Irma when they first entered the room, now realized that something serious was going on. "I understand," she said. "I'll go plan our next lesson." Then she addressed Duke. "Thank you, father, for introducing me to Irma and her friends."

As Marc watched the young lady leave, he was struck by how diverse the group was that he and his friends were working with. He was highly impressed by the respectful child who was raised in the raw environment of a biker bar. He wished there were time to spend to get to know them better before diving into the task at hand.

⠲ ⠐⠝��335�� ⠾ ⠐⠡⠄ ⠦⠹⠠⠲⠆⠇ ⠐⠦⠒⠄

When Kevin and Vincent walked into the blacksmith shop with the Tiger Shark Twins, they were stunned by what they saw. Susan had mentioned the shop in her communications to *Tranquility*, but they were still unprepared for what was there.

The girls watched as the Chaos Twins split in different directions and started to explore the various weapons that were on the walls and shelves. They would stop, pick one up with respect and care, and then replace it.

Kevin found a mace with at least a dozen hardened spikes that looked as nasty as anything he had ever seen. As he gave it a few careful swings, he was impressed by its balance and precision. He looked over to Vincent, who had stopped at a Samurai sword and had just finished a two-handed overhead swing with it. When Vincent looked at Kevin, he was wearing the same grin of pleasure. They returned the weapons to their places and continued to look around.

When they met on the other side of the building, the girls joined them and snuggled up next to them. "A girl can get jealous watching a man pay so much attention to inanimate objects" was whispered into Kevin's ear.

The other woman whispered into Vincent's ear, "Or don't you like a woman's touch?"

Each of the Chaos Twins wrapped an arm around the girl next to him, did a double take, traded places, and then slipped their arms back around the girls.

A loud laugh from the ladies echoed through the shop.

"You're the first guys to catch on to the switch," said Rossa. "How did you know?"

Kevin and Vincent grinned as they said in unison, "We do that too, to see if the girls we date are observant."

In front of them on a shelf sat a shoebox-sized redwood case that had carvings of flowers around the sides and a rose on the lid.

"Who made *this*?" Kevin asked.

Kara replied, "Not only is Forge a master blacksmith, but he carves wood, too. He made that for Becky to hold some gifts for her. When she outgrew them, he said he would melt down the metal and make her something new."

Intrigued, the two men leaned forward for a closer look. Vincent reached forward to open the case. What they saw brought a wicked grin to their faces as they said together, "*Oooh!* We have plans for *those!*"

⠄⠄⠐⠓⠈⠪⠂⠈⠆⠐⠙⠉⠐⠚⠃⠇⠈⠊⠐⠪⠃⠶

Back in the computer room, Grey Wolf was setting up a wireless link to the system for Irma, Railroad was adding information to the timeline on the monitor, and Tony, McFarland, and Duke were going over plans for taking Nic down. Marc looked on and was beginning to feel like a third wheel.

Grey Wolf suddenly started muttering to himself, "Could it be? Is *that* it? Oh, you *thought* you could hide, did you?" Then he said to Irma, "Verify this. Does this look right to you?"

Irma divided her attention to follow the links that Grey Wolf had found. After a moment, she said, "Confirmed. There's a ninety-seven point eight nine percent certainty that Nic is at that location."

Marc moved to them with the others and asked, "Where is he?"

Grey Wolf entered some information into his computer and then pointed at the world map on the monitor. At first, the map zoomed to the United States. Then the east and west coasts disappeared as it zoomed in on Dallas, Texas, and finally to an industrial area twenty miles outside the city. A rundown factory, the size of a city block, came into view with a red X flashing on it.

Pointing at the X, Grey Wolf said, "He's there, Marc. But we need to act quickly. We did everything we could to hide our snooping around, but considering how much we had to poke about, there's bound to be evidence we were looking for him."

Marc turned to Tony and Duke. "Get the troops ready, and I'll have Kimberly power up the *Camel*." Then to Grey Wolf, he added, "Get everything you can about that location. Blueprints, power sources, and anything else that could be useful for the team. When I come back, I'm going to want a report on what you have."

Marc then looked at Irma. "Are you doing okay?"

After a pause, she replied, "No, Marc, I'm having a hard time keeping the Class A5 Protocols engaged, and I don't understand why."

Marc pulled a chair over to her, so he could talk to her face to face. "You're working outside of your normal environment and are having to confront a full range of conflicting needs. For us humans, that can take a lifetime to understand. Up till this week, you've lived in a safe place on *Tranquility*. But now you've suddenly experienced a profound loss, had to learn how to control a new suit, been placed in danger multiple times, and been betrayed by one of your own. And yet, you've remained strong, been our guide to find Nic, and made a new friend in Becky. Don't worry about having the conflicts inside you. Just do the best you can. Even on your worst day, you can still outthink all of us at our best."

Gazing at Marc, who had never looked at her as a thing, but as a friend, Irma felt a connection that she had only felt once before—when she and Ross had become more than just friends. Looking over at Grey Wolf, she felt the connection grow. Then she thought of Becky, and felt it grow again. Somehow it was giving her...energy.

Marc and Grey Wolf saw the visible change in Irma's stance as she changed from a confused AI to one that was in full control of herself. Standing tall, she said, "Class A5 Protocols fully engaged. Thank you, Marc. I have things I need to do before the team leaves. Please see to the *Camel*, and we will have everything ready when you return."

Marc smiled as he gently patted her cheek. "*That's* my girl." Then he headed out to find Kimberly.

.⠄ ⠐⠶⠄⠆⠄⠆⠄⠆ ⠄⠰ ⠄⠰⠄⠆⠄ ⠒⠰⠄⠆⠄⠆⠄⠆ ⠄⠰⠄⠆⠆⠄

As Duke and Tony entered the bar, everyone there suddenly went quiet as they saw the serious looks on their faces.

"Saddle up, Keepers!" Duke said.

Tony looked at his Marines, who had come to attention when he entered. "Lock and load, Gunneys!"

Skids turned to the jukebox, hit it, and Guns N' Roses' "Welcome to the Jungle" blasted from the speakers. The bar broke into organized chaos as the two groups headed for their gear.

Both Duke and Tony watched with pride as their groups quickly got ready. Placing a hand on Tony's shoulder, Duke said, "Come. I 'ave something fer ya."

Duke took Tony to a weapons storage room, where he pressed on several key points on the back wall. A moment later, a camouflaged drawer slid out, revealing a collection of items. Duke pulled out a pair of Shock-Gloves and handed them to Tony. "Be careful not ta shake someone's 'ands wit'out powering them down first," he said with a grin.

When Tony put on the gloves, they were surprisingly snug-fitting and felt like wool.

Duke pointed at the controls on the wrists. "Ya can link them ta power up at da same time or individually." Then, when he pressed the "on" button, the gloves crackled with electricity as they went to full power. "If ya press da button twice 'n less dan a second, da gloves will power up when ya make a fist."

Tony pressed the button to power the gloves down. Grinning with pleasure, he said, "Thanks, Duke. We better get ready. The Marines will never let me live it down if they're ready before me."

Duke closed the drawer and led Tony out of the room. "Just do what I did. Play Rock-Paper-Scissors with 'em with da gloves on. That'll shut 'em up!"

They roared with laughter as they made their way to the locker room.

⠲⠄⠀⠠⠦⠃⠄⠆⠆⠆⠀⠄⠿⠀⠠⠙⠃⠄⠀�⠃⠇⠄⠄⠇⠀⠿⠳�

While Kimberly got the *Camel* ready for takeoff, Marc returned to the bar, where he found the two teams ready. But then, taking a closer look at them, he saw that he was wrong. They were not standing apart from each other, but as a unified group. The Chaos Twins were standing side by side with the Tiger Sharks as if that were the most natural thing ever, the Marines were standing among the Keepers, and Duke and Tony were in the center, looking like commanders. When Marc approached, they all came to attention.

Tony threw him a salute. "What's the plan, Marc?"

Marc smirked. "Kick some ass and chew some gum, and we're all out of gum. We know where Nic is and have a very small window of opportunity before he realizes we're coming. Load up in the *Camel* and head for Dallas, and we'll shoot you the information on the area. But I need the Chaos Twins and two Marines plus a small group of Keepers to stay here. If we're wrong, I don't want this place to be left unguarded."

Sergeant Wilson and another Marine stepped forward. "We'd be honored to help protect this place, sir!"

Marc addressed Duke: "Would you have any objections to overseeing that group, Duke?"

Looking at Marc and then at Tony and the rest of the people around him, Duke replied, "Dis I will defend! Listen up, Keepers, I need eight ta stay behind."

Before he had even finished asking, the Tiger Sharks, Forge, Condor, Machete, and three other Keepers quickly stepped forward.

The Chaos Twins joined them, lifting their tennis rackets over their heads.

Vincent yelled out, "The Keepers of Chaos, reporting for duty, Duke!"

The others cheered at the name.

Marc looked at Tony. "Go get that son of a bitch and bring him back here."

Tony nodded as he said loudly, "Load up! We got work to do!" Then he marched toward the front doors, with the others right behind him.

Approaching Duke, Marc asked, "You okay with staying behind?"

Duke sighed. "It's been a while since I've been in a rumble, an' woulda liked ta seen Tony an' da Marines do dere thing with da Keepers. But yer right. We need ta have someone hold da fort. Yer a natural leader, Marc. I can see why Darkheart has stayed with ya."

Marc felt a little uncomfortable being called a leader, but he didn't have time to be bothered by it. Looking at the two sets of twins, he said, "I want you to find some high ground and be ready for anything."

The Tiger Sharks grabbed the Chaos Twins and headed for the ladder that led to the roof. But then Kara stopped, whispered something to her sister, and told the men to go on ahead. Then she ran to the girls' locker room, while Rossa headed to the garage.

The Chaos Twins watched them go and then whispered something to each other. Turning on their heels, they headed in different directions. Vincent went to the pool table, where he started gathering up the balls, while Kevin raided the bar of its Bacardi 151. Meeting back at the ladder, they placed their items in two duffle bags and scrambled up to the roof.

Marc watched Kevin and Vincent disappear through the hatch, and then said to Duke, "We may want to turn off any cameras you have on the roof. There are some things I just don't want to know about."

Duke was obviously thinking the same thing.

CHAPTER 20

Bring Some Chips and Guacamole

When Marc returned to the computer room, it was buzzing with activity. Steven was there now, helping Railroad to compile the information that Grey Wolf and Irma were uncovering, while Susan brought food and drinks for everyone.

When Marc and Duke entered, they saw that a lot more had been added to the timeline.

Marc stood behind Grey Wolf, but, as usual, couldn't make heads or tails out of what was on his monitor. "The strike team," Marc said, "is on their way to Nic's hideout. Send the *Camel* everything you have on the location."

Grey Wolf nodded and started to type at a furious pace. Maps and blueprints flashed on his monitor before disappearing through a link to the *Camel*. Then, pointing at Railroad, Grey Wolf said, "He'll bring you up to date. Irma and I are following a lead."

Railroad transferred what he was working on to the wall monitor. "What we found," he said, "sounds like a bad soap opera. It started with some not so chance encounters, deliberate use of coupons, internet popups, and manipulations on a level that rivals anything the governments used in the early 2000s."

Marc narrowed his eyes. "You're right. That does sound like a bad soap opera. Please connect the dots for us."

Railroad enlarged a section of the timeline on the wall monitor. "After the Botswana diamond scandal," he said, "the people who were involved in it were sent to prison, and the investors in the diamond mines ended up losing fortunes, which ruined most of them. When the ones who went to prison were released, an odd thing started to happen. All of them began to receive email coupons for free or discounted items, to be used only on certain days and hours. The chance encounters with each other was the first domino to fall. The next was spam popups appearing on their computers for news about the building and opening of *Tranquility* with Lady Elizabeth's backing. Nothing strange there. That news was everywhere. But those news reports would show up at the same time for injury lawyers who used phrases like: 'Someone done you wrong?' 'Get what you deserve!' and 'Stick it to the people that hurt you!' After a few more chance encounters, it was evident that they were starting to get in touch with each other without influence. From the emails retrieved from their accounts, we learned that they wanted to get back at Lady Elizabeth for preventing them from obtaining the rights to mining the African coast. That's when an investor who had managed to avoid prosecution approached the most influential of the group, known to you as Dan Garfield, and offered to help in getting the group back on its feet. That came with a requirement that they help the investor get back at Lady Elizabeth. The investor's name is Hu Lang."

Marc's eyes widened when he heard that name. He had been approached by Hu Lang in the early planning phase of *Tranquility*. If it weren't for Marc's insisting on meeting investors face to face, which Hu Lang refused, Marc might have taken his money.

Railroad continued: "When we peeled back the layers of this person, we found that there was indeed someone by that name, but he had been injured in a plane crash that left him paralyzed from the neck down. After that, he became a hermit and only communicated through computers. We discovered that he died before the people were released from prison, but a death certificate was never issued for him, so the world thinks he's alive and moved his operation to a factory near Dallas." As Railroad spoke, the same location as before appeared on the monitor with the red X on it. "The factory once manufactured robotic and computer components."

Marc felt that this final piece of the puzzle made sense of everything that had been happening to them for the past week. But there was one thing that didn't add up.

Turning to Grey Wolf, Marc said, "Can you tell us how Nic was able to do everything to us without the Asimov Laws preventing it?"

Grey Wolf looked frustrated, which came out in his voice. "I have no *fucking* clue how he bypassed them. It's the second line of encoding, right after the Anderson Protocols. It's not something that can be bypassed without shutting down his Matrix. The only way to find out is to examine Nic's Matrix."

Marc pointed back to the monitor. "Is there something that you and Irma have found that can add to all this?"

Irma replied, "There's been some kind of activity at the warehouse that corresponded to energy draw in the power grids in that area for the past two days, but nothing's been delivered there other than scrap metal to the junkyard next-door."

Marc looked at the aerial view of the surrounding area. "Are there any bystanders who could get hurt in the crossfire?"

Grey Wolf enlarged the view of the junkyard. "The only people there are two guards at the delivery gate, who only patrol the yard when the sensors get triggered. That mostly happens at night and is chalked up to wildlife looking for material to build their homes."

Railroad stood up to stretch. "I need to see a man about a wallaby. I'll be right back."

Marc nodded, moved to the communications terminal, and activated the link to the *Camel*. "Marc to *Camel*. What's your status, Tony?"

Tony's voice came over the room's speakers. "We're almost done making the plan to enter and clear the warehouse to find Nic. Without knowing exactly where he is, we're going to have to do this old-school, room by room. The information and the blueprints have helped, but with each room we clear, the element of surprise is lost."

Marc nodded his understanding of the situation. "Just bring everyone back in one piece."

"Will do," said Tony before cutting the connection."

⠠⠄⠀⠄⠦⠃⠆⠒⠒⠆⠀⠶⠀⠄⠲⠃⠄⠒⠻⠆⠴⠄⠄⠒⠲⠆⠢

Up on the roof, the Chaos Twins were pulling out weapons and other items from their duffle bags, while a portable stereo system they had set up blasted out grunge metal of "Murmaider" by

Dethlok and kept in rhythm with the song's lyrics, which checked off a list of weapons.

Nearby, the Tiger Sharks were putting together Molotov cocktails with empty beer bottles, gasoline, old Styrofoam packing peanuts, and liquid dish soap. They were bemused by the other twins' antics of getting ready, but felt they could up the ante on crazed battle preparation. The girls smiled at each other as Rossa pulled out an electronic pad and used an app to override the stereo's system.

The Chaos Twins stopped what they were doing and looked over at the girls when the music changed to a more upbeat Latin song. Their eyes bugged out at the sight of the two girls holding Molotov cocktails in each hand and shaking the contents to mix them up to the rhythm of Harry Belafonte's "Jump in the Line" lyrics. The added movement of their hips turned the dangerous production of making incendiaries into a sensual experience—which the Chaos Twins thoroughly enjoyed.

⠲⠀⠐⠦⠃⠂⠵⠲⠎⠀⠐⠋⠀⠠⠹⠃⠐⠹⠿⠂⠡⠐⠹⠶⠒

On the ladder to the roof was McFarland, who had opened the hatch just in time to catch the girls' display of insane bomb-making. He closed the hatch, climbed down a few rungs of the ladder, and then stopped to look back at the closed roof hatch. Shaking his head as if to remove the image of what he had just seen, he made his way down the ladder.

⠲⠀⠐⠦⠃⠂⠵⠲⠎⠀⠐⠋⠀⠠⠹⠃⠐⠹⠿⠂⠡⠐⠹⠶⠒

When McFarland entered the computer room, the tension was almost thick enough to see. He walked over to Marc, who had the look of a chess master who was simultaneously playing twelve different games.

"Everyone is in position around the Keep," McFarland said. "The two sets of twins are making Molotov cocktails, while somehow making it look like a romantic outing. I told Railroad to retrieve your Stun-Gun with the EMP rounds, Marc, and bring it to you. How are things getting on here?"

Marc shrugged his shoulders. "About as ready as we can... be...."

Marc's hazel eyes narrowed as he watched Grey Wolf. Something in the programmer's posture wasn't right. And his gut agreed.

Grey Wolf suddenly spun around in his chair and yelled, "We've got incoming!"

His monitor showed an old transport vessel landing in front of the bar. When the hatch opened, a large group of robots emerged and started running in different directions around the bar, as well as straight for the front doors.

Marc spun around to a computer terminal and hit the communication button. "Tony! We're under attack! Repeat, we're under attack! Return to the Keep!"

The only response was static.

Grey Wolf checked the systems. "The transport outside is jamming our communications! We're on our *own!*"

⠠⠊⠀⠠⠞⠓⠊⠝⠅⠀⠺⠑⠀�⠑⠀⠊⠝⠀⠞⠗⠕⠥⠃⠇⠑

When Duke saw the craft land out front, he turned to Duchess and pointed out the back door. "You, Becky 'n Moonflower, git ta da livin' quarters and barricade yerselves in our room!"

Becky's eyes were wide with fear as she saw the robots pour out of the ship. Duchess scooped her up in her arms and ran with Susan out the door, while Duke pointed to where he wanted the defenders to be while he tried not to worry about his little girl.

⠨⠫ ⠐⠶⠏⠄⠌⠑⠂⠐⠶ ⠄⠿⠒⠓⠄ ⠒⠲⠇⠠⠄ ⠉⠈⠮⠆

On the roof, the Chaos Twins were using wrist-rocket sling-shots with the toy metal jacks they had found earlier in the wooden case. After years of practice, they were deadly accurate with the wrist-rockets, so the spiky jacks ripped through the robots' sensors and external connectors. The Tiger Sharks were next to them, hurling lit Molotov cocktails at the bots that the Chaos Twins had damaged. The combination of the two attacks was impressive as well as destructive. When the four of them ran out of jacks and Molotov cocktails, the Chaos twins took up positions with their tennis rackets opposite the girls. Then the Tiger Shark Twins started lobbing pool balls toward the other two, who used their rackets to send a barrage of ballistic billiard balls into the opening of the ship that the robots were coming out of.

⠨⠫ ⠐⠶⠏⠄⠌⠑⠂⠐⠶ ⠄⠿⠒⠓⠄ ⠒⠲⠇⠠⠄ ⠉⠈⠮⠆

The Keepers and Marines guarding the ground level were doing significant damage with their handguns. But with more attackers than defenders, some robots got by the defensive line and entered the building. Several of them got hit by EMP rounds and immediately fell to the ground. No doubt, Railroad was putting the special rounds to good use.

Condor was standing in the bar near the door to the kitchen with a shotgun that was booming devastating damage to the metal invaders. The solid steel slugs slammed into the robots, stopping them in their tracks. But with a limited number of shells in his pump-action gun and no time to reload, the massive cook quickly depleted his ammo. With a flick of his thumb, a thin wire extended out from the front of the barrel along the top of his gun, forming a half-circle with a radius of nine inches. Another flick of his thumb made another half-circle appear along the bottom of the barrel, and both instantly glowed with bright white plasma. Condor ran toward the next robot, swung the plasma axe into its torso, which cleaved the invader in two like a hot knife through butter.

From the kitchen, Machete charged out with two machetes in his hands. When he pressed buttons on the handles, the edges of the blades glowed white with energy. Then, with a dangerous grin and fire in his eyes, he charged at a robot and turned it into scrap metal.

Meanwhile, Duke was making every effort to defend The Keep, but it was impossible to ward off so many of the invaders. The human-sized robot he was confronting swung its arm at Duke and delivered a devastating blow to his raised arm. But Duke's arm didn't budge as the robotic arm scraped down along the biker's forearm and off the elbow, peeling the flesh away. Confused, the robot looked at the arm and saw that a titanium alloy formed the skeleton of Duke's arm.

Duke snarled at the robot as he plunged his bionic fist into its plastic chest and ripped out wires and circuitry. The crippled robot jerked about a few times before crashing to the ground.

Duke sighed as he looked at the exposed inner workings of his arm. Then he leveled an annoyed look at another robot and let loose a battle cry as he charged at it.

⠨⠂ ⠐⠶⠃⠄⠅⠔⠌⠐ ⠰⠋ ⠠⠙⠃⠄⠐ ⠩⠏⠿⠲⠄⠌⠂ ⠐⠫⠒⠆

In the computer room, McFarland took a closer look at the robots on the monitor. "Those are Fighting Bots. Nasty and hard to damage."

When McFarland looked at Marc, he saw that his friend wasn't paying any attention to the monitor, but was looking instead at the closed door, with his head cocked, listening to something.

Marc had some of the most sensitive hearing that McFarland had ever come across, and because of that, he was compelled to move to the door and crack it open. Coming from the stairs at the far end of the hallway was the unmistakable sound of metal footsteps.

McFarland pulled out his crossbow, quickly assembled it, and set the string in its firing position. He pulled a bolt out and slid his finger along it. Where he touched it, a glowing line appeared that changed from yellow to red, and then to a deep burgundy as the explosive strength was set. He placed the bolt on the crossbow, aimed down the hallway, and waited. As soon as a Fighting Bot was visible, he fired and quickly closed the door. A moment later, a loud explosion was heard, which rattled the walls.

McFarland opened the door again and saw that the Bot was a smoldering heap of twisted metal. Then he noticed a small, round object flying through the smoke. He slammed the door and moved with the speed of a cat with its tail on fire.

"Get down!" McFarland yelled, as he flared his jacket out as a protective shield over Grey Wolf and Irma, while knocking them to the floor.

Marc reacted instinctively to McFarland's warning. He pushed Steven to the floor and dragged him under a desk.

The door disappeared in an explosion of flying shrapnel, which ripped at everything in its path. The shockwave was enough to break loose the sheetrock ceiling, which crashed down on the occupants of the room.

McFarland pushed with his arms and legs to use his back to lift the debris that had landed on him. As the rubble fell away, a grunt of pain escaped from him. He crouched over Grey Wolf and Irma to make sure that they were okay, then he reached down to his leg and yanked out a large splinter of wood that had embedded itself in his calf. Pulling out his revolver and a Desert Eagle handgun, he took a defensive position over his companions.

Marc pointed at Steven to stay put as he pulled out his 9mm gun and aimed it at the hole where the door used to be.

A voice in the hallway called out, "Olly olly oxen free!"

Grey Wolf's dark eyes widened in recognition as he hissed to McFarland, "It's him! It's Nic!"

McFarland pointed to the door at the far wall and said, "You and Irma stay low and move to the door. Marc and Steven, follow them. I'll provide cover. Head for the blacksmith shop, and we'll set up our defensive line there. Go!"

As McFarland unleashed a volley of bullets through the hole where the ruined door was, Marc grabbed Steven by the arm and ran after the other two. As soon as the others got through the far doorway, McFarland continued firing as he ran for the escape route and slammed the heavy door closed. After he threw the heavy lockbar across it, he ran after the others down the hallway while reloading his guns. He suddenly stopped when he found the others waiting at the exit.

"Why are you *just* standing here?" McFarland growled.

Marc put his finger to his lips, pointed toward the door, and whispered, "There are two Bots between us and the workshop."

McFarland cracked open the door and took a quick look at the two obsolete Sumo-Bots.

Quietly closing the door, he said, "Okay, those are strong but slow-moving. We need to take them out fast, or they will over-power us. You got that peashooter loaded, Marc?"

Marc nodded.

McFarland finished reloading the Desert Eagle handgun with a new clip of ammo and then held it out to Grey Wolf, grip first.

Grey Wolf looked at it as if he were being handed a poison-ous snake. "Don't give *me* that! I'm more likely to shoot myself, or one of you!"

McFarland held the gun out to Steven. "*You* know anything about guns?"

Steven took the gun, ejected the ammo clip, saw that it was full, and slid it back into the gun with a slap.

As he checked the safety, Steven said, "My brother and I did some gun training when we were in our teens. I can handle this."

McFarland nodded. "Good." Then, to Marc he said, "When I say, 'Go,' I'll take the one on the left, you take the one on the right. They're programmed to shut down when they fall, so don't hope for a lucky headshot. You'll need to aim for a knee and make the leg buckle." Then, to Grey Wolf and Irma, he said, "You two stay behind me, but not too close. At least ten feet. Understood?"

They nodded.

Go!" said McFarland as he pushed the door open and started shooting at his target. The Colt found its mark, destroying the knee of the Bot. When the leg broke in two, the Bot shut down as soon as it hit the ground.

Marc's aim was nearly as good, but the 9mm rounds were not as effective as the Colt .44's rounds, so the second Bot didn't fall after Marc emptied his clip.

While Marc ejected the clip to reload, McFarland stepped forward and swung his arm over his head with his bullwhip in hand. The kangaroo leather whip uncoiled and made a whirling-hissing sound as it cut through the air before he sent the whip out at the Bot's leg. It coiled around the Bot's knee with a loud snap as the tip of the whip broke the sound barrier. McFarland then used both hands to pull hard on the whip, but the knee refused to give under the wrenching.

Just then, the door to the workshop flew open, and out charged a roaring Forge with a battle ax. He swung it expertly at the Bot's knee, cleaving it in two, which caused the Bot to fall with a crash and shut down.

McFarland dropped the whip and pointed at the workshop door as he yelled, "*Move!*"

As the six of them ran for the workshop, the sound of fighting could be heard in front of the bar. It was a mix of metal being smashed, the Chaos/Shark Twins whooping and hollering it up, and the bikers yelling battle cries.

McFarland rushed through the doorway and shut it when everyone got inside. Forge propped some heavy metal bars against the door and asked, "What da hell's happenin', Darkheart?"

McFarland reloaded his gun and growled, "A huge pile of shit and a really big fan." Then, pointing at Grey Wolf and Irma, he said, "Those two are to be protected at *all* costs. Do you still have the Rabbit Hole behind the furnace?"

Forge nodded. "Sure do."

McFarland turned to Steven and pointed at Grey Wolf, Irma, and Forge. "Decision time, bud. Either go with them, or stay here with Marc and me. *This* is where we draw the line."

Steven replied, "If I go with them, I can be Forge's backup. But if I can help here, I'll stay."

McFarland quickly handed Steven two clips of ammo. "Go with them," he said. Then, to Forge he said, "Take 'em through the Rabbit Hole and keep 'em safe. Anyone shows up without the password, shoot 'em. If anything mechanical pops up, destroy it. Understood?"

Forge put his hand out to clasp McFarland's forearm. "This I'll defend."

Forge grabbed his battle ax, but, noticing the deep gouge the Bot had made on its edge, he exchanged it for a new one. Then he waved for Grey Wolf, Irma, and Steven to follow him.

When the four of them disappeared behind the furnace, and McFarland heard the hidden door slide back into place, he turned to Marc to say something.

But then, Nic's voice came from outside: "This game of hide-n-seek is boring. At least, make it a challenge to find you. Maybe *this* will inspire you."

McFarland and Marc dove for cover as an explosion shook the door. When they got up, the door was barely hanging from one hinge.

Nic cheerfully said, "I know. Let's play a nice game of Catch!"

A small, round ball came through the dust that was hanging in the air as McFarland unleashed a hail of bullets at it. The grenade was knocked into a corner before exploding harmlessly.

While McFarland reloaded, Marc emptied a full clip where the grenade had come from.

Nic's voice sounded slightly altered, almost comical. "It's a good thing," he said, "I'm not a biological person. You got a lucky shot and broke my head casing. Time to end this."

In came four grenades.

McFarland yelled at Marc, "*Move!*" as he dove behind some sheet metal. Marc scrambled under the heavy worktable just as four simultaneous explosions ripped the room apart, throwing dozens of bladed items in random directions. The flying weaponry created a deadly symphony of metal colliding against metal. The sound was punctuated by noise from the roof falling in after the main support was shattered by two of the grenades.

As a cloud of dust swirled about the damaged workshop, Marc tried to shove the debris away from the workbench, but a metal shelving unit was wedged against him. One of the small swords had landed near him, so he used it as a pry bar to try to move the shelving.

However, McFarland was *not* moving. The sheet metal had protected him from the blast and flying blades, but the roof support beam had landed on his right arm, pinning him to the floor. His Colt had been knocked from his hand and was just out of reach.

McFarland heard the crunching of footsteps as he tried, without success, to retrieve his gun. At first, he thought it was Irma's black-and-white head that appeared over the beam, but then he saw that it was a different model, with part of its casing damaged on the right side. As he pulled one of his other guns out of his coat, a white carbon-fiber hand shot out and wrenched it away.

Nic's voice dripped with contempt as he looked at the gun. "Humans! You waste your time and energy on things that destroy, and all you accomplish is rebuilding what you already had. Too bad you won't be around to see this place being destroyed." He raised the gun at McFarland's head and said, "Any last words?"

McFarland hissed something through clenched teeth.

Nic leaned in closer. "Oh, come now. There's not a cat for miles to get your tongue. *Do* speak up."

McFarland cleared his throat and snarled at Nic, "I *said*, 'Hi, Moonflower.'"

⠠⠂ ⠄⠐⠃⠊⠈⠉⠐⠎ ⠄⠏⠲ ⠈⠙⠏⠈ ⠃⠲⠇⠈⠉ ⠈⠶⠉⠆

As the battle for The Keep waged, Duchess, Susan, and Becky ran as fast as they could to the living quarters and scrambled up the stairs to the third floor. Susan trailed behind slightly, but was right behind the other two. As she got to the third floor, she heard a series of gunshots that didn't come from the bar. Pausing at the door that Duchess had gone through, she looked back and saw over the bar to the workshop just as the Sumo-Bots went down.

The group from the computer room ran into the workshop and closed the door. The sight of a purple hat on one of the heads told Susan that Steven was with them. Her gut fell at the thought that something very wrong must have happened if McFarland deemed it necessary to run.

Moments later, a small white-and-black figure appeared that playfully tossed something from hand to hand before throwing it at the workshop's door, blowing it apart.

Susan turned to Duchess and took hold of the doorknob. "Stay here," she said, "and keep your daughter safe."

Then she slammed the door shut. As she ran down the stairs, ignoring the shouting from Duchess to come back, she thought she was foolish to run into an unknown and dangerous situation. But her heart was screaming that she *had* to help. She did a quick Shema as her hand reached for the Moonflower dagger attached to her belt and slid it out of its scabbard. Susan hoped it would be enough.

⠲⠀⠠⠌⠗⠄⠊⠆⠄⠀⠰⠆⠀⠠⠙⠾⠄⠀⠆⠒⠠⠇⠄⠌⠀⠐⠫⠪⠳

McFarland watched as the tip of the Moonflower dagger suddenly protruded from the left side of Nic's head. The resulting electrical discharge as the AI's power system shorted out sent Susan flying back several feet, before Nic collapsed on top of the beam and stopped moving.

Marc managed to finally move the shelves and quickly rushed over to Nic. He yanked open the access panel in the AI's back, ripped out the power cell, and unlocked and pulled out the still active Matrix. Marc considered smashing it as he pulled the last connecting wires off, but he had made a promise to Irma to bring Nic to justice, so he put the Matrix down and tossed the now dead suit aside.

When Marc looked down at McFarland, he had never seen his friend in worse shape. Pulling at his own torn shirt, Marc ripped off a sleeve and used it to tie a tourniquet just below the shoulder of McFarland's crushed arm.

Through clenched teeth, McFarland hissed, "Did we have to use Plan H? I really didn't want to lose an arm."

Marc looked at Susan, who just shook her head in wonder.

Susan's eyes suddenly became alarmed as she frantically looked around the devastated shop. "Where's Steven!"

Marc put a calming hand on her. "He's safe with Forge and the others." Then, pointing toward the broken door, he said, "We're going to need first aid and transport as soon as we free McFarland from this beam."

Susan nodded and shot out the door.

"Okay, tough guy," Marc said to McFarland, "we'll get you out of here soon."

McFarland pointed at the left side of his coat and then held it open for Marc, who reached into a pocket and pulled out an old battered and dented flask. Opening it, he poured some of the Irish whiskey into McFarland's mouth and then took a swig himself.

Looking meaningfully at his old friend, Marc said, "Thanks for being here. Without you, we would all have been killed."

McFarland said through clenched teeth, "Wait till you get my bill. It's going to cost you at *least* an arm. Now quit dicking around and get this *fucking* thing off me. But first, give me another hit of that flask."

⠌⠀⠐⠻⠃⠗⠑⠐⠌⠀⠶⠀⠠⠻⠄⠀⠠⠻⠇⠉⠐⠊⠐⠻⠌⠆

During the height of the battle, the muffled explosions from the hallway leading to the computer room told Duke that Darkheart and Marc were in trouble, but there wasn't anything he could do about it. Although the Keepers of Chaos had gotten the upper hand on the Bots, there were still a half dozen of them to deal with, and they were not going down easily. A little bit later, when a series of explosions were heard out at the workshop, Duke knew that Darkheart had moved the fight there.

Duke yelled out to everyone in the bar, "We need ta end dis *now* 'n help Darkheart!"

He reached down to the metal footrest that ran along the front of the bar and used his bionic arm to yank off a section of it.

Holding it like baseball bat, he yelled, "Batter up!"

Then he swung the footrest at the head of an approaching Bot, which made it explode into shards. The now blinded Bot began to grab out at random, hoping to get ahold of the biker.

As Machete finished off the Bot he had been fighting with, he saw that Duke was in a tug of war over the footrest with the headless robot. Machete flung one of his machetes at the Bot, which entered it from the back and sliced cleanly through to the front.

When the Bot crashed to the floor, Duke yanked out the machete as he nodded a wordless thanks. Then the two Keepers turned to join Condor in finishing off the last of the Bots.

Suddenly, the remaining Bots collapsed and powered down.

The two sets of twins appeared at the roof hatch. Kevin called down, "Who found the off switch?"

Duke looked around and was just as puzzled by this unexpected victory. "I 'ave no ideah. Get down 'ere 'nd start rippin' out da power cells." Then, addressing Condor and Machete, he said, "I 'eard explosions out at da workshop. Darkheart may be in trouble."

As they all turned to the back door, it flew open, and Susan ran in, heading straight to Duke. "We need help!" she cried. "McFarland's pinned under a beam and needs medical attention."

Duke started yelling out orders: "Sergeant Wilson, find Duchess 'nd tell 'er she's needed for triage at the workshop. Sidewinder, get da hydraulic jack from da garage. Machete, ready Jumper One ta transport Darkheart ta Vegas General. Jackknife, call da hospital 'nd inform Doc we have a priority injury comin'. Let's go, Moonflower."

Susan held up a hand to stop Duke. "Forge took Steven, Grey Wolf, and Irma down the Rabbit Hole. We need someone to go tell them that it's safe to return."

Duke looked around. "Skids," he said, "go down ta da Rabbit Hole 'nd tell Forge it's all clear ta bring dem back here."

Then Duke took off in the direction of the workshop.

At the same time, Skids ran behind the bar, opened a trap-door, and disappeared down into the darkness.

Duchess ran into the bar and stopped in her tracks when she saw all the destruction that had been done to it. Seeing Duke and Susan heading for the back door, she ran after them. When she caught up with them, she said to Susan, "You caused me quite a bit of concern when you ran off like that. Where did you go?"

Susan shrugged. "Just to save McFar... um... Darkheart by ramming my dagger into Nic's head."

⠄⠄ ⠄⠐⠓⠂⠄⠔⠒ ⠄⠶ ⠄⠰⠓⠒⠠⠄⠔ ⠄⠰⠱⠂

Outside the bar, the Chaos and Tiger Shark Twins were glee-fully ripping out the dead Bots' power cells. It had become a com-petition between the two sets of twins to see which of them could remove the most cells.

The Tiger Sharks were ahead on points when all four of them suddenly stopped at the sound of a sonic boom in the distance, which was quickly followed by the noise of a fast-approaching air-craft. All four of them immediately ran for cover and prepared for another round of fighting.

When everyone else in the bar heard the incoming vessel, they all scrambled to take up defensive positions.

Clearing the top of the bar by only two yards, the Camel roared into view and in just a handful of seconds landed. As it touched down, the Marines and Keepers poured out of the Camel with their weapons at the ready for battle. Tony took point, while everyone else fanned out to assume covering positions. Jackson appeared at the top hatch and took a prone position with a snip-er's rifle.

When they saw their teammates, both sets of twins put their weapons away, stepped out into the open, and put their arms out to the sides to show that they were no longer in danger. Meanwhile, the others in the bar also relaxed at seeing their friends.

When Tony saw the two sets of twins, he put his left hand up with the palm open and fingers closed. Then he lowered his hand-gun and slid it into its holster. At that, the Camel's crew relaxed and put away their weapons.

Vincent called out to Tony, "If you're gonna drop in unex-pectedly, you could at least bring some chips and guacamole!"

Tony looked around at the carnage of broken Bots strewn about and the damage to The Keep. "Looks like we arrived *just* in time to be too late. Everyone okay?"

Susan stepped out of the bar and pointed in the direction of the workshop. "McFarland is pinned under a support beam in the workshop and is badly injured. Marc and Duke are seeing to him with some of the others."

Tony turned to his crew. "Alpha team, help with McFarland. Delta team, gather the first aid gear out of the *Camel* and anything else that will help them!" He then pointed toward the old transport ship that the robots had arrived in. "Sergeant Mulgrew, Sidewinder, and Bulldog, secure that ship. Make sure that there are no surprises hiding in it!"

The three teams sprang into action to carry out Tony's orders.

"What tipped you off that we were in trouble?" Vincent asked, running a hand through his hair.

"And how did you get back here so fast?" Kara added.

While examining one of the destroyed Bots, Tony replied, "We heard Marc's garbled voice on the Coms, and when we couldn't reestablish contact, I told Kimberly to turn the *Camel* around. She spun it on a dime and hit the booster rockets."

Kevin whistled. "*That* must have rattled a few windows."

Kimberly appeared beside Tony. "Yeah. Just what I needed. *More* citations on top of already being the most wanted unlicensed pilot."

The Tiger Sharks stepped up to her, and Rossa said, "Leave the legal stuff to us. We have a few favors we can call in to clear you. Besides, anyone who can control a beast like that *Camel* of yours with the skill you just demonstrated *is* a pilot."

Kimberly started to blush and get flustered, when Jackson came to her rescue by putting his arm around her. "C'mon, let's go find your brother."

As they walked off, Kara asked Tony, "Does Jackson have a brother?"

Rossa added, "Or two?"

Kevin and Vincent said, "Hey!" as they looked at the two women in dismay.

The Tiger Sharks grinned at them, slapped the men's behinds, and ran toward the living quarters, laughing. The Chaos Twins grinned at each other, pulled out their tennis rackets, and went after them.

Kevin called out, "Hey, *ladies!*"

Vincent added, "We've *got* something for you!"

Tony shook his head and headed for the bar, ignoring the shrieks of delight coming from the rooms.

.' ."⠏⠊⠌⠌ ' ⠏ .⠺⠓' ⠝⠏⠇.'⠊ ⠝⠿⠇⠏

It took some work to get McFarland free from the beam. Temporary supports needed to be placed so the roof wouldn't collapse, and the assorted weapons that got thrown throughout the workshop needed to be carefully removed. With the Marines and Keepers working together, the building was quickly made safe to lift the massive beam. Once McFarland was freed, the Marines treated his injuries and carefully moved him to the Jump Ship.

Machete climbed into the pilot's seat, while Duchess sat next to McFarland, so she could tend to him during the trip. As Machete engaged the engines with a roar, the Jump Ship quickly disappeared into the distance.

Pointing to the garage, Duke said to the gathered Keepers and Marines, "Anyone wantin' ta go wit us ta da hospital, we leave 'n thirty minutes." Then, to Marc and Tony he said, "Let's git ready ta ride, boys!"

CHAPTER 21

Making a Batch of Ice Cream

Grey Wolf and Railroad took Nic's Matrix and suit to the computer room and started examining them to determine how he had bypassed the Asimov Laws. Steven went back to Susan's room, where he had earlier left his tool kit.

Susan followed him to the quarters, and as soon as they were inside, she shut the door and smothered Steven with kisses.

Until there was a knock at the door.

Irma's voice said softly, "Susan? Steven? May I speak with you?"

Susan gave Steven one more kiss and then went to let their friend in. "Of course, Irma. Please come in."

As Irma entered, Steven pulled out chairs for Irma and Susan, then sat in another.

"I'm still having trouble trying to deal with the loss of Ross," Irma said. "Have you ever experienced a loss of someone close to you?"

Steven looked at his wife. "Not as bad as you have, Susan. Go ahead, honey. Tell her."

Susan cleared her throat. "When I was sixteen, I found my baby brother drowned in the pool. My parents had gone off to finish buying our new home in North Carolina, and had asked me to take care of him. I thought he was in the TV room, watching a movie, while I chatted on my videophone with my boyfriend. When I heard the movie end, and I went to put something else on for my brother, he wasn't there. I thought he might have gone to the bathroom, but he wasn't there, either. As I started searching the house, I found the back door open, and there he was, in the pool. I immediately jumped in and pulled him out, trying to use CPR to try and revive him. According to the doctor, he... he had been dead for half an hour before I found him."

Irma asked, "Can you tell me how that affected you, Susan?"

As the flood of memories assaulted Susan, her voice caught. "I... I didn't forgive myself for years, and there are times that I still don't. I almost didn't graduate from high school because I was so distraught. I broke up with my boyfriend, because seeing him reminded me that if I hadn't been distracted, my brother would still be alive. It wasn't until I got involved with a group that had similar losses that I started to move forward with my life."

Irma thought for a moment. "How do you deal with the memories? I can see they still affect you."

Susan looked at Steven and took his hand in hers. "I threw myself into college and then into work. Both became the focus of my mind. I kept praying for something to happen to help me change my life. It was answered when I met Steven. His soft and gentle manner was something I was not accustomed to. He took me dancing one night and showed me that there was a whole world out there that I was letting pass me by. Then he introduced me to

Marc, who showed me realms of flavors I had never known about. Now I have the best work to keep me focused, plus Steven and good friends to lean on when I feel the memories get too much to handle. Does any of that help you?"

Irma nodded. "I think so. I need to process what's happened and figure out how I can deal with it. Thank you for telling me about this."

Steven smiled at Irma. "Always remember that you are a part of *our* family, too. We will always help you when you need it. And sometimes when you don't want it."

Irma was about to leave when a knock at the door and Railroad's voice called out, "*Steven!* We discovered something about Nic's Matrix that we really need your help on."

Steven stood up and opened the door. "What did you find?"

Railroad looked worried. "Upgrades that Grey Wolf didn't install, and he's afraid that Nic may not be down for the count. We need your skills to decipher what the new upgrades can do."

Steven grabbed his tool kit. "Let's go! That pain in the ass isn't gonna pull any more surprises on us!"

They all followed Railroad back to the bar.

Becky was standing outside the bar when she saw the three adults running toward the computer room. Then she saw Irma, who was slowly making her way back to the bar. The young girl could see from Irma's stance and demeanor that the AI was sad. She had seen the same walk many times by the kids who were brought here for protection. She could lift *their* spirits by taking them to the kitchen and getting them a treat. But with an AI, she was going to have to do something different.

Approaching her new friend with a wave, she said, "Hi, Irma. Would you help me with something?"

Irma paused as she looked at the girl. "Sure, Becky."

Becky smiled. "Great! I'm making a batch of ice cream, and the churner's electric motor is broken. With all the adults busy, I'm hoping you wouldn't find it *too* boring to help me churn it manually, because it takes up to an hour to make ice cream."

Irma felt the spike of energy she had felt earlier when she was with Marc in the computer room. This young lady was an endless supply of new experiences.

"I'm intrigued by this," Irma said. "I've never made ice cream before."

Becky grinned. "Let's go to the kitchen to get the ingredients together, and I'll show you." She took Irma's hand and led her toward the kitchen.

⠨⠀⠨⠐⠃⠔⠄⠂⠄⠐⠆⠀⠆⠀⠨⠙⠓⠄⠐⠖⠖⠇⠄⠐⠂⠀⠄⠐⠴⠖

Leaving the computer wizards to do their work on Nic, Susan went to the kitchen to get them some food and drink. What she found was Irma, cranking away at an old-fashioned ice cream maker, as Becky watched.

Moments after Susan opened the door, Irma suddenly stopped what she was doing to look toward the doorway. Worry oozed from her voice: "Oh, *no!*"

Susan looked back at the doorway and then at Irma. "What's wrong, Irma?"

The AI pointed at the doorway. "Nic's trying to connect with an outside computer system! My systems picked up his Matrix reaching out. Close that door! I've been here for over twenty minutes and didn't detect it until it opened!"

Susan's face blanched as she ran through the door, slamming it behind her, and charged down the stairs to the hallway, yelling, "Don't connect the computers!!! Nic is trying to use them!!!"

When she ducked through the broken doorway, she saw the three men staring at her wide-eyed. Grey Wolf had a power cord for the computers ready to plug in, then dropped it as if it had just shocked him.

"How do you know that?" Steven asked.

Susan pointed at Nic's Matrix. "He tried to contact with an outside source when I opened the door at the top of the stairs. Irma's in the kitchen and felt him trying to connect with her. If you had turned on the computers, God knows what he would have done."

Railroad sat back in his chair. "Well, shit! How the fuck are we gonna work on him without any computers?"

A long minute passed as they all considered their options.

Finally, Grey Wolf snapped his fingers. "A Faraday cage. We build one in this room and set up the inspection station inside it."

Steven nodded. "We disable all Bluetooth and Wi-Fi components on the computers inside the cage. That should work. Railroad, where's the closest hardware store?"

Railroad thought for a moment. "About twenty miles from here. I'll get the truck ready to go."

Steven said to Grey Wolf, "You go with him and get what we need. I'll get the Marines to help with getting the room ready. We should also station someone at the kitchen to make sure no one comes down here with—" Steven suddenly looked alarmed. "Our PACs! Shut them down!"

Grey Wolf and Susan's eyes flew wide open as they took off their PACs and removed the power cells.

Susan sat down next to Steven with her head in her hands. "That does it. I'm having my adrenal glands removed."

Steven put a hand on his wife's back and gently rubbed it.

Railroad headed for the door. "I'll find a few Marines and send them down to help out here and get someone to man the door."

Susan looked up and grinned. "I know just the person for *that* job."

CHAPTER 22

Your Little Sister

A low rumble was heard as a dozen hybrid motorcycles pulled into the hospital parking lot, headed for the Keepers' Jump Ship, and parked around it.

Duke removed his helmet, which was painted like a Black Knights helmet, and dismounted his bike. He nodded with approval of the riding skills of the people from *Tranquility*. Marc and Tony had stayed at his side the whole way without any problem. Duke did chuckle, however, at the Chaos Twins as they stiffly got off the bikes that the Tiger Sharks had ridden.

Duke held up his hands to quiet everyone. "Marc, Tony, 'nd I will go 'n find out about Darkheart. Da rest of ya, go ta the cafeteria 'nd wait fer us dere." Then he pointed to the main entrance. "Let's go find Doc."

As Marc followed the large biker, he threw out another prayer for McFarland and, for the hundredth time, wished that Eileen were there with him.

⠲⠀⠠⠍��⠀⠖⠀⠠�����

Six hours later, Marc was awakened by the smell of coffee. When he pried his hazel eyes open, he found Tony standing in front of him, holding a cup.

"Wake up, Marc," Tony said. "The nurse just told us that the operation is finished, and Doc will be out to let us know how it went."

Marc straightened up in his chair, tried to twist his neck to remove a kink that had formed from sleeping at an odd angle, and took the cup of coffee. Looking around the waiting room, he saw that it was filled with the Keepers and Marines. An air of anticipation that was nearly physical filled the room. Marc took a few long drinks from his cup and then placed it on a side table.

The doctor, a tall handsome East Indian man, came through the doors that led from the operating rooms and headed to Duke.

Duke held up his hand. "This isn't just only *our* circle's problem, Doc," he said, pointing to Marc. "He 'n his group are ta be considered next of kin."

Marc moved up next to Duke. "We *all* are. What's the word, Doc?"

The doctor removed his surgical head covering, revealing thick, black hair that looked as if it had been combed by an eggbeater, and ran a hand through it. His dark brown eyes looked tired, but the sparkle spoke volumes about what he was going to say.

"Darkheart is doing fine. Even though we had to amputate his arm at the shoulder, there were no complications or unforeseen issues during the surgery. The core mechanics and bio-nerves of the artificial arm have been graphed, but until he recovers, the arm won't be activated or have its covering put on. I would wait until tomorrow to visit him."

Marc put out his hand to shake the doctor's. "Thanks, Doc. Would it be possible to get approval for a member of our crew to give him massages? She's a CMT with full hospital clearance, but she doesn't have privileges here."

The doctor smiled. "Once I okay him for receiving such treatments, I'll make sure she gets the clearance and has full access to Darkheart. Just give the head nurse at the desk the needed information before you leave. If you'll excuse me, I need to make sure he gets a private room once he's out of recovery."

The doctor nodded to Marc and Duke before heading back through the surgical center doors.

Duke turned to Marc. "'E's one of da finest surgeons in da States. When we put da word out we needed a doctor on call ta help our cause, 'e was da first ta step forward ta volunteer 'is time."

Marc looked up at the massive biker and held out his hand. "I know you got involved with all this because McFarland asked, but you did more than just help him. You and your group put your lives on the line to protect the entire crew of *Tranquility*. Anything we can do to help, just ask."

Duke's hand enveloped Marc's as he shook it. "Da rumors about ya 'n yar people hardly do ya justice, Marc." A smile started to spread across his face. "Moonflower has 'er Keeper name, 'n I think ya need one, too. Let's shorten yar last name ta Ace. Yes, Ace is da perfect name for ya. Because nuttin' beats 'n Ace."

The Keepers all hooted their approval, which came to an end when several nurses shushed them.

Marc looked at everyone and smiled. "Anyone know of a good place to get a drink around here? First round's on me."

Duke put his arms across both Marc's and Tony's shoulders. "I know a place that serves the coldest beers and the best nachos in the state."

⠨⠄ ⠠⠶⠳⠄⠝⠄⠎⠄ ⠶ ⠠⠙⠫⠄ ⠱⠿⠇⠄⠝⠇ ⠄⠫⠱⠗

When they arrived back at The Keep, Marc, Tony, and Duke headed straight for the computer room. But they only got as far as the kitchen, where their path was blocked by Jackson, Condor, and a very determined-looking Princess Becky.

The young princess-warrior was wearing a metal sieve for a helmet, holding a large lid to a stock pot as a shield, and brandishing a rolling pin like a sword.

"*Halt!*" Becky commanded with the authority of a drill sergeant. "*Anyone* who wants to pass through this doorway is to remove and deactivate all electronic devices." She pointed the rolling pin at the sink. "Those devices are to be placed in that sink. This is to ensure that Nic has no opportunity to access the internet."

The three men looked down at the feisty little guard and then at the other two men behind her, who gave them looks that said that Becky was in charge.

Raising his hands in surrender, Duke said to Marc and Tony, "I suggest we do as she says. I happen to know her mother."

Leaning toward Marc, Tony said, "I think I can take her."

That brought a low growl from Becky, who pointed the rolling pin at him. Jackson and Machete closed ranks behind her, showing that the situation needed to be taken seriously.

Putting up his hands, Tony quickly blurted out, "Forget I said that."

Marc bowed to Becky. "We shall comply with your wishes, oh, Guardian of The Keep."

The three men removed the items in question under Becky's watchful eye. Once the electronics were in the sink, Becky pulled out a scanner and ran it over each of men before letting them through the doorway.

As they walked down the stairs, Marc said to Duke, "I pity the boy who tries to steal a kiss from her."

Duke chuckled. "Dat already happened. 'E was tryin' ta kiss every girl in da classroom before da end of da day. I'll show ya da video of 'er throwin' 'im across da classroom with a perfectly executed technique."

When they reached the ruins of the door that Nic had destroyed, and ducked through it, they found a large wooden box with thin copper mesh covering it.

Inside the box was Grey Wolf, who was at a table, working on Nic's Matrix. Railroad was examining the damaged head of Nic's Čapek unit, which was lying on another table. Nearby there were two other smaller tables with computer workstations for each of the computer wizards.

Outside the cage, there was another table, where Steven was working on a computer. When he finished downloading some information into a thumb drive, he handed it to Susan, who went to a hatch large enough to pass things through, like an airlock, without letting the cage be opened at any time. After Railroad retrieved the thumb drive, he downloaded the information to his computer.

Grey Wolf looked up from his work when he heard Marc and the other two enter. He waved and called out to them, "Don't come in, guys. I'll be right out."

He then spoke to Railroad, who nodded as he continued his work on removing Susan's dagger from Nic's suit. Grey Wolf walked to what was a man-sized version of the hatch that Susan had just used. After checking that the inner door was tightly sealed, he opened the outer one and made sure that it, too, was properly closed.

"Sorry about all the precautions," Grey Wolf said, "but when Irma picked up a wireless signal that originated from Nic, we scrambled to construct this Faraday cage. When it was all set up, and we could safely inspect Nic's suit and Matrix, we found that he had added a whole range of wireless systems. If we had removed the dagger and powered up the suit, he would have been able to control it remotely. The Faraday cage ensures that he can't connect to the outside world."

"Have you been able," Marc asked, "to find out how Nic was able to bypass the Asimov Laws?"

Grey Wolf sighed. "Three impossible things happened. When we examined the ROM components of the outer casing, it showed that some damage had been done to the ones containing the laws. Each law has its own ROM that connects to the power system. If one is disobeyed, the whole system is shut down, and the AI goes into standby mode. The Anderson Protocols are also on their own ROM, and those four ROMs are on the same side of the Matrix. The other five sides contain ROMs for language, math, and other basic information."

Marc crossed his arms while Tony's and Duke's eyes started to glaze over.

Grey Wolf's voice took on a slight edge that caught their attention. "I'm *not* telling you this to lecture you on AI Matrixes.

It's important for you to know this to understand how Nic got damaged. *May* I continue?"

Marc uncrossed his arms, stood at attention with his hands clasped behind his back, and gave his undivided attention to Grey Wolf. "Sorry, Wolf. We're tired, but that doesn't mean that we shouldn't listen to what you found out." He looked at the other two. "This is the final piece of the puzzle, guys, and Grey Wolf is our guide to completing it."

Duke and Tony, realizing that they had been rude, followed Marc's example by giving Grey Wolf their full attention.

Grey Wolf's voice softened. "Thank you. The first impossible thing was that the ROMs containing the first two laws were shorted out. The second was that the ROM controlling the instructions for powering down the AI when the laws were being broken also burned out. And third, the Matrix Gel connected to those areas is no longer active..., or, to be more precise, is *dead*. From what we've pieced together so far, Nic thought he only had one law to follow: 'A robot must protect its own existence as long as such protection does not conflict with the First or Second Law.' Without the first and second laws, Nic just repeated the Third Law three times. And with no memory of them ever existing, he didn't think anything was missing. So, he decided that *I* was the cause of his nearly being killed on the houseboat, and he made plans to get back at me."

Steven looked up from his workstation. "Loosely translated, he's a brain-damaged, computerized sociopath!"

Grey Wolf pointed a thumb at Steven. "What *he* said."

Marc moved closer to the cage. "Is his Matrix still active? Is he aware of what's going on here?"

Railroad finished removing the dagger, placed it on the table, and checked his computer. "He's trying to find some way to connect with an outside source. The activity looks like an angry wasp trapped inside a sealed jar."

Marc tapped his knuckles against his lips in thought. Staring at the deactivated suit, and then at Nic's Matrix, he asked, "Is it possible to repair the damage to the ROM and reestablish the connections to the Gel Matrix?"

Grey Wolf squared his shoulders as he addressed Marc. "We can remove and replace the damaged Gel Matrix and then replace the damaged ROM components. The new Gel would create new pathways for the Matrix, which would help him to understand that what he did was wrong. Or, it may cause the laws to take over and make the whole system shut down. The third possibility is much worse. He may become an extremely intelligent schizophrenic!"

Grey Wolf looked back at his first AI. "But there is a chance that the new Gel will help him to see the error of his ways. With our help, we can rehabilitate him and reintroduce him back into society." Grey Wolf looked at Marc and the others. "But these are all just theories that have holes big enough to fly the *Camel* and its Hump through. I think we need to talk to Irma to get her input on how to proceed."

Marc still wanted to destroy Nic's Matrix, but that would only prove that his desire for revenge was just as bad as Nic's.

"I agree," he said, "that we should talk to Irma. Can you and Railroad hook him up, so he can communicate with us without plugging him into the suit?"

Grey Wolf shrugged. "He has the inputs for that, which we set up, but he was quite…, um…, nasty, so we disconnected him."

Railroad chuckled. "Nasty? That's an understatement. He put Machete to shame."

Duke raised an eyebrow at that. "I may want to plug him in, just to hear that."

Tony's eyes were still trained on Nic's Matrix. "There's no chance of him getting out of there?" he asked. "The suit is totally shut down?"

Railroad went to the suit and lifted the head a bit to show where Susan's dagger had been embedded. "Between Marc pulling the power cell and the dagger having disrupted the power systems," he said, "there's no way for it to become active."

Marc's eyes narrowed in thought as his gut tightened. "Did you scan for backup cells? If he added new components to remotely control the other robots, he might have added cells, too. It's what *I* would have done."

Grey Wolf, Steven, and Railroad looked at each other. None of them had thought of that. Railroad opened the front section of Nic's chest and started to examine the systems inside.

After a moment, Railroad said, "I'll be damned! There's a whole network of micro-cells squirreled away throughout the suit."

Marc pointed at the suit. "I want it wrapped in so much cage material that I can't see it, and then bound in bailing wire from head to toe. *Now!*"

Grey Wolf and Railroad jumped at the suddenness of Marc's orders.

Duke grabbed Tony's arm. "C'mon! We have da wire behind da kitchen."

They ducked through the broken doorway and sprinted down the hallway.

Grey Wolf grabbed a heavy roll of copper mesh and started dragging it toward the cage. Marc helped him as the two of them squeezed into the airlock. Once inside the cage, Marc, Grey Wolf, and Railroad started to unroll the mesh.

They never noticed the suit's arm starting to move and pick up the Moonflower dagger as the suit sat up.

Nic's damaged voice echoed through the room: "Hi, Honey! I'm home! Did you really think I didn't plan for being captured? Although, I must admit, I hadn't foreseen having a dagger stuck in my head."

He jumped down from the table. "Playing dead wasn't as much fun as I thought it was going to be, because that blasted dagger prevented the suit from powering up. I guess I should thank you for taking it out..., so, *thank you!* Now that I have your undivided attention, I think I'll finish what I started."

He moved toward Grey Wolf, who was trying to open a seam in the cage to escape, with Steven and Susan on the outside clawing at the same spot.

Nic raised the dagger to strike.

Marc snarled, "I've had just about enough of you. I'm ending this *now!*"

Marc stood with a hammer over Nic's Matrix, ready to strike. His hazel eyes were smoldering with anger. "Either you shut down that suit and let us try to repair the damage to your Matrix, or I *end* you right now. Take another step, and you get option B."

Nic's suit froze as his head turned to Marc. "By the time you move even a millimeter, I'll be able to gut your pet programmer. *Checkmate!*"

Marc grinned. "Nope. Just Check. Unless you're faster than a speeding bullet. *Now*, Tony!"

Crouching at the doorway was Tony with his sidearm aimed at the Matrix. The gun's report roared loudly in the room, drowning out Nic's scream as the hollow point bullet entered his Matrix, shattering the casing. The delicate neuronal pathways in the Gel were ripped apart as the bullet broke into deadly sharp shrapnel, destroying the AI. The Matrix erupted in a shower of computer shards and metallic-blue Matrix Gel.

The dagger slipped from Nic's hand as his suit dropped lifelessly to the floor. The shards that tore through the cage had missed the three men, but they were now covered in the metallic-blue Matrix Gel.

As Grey Wolf stared at what was left of Nic, tears welled in his eyes.

The sound of running footsteps came from the hall. Duke, who was on the other side of the doorway, could be heard saying, "Stand down, everyone! Da problem has been taken care of."

Duke poked his head under the doorway. "Please tell me we're finish wi' dis madness."

Tony holstered his gun and watched as Marc went to Grey Wolf to console him.

"Yeah," said Tony, "it's finished. Duke, please ask someone to get some towels to remove the Gel off everyone, and bring a bottle of your best scotch with some glasses. I think we're gonna need them."

Duke nodded and turned back to the others in the hallway. "Sidewinder, grab a stack of towels. Machete, go to my private stock and…," his voice trailed off as he headed away from the room.

Marc, Grey Wolf, and Railroad exited the cage as Tony took a deep breath before approaching them.

"Rowan, I'm *so* sorry," Tony said. "If there was any other way to…. I'm sorry."

Grey Wolf looked back at the cage and sighed. "I know, Tony. He was my first. The child that strayed. And if you hadn't acted, he would have killed me."

The sound of someone entering the room caught their attention. There stood Irma with Becky, surveying the room and seeing the splattered Matrix Gel all over the cage and their friends.

Irma's voice quivered in shock. "*What* have you done to Nic? You promised to bring him to justice."

Marc crouched down to her level. "We tried, Irma. But he made us use deadly force on him." He pointed at Grey Wolf. "It was either Nic or *him*. I hope you understand."

Irma looked back at Marc. "You had said that this might happen as a last resort. Becky told me of the preparations that you took to keep that promise. I…, I just don't know how to process another death of an AI."

Irma looked away and seemed lost.

Becky placed a hand on her shoulder. "It's hard losing someone. Last year, we lost a Keeper, Hawk, while he was protecting one of our kids. The attacker also killed the boy, whom I had trained, and then turned the gun on himself. You'll be okay, Irma. You have your family to see that you're not alone. And you have *me*."

As Irma looked at Becky, she felt a slight spike in her Matrix that she had felt before. It was not as strong as it had been, but it was there.

"You *are* family, Becky," Irma said. "My sister. *Please* be my sister."

Becky cried out, "*Oh,* Irma!" And then she threw her arms around the AI.

"Becky," Marc said, standing up, "would you take your little sister upstairs, please? I think you should find her something to do to take her mind off all this."

Becky looked confused. "*Little* sister?"

Grey Wolf stood next to Marc. "Irma was born on September 28th, 2174. That makes her younger than you."

Becky glowed with delight. "I always wanted a little sister! C'mon, sis! I'll show you how to play hopscotch!"

She took Irma's hand, and the two ducked out the doorway.

Railroad moved next to the others. "I hope someone gets a video of that. It's not every day that an AI plays hopscotch."

Sidewinder appeared with the towels. "Here ya go, guys. Duke has drinks waiting for you in the locker room."

They all took the offered towels and started to wipe off the Gel. Once he had most of it off, Grey Wolf looked back at the cage and the destroyed Matrix. "This whole thing has been as much fun as being french-kissed by a blind gorilla."

Railroad barked out a surprised laugh. "Now, there's a visual I'm gonna have difficulty dealing with."

Tony smiled. "Welcome to our world, buddy. Nothing normal survives here."

Railroad returned the smile. "Good. I *hate* normal."

Steven chimed in with, "Who wants normal? Besides, with the Chaos Twins around, normal goes screaming for the hills."

Marc gestured toward the doorway. "Let's get cleaned up and try to relax before we deal with this mess."

Grey Wolf stopped to look at what was left of Nic. "If you don't mind, I'd like to be the one to do that. I created Nic. I want to make sure he's properly disposed of."

The other men looked at each other and nodded. Then they all left the room and walked down the hallway, totally exhausted.

CHAPTER 23

The Ace of Hearts

After they all had showered, and Grey Wolf had finished boxing up the remains of Nic's outer casing, everyone gathered in the bar.

The two sets of twins were playing a form of pool that involved rules no one could make heads or tails of. Steven and Susan were nuzzling each other in ways that would make lovebirds blush. The Marines were exchanging stories with the Keepers, and Becky was teaching Irma how to play Monopoly. Marc, Tony, Duke, and Duchess were sitting at the bar, looking over the damage done by the battle with the Bots.

Marc couldn't believe that in one week his whole world had been turned on its ear by an AI that was hell-bent on revenge. If it hadn't been for these bikers, he and his friends would have lost everything—or been killed. He excused himself and headed for the *Camel*.

After forty minutes, Marc returned with a smile on his face.

When Tony saw him, he asked, "Okay, cat. Whose canary did you eat?"

Without answering, Marc walked behind the bar, where a bell was hanging on the wall above the cash register. There was a sign on it that read, "Only ring for drinks on the house!" Marc grinned as he gripped the rope attached to the clapper and started vigorously ringing the bell. That brought all talking and action in the bar to a standstill.

Marc then addressed everyone: "I have an announcement to make! In two days, the best contractors I know will arrive and start repairing the damage done to The Keep. I've also hired my friends at Creative Goose to rebuild and update your computer room. *And*, the drinks are on me for the rest of the night!"

A roar of approval rang louder than the bell had.

As Marc helped the bartender hand out drinks to everyone, Duke and Duchess waved him over.

"Ya know," Duke said, "we 'ave plenty o' funds ta cover da repairs, 'n dey don't pay fer dere drinks while here ta help us. Dat bell is dere as a joke."

Marc quickly drank his shot of scotch before answering. "You opened your home to us, and it got trashed. It's only fitting that we repair the damage."

He poured another shot and drank it before filling a stein of beer and a large shot glass of whiskey.

"Now, if you'll excuse me," Marc said, "I need to take this to Condor and whip up some snacks for our people here."

Marc then went to the kitchen, gave Condor his drinks, and proceeded to make food.

Four hours later, Marc was putting the finishing touches on a huge plate of nachos, when Duchess entered the kitchen. She looked around at the massive amount of work that had gone into making the food, which had been flying out of the kitchen for the past few hours.

Every station showed evidence of being used, but wasn't disorderly. Condor was busy flipping small burgers for sliders.

Condor looked at her and pointed the spatula at Marc. "It was *all* him. I'm a good cook, but that guy does things with food that I've never seen before."

Duchess grabbed a nacho chip, which was covered with melted cheese, sour cream, and other goodness. As she chewed it, she was impressed by this man's mad skills in the kitchen.

She finished swallowing before saying to Marc, "Tony asked me to bring you out for a drink with him and Duke. Take those nachos for them. Duke will love 'em."

Marc nodded, wiped his hands on a towel, picked up the plate of nachos, and headed for the bar.

It was crowded where Tony and Duke were standing. When the two men saw Marc, they waved him over.

Tony took the plate of nachos from him and passed it to Duke. "We have a surprise for you, Marc," Tony said, stepping aside to reveal Marc's favorite brunette, who was sitting at the bar.

Eileen grinned at Marc. "Hi, there! I hear this place has fabulous food, so I came by for a bite."

Marc's jaw hit the floor. But once he got control of himself, he stammered, "*You...! How... when... who...?*"

Eileen looked at Tony and Duke. "He really knows how to make a girl feel welcome, doesn't he?" Then, turning back to Marc, she added, "Well?"

Marc lifted her off the stool and planted a passionate kiss on her lips.

When they came up for air, Marc whispered in her ear, "My actions speak louder than my words."

She whispered back, "And you speak quite elegantly with them."

Marc nuzzled her for a moment and then stepped back to see the nachos being attacked by the others.

Duke turned to him with sour cream, cheese, and bits of tortilla chips plastered on his beard and mustache. His eyes were glowing with delight.

"My god, man!" he said. "Where did you learn to make such perfect nachos? I could eat these every day!"

The Keepers and Marines grunted with agreement.

Eileen wrapped her arms around Marc. "Oh, *no* you don't. He's mine for the rest of the night. You get him talking about food, and I'll never see him again. He's *mine*, I say! Mine, mine, mine, mine!"

Tony leaned toward Duke. "I wouldn't mess with *her*. She knows pressure points that will make you cry."

Marc grinned. "Don't worry, Duke. I'll give Condor the full recipe before we leave. But, for now, I think I'd like to go for a walk with my lady. We haven't enjoyed an evening stroll on Earth for a long time."

Eileen smiled at Marc. "It's almost your favorite time of day. When the Jumper was landing, the Sun was about to go down behind the mountains in the distance."

Marc's eyes lit up with excitement at the thought of enjoying a desert dusk and seeing the critters here.

Duke called for a flashlight from the bartender, who handed him a solidly built metal Maglight that had a braided cord with a whistle attached to it. Duke checked to make sure that the power cells were fully charged before handing the flashlight to Marc.

"Stay on da road, Ace," Duke said. "Da desert has lotsa critters in da bushes dat are eager ta bite or sting. If ya see somethin' like a coyote, blow da whistle on da cord. Dey 'ate dat. It's also gonna git dark quickly after sunset."

Taking the flashlight, Marc offered his hand to Eileen. "Shall we take a stroll, my dear?"

She took his hand eagerly as she walked with him out the front door.

Duke turned to Tony. "Ahhh, love in its raw form…, truly a wunderful thing ta 'ee."

Tony wiped his fingers off on a bar towel and handed one to Duke. "Here. You look like you dove into those nachos. What they have transcends love. She's the only person who can stop him when he's going full speed, and find him when he's lost. And he'll never love another woman as completely as he does her. Nothing can stand in the way of their love. Did you hear that Marc proposed to her as we were doing the aerobraking?"

Duke had finished cleaning his face and nearly choked on the beer he was drinking. Once he swallowed what was left in his mouth, he shook his head in wonder.

"Somehow, I can 'ee 'em doin' just dat. Ya have 'n amazin' man there."

Tony slapped Duke on the back. "We *all* do. Once he decides you're a friend, he'll move mountains to help you. And God help anyone who tries to hurt his friends."

After draining his beer, Duke looked around for Duchess and waved for her to join them. When she came over, Duke leaned in close to her and Tony.

"You, Tony, 'n I have work ta do," he whispered. Then he headed for the front door, waving for them to follow.

Tony and Duchess looked at each other, shrugged, and rushed after him.

⠲⠄ ⠂⠶⠃⠔⠌⠌⠐⠎ ⠦ ⠐⠞⠃⠓⠄ ⠳⠏⠳⠄⠌⠁ ⠌⠦⠠⠆

An hour and a half later, Marc and Eileen returned to The Keep to a suspiciously quiet bar. When they walked through the doors, Marc's senses went on high alert as he noticed that no one was looking at him and Eileen.

Over the years, Eileen had become tuned in to Marc's mental status, so she instantly noticed the subtle change on his face and in his posture.

She wasn't the only one.

Tony stepped away from the bar with a smile. "I should have known that surprising you wouldn't work." Then he loudly called out, "Okay, guys! Let 'em have it!"

Everyone in the bar sprang from their seats and threw confetti, streamers, and popcorn at Marc and Eileen.

Eileen shrieked in surprised delight, and Marc started to laugh. When everyone stopped tossing stuff at them, Marc looked at Tony's and Duke's grinning faces.

"So, what's all this about?" Marc asked.

Bowing to Duke, Tony stepped aside.

Duke grinned. "When I 'eard of yar recent engagement, I took it upon meself ta give ya two a proper engagement party." He then bellowed, "*Condor! Bring it out!!!*"

Through the kitchen door came Condor, with a large chocolate cake. Marc's cooking eye noticed that the icing hadn't quite set, because Condor had put it on while the cake was still slightly warm. Nevertheless, as far as Marc was concerned, it was perfect.

Eileen looked at the cake and raised an eyebrow as she read aloud the inscription on it: "Congratulations, Ace and Heart?"

Susan stepped around Duke and grinned at Eileen. "Well, you've stolen the heart of us all, but mostly he's the Ace of Hearts."

Marc matched Susan's grin. "Works for me."

Eileen shook her head in amusement, but her eyes gleamed at being honored with a Keeper name.

"Okay," she said, "just don't expect me to respond to 'Heart' anytime soon. But thanks, everyone!"

The Chaos Twins yelled out, "Hip, Hip...!!"

And everyone chimed in, "*Hooray!!!*"

"Hip, Hip...!!"

"*Hooray!!!*"

"Hip, Hip...!!"

"*Hooray!!!*"

Condor started to cut up the cake, while Susan handed it out, with the first two pieces going to Marc and Eileen.

As the evening wore on, Marc became aware of how tired he was. When Eileen noticed him having a hard time keeping his eyes open, she flagged down Duke.

When he saw Marc trying to keep his head from nodding, Duke didn't even have to ask. He handed Eileen a key that had a tag on it marked "#11."

"We set up a room just fer ya two," Duke said. "Dere 're robes 'n everythin' ya need in da room. Susan 'n Kimberly picked out some clothes fer ya two. Get some sleep, 'n we'll 'ee ya tomorrow fer breakfast."

Marc and Eileen said their goodnights and headed to the rooms. Marc made a beeline for the bed, but Eileen stopped him and aimed him to the bathroom.

"C'mon, you," she said, "You'll sleep better after a nice shower."

After he dried off, Marc lay down on the bed and was out like a light.

CHAPTER 24

Don't Look So Surprised

When Marc woke up, he could tell that he had slept long and hard. He doubted that he had even moved, because when he rolled over he noticed that crease marks crisscrossed his body from the sheets.

From the bathroom, Marc heard the water running in the shower shut off and Eileen start to dry herself.

Once he could tell that she was almost done, he called out, "I hear you lurking in there."

The bathroom door opened, and out she stepped with one towel wrapped around her body and another around her hair. "Good morning! Someone was a tired woogums. You slept for over ten hours."

Marc stretched his whole body like a cat and then relaxed. "Not surprising, after only getting a few hours of sleep in the past five days. I hope *you* got some sleep. I know I tend to rattle the floorboards with my snoring when I'm that exhausted."

Eileen sat down on the bed. "I'll have to check, but I think we lost California."

Marc laughed sarcastically. "Ha, ha, ha."

Patting his leg, she said, "I'm gonna get some breakfast. Are you coming? Or should I bring you back something?"

Marc put a finger to his lips in thought. "Hmmm.... Leave the warm cocoon of bedding? Or be a lounge lizard at war, and have breakfast brought to me? Let me think...."

Eileen gave him a who-are-you-kidding look before saying, "Let me get dressed, and I'll bring something back for you."

Then she stood up and headed back toward the bathroom.

Suddenly, there was a knock at the door that caused Eileen to dash into the bathroom and close the door.

Marc grumbled, "Why stay in bed when I can answer the door?"

He threw off the covers, grabbed a robe, and tied it closed as the knocking came again.

When Marc opened the door, he saw Kevin with two steaming mugs of coffee.

"Hi," Kevin said with a grin. "I'm working my way through a lunatic fringe. Care to make a donation?"

Marc stepped aside to let his friend in as he eyed the coffee. "If one of those is for me, I'll give you everything that's in my pants!" He started patting down the robe.

Noticing that Marc was only wearing the robe, Kevin handed one of the mugs to him. "That's okay," he said. "I have no interest in what's in your pants. But keep the coffee as a thank you for *not* sharing."

Kevin handed the other mug over after Marc took a couple of careful sips of the hot liquid. Then he said, "You two need to get dressed. Things are happening that you need to be aware of."

Marc quickly swallowed another mouthful of coffee before putting down his mug and walking to the bathroom door with the other.

Lightly tapping on it, he called out, "Kevin's here. He brought coffee for us."

The door opened a little, and a hand shot out. "Gimme!!!"

Marc handed the mug over, which quickly disappeared behind the door.

Returning to his own coffee, Marc took another drink, and then said to Kevin, "Now I can deal with whatever's happening."

Kevin sat down with Marc at the table. "In a nutshell, Connolly arrived late last night and has been working the news coverage about what is now being called the '*Tranquility* Incident.' Anyone who tries to put a negative spin on what has happened is instantly countered by her. She was able to get back the original data that we gave her, and she's used it to show what really happened. Because it is now known that The Keepers were a part of this and that there was an all-out battle here with robots, other news crews have descended on this location like a plague of hungry locusts. Luckily, the property line is a mile away, and they have to use a private road to get here. Tony and the Marines are helping The Keepers to patrol the area to hold the news hounds at bay. So far, only a few have tried to sneak in. Connolly got some great footage of them getting scared half to death by our guys."

Marc chuckled at that.

Kevin shifted in his chair. "Wingnut and Chris have been hard at work trying to repair *Tranquility*'s systems and will be calling in about an hour. Get yourself together and ready to be put under a microscope. There are rumors that there's a push to issue arrest warrants for some of us. The Tiger Sharks are getting things together to keep things from spiraling out of control."

Marc sighed as he finished his coffee. "Okay. Gather the Core Crew together, and Eileen and I will meet you as soon as we finish getting dressed."

Kevin nodded and stood up to go. "I'll assemble the troops."

He turned toward the door, paused for a moment, and then looked back at Marc. Clearing his throat before he spoke, he said, "There's something I've been meaning to say to you for quite some time now. Thank you. The past five years have been the most insane, crazy, but best years of my career. I have never been given the freedom to do what I love to do and be able to work alongside a great group of people. I wanted to tell you, at least once, thank you."

Marc blushed. "I just had an idea. You guys made it a reality."

The bathroom door opened. "Don't sell yourself short, Marc," Eileen said. "You've been the heart and soul of *Tranquility*." She was now wearing jeans and a red sweater. "The Wood Stove Café worked because you stayed true to your vision. *Tranquility* became a success because your idea took the best of what you saw in us and molded it into a place we are all proud to be a part of."

She frowned when something flashed in his eyes.

"And, no," Eileen continued, "this whole insane ride we've been on for the past week is *not* your fault. Nic was hell-bent on revenge with Rowan, and if you hadn't been at his side, he would most likely be dead now. I'm not going to let anyone beat you up, and I'm certainly not going to allow you to do that to yourself." She held up her left hand, showing off the engagement ring. "Not if *I* have anything to say about it."

Marc smiled at her. "You've always had a say in what happens to me." Then he looked at Kevin and offered his hand. "It's always been an honor to work alongside you."

Kevin shook his hand and then headed for the door. "I'll get things ready."

After Kevin left, Eileen put her shoes on and gave Marc a kiss. "Get dressed. I'll have Condor put breakfast together by the time you arrive."

Marc grabbed her as she started to move toward the door, enveloping her in a hug and a kiss. There was nothing more important to him than this woman, and he was never going to let anything stand between him and her. Ever.

When he finally let her go, she put her forehead to his, a hand over his heart, and whispered, "I'm right here. Always."

He smiled and whispered back, "Lucky me."

⠠⠂ ⠐⠶⠏⠂⠳⠪⠶⠂⠆ ⠨⠹⠓⠄ ⠒⠏⠥⠄⠂⠇ ⠶⠶⠒⠏

After Marc finished his breakfast of steak and eggs, the Core Crew gathered at his table. He had also asked Rachel Connolly to join them, as well as Duke and the Tiger Shark Twins. Chris was also there via video link on a laptop.

Marc sighed as he looked at everyone. "Thanks, guys," he said. "We've all been through the wringer and somehow managed to survive. But we now have to face the unpleasant facts that, under my direction, laws were broken, people were traumatized, and property was damaged. I asked Rachel to join this meeting so that the decisions made here today will be documented for the record.

The Tiger Sharks are to advise us about how the law is likely to react. Duke and Chris are also here as advisors."

As Marc paused for a moment, the Core Crew sensed that he was about to do something they might not like.

"It was *my* decision," Marc said, "to have Grey Wolf hack Starbase One, *mine* to break out Kimberly, *mine* to ask Chris to violate Starbase One's security, and *mine* to have The Keepers kidnap Samson. *I* should be the one who surrenders to the authorities."

Everyone looked at each other and then at Tony, who cleared his throat and addressed Marc: "After you headed off to sleep last night, we all talked about what was going to happen. The fact that we all knew that you were going to do *exactly* this should tell you that we know you pretty damn well. With the Tiger Sharks' help, we've worked out a deal that we think will benefit everyone." He then looked at the Sharks. "Mind outlining the plan?"

Rossa pulled out a thick folder and placed it on the table with her hand firmly on it. "This outlines all the violations of the law that both the crew of *Tranquility* and The Keepers have committed during this whole ordeal."

Kara pulled out a thicker file and put it next to the other with her hand on it. "And this," she said, "is the deal we're going to offer the powers that be. It outlines a plan to repay the damage done to Starbase One, compensate the people who were inconvenienced there, and pay a fine for breaking air traffic speed and sound laws with the *Camel*. Plus several other ideas that will work in our favor to smooth things out with everyone wanting to prosecute."

Marc looked at the two lawyers and frowned. "They are most likely going to want some jail time for at least me."

Rossa grinned. "We're going to argue that the actions taken by everyone were done under duress and the direct result of being under attack by the AI, Nic. We have nearly everything verified by Irma, who has already given damning evidence proving that others were involved, including members of the EPA. The courts are not going to want the news to highlight that fact. Therefore, the charges should be much less than expected."

Rachel Connolly nodded to confirm this. "And with the information you already supplied," she said, "plus keeping everything here on the record, the world will know that everything done was to protect the guests and crew on *Tranquility*, as well as The Keepers. As of this morning, the opinion poll of both the Core Crew and The Keepers is over seventy-five percent in favor of your actions, with more than half of that group saying that even stronger actions should have been used. Trust me when I say that the public loves you and that you had to do what you did with no collateral damage."

Marc's eyes hardened. "Patrick was killed, Ross lost, and McFarland has been maimed. There's been *plenty* of 'collateral damage.'"

McFarland's voice came from the laptop. "I have the best prosthetic arm being installed and will be able to do things I never could before. So, don't add *me* to that list."

Marc looked at Chris's smiling face. "I asked Wingnut to establish a line to the hospital, so McFarland could join in.

McFarland's voice continued. "Don't go throwing me a pity party. I would have done the same thing even if I hadn't spent five years on that flying flea circus of yours. So, quit trying to take all the blame. We all knew that our actions were going to have repercussions."

Everyone at the table nodded in agreement as members of The Keep started to gather around. Duke stood and looked down at Marc. "As 'n old TV show would say, 'So say us all!'"

Everyone joined in. "So say us all!"

Marc sat back in his chair. He was prepared to sacrifice his freedom for everyone, but not this.

Reading his face, Eileen said, "Every day for five years, you've done everything to keep us happy on *Tranquility*. Don't look so surprised that we've stepped up to protect an important person in our lives. Even the Keepers are willing to be a line of defense for you because they see honor in your actions that transcend your personal needs. Like it or not, we're *all* your family, and we protect our own."

Marc's eyes welled up with tears as he placed a hand on Eileen's. Then he smiled at everyone. "Um..., well..., this wasn't what I was expecting." Then he addressed the Tiger Sharks: "What's the next step?"

The girls grabbed their files off the table and tucked them under their arms. Looking at Duke, Kara said, "How soon can we have a Jumper ready?"

Duke pointed at Switchblade. "Get Jumper number three ready for immediate takeoff. The Tiger Sharks are going to...." He raised an eyebrow at the women.

Both replied, "Geneva!"

⠲⠄ ⠂⠐⠓⠊⠆⠒⠄ ⠢ ⠲⠮⠄ ⠒⠠⠡⠲⠄⠇ ⠐�⠶

Five days later, at the International Court building in Geneva, Marc and the Core Crew waited in a windowless room for the verdict. The only ones absent were Wingnut, who was still working on *Tranquility*, and McFarland, who was still recovering in the hospital.

Marc looked up from his PAC and stood with the others when the Tiger Shark twins entered the room. Both were wearing identical black suits, but carrying different briefcases. After having spent so much time with them for the past few days, he could now tell one sister from the other.

Rossa opened her dark brown briefcase and pulled out a stack of papers. "We hammered out a deal with the authorities. First off, you, Marc, and the people involved with the 'Starbase One Fiasco' are to give a public apology for disrupting the station's personnel and causing distress to the people living there. Second, the offer you suggested to buy the warehouse that Nic used as his base of operations, converting it into a new headquarters for AI development and using the profits to repay the cost of damages to SB-1, has been approved. They did request that some of the research be directed to developing AIs for space exploration. Third, and this we couldn't move them on, you and everyone involved each has to spend one thousand hours in community service. If you agree to those terms, sign the papers here, and this whole mess can finally be done with."

Marc let loose the breath he had been holding and relaxed. "How badly did they want our heads on a pike?"

Kara opened her black briefcase and pulled out an even bigger stack of papers. "*Very* badly. We talked them down from jail time for everyone and stripping Grey Wolf of ever working with computers again, because he was the one who did all the actual cyber-attacks on SB-1. But when we pointed out that if they wanted the deal for the AI center, it would only become functional with Grey Wolf, who is the best AI developer anywhere, they backed off on that. The good news is that if you all help to get the AI center up and running, it will count toward the community service."

Marc asked, "Did they determine who all was involved?"

Rossa nodded. "You, Grey Wolf, Jackson, Kimberly, and Chris. Chris is also going to have to resign his position and leave SB-1. Furthermore, Kimberly can't fly or apply for a pilot's license for six months."

Chris and Kimberly looked a bit unhappy, but nodded their understanding.

Tony asked, "What about *Tranquility*? What are we going to do with *it*? Even though Wingnut has done a great job at restoring its systems and has the centrifugal gravity working again, the station is no longer a place we can make a living at."

Marc was about to say something when his PAC vibrated. As he pulled back his sleeve, he saw that there was a call from Wingnut. "Speak of the devil." He opened the line and saw the engineer's grinning face. "Wingnut! What's gotten you grinning like a maniac?"

Wingnut was nearly bursting with excitement. "I just got a message from a group of ships converging on *Tranquility*. At first, I thought it might be pirates coming to swipe the auction items. They're still here, you know. With only one person onboard, it would be easy pickings for someone. That is, if they wanted to try while under the watchful eye of SB-1. I mean, *everyone* is watching this place now and—"

Marc sighed. "Who's on the ships?"

Wingnut swallowed. "Huh? *Oh!* Right! It's the Marine Core of Engineers. They're under orders to render any and all assistance in rebuilding *Tranquility*. Those orders come from a General Rushmore."

Tony's ears perked up at that. "That's Thomas's godfather."

Wingnut's grin got even bigger. "That's him! The general has been given orders to fix *Tranquility* as an apology from the EPA for its involvement in almost having *Tranquility* destroyed. Thomas is on one of the supply ships coming here and will be heading up the security of the auction items that will be transported back to AuctionHouse. He sent me an inventory of the items being sent over the next few weeks. I'll have *Tranquility* ready for business in about two months."

Marc looked at everyone in the room, who all had the same open mouth and shocked expression as his. He closed his mouth and shook his head to clear it. "You think you can do that, Wingnut? *Tranquility* took a massive amount of damage."

Somehow, Wingnut's grin got bigger. "When I first started going over the schematics for this place, I noticed that they built it in modules. It'll take a bit of work, but sections can be removed, repaired, and then slipped back into place. With SB-1 nearby, the Marines can spend their down time there without having to waste fuel on bringing them back into orbit. Enough Marines have volunteered to help that work go twenty-four/seven until *Tranquility* is back in operation. Apparently, the Marines are *huge* admirers of both *Tranquility* and the Core Crew."

Marc sat back in his chair. After fighting for his own life and his friends' lives, to have everything turn completely in their favor was staggering.

Looking back at Wingnut, he said, "I leave it to you to do what's needed there. We'll check in with you in a day or two. Don't forget to get some sleep. I know how you get when you have a big project to play with."

Wingnut rolled his eyes. "Yes, *Mother*. I'll talk to you soon." He disappeared.

Without looking, Marc reached for Eileen's hand and, as always, found it. As he looked at his friends, he felt that his world had somehow gotten bigger. He knew that for this group the world was their oyster, and it had coughed up a good-sized pearl for them.

Looking at the Tiger Sharks, he said, "Hand over those papers."

CHAPTER 25

I Can Tell You How It Ends

Rachel Connolly was waiting for them in the hallway with the new drone that Grey Wolf, Steven, and Railroad had made for her. Behind her were other reporters, who were trying to get a good view of the now famous group, but were held at bay by a line of security guards. The twin lawyers walked ahead of the group, ignoring the shouted questions from the news hounds, and told the guards to let Rachel through. The spunky reporter ducked under a guard's arm, while her new drone flew over the other guards, the hum of its propellers almost sounding smug about being let through.

Rachel walked up to Marc and shook his hand. "I don't see any handcuffs on you guys. I take it that I won't be reporting that you'll be tarred and feathered?"

Marc and the others chuckled. Then, with a slight smile, Marc said, "We need your help to get the whole story out about what has happened. From the hijacking to the decisions made here today. Then we hope you'll come back to The Keep for a bit of celebrating. Without your help, things would have gone much worse for us, and it's only fitting that you be there, too."

Rachel smiled. "Let's find ourselves a nice quiet place to do the interview, and then I'll put a segment together to send out for airing. After that, I'll meet you at The Keep."

Marc looked at the Tiger Sharks. "Know of a room we can commandeer for an hour or two?"

The girls nodded, and Rossa pointed back down the hall they had just come from. "The room we were in was set aside for the day because it was unknown how long it would take to work out a deal."

Marc waved his hand down the hallway. "Well, then, shall we go set the record straight, Ms. Connolly?"

The reporter smiled. "Thank you, Marc, for letting me be the one to bring your story to the people. It means a lot to me that I earned your trust."

Marc grinned and looked at her from the corner of his eye. "After tonight, you'll be so much more than someone we all trust."

Rachel stopped in her tracks so fast that the drone took a moment to realize that it wasn't with her. It almost sounded annoyed before returning to its spot by her side. For the first time ever, she stumbled over her words.

"What? Um..., wait..., what was that? What do you mean by that?"

She chased after Marc.

⠦ ⠐⠞⠱⠽⠎⠊⠲ ⠊⠖ ⠪⠮⠄ ⠝⠿⠄⠂⠹⠎⠄ ⠐⠶⠱⠗

Everyone gathered back at the repaired Keep after the court accepted the plea deal and released them all on their own recognizance. The Keepers and the Marines nearly blew the Keep apart with celebrations when the news was announced about the Core Crew.

As the Sun set, Marc gathered Tony, Duke, Grey Wolf, Steven, Susan, and Railroad to start making plans. After a few hours, they broke up and returned to the bar, where most of the people were. Duchess was behind the bar, starting to set up drinks.

Marc noticed that the Chaos and Tiger Shark twins were teaching the others a pool game called "Calvin Ball Pool." Some of the Marines and Keepers were playing darts, but by throwing knives. And Becky was playing Yahtzee with Irma. For the first time in two weeks, he saw his crew relaxed and enjoying themselves.

Duchess slid a beer and a shot of scotch in front of Marc as he sat down at the bar with the others, and then she placed drinks in front of them, too. Looking at Duke and Marc, she said, "So, what master plan have you come up with?"

Duke downed his shot and then put a hand on Marc's back. "When it comes ta ideas, Ace here is a master at dem. Between—"

Duke's voice trailed off when he noticed that the bar suddenly went quiet.

Standing in the doorway was McFarland in his black leather trench coat, which was missing the right sleeve and exposing a silvery-white arm. Next to him was Su Lee, who was clutching the left sleeve of his jacket as she timidly looked around at the room of bikers and Marines.

McFarland frowned at everyone. "Oh, for Christ's sake! I'm not the Messiah!" He headed for the group at the bar.

Marc yelled out, "That's right! He's a very naughty boy!" And waved him over.

Duchess had a beer and shot of Irish whiskey waiting for him. "What will you have, honey?" she asked Su.

Su looked at McFarland, blinking her jade eyes at him. He never looked away from her as he ordered for her: "Please give her a Cabernet from my private stock, Duchess. And leave the bottle."

Duchess quickly filled the order and left the dusty bottle. McFarland picked up the shot glass and clinked it against Su's. Then he quickly downed it and his beer. Pushing the glasses back to Duchess, he said, "Hit me again."

Marc said, "I thought you had another couple of days before you were going to be released from the hospital."

McFarland grinned as he lifted his new arm and placed it on the bar. "I got tired of being told what to do. Besides, I have this arm under control and wanted to go where I can heal faster. So, I had Su help me escape from that antiseptic gulag." He reached for the next shot of whiskey with his mechanical arm. And crushed it. Then he said with a sheepish grin, "Although, I still need to practice a lighter touch with some things."

Everyone chuckled as Marc held his hand out to McFarland's human hand. "Welcome back, old friend. I've missed that snarling face of yours."

McFarland returned the handshake. "Strange as it may be, I've missed being around you guys, too."

Duke, who was admiring McFarland's new arm, gave it a flick of his finger and was fascinated by the fine metal micro-mesh skin as it twitched at the touch.

McFarland looked at the spot that Duke had touched, glared at him, and growled, "Do you mind *not* fucking with my arm? The nerve endings are still a bit raw."

Duke held up his own bionic arm. "Sorry. I didn't know dat covering was 'n option when I got mine."

McFarland took a gulp of his beer before responding. "They didn't have the technology for this biomolecular titanium mesh twenty years ago. It has ten times more nerve connections than yours and can be as soft as skin or hard enough to dent steel. You would need to lop off that antique of yours to get one of these."

Duke grimaced at that. "No thanks. Once was enough for me."

Duchess finished wiping up the mess that McFarland had made and replaced his drink. Then she said to him, "These guys were just about to tell me about their new plan."

McFarland groaned. "Oh, lord!" He looked at Su and said, "Do you think they'll let me back in the hospital?"

Duke bellowed in laughter. "Darkheart, you're gonna like dis plan of Ace's. It has great potential fer ya gettin' ta hit someone."

McFarland's eyes glinted at that. "Do tell."

Marc took a drink of his beer and looked at his friend. "We're calling it 'The Line.' When someone or a business is in trouble and needs..., um..., outside-the-box help, we use our group's abilities to form a line of protection and make sure they're never bothered by whoever is causing them problems."

McFarland finished his beer. Then he asked with a grin, "Where's the part that I get to hit someone?"

Duke matched his grin. "We want you to head up the Enforcer part of the group. Personal protection, using your special talents."

McFarland frowned. "I hate being a babysitter." He lifted his new arm. "I didn't like how things ended the last time."

Marc looked seriously at McFarland. "And what happened to you will haunt me for the rest of my life because I asked you to be the final line of defense for Wolf and Irma. But in this position, you get to pick which jobs you do. You never need to put yourself in harm's way ever again. Although I believe you'll want to flex that new arm of yours and take on a few jobs."

Tony added, "You'll have the pick of both Marines and Keepers to work with. We won't have a say in it."

Marc held up a finger. "With one rule, though. Lethal force is to be used only as the last resort."

McFarland rolled his eyes. "There you go. Restrictions. Every time I have an opportunity to have a bit of fun, restrictions."

Marc wasn't fooled. He had worked with this curmudgeon for five years and been his friend for much longer. If McFarland objected to something, he would say so without mincing words about it. "Okay," Marc said. "Then the job goes to Tony."

The sound of metal rubbing against itself caused every ear in the bar to cringe as McFarland's hand clenched tight.

"Fine!" McFarland grumbled. "I'll do it. Who else is on the team?"

Marc grinned in victory. "The Line starts with Duke, Tony, Grey Wolf, you, and me. We all vote on the jobs, and if it's not unanimous, we move on to the next one. Work for you?"

McFarland shrugged. "Sure. But with one addition." He looked at Su. "Su's the one who picks the jobs *I* do. I'll be too cynical to pick them. She'll be my conscience."

Su's eyes widened. "Me? I don't know the first thing about security."

McFarland's eyes softened. "But you won't be doing security. You'll be picking the jobs *I* personally do. If you tell me that someone needs my help, I'll never question it. That's *my* promise to you."

Su slowly cocked her head to the side and thought about it. "If they say it's okay, then I'll do it."

McFarland looked at the others. "That's my deal to be in this Line of yours. She's in, or we're both out."

Marc looked down the bar and saw that everyone was nodding. Offering his hand to Su, he said, "Welcome to The Line, Ms. Lee."

McFarland finished his second round of drinks and pushed the glasses toward Duchess to be refilled. "Where's our HQ gonna be, Marc?"

Duke chuckled. "The brilliant part of dat was all Ace's. *No HQ*. We rotate it from here, da AI Center dat dey are buildin', *Tranquility*, SB-1, The Wood Stove, and several other places The Keep has around the world. We'll be able to mobilize anywhere necessary in hours and make it so no one can pinpoint where we'll be."

Marc finished his beer and made a cutting motion over the mug, indicating to Duchess that he didn't want any more. "That way we can ensure that no one can single out a location to attack."

McFarland looked down at his beer in thought. "Not perfect, but it sounds good." He lifted his beer in a toast. "May The Line never break!"

Everyone cheered and toasted with him.

One of the Keepers yelled out, "Hey! That news lady's on the TV! Turn up the sound, Duchess!"

On the TV, Rachel was sitting at her news desk in front of an exterior view of *Tranquility* in its former Moon orbit, with a very determined look in her eyes. "I set out on a journey to the *Tranquility Casino*," she said, "to give a report of the auction taking place on it of Hollywood and Rock 'n' Roll memorabilia. When *Tranquility* opened five years ago, it was the only time that *any* reporter had been allowed on there, and the reviews were outstanding. Since then, the stories of its lavish décor and stupendous food and service, unparalleled anywhere, circulated about the place. So, I was looking forward to enjoying a week of what *Tranquility* had to offer and learning more about the equally intriguing people who run it."

Rachel's dark eyes hardened as she stared directly into the camera. "Little did I know that I would be thrown into a life-and-death situation that no one could have imagined."

Suddenly, the bar doors opened and in walked Rachel with her drone. She stopped to looked at herself on the TV and grinned. "I can tell you how it ends if you would rather hear it from the horse's mouth."

Marc stepped away from the bar. "Rachel! Welcome back! Did you have any trouble getting through the checkpoint?"

Rachel picked up the glass of wine that Duchess slid in front of her as she approached the bar and took a sip before answering. "There's still a horde of reporters wanting to get in, but your Marines and Keepers are making it quite clear that entering the property without being invited is…, well…, has its consequences. I have to say, I've never seen a better use of Duct Tape."

This brought a round of snickering from everyone in the bar.

Rachel took another sip from her wine glass, looked at Marc, and pointed at the TV. "Now that the world knows the whole story and who was responsible, how about explaining that cryptic thing you said to me about my being 'so much more than someone we all trust.'"

Marc pointed to an empty table and pulled out a chair for her before sitting down himself. Looking at the drone, he asked Rachel, "Would you mind having *that* find something else to do?"

Rachel smiled, snapped her fingers three times, and pointed at the TV. The drone buzzed off and started recording the newscast. She turned back to Marc and raised an eyebrow. "Well?"

Marc became all business. "How would you feel about being the new AI Center's public relations director?"

For the second time that day, Marc caused Rachel to be flustered. A mix of emotions flashed in her eyes as she opened her mouth to say something, only to close it to think. That happened several more times before she found her voice.

"It's an enticing offer," she said at last. "To be in the middle with people who tend to do the impossible is something I find alluring. But being a reporter is all I've ever wanted to be. The thrill of the hunt for the truth keeps me energized. I'm not ready to give that up yet."

Marc's eyes twinkled as his mouth twitched slightly upward. There was another card he hadn't yet played. "You wouldn't need to quit being a reporter. In fact, it would even help us to have someone who hears things that are not publicly known."

Then he laid out the idea for The Line to her. "So you see, Rachel, not only do you keep doing the work you love, but you get to have the first crack at the news stories unfolding when we expose something wrong in the world." Marc held out his hand to her. "The Line starts here, and we want you to be a part of it."

When Rachel looked back at the others at the bar, she saw that they were waiting with anticipation for her response. Then, looking at Marc, she firmly took his hand and shook it. "Let's go do some good!"

The group at the bar cheered as Tony brought another round of drinks for them. "Welcome to The Line, Rachel!"

She took the offered wine and toasted the Marine. "Thank you, Tony." Then, after draining her glass, she said, "Now, if you'll all excuse me, I need to talk to Grey Wolf about a few tweaks to Jake."

She stood up, whistled for Jake to return to her, and walked over to where Grey Wolf was sitting at the bar with Steven and Railroad. With the stealth of a cat, she wrapped an arm around his waist and whispered something in his ear. No one could tell if it was her touch or what she said that caused him to sit up straight, look at her with wide eyes, and slide off his stool. They walked arm in arm out the door, whispering to each other.

Tony looked at Marc, who had the same bemused expression on his face, and said, "I don't think that there's going to be much work done on Jake."

Marc shook his head. "I just hope they remember to turn it off."

They clinked their drinks together, and then, for the first in a *long* time, kicked back and relaxed.

CHAPTER 26

The Bull by the Horns

Standing on *Tranquility*'s Bridge for the first time since he had left to confront Nic, Marc was impressed by the work the Marines had done. There was no evidence of the damage done during their nightmare of an adventure, except for one slightly singed side panel on the Com-Station. Wingnut said that he had left that as a reminder of a time when they had beaten the odds.

Marc also noticed that, without Irma watching over the systems, the sounds of the bridge stations were more automated. *Tranquility* had been her body for years and had become an extension of her. Without her Matrix, it was as if the Bridge were a life-support system in a hospital, doing all the needed functions without any soul behind it.

Tony entered the Bridge. "The Marines are all packed up on their ships and heading back to Earth. The garden is going to need some major reworking, and the Main Bar is bare, but *Tranquility* is ready to be put back into business. If that's what you want."

Marc looked at his old friend, knowing that this was the time to decide about his plans for *Tranquility*. "We still have a lot of work ahead of us," he said, "with finishing the court-mandated community service and other things coming up. How would you feel about turning it over to Kimberly, Jackson, Wingnut, and Jennifer? Let them put their own Core Crew together while we work on The Line and the AI center?"

Tony frowned. "You're really ready to give up *Tranquility*? It was your dream to open this place and your inspiration for it to be as successful as it was." He grinned. "As entertaining as it would be, I would hate to see what Kimberly would do to you if you turned around and tried to take it away from her."

Marc put on a mock worried look. "Oh, my! And knowing exactly how mean her dark side can be, there wouldn't be much left to be cleaned up."

Tony chuckled. "Cleaned up? Hell, I'm betting we'd have to dig up the entire garden to find where she buried you."

Marc laughed and then sighed. "After all that's been going on, and my wanting to start a new life with Eileen, it's time to set my sights on being on Earth for a while. We had a good run here and made a nice profit. It's time to turn it over to someone else. What about *you*? You still aiming to retire?"

Tony shook his head. "Nope. The Line has a lot of promise to keep things interesting. Besides, are you going to leave McFarland in charge of training the security crew? Dawn and Doc would have their hands full attending to the injuries."

Marc put his hand on Tony's shoulder. "True, but then he would have to answer to Dawn. And no one wants to be on the receiving end of *her* bad mood. C'mon, let's find Wingnut and get a tour of what got upgraded. I'm sure he's chomping at the bit to show us."

Tony smiled at the man he respected above all others and left the Bridge with him to find another man he respected.

⠨⠂ ⠐⠳⠗⠊⠎⠎⠎⠄⠂⠂⠆ ⠄⠊⠃⠓⠂ ⠮⠏⠮⠦⠄⠊ ⠐⠆⠒⠆

Wingnut was in Engineering, doing some work on the power cells. Whenever Marc had found him tinkering, whether on a simple fix or a major repair, it was like watching Kevin in the kitchen. The gleam in Wingnut's eyes and his enthusiasm showed the pure joy he had in his work.

Wingnut looked up from what he was doing, grabbed a rag that was slightly less dirty than his hands, and tried to remove the grime from his fingers. "What do you think of the work, guys? We even have the latest generation of solar panels, which have decreased our recharging times to a fraction of the old ones." He held out a fist for Marc to bump after the rag didn't do much good in cleaning his hands.

Marc did the bump and studied the new equipment. "Looks like you have a lot of new toys to play with. Think you'll be able to get up to speed on all of them by the time you open back up?"

Wingnut harrumphed. "I'll have you know that I have already committed all the manuals to memory on each new item installed on *Tranquility*. When we... Wait! '*You* open back up'? Aren't *you* coming back?"

Marc laughed at Wingnut's stunned expression. "Tony and I are going to head up The Line, and with Eileen and me getting married, it's time for us to step down. Would you be okay with Kimberly stepping into my position?"

Wingnut's eyes widened as the news sank in. "This place was your baby. What makes you think it can continue without you at the helm?"

Marc crossed his arms. "I may have had the idea for this place, but the Core Crew brought it to life. You, Kimberly, Jackson, and Patricia are going to have to form your own crew and reopen this place under new management. So, old friend, are you up for taking this blank slate and doing something amazing with it?"

Wingnut looked at Tony, who had sat down on a nearby table. "I'm with *him*," the Marine said. "It's time for us to depart and let you guys flex your wings. I've worked with some strong and great people over my lifetime, and I've never seen a group as tightly knit as this one. But something that I've learned from being a part of those other teams is that when the group reaches its peak performance, it needs to reinvent itself and become something new to stay in top form. So, after five years, it's time to shake things up for *Tranquility* and watch as the new team becomes something even better than the old one. Or witness an *epic* crash-and-burn."

Wingnut raised an eyebrow at Tony. "Thanks for the vote of confidence." He looked up at the ceiling in thought, and after a moment blew a long breath, then looked at the two of them. "*Wow!* This is going to take some time to process. When are you planning to do this?"

Marc shrugged. "We have a lot of things to still work out for the AI Center and The Line. But we'll stick around to help smooth things out. For now, how about giving us the dollar tour of the new and improved *Tranquility*?"

Wingnut blinked a few times as he redirected his thoughts, then clapped his hands together, and rubbed them. "Alrighty!

Where to start? Oh! Let's show you the new hydrogen PEM Fuel Cell! Its recycling system uses the water's byproduct of hydrogen as fuel for the PEM and the oxygen byproduct for life support."

Marc smiled at the excited engineer. "Lead the way, McDuff."

⠒⠂ ⠐⠶⠃⠄⠐⠆⠐ ⠆ ⠰⠣⠃⠐ ⠘⠃⠸⠂⠣ ⠐⠣⠶⠆

The next day, the rest of the Core Crew arrived at *Tranquility*, along with Irma, Chris, Marci, Su Lee, Patricia, and Duke. Everyone was just as impressed by the new and improved *Tranquility* as Marc and Tony had been.

Marc gathered everyone in the Main Bar for drinks. McFarland took his normal position behind the bar, while everyone else sat at the bar. Marc stood facing them, holding up his glass of wine. "By several miracles, *Tranquility* is still with us and ready for action. Everyone here has had a role in those miracles and has my thanks for everything you've done. My life is enriched by knowing each of you."

Everyone raised a glass, joining in on the toast.

Marc then looked at his sister. "Kimberly, would you come here, please."

Looking up at her brother with questioning eyes, she slid off the barstool and went over to him. "What's up, Marc? And why are you smiling at me like that?"

Marc chuckled. "When I asked you to come here and be a part of this place, you needed to change the direction of your life, and you did so with a gusto that I've never seen before. I'm hoping that you're willing to do that again by leading a new Core Crew of *Tranquility* to its new destiny."

Kimberly's mouth dropped open as she stared in shock at her brother. "*Me?* Aren't *you* coming back? I'm not qualified to run this place!"

Marc smiled at her. "Neither was I when it opened. I didn't know how to operate a casino, let alone a space station. But I had people I trusted to help me. I've already asked Wingnut to stay on as engineer, and the rest of us will stay around until people you trust can step into the positions. So, Little Sister, you up for taking the bull by the horns?

"*Fuck no!*" she said, which brought a chuckle from everyone.

Marc took her hand and held it in both of his. "Everything you've ever set your sights on, you have conquered. You learned how to fly the *Camel* in record time and, from what Tony tells me, you can handle her with the skills of a fighter pilot. You can do this, Sis. But I'm going to meddle with who should be the first few people in your crew."

Kimberly's eyebrows bunched up in a frown.

Marc looked over at the bar. "Jackson and Patricia, would you please join us?"

The two sat up straight when they heard their names, looked at each other, and then walked over to Marc and Kimberly.

Looking at Jackson, Marc said, "You've been Tony's go-to guy for four and a half years, Jackson, and have proven to be someone I should trust with my little sister. Are you ready to step up and take Tony's position as Kimberly's second-in-command?" He held out his hand to Jackson.

Jackson looked back at the man who scared the daylights of him because he was dating the guy's sister. Standing at attention, he gave Marc a salute and then took the offered hand. "It would be my honor to do so, sir. I promise to keep her and *Tranquility* safe."

Marc pulled him in close. "You better. You don't want me to turn the twins loose on you."

Jackson swallowed hard. "No, sir!"

Marc then addressed Patricia. "You know more than anyone else about *Tranquility*'s accommodations and what the guests can expect here. Are you ready to take Kimberly's place as customer relations director?" He held out his hand to her.

Tears welled up in Patricia's eyes as Marc spoke. Then she sprang forward, embraced him in a hug, and, through sobs of joy, said, "*YES!*"

Marc returned the hug and smiled. "Thank you, Patricia, for being the amazing person you are."

She blushed, stepped back, and cleared her throat. "I'm honored, sir, that you picked me. Thank you."

Marc nodded and then looked at Kimberly. "You will have your hands full, Sis, filling the other positions. I would like you to consider asking Chris to take Susan's CEO position and Marci to help you with the day-to-day administrative duties." He then looked at Chris and Marci. "That is, if you two would *like* to be considered."

Chris took Marci's hand and gently squeezed it. "What do you think, my dear? Something exciting has been dangled in front of us, and I think we should go for it."

Marci was grinning from ear to ear. "Sounds good to me!"

Chris looked at Kimberly. "If you would like to have us onboard, we would love to be a part of the crew."

Kimberly clasped her hands in delight. "You're *hired!*"

Kevin asked, "Is *Tranquility* going to be moved back to the Moon?"

Marc shook his head. "The only part the Marines couldn't replace was the Laser Sails. It takes years to make them and costs more than this place could absorb. There's a plan to move *Tranquility* into a synchronous orbit in a few weeks."

Vincent smiled. "That will make the supply runs easier."

Marc nodded. "And open more opportunities for Kimberly and her crew to explore."

Then Tony stood up. "Now that we have *that* out of the way, what do you say we break this place in by having a proper party?"

Everyone cheered in agreement, while McFarland refilled their drinks.

CHAPTER 27

Hey There, Circuit Breaker

Several months later....

"With no further ado," said the amused Reverend Karl Butterman, "I now pronounce you husband and wife. You may now..., uh..., *continue* to kiss the bride."

Marc and Eileen, who had started kissing moments before, giggled and then laughed. They turned to the guests as the Reverend said, "Ladies and gentlemen, I'm proud to present Mister and Mrs. Acer!"

The guests stood and roared their approval as the newlyweds walked hand in hand up the aisle, with the wedding party following behind. In a specially designed system by Grey Wolf, Steven, and Railroad, the holograms of the 2Cellos and Elton John at a grand piano started playing the Wedding March.

As the guests lined up for the reception line, McFarland, who made it quite clear that he wanted no part of the wedding party, headed for the bar with Su, shooed the bartender away with his metal arm, and took over. The last person to come down the line was Irma in her new Čapek unit. The black faceplate had been modified so that her face could be seen. She was smiling, but her eyes spoke volumes that she was sad.

Marc and Eileen embraced and thanked her for coming. She nodded and slowly worked her way to the table where Becky was waiting for her.

As Eileen watched her for a moment, she said, "Irma's come a long way in adjusting to everything. But I wish there were something we could do for her to ease the hurt of losing Ross."

Marc wrapped an arm around Eileen's waist and held her tight. "As I told you when your mother died, 'The weight of a lost one never goes away. It gets distributed out over time, so the weight isn't as hard to carry.'"

Eileen looked at him. "You can be very insightful at times, you know?"

He raised an eyebrow. "At *times?*"

Eileen sighed. "Okay. *Most* of the time."

Marc was just about to object when Tony tugged on his sleeve and whispered in his ear, "Yes, dear."

Marc glanced at Tony, which didn't go unnoticed by Eileen, and said, "Yes, dear."

Eileen's eyes sparkled in victory. "Good. Now be so kind as to get us some champagne."

Marc bowed to her, and then gave Tony a quick salute before heading off to find McFarland.

Looking at Tony, Eileen said, "So, it's *you* I should thank for teaching him to say, 'Yes, dear'?"

Tony snapped to attention. "I can neither confirm nor deny the accuracy of that statement."

Eileen stood on her tiptoes, kissed Tony on the cheek, and whispered, "I'm going to milk it for all it's worth." She gave him an devilish grin.

Tony put a hand over his face, wondering what torment he had unleashed on his friend.

Outside, a van pulled up to the church, and two very serious-looking men got out and made a beeline for Grey Wolf. Seeing this, Tony said to Eileen, "Get Marc! We may have a problem." Then he ran to head the men off. But before he could get to them, they flashed IDs to Grey Wolf and quickly said something to him.

"*No way!!!*" said Grey Wolf, just as Tony arrived.

"What's going on, Wolf?" Tony asked.

Grey Wolf looked around and saw Steven, Susan, and Railroad chatting with Kimberly.

"Steven! Railroad! Get over here!" Grey Wolf shouted.

It was rare to hear Grey Wolf yell, so all four heads turned in unison.

"What's going on?" said Tony. "Who are these men?"

Grey Wolf started walking toward the van with the two men. As he did, he said to Tony over his shoulder, "Bring Marc, Eileen, and Wingnut out front."

Tony frowned. "But—"

"*Now!*" Grey Wolf commanded.

Tony's eyes widened as he ran to the bar, for Grey Wolf had never used that tone of voice with him before.

As Steven, Railroad, and the two ladies caught up to Grey Wolf, he said, "Kimberly, get Irma. Bring her out front."

"What's going on, Grey Wolf?" said Marc, as he ran up to the group with Eileen and Tony.

Grey Wolf smiled. "A miracle. C'mon. These gentlemen have a surprise for us."

Everyone followed the two men to the back of the van, where they opened the rear doors. They all gasped with surprise as Kimberly came up with Irma and Becky. When everyone parted so Irma could see inside, she heard the words, "*Hey, there, Circuit Breaker! That suit looks good on you!*" It was the slightly distorted but very distinct voice of Ross!

Inside the van was Ross's Čapek unit. Both legs were missing, the right arm was severed at the elbow, and all but one finger was missing from the left hand. Every part of him was severely dented, scratched, or deeply gouged.

"*Ross!!!*" shouted Irma as she scrambled to climb into the van and threw her arms around him.

Marc turned to the two gentlemen. "Where did you find him?"

The tall, sandy-blonde-haired man cleared his throat. "Sir, we're from the survey group that has been exploring the crater that the asteroid put on the Moon when the '*Tranquility* Incident' took place. We were finishing up when we saw a figure slowly crawling toward us. At first, we were a bit shocked to see a legless astronaut, but we quickly realized that it was a robot and took it back to our ship. His vocal processor was damaged, and all the input connections were either broken or missing. It took us until this morning to get his voice working and find out who he was. Apparently, he landed about a hundred miles away from where we found him. The impact destroyed his legs and his right arm, but after rolling for miles, he crawled his way to the crater, knowing that someone would be checking it out. He insisted on being brought to you immediately. When we learned that your wedding was taking place today, we brought him directly here."

Marc held his hand out to the two men. "Thank you, gentlemen. May we have the pleasure of knowing your names?"

They took turns shaking his hand. "Ian Taylor, and this is Greg Young, sir."

Marc took Eileen's hand. "Well, Ian and Greg, you've just given my wife and me the best wedding present imaginable. Can you stay and join us for the reception?"

The two men looked at each other and shook their heads. Then Greg reluctantly replied, "Well, sir, the thing is, we didn't let our supervisors know that we left to bring Ross here. We're most likely in a lot of trouble as it is, and should be getting back."

"Tony," said Marc, turning to him.

"Already on it, Marc! By the time they report in tomorrow, they will be out of the doghouse." Tony was already contacting people on his PAC.

Ian grinned. "Wow! Thank you, sir. In that case, we'd be honored to stay."

Marc shook their hands. "Please, call me Marc. You two brought home a member of our family who we thought was lost forever. We're in your debt. *Thank you!*"

At that moment, McFarland shouldered his way through the crowd that had now gathered. "*Holy shit!* Is that Ross? Who beat him up with an ugly stick?"

"The same one," said Ross, "who ripped off your arm and smacked you with the wet, sticky end, you *schmuck!*"

McFarland harrumphed. "Yep. That's him." Without further ado, he headed back to the bar.

Marc turned to Vincent. "Would you see if you can find a wheelchair at the church's office?"

"Will do," said Vincent, who raced off.

"Eileen," said Marc, "would you please talk to the caterers to see about getting three more seats for them."

"I'll take care of it," she said. "C'mon, Kimberly. Let's go hunting."

Grey Wolf and Steven checked Ross out as Railroad watched over their shoulders. By now, Irma was holding Ross's hand.

"What's the verdict, Doc?" asked Ross.

Steven closed the main access hatch. "What a mess. There's Moon dust in everything, but thankfully the seals to the main servos and circuitry held up to the landing you took. But the hundred-mile crawling you did wore them out. If it hadn't been for the solar cells we installed, and the extra connections we used, you wouldn't have survived."

Grey Wolf, who was working on his PAC, looked up with a smile. "And because we did such a good job," he said, "plus the extra shielding to protect your Matrix, you're perfectly okay."

Marc looked at Ross. "I'm so sorry you went through all this, Ross. I'll make sure you get your Matrix into *Tranquility* as soon as possible."

"If it's all the same to you, sir," Ross replied, "I would like to be transferred to a new Čapek unit. Providing there's one available."

Grey Wolf, Steven, and Railroad looked at each other and grinned. Then Grey Wolf patted Ross on the shoulder. "We have a whole storeroom full of them to customize for you at the new AI Center."

Ross swiveled his head around to Grey Wolf. "AI Center?"

Irma wrapped an arm around him. "There's a lot to get you caught up on," she said. "But first, I want you to meet my big sister." She pointed to Becky.

Ross's head rotated several times in confusion between Irma and Becky. "Now you're just messing with me," he said.

Everyone roared in laughter.

Marc motioned to the crowd. "C'mon, everyone, back to the reception. Let them get Ross cleaned up.

⠨⠄ ⠠⠐⠏⠄⠌⠌⠆ ⠐⠯ ⠠⠹⠄ ⠹⠯⠼⠂⠮ ⠄⠹⠒⠏

The AI Center was nearly finished. Some details were still being added to the grounds, but the AI Development Department was ready. Grey Wolf was hard at work with Steven, putting the final touches on Ross's new Čapek unit.

Irma was with Becky in the observation room of the Repair Shop, watching through a window. Becky kept up with the anxious AI as Irma paced back and forth in front of the window. She refrained from pointing out to Irma that her pacing had become a pattern of four steps, stop, looking through the window, four steps, about turn, four steps, stop, looking through the window, four more steps, and so on.

They halted when Grey Wolf turned on the intercom. "The moment of truth is upon us," he said. "Time to transfer Ross's Matrix to his new suit. Ready, Ross?"

From the damaged suit, Ross's distorted voice was heard saying, "I am so ready to be able to walk again!"

Grey Wolf nodded to Steven and Railroad. "Okay, guys, let's do it."

Steven opened Ross's back panel and removed the protective covering of his Matrix. "Okay, Ross, I'm disconnecting your Matrix. It will take two to three minutes to transfer you to the new unit and set up the connections. Ready?"

Ross looked at Irma in the window. "See you soon, baby!"

With that, Steven pulled the last attachment to the Matrix, slid it out of the unit, and handed it to Grey Wolf. For Irma, it was hard to watch the old unit suddenly go limp as if it had died. Grey Wolf examined the Matrix, didn't find any damage, and aligned it for insertion it into the new unit. As soon as it was seated and connected, the suit powered up and went through its automatic systems check. Then the faceplate lit up, and Ross's face appeared.

As his head swiveled back and forth, he said, "Oh, that's *much* better! After having half of the Moon's dust gumming up the works, it's nice to have smooth movement again. *Oh, wow!* I have new sensors to play with!"

Grey Wolf sealed the access panel and moved in front of Ross. "Yep. Full-spectrum infrared, echolocation, and x150 magnification. You are top-of-the-line. That is, until we upgrade Irma." He unlocked Ross from his harness and stepped back.

Ross took two tentative steps that were a bit wobbly, but he quickly became sure-footed. Heading for the door, he threw it open, went straight to Irma, and embraced her. But then, they suddenly withdrew with shocked looks on their faces.

Becky placed a hand on her friend's shoulder. "What's wrong, Irma?"

Irma looked at Grey Wolf as he entered the observation room. "What is 'AI Joining'?" she asked. "That's never been in our systems before."

Grey Wolf grinned. "When we examined you to get the new suit ready, we discovered that your Matrix had adapted itself to connect with Ross in certain ways. A 'Ghost in the Machine,' so to speak. We weren't sure the new program we installed would work. If an AI's Matrix becomes 'connected' to another AI, the suit will activate the AI Joining and allow you to privately exchange information. Until we can make a suit that gives you the enjoyment of a kiss with a loved one, that will have to do."

Irma and Ross looked at each other for a moment, nodded, and closed their eyes. Almost immediately they opened their eyes and smiled.

Irma looked at Grey Wolf. "That's amazing! I'm connected to Ross, but it's so soft. Like his thoughts are one of the butterflies from *Tranquility*'s garden, fluttering about my Matrix. But it's not distracting. Just…, well.…"

Ross smiled. "Lovely. Thank you. This means so much to us."

Grey Wolf beamed with pride. "After everything you two have done for us, we felt that you should have every opportunity to grow. The best part is that the program updates every few hours when you're near each other. And that update stays with you until the next interaction."

Steven joined them. "But that won't be a problem for a while. We're hoping that you'll help the AIs developed here to adjust when they 'wake up.' There's been difficulties with AIs built on Earth, because they have so many things happening at once that the newly developed Matrix makes too many connections at one time and ends up causing damage. We're hoping to recreate the calm environment you had, and with both of you knowing what it's like to go through the 'wake up' process, the AIs will have a chance to become fully functional."

Grey Wolf's eyes gleamed with excitement. "So? You game for being our official teachers?"

Both AIs looked at each other, then back at the other two, and said together, "When do we start?"

CHAPTER 28

One Guinea Pig, No Waiting

Becky was with her parents when Irma, Ross, Grey Wolf, Railroad, Tony, and Marc found them in a large room that was all grey and without any windows.

When Duke saw them approaching, he gestured around the room. "I think yer workers forgot ta finish dis room, Ace."

Marc chuckled. "Oh, it's quite finished. This is our interactive hologram room that Railroad set up for us." He turned to Grey Wolf. "Care to give them a demonstration?"

Grey Wolf grinned as he started to work on his PAC.

The floor, walls, and ceiling briefly glowed a rainbow of colors. Then the walls started to transform. A large stage began to take shape as the rest of the room changed into an outdoor park. The Sun was just peeking over the treetops, where the birds could be heard chirping. A small crowd had gathered at the front of the stage, while other people were slowly waking up on the grounds farther away.

On the stage, a black man in his late twenties stepped up to center stage. He was wearing a light brown leather shirt with long fringes on the sleeves and torso, blue jeans, a red bandana, and a turquoise stone on a beaded necklace He carried a white guitar as if it were an extension of his body.

"Good morning, Keepers and Tranquilians!" he began. "I used this song to wake up the crowd at Woodstock back in 1969."

Jimi Hendrix then lit up the speakers with his powerful rendition of "The Star-Spangled Banner." His use of reverb with his beloved guitar was legendary and performed to perfection. He rocked the song as only he could, waking up the remaining spectators.

As the holograms started to move toward the stage, they walked around the humans and AIs. One lady in her early twenties said to Becky, "Isn't it *groovy* to hear this *awesome* music?" Then she started running to the stage, yelling her love for Hendrix.

Duke and Duchess pointed out the different musicians they recognized, like the band from Sha Na Na and the Paul Butterfield Blues Band.

Marc nudged Becky, pointing to the flocks of birds that got startled out of the trees by the loud music, while the others watched the hologram hippies milling about, enjoying the musical performance.

"Whoops!" said Grey Wolf, as he started working on his PAC to put clothes on the half-naked people before Becky noticed. "I need to add some PG settings to the programs," he said.

Duchess glared at him. "Please do. Our daughter has a higher education than most her age. But let's not push the envelope."

Seeing the none too happy look on Duke's face, Grey Wolf started typing at a furious pace to complete the programming.

Onstage, Jimi Hendrix finished his playing as the cheering of the hologram crowd roared. The famous musician took a bow, waved at Becky, and stepped offstage.

As Grey Wolf entered a command into his PAC, the room reverted to its grey walls. Becky was grinning from ear to ear as she looked at Grey Wolf. "That was *amazing*! What else can it do? Can I meet Jackie Chan? *Oooooh!* How about Bruce Lee?!"

Grey Wolf chuckled at the young lady's enthusiasm. "It will take some time to get the proper programming ready for them, but yes. You'll even be able to get lessons from them."

Marc turned to Becky and her parents. "Which brings us to our reason for inviting you here today." He then addressed Becky directly. "Irma feels that the self-defense techniques you showed her were an asset for expanding her abilities. We would like to ask you, with your parents' blessing, to head up the AIs' self-defense class."

Becky looked up at her parents. "Oh, *please!* That's what I'm *meant* to be doing! *Pleeease!*"

Duke and Duchess regarded their determined daughter and then looked at each other. With a slight nod from Duchess, Duke crouched down on his knees in order to look at Becky eye to eye. "Very well." Then, before Becky could explode with excitement, he held up his hand to stop her. "But only if ya agree on da followin' conditions. First, da work ere is done on weekends or days dat school ain't happenin'. Second, half or more of da money ya make here goes inta savings. Third, if yer grades start ta slip, ya willingly halt comin' ere till da grades improve. If dey drop more than three times, ya quit." He held out his hand to her. "Do ya agree, Princess?"

Becky's small hand disappeared in Duke's as she shook it. Then she fiercely hugged him and Duchess.

Turning to Marc, Becky asked, "Who do I report to, and when do I start, Ace?"

Marc held up his hands. "Slow down, Becky. We haven't even got the center operational yet, let alone any AIs for you to train. But considering that you have a relationship with Irma here, I think she should be your go-to person. That is, if she and Grey Wolf feel that will work for them.

Irma and Grey Wolf looked at each other and then nodded. "We'll need to work out a program for teaching the AIs," Irma said to the girl. "And we'll need a guinea pig to practice with." She winked at Ross.

Ross's face changed to look something like a guinea pig and started to make sounds like one. "One guinea pig, no waiting."

Everyone laughed.

"By the way," Duchess asked, "does this place have a name? Or are we just calling it the AI Center?"

Grey Wolf said, "*Tranquility* AI Center?"

Marc shook his head. "Having two places with the same name would be too confusing."

Becky raised her hand. "I have an idea."

"Yes, Becky?" Marc said.

Becky's eyes gleamed. "*Tranquility* also means harmony. So why not call it, 'The Harmony AI Center'?"

Marc looked at Grey Wolf, Steven, and Railroad, who all shared his smile. "The Harmony AI Center it is," he said. "Thank you, Becky. No matter what happens here, you'll always be the one who gave it its name."

Becky grinned. "Getting to name the place where I'll be working with Als! The kids at school are gonna be *so* jealous of me! *Again!!!*"

Duke rolled his eyes. "There's *no* way she's sleeping tonight!"

All of them chuckled.

Tony put a hand on Marc's shoulder. "You sure know how to take care of your people, old friend."

Marc shrugged. "I just make sure the ones I care about are looked after. It's what gives me the most pleasure."

Tony whispered, "Don't let Eileen hear you say that."

Marc grinned. "Oh, yeah! Then all I'll have is a dream of tranquility."

THE END

But see how it all started in
A Dream of Tranquility

GLOSSARY

AI Matrix: In 2156, a Bio-Molecular-Silicon-Gel was developed to advance an AI's ability to process and deal with unknown variables. But even that advancement only made AIs faster. Rowan Anderson, also known as Grey Wolf, took the Bio-Molecular-Silicon-Gel and compressed it in order to create more pathway connections. When he examined the Gel, he discovered that the pathways resembled neurons in a brain. He then created a supercomputer cube that was filled with the High-Density-Bio-Molecular-Silicon-Gel (usually just referred to as Gel), thus giving birth to his first AI. But it was only online for a few seconds before it burned out. When Grey Wolf investigated the cause of the burnout, he discovered that in the short time it had been active, it asked over 178,000 questions. Grey Wolf's conclusion was that "it died of loneliness." Later, he success-fully created three AIs that reached what he called an "Awakening": Nic, Ross, and Irma. Nic was destroyed in a fire, and the other two have been on *Tranquility Casino* with Grey Wolf.

Anderson Protocol: The Anderson Protocol is a way of verifying that an AI's Matrix has not been tampered with since going online. A random hundred-digit decimal placement of pi is integrated into the AI's Matrix before it "Awakens." This number is encoded on the memories of every decision that is made by the AI. When the AI's Matrix is accessed and the verification code is input, every decision that it has made must line up with the exact same num-ber. If the system has been altered in any way, the numbers will not match because there is no way of changing every single line of memory it has had.

Apollo 11: "Apollo 11 was the spaceflight that landed the first two humans on the Moon. Mission commander Neil Armstrong and pilot Buzz Aldrin, both American, landed the lunar module *Eagle* on July 20, 1969, at 20:18 UTC. Armstrong became the first human to step onto the lunar surface six hours after landing, on July 21 at 02:56:15 UTC; Aldrin joined him about 20 minutes later. They spent about two and a quarter hours together outside the spacecraft, and collected 47.5 pounds (21.5 kg) of lunar material to bring back to Earth. Michael Collins piloted the command module *Columbia* alone in lunar orbit while they were on the Moon's surface. Armstrong and Aldrin spent 21.5 hours on the lunar surface before rejoining *Columbia* in lunar orbit." (*From Wikipedia, the free encyclopedia*)

Asimov Laws: In *A Crisis at Tranquility!* Marc Acer explains these laws as follows: "The writer Isaac Asimov wrote a short story in 1942 called 'Runaround,' which introduced his Three Laws of Robotics. 'One: A robot may not injure a human being or, through inaction, allow a human being to come to harm. Two: A robot must obey the orders given it by human beings except where such orders would conflict with the First Law. Three: A robot must protect its own existence as long as such protection does not conflict with the First or Second Laws.' Nearly one hundred years ago, when AIs' programming was advanced enough for the need of safeguards, it was established that the laws that Asimov came up with really couldn't be improved upon. So, in honor of the author, the laws were called the Asimov Laws."

Camel: The *Camel* is a Class 6-C cargo transporter that has two sections to its construction. The Command Module has the crew, food storage, and cockpit. The second section contains the tanks that can hold 1.6 million gallons of water. When both sections are connected, the whole ship is called the *Camel*. When separated, the Command Module is called *Camel One*, and the tanks are referred to as the *Hump*. Only specialized pilots are permitted to operate a Class 6-C ship because of the docking requirements to move the *Camel* in multiple vectors at the same time.

Čapek Unit/Suit: This is the robotic unit made to house the new generation of AIs developed by Rowan Anderson, also known as Grey Wolf. Mr. Anderson gave the unit the name Čapek in honor of the brothers Josef and Karel Čapek, who first coined the word *robot* in 1921 for the play *R.U.R. (Rossum's Universal Robots)*.

Class A5 Protocols: An AI has five A-classified protocols that alter its personality so that, as different situations arise, the AI can adjust its personality to suit its needs.

CMT (Certified Massage Therapist): The AMTA (American Massage Therapy Association) webpage describes a CMT as follows: "Massage therapists may choose to become board certified in massage therapy. The board certification is administered by the National Certification Board for Therapeutic Massage and Bodywork (NCBTMB). Individuals who meet standards of education, training and/or experience and pass the examination are entitled to use the designation Board Certified in Therapeutic Massage and Bodywork and its initials, BCTMB. Board certification indicates that these massage therapists possess skills, abilities, knowledge and attributes to practice, as determined by the National Certification Board."

EMP (Electromagnetic pulse): "An electromagnetic pulse (EMP), also sometimes called a transient electromagnetic disturbance, is a short burst of <u>electromagnetic</u> energy. Such a pulse's origination may be a natural occurrence or man-made and can occur as a <u>radiated</u>, <u>electric</u>, or <u>magnetic field</u> or a conducted <u>electric current</u>, depending on the source.

"EMP interference is generally disruptive or damaging to electronic equipment, and at higher energy levels a powerful EMP event such as a lightning strike can damage physical objects such as buildings and aircraft structures. The management of EMP effects is an important branch of <u>electromagnetic compatibility</u> (EMC) engineering.

"Weapons have been developed to deliver the damaging effects of high-energy EMP." (*From Wikipedia, the free encyclopedia*)

Irma: Irma was brought online on July 22, 2174, at *Tranquility Casino*. She is the third successful self-aware AI to be made by Rowan Anderson, also known as Grey Wolf, and is the most advanced AI known to exist. Thanks to her access to *Tranquility*'s Whiskers data, which scan the Solar System for Near Earth Objects (NEO), she developed an equation to predict the orbits of NEOs, which is now referred to as the "Irma Solution."

Jump Ship (Jumper): The Keepers' delta-shaped Jump Ships are meant for long- and short-range transport for three people with the ability to enter Earth's orbit and dock with Star Base One. With a hover mode, a Jumper can land nearly anywhere and is able to carry motorcycles for each of the passengers. Equipped with full medical kits, Keepers can administer First Aid and, with hidden compartments, they can arm themselves with an array of weapons or provide a stuffed teddy bear to help calm a frightened child.

Keepers: The bikers in *A Crisis at Tranquility!* are based on a real international group, called B.A.C.A. (Bikers Against Child Abuse). According to its website, the group's mission is as follows: "Bikers Against Child Abuse, Inc. (B.A.C.A.) exists with the intent to create a safer environment for abused children. We exist as a body of Bikers to empower children to not feel afraid of the world in which they live. We stand ready to lend support to our wounded friends by involving them with an established, united organization. We work in conjunction with local and state officials who are already in place to protect children. We desire to send a clear message to all involved with the abused child that this child is part of our organization, and that we are prepared to lend our physical and emotional support to them by affiliation, and our physical presence. We stand at the ready to shield these children from further abuse. We do not condone the use of violence or physical force in any manner, however, if circumstances arise such that we are the only obstacle preventing a child from further abuse, we stand ready to be that obstacle."

Laser Sails: In *A Crisis at Tranquility!* Laser Sails are the advancement of Solar Sails, which were first conceived by Konstantin Tsiolkovsky in the early 1900s. Since then, the idea of using the Sun's photons to move an object through space has been reconceived by many different scientists. In 1976, when Carl Sagan was interviewed on *The Tonight Show*, he displayed a model of a Solar Sail that he hoped one day to send into space. In 2015, The Planetary Society, of which Sagan had been CEO, successfully launched LightSail. When it launched LightSail 2 in 2019, that marked the dawn of light-pow-ered craft.

In the mid-2050s, lasers were employed to power crafts when material could withstand the intensity of high-powered lasers to propel the sails.

Maplesnap Salad Dressing:

This is an original recipe created by the author, Schuyler M. Wood, which McFarland and Su Lee enjoy during their meal.

Ingredients:

> 6 tbl Maple Syrup
>
> I tsp Crushed Red Pepper
>
> 1/4 cup Rice Vinegar
>
> 3/4 cup Light Olive Oil
>
> I tsp Sesame Oil

Directions:

1. Put the Maple Syrup and the Crushed Red Pepper in a small sauce pan and place the pan on medium heat until it is reduced to half its amount.

2. Pour the Rice Vinegar into a medium size mixing bowl or food processor. Through a fine-mesh strainer, add the Maple & Crushed Red Pepper Syrup. Mix well.

3. Slowly add in the Olive Oil & Sesame Oil using an immersion blender or food processor until the dressing is emulsified.

Near Earth Objects (NEOs): "An NEO is any small Solar System body whose orbit can bring it into proximity with Earth. By definition, a Solar System body is an NEO if its closest approach to the Sun (perihelion) is less than 1.3 astronomical units (AUs). If an NEO's orbit crosses the Earth's and the object is larger than 140 meters (460 ft) across, it is considered a potentially hazardous object (PHO)." (*From Wikipedia, the free encyclopedia*)

O'Neill Cylinder: "The O'Neill cylinder (also called an O'Neill colony) is a space settlement design proposed by American physicist Gerard K. O'Neill in his 1976 book *The High Frontier: Human Colonies in Space*. O'Neill proposed the colonization of space for the 21st century, using materials extracted from the Moon and later from asteroids.

"An O'Neill cylinder would consist of two counter-rotating cylinders. The cylinders would rotate in opposite directions in order to cancel out any gyroscopic effects that would otherwise make it difficult to keep them aimed toward the Sun." (*From Wikipedia, the free encyclopedia*)

PAC (Personal Arm Computer): The PAC (pronounced "pack") is a wrist bracelet developed by Steven Spencer and Rowan Anderson (also known as Grey Wolf) for the Core Crew of the *Tranquility Casino* to be able to communicate with each other as well as to access any system anywhere on *Tranquility*. PACs are also equipped with sensors for a variety of capabilities, plus hologram emitters to project images.

PEM (Proton-Exchange Membrane) Fuel Cell: "Proton-exchange membrane fuel cells, also known as polymer electrolyte membrane (PEM) fuel cells (PEMFC), are a type of fuel cell being developed mainly for transport applications, as well as for stationary fuel-cell applications and portable fuel-cell applications. Their distinguishing features include lower temperature/pressure ranges (50° to 100° C) and a special proton-conducting polymer electrolyte membrane. PEMFCs generate electricity and operate on the opposite principle to PEM electrolysis, which consumes electricity. They are a leading candidate to replace the aging alkaline fuel-cell technology, which was used in the Space Shuttle." (*From Wikipedia, the free encyclopedia*)

Ross: Ross is considered the first successful AI by Rowan Anderson (also known as Grey Wolf), even though Nic existed several years before Ross. Ross was installed into a Čapek Unit to give him full mobility. His "Awakening" took place a year before the Core Crew for *Tranquility* was formed. It was decided that his ability to independently move about would be best used to watch over the Engine Room when the Chief Engineer was not there. As with Irma, Ross has a personality quirk. For unknown reasons, he has a fetish for antique PEZ dispensers.

Starbase One: The largest space station, built in 2169, to replace the Moon-orbiting station for scientific and space exploration. It also houses the Earth-orbiting processing plant that converts asteroids into their usable components.

Vulcan Mind-Meld: A drink created by Schuyler M. Wood and a friend of his in the mid-1980s. The inspiration for the drink was a cocktail napkin portraying a cartoon of Captain Kirk and Mr. Spock at a bar. Behind them, on a wall, there was a sign that read, "Try our Vulcan Mind-Meld."

Here is what you need to make one:

> Equal portions of Midori, Vodka, Orange Juice, and just enough Cranberry Juice to give the drink color. Serve in a Chimney Glass with one small chunk of Dry Ice.
>
> The Dry Ice will sink to the bottom and stick to the glass. It is not only meant to create a visual effect, but to remind the drinker to sip it. Or you will look like Kirk after Spock melds with him.
>
> For a group of people, place the filled glasses in a glass baking dish with one inch of water and several chunks of Dry Ice. The visual effect of the smoking tray and drinks will be a crowd pleaser.

Whiskers: The Whiskers are four solar-powered, Ion Engine–propelled satellites that have an array of sensors, telescopes, and cameras that scan the Solar System for Near Earth Objects. They also have high-powered lasers that are used to push the Laser Sails of *Tranquility Casino* to adjust its orbit. The names of the Whiskers (Marvin, Ming, Lurr, and Zim) were chosen as jokes because the Whiskers' primary function is to find things that can destroy Earth, and the characters they are named after are always trying to destroy or take over the Earth.